MY LIFE TO TAKE

A DEMON'S LOVE BOOK #2

M. A. FRÉCHETTE

When his mere presence bends iron, does her broken soul stand a chance?

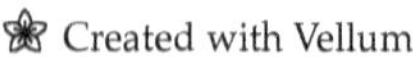 Created with Vellum

This one is dedicated to you, mom. Everything I've been able to accomplish is thanks to your love and support—I never would have gotten this far without you. Since finding out I write books, you've been my number one supporter, and always encourage me to keep going. Thank you for not only being my mom, but for always being the greatest mom.

1

———————

A NEW LIFE

Celina sighed and placed her book on the coffee table; she couldn't focus on the words. The polished wood of the surface shimmered in the flames of the hearth burning close. Inside her own bedroom, she should feel safe, yet every shadow lurked above her as though wanting to pounce and devour.

One month had passed since she was brought to the dark realm, and with each minute ticking by, her heart weighed heavier.

Nalie, the Viscus demon charged with her care, watched her in silence. Her icy-blue irises glowed with curiosity, likely waiting for Celina to share. Demons, as Celina found out, were not the types to open up. Still, she couldn't deny it made her feel less lonely to have someone with her.

Celina swallowed hard. "Can I ask you something?"

"Yes."

"Something you won't share with your king?"

Nalie stiffened but gave a curt nod as her vertical pupils thinned. "If it is a matter of confidence, then I shall not share the information with anyone. Not even with Mekaisto."

Hearing his name caused Celina to shudder, and she

shifted on the sofa, trying to hide her reaction. "I'm not sure how to deal with anything that's happened. Kai is giving me time to adjust, but I don't think he understands trust may not be something I'll ever be able to give him after what he did."

It had started with revenge, but by the end, was revealed to be a lie. Her entire life was fabricated under Kai's doing. Just thinking about it churned her stomach, but more than anything, it broke her heart. Meeting him in a bar when she was sixteen years old; he'd been waiting for her there. Years of dating until he proposed. And as soon as he slipped the wedding ring onto her finger, he separated her from the rest of the world, so slowly she didn't notice until it was done.

Celina ran her hand over her abdomen, the baby bump more prominent since arriving in the realm. She had wanted children with her husband, Thomas, and as it would happen, her wish was granted. Just not the way she'd planned.

Be careful what you wish for.

Nalie leaned, her platinum hair falling forward. "You no longer trust the king?" She frowned, staring off into the distance. "Does this have to do with what humans call love? Does it matter so much?"

"It does. It's hard to love someone you can't trust." Celina got to her feet and paced. "When Kai told me the truth, I wanted to believe he did it out of love." She scoffed. "I know it was. But his idea of love is... warped. Now that I've had time to think about it, I don't know if I can forgive him."

"Demons... we do not understand what forgiving is. We remember, take revenge, and kill." She shrugged. "He lied to protect—"

Celina raised her hand. "No. He lied at the end to protect our child, but those years before his lies were to take what was his: me. There's no excuse for that."

The flames inside the hearth flickered, and Nalie stared at it, the embers bursting hotter. "You made a deal with the king, and the contract will keep you here. Willingly or not."

"I killed people," she whispered. "I know it doesn't mean much to demons, but it does to me." Her heart hammered as memories of what happened flashed through her mind. The Lumen member who'd lunged at Celina, murdered by her hand when she pulled the trigger. "I thought I was avenging my husband. I allowed demons to murder people. I took lives, too." She swallowed hard, recalling how she'd shot Emily Pierce in the head, thinking she was achieving her revenge. "I lost people. And the whole time…"

The whole time Thomas had been Kai. Mekaisto, the king of the dark realm. The Devil.

Voices carried over from outside Celina's living quarters, and she held her breath. Kai hadn't visited her for a while, and it helped while she tried figuring out her feelings. She dreaded facing him, too afraid her heart would win over her mind. Love winning over the logic of betrayal. She loved Thomas, loved Kai, but hated them both.

"Have you spoken to others about this?" Nalie asked, getting to her feet and glancing toward the door at the continued ruckus.

Celina shook her head. "There isn't anyone here I can trust. I feel so alone." Her shoulders sagged.

"You should speak to your husband. Tell him what is plaguing your mind and allow him to bed you. It will make things right."

Heat crept into Celina's cheeks. "It doesn't work like that. But you're right. Eventually, I'll have to talk to him and decide."

"A decision?"

Celina stared at the demon who had taken care of her health since arriving in the realm. "Whether I can stay with him."

The ghost of a smile touched Nalie's lips. "You believe you can escape the king? We are possessive beings, and you are his. Even if you left this realm, he would find you, wherever you go."

Ice flowed through her veins at Nalie's words. She was right; Kai would never let her go, and it made the hurt even worse.

Continued shouts echoed from below, and Celina frowned. "What's going on down there?"

Nalie seemed to hesitate. "All Sanguis were summoned. However, some did not answer the call. It has been a few days, and their leader, Adam, is worried. Shiriki was tasked with finding their whereabouts."

The thought of how Shiriki got his answers sent a shiver down Celina's spine, and she trembled. The demon had tortured her without a second thought despite knowing she was under Kai's protection. Shiriki was infamous for obsessing over how souls worked, and he would do anything—from dissecting to boiling live victims of any race—to find the answers he sought. "I... er, I need to take a shower."

Nalie gave a small bow. "I will return shortly."

Celina stood in the same spot for a few minutes after Nalie left, lost in thought. It was like being home again. Free yet trapped within a beautiful place. She wanted to kick herself for not realizing Kai was Thomas the whole time. But how could she have known? He had lied to her at every turn.

Curling her hands into fists, she marched to the bathroom, slamming the door behind her. Her mind and heart were at odds with each other, and over two different people even though they were the same. The memories she had of Thomas twisted inside her, changing them into the demon she'd made a deal with. The demon she fell in love with.

Celina grasped the handle of the glass shower door, and it opened with a squeak. She turned on the faucet and slipped out of her white nightgown. As the water warmed her skin, her memories flew to the last time she'd showered with Kai.

When she had realized she loved him despite the situation. Did she feel the same as before?

She focused on a few drops beading across the tiled wall. Kai had built these chambers for her. A bathroom wasn't a necessity for demons, but it was for her, and he wanted to give her a private space of her own. He still surprised her with kindness, showing he loved her. With a loud sigh, she grabbed the shampoo bottle sitting in the corner and lathered a thick amount into her hair. The sound of the water flowing put her in a daze, and her movements slowed. She stepped underneath the cascade and sighed as the soap rinsed off her body.

Her hand slid along her bump. Thomas's son… Kai's son.

He had let her believe the lies, then allowed her world to crumble in a cascade of horrible truths. But Kai had done everything to save her and their unborn baby. A sob tore through her chest as she leaned on the white tiles. Love didn't mean the same thing for demons.

I'm here to carry his son, and that's it. Just a vessel…

The room trembled, and she gasped as Kai's energy encircled her. She shook her head, trying to get the thoughts out of her mind. He could slither through her train of thoughts, and she was sure she'd felt him a second ago. She turned the water off, and a shiver ran through her.

Curling her toes into the fluffy mat, she eyed the steam covering the mirror.

Kai was destined to take her life and soul one way or another.

She took out her rage and frustration on her tangled hair, brushing through the knots. Hissing at a painful snag, she tugged hard through her red locks. Once finished, she leaned on the cool marble countertop, focusing on her breathing.

She stared at herself in the mirror. Was anything Thomas—Kai—told her true? Her hands curled into fists. He'd tucked her away where they first met at his tree, keeping her secluded from everyone. Year after year, she talked about children, and his mood soured, to the point where she'd been nervous about bringing it up. Both the man she'd known as her husband, and the demon who came after, tricked and manipulated her. She was a means to an end for an heir Kai needed when *he* was ready. Nothing more.

She clenched her teeth and punched the mirror. Pain shot through her arm, and she swore. Hundreds of different reflections stared back with the same gray irises as the demon who'd fathered her. Shattered pieces showed how she felt inside—broken.

An image flashed inside her mind, bringing a frown. Blurred and dark, at first, the scene focused. Her pulse sped as it spun, and she was facing a wall covered in graffiti.

No, not graffiti. Symbols?

They inched closer, and she squinted in the low streetlight as she read, 'The traitor is within their midst.' The image disappeared, and she staggered as though thrown out from her own mind. She pressed her hand on the wall inside her room, panting.

What the hell was that?

She walked through the living room as she flexed her wounded hand. Built in an open concept, the home had an apartment feel to it. Dark earth tones gave the place a warm ambiance, but she felt cold.

The edge of her vision blurred as a dizzy spell hit her, and she forced her lips together to keep from throwing up. The attacks were becoming frequent. Carrying a baby who was more demon than human was poisoning her, and it's why she was in Kai's realm. But she was dying, and no one was telling her anything.

She took a deep breath and placed her hand on her belly.

It's okay. We're okay.

She rummaged through a drawer and slipped on a black dress that ended above her knees. After pushing aside a few discarded blankets, she found her flats. She was grateful she didn't need to bend over to put them on. At about five months pregnant, she wasn't sure she'd manage.

Nalie had explained demon babies grew faster than human ones, but because Celina's son was a quarter human, she had no way of knowing when he was due. One thing was for certain: since arriving in the dark realm, her son seemed to have grown much bigger.

She stepped out into the hallway. The wood was partially covered with a red rug traveling the length of the upstairs. Well, what she could see. She didn't get to explore as much as she'd like.

She'd thought him overprotective as Thomas, but Kai had become worse since bringing her to his realm.

Her hand slid along the polished banister as she stepped down the curving stairway. The smell of warm bread made her stomach growl, and she followed the scent. Once she reached the main floor, she took time to look at her surroundings, ignoring the hunger pangs.

It was a gorgeous place, a genuine mansion with crown molding and chandeliers in the common areas. The rooms she'd seen were spacious, with high windows and upholstered furniture made of oak. The house she'd shared with Kai as her husband had been beautiful, but nothing like this place.

A wall moved, and she muffled a scream when a dozen eyelids flew open, staring at her. A few blinked but nothing happened. "I'll never get used to you," she spoke to the irises All they ever did was swivel and stare.

Kai had eyes everywhere, so to speak. He knew when she left her private chambers, and he'd know if she left their home.

A delicious smell called to her, and she followed. An open entryway with a high ceiling led into the kitchen, a small one since it wasn't meant to be an eat-in. Kai had a formal dining hall for that.

Strange yellow-spotted pink fruits sat in a bowl on the counter, but she skipped those. No way to know if they were meant for human consumption.

I'm half, though.

The thought remained traumatic. Finding out in a letter from her late mother that Shiriki was her biological father had been a shock. The first Viscus and the only demon save for Kai that other demons feared.

She longed to return to simpler days when it was just Thomas and her… the way she had known him. But finding out what he had done, even as Thomas, tainted memories of their marriage.

She grabbed a piece of bread and bit into it. Grateful to be fed, her stomach stopped churning, and she closed her eyes. She trudged toward the staircase, but energy pressed against her, enough to make her wince. The wide hallway seemed to shrink as she turned and faced Shiriki.

"You should not be alone," he said with a grin.

Speak of the other devil.

She averted her gaze, staring at a painting instead. "I'm allowed to walk around."

"You are not safe as long as your demon blood is reacting to the realm's essence. It is fighting your soul, making it weak." He moved toward her. "It will be dealt with. Mekaisto knows he will simply need to proceed with taking your life and soul. Just a matter of time. In case you have not caught on yet, there is a price to pay when dealing with our kind, pet."

She wished she could punch his smile away. "Is that what happened with my mother?"

"It is complicated." An unknown emotion flashed across his gaze. He materialized inches from her, and grabbed her wrist, turning her hand to look at her wounded knuckles. "Feeling angry?"

Before Celina replied, a woman walked down the corridor toward them. The Viscus demon wore tight clothing revealing her curves, and every step seemed to emphasize her hips. Her blue hair fell loosely on her bare shoulders. "Adam has provided a list of the Sanguis who are missing. There are more than we suspected."

Another attack?

"That will be all, Tess." Shiriki turned to Celina. "I will see you again. And sooner than you would like." Without another word, he left the two alone.

The Viscus approached Celina wearing an icy smile. "I must admit, every time I see you, I am surprised you are Mekaisto's wife." Her gaze traveled along Celina's body with a sneer.

Celina bristled. "What does that mean?"

"Just was shocked when I realized it wasn't a rumor. I mean, once upon a time he summoned Viscus demons to his bed. He had high standards. I never imagined the female he chose is a half-breed."

This wasn't the first time a demon baited Celina for a reaction, trying to prove she was too human to be in their realm. They feared she would corrupt their king, make him soft.

Fists tight, she clenched her jaw. "Back. Off."

Tess's eyebrows shot up, her expression losing its flirt. "Are you challenging your betters?"

"I'm sure anyone is better than a desperate whore."

Tess shrugged, but her irises glowed brighter. "Being with a child makes it harder to please, assuming you ever could." She scoffed. "You do not seem willing to be here. Perhaps you should leave if it is the case?"

Celina kept a neutral expression, hoping she didn't give any hit the taunt hit a sore spot. Even if they fixed their relationship, was she enough for Kai? Silence hung heavy between them. When Celina said nothing, Tess turned and left.

Her jaw throbbed from clenching her teeth too hard. She'd already heard the rumors. Kai used to have rooms reserved for his favorites. The thought of him returning to his realm while they were married was enough to make her nauseous. Not wanting to stay somewhere Shiriki would catch her alone, Celina marched to the common living area inside the mansion.

Can I forgive him for everything? Can we start over?

2

SUMMONED

The dark wooden floor creaked beneath her feet, and Celina stopped near the window looking out into the garden. From her angle, the meeting area was visible, but empty today. Built from white stone, it stood on four columns in an open concept, allowing the garden to connect to its furnishings. Focusing on the eerie vegetation, she pressed her lips together, glancing toward the door leading outside. She wanted to go out, but Kai kept her indoors. She'd even had to argue leaving her bedroom. Protective was an understatement and sometimes bordered on controlling. He'd explained his realm was even more dangerous than usual at the moment but hadn't elaborated.

Nothing has changed.

She strode to the door, pressed on the long silver handle, and stepped outside. The thrill of going against Kai's orders curled a smile on her lips. She refused to let him control her any longer. Period.

The physical pressure took time getting used to, but she kept her mind off the tightening in her chest. A bush caught her attention, the stems wavering as a few petals sparked as though a crackling fire burned within. She reached out but gasped when a hand caught her wrist, holding her back.

Red irises observed her with amusement. With a grin, Brihan touched the petal, and the stem wrapped around his finger, teeth snapping and tearing off flesh. He wrenched away, his flesh healing instantly, and Celina took a step back.

"They're pretty, but tricky little things." His eyes returned to their usual green, and he smiled.

"Thanks." She glanced toward the mansion, her heart hammering. If Kai found out what almost happened, he'd never let her out of her room again. "Please don't—"

"We should get you inside before someone finds out," he added with a wink.

Brihan, a Sanguis demon, had been kind to Celina from the minute she woke up in the dark realm. He was one of the few of Kai's subjects who didn't despise her for who or what she was. Despite not seeing him often, he'd become a good friend.

She followed him inside. "That plant was so beautiful. I never imagined it would be dangerous."

Once the door was closed, he turned to her, his eyes gleaming. "This is the dark realm. Everything is deadly." He glanced over his shoulder. "And speaking of deadly, Mekaisto would like a word with you."

"And he couldn't come to see me himself?" Still, the thought of facing him made her shiver. She wasn't ready. She straightened and held her head higher. "Tell him I'll... see him when I'm ready."

His eyebrows rose until they disappeared behind his blond bangs. "You want me to tell the king you refuse?"

"Yes." She swallowed hard. He was no longer the demon she'd formed a deal with. No longer Thomas. He was a stranger, and if he wanted to talk to her, he'd have to wait until she was ready.

Brihan gave a quick bow, and strode away, muttering under his breath about Mekaisto flaying him.

Celina took a few strides forward and called, "Wait." When he halted, she approached. "Tell him he can meet me here. I don't want him to punish you for my answer. I'll let him know myself, okay?"

Relief crossed his features, and he dashed away as though terrified she'd changed her mind and send him with the message instead.

One way or another, she'd have to face Kai, and it might as well be sooner than later.

The fire sparked in the hearth, flames dancing, creating lithe shadows on the walls. Lamps on the end tables flickered, and Celina stiffened. She stared outside at the treacherous garden, but glanced at Kai's reflection in the glass, standing behind her.

Despite seeing his demon appearance often, it sent a jolt through her. Black hair reached his shoulders, his glowing red irises contrasting against the black vertical pupils. Dressed in black, he favored a Victorian style, with a vest over his dress shirt and well-fitted trousers.

She turned to stare at him, her breath catching in her throat.

"We need to talk," Kai said in a husky voice.

She took several steps back. "No."

"No?" he repeated in a dark tone, yet an amused expression changed the way his irises glowed.

"I'm not one of your subjects, and it won't be like it used to when you were… the demon I made a contract with. I don't want to be nervous or scared, and—"

"If you were not nervous or scared, it would make you a fool."

"Yeah, I found that out when you told me the truth," she said louder than she'd planned. She took a deep breath. "I'm not ready to talk yet."

"Then it is a good thing I only need you to listen." His smile widened as she glared at him.

She crossed her arms. "Sure, why not? Not like I've ever had a choice in anything." Her own tone surprised her, but she didn't waver.

He stared at her with an unreadable expression. "I swear—"

"And I should believe you because you never twist everything to your advantage?"

"I could not tell you the whole truth yet."

"How convenient for you."

He stalked toward her, every step measured, and she froze in place. Grabbing her wrist, he pulled her close to bring his mouth to her ear. "Do you want me to apologize?" Darkness seeped from him, turning the walls and ceiling pitch black. "I will never say I am sorry for saving you and our child."

"You had to lie to save us, I get that. It's something I have to live with, and I hate it, but I understand. You had to make a terrible choice. Tainting my soul had to be done. But what about our life together before that?" she whispered. "Aren't you sorry for secluding me like you did? Driving me from my friends? Making me scared of bringing up anything child-related?"

"I am sorry for all of it. But—"

"You're a demon? I got that…" She wrenched away from him and took a seat on the sofa. Grabbing the soft cushion, she held it close to her chest.

"Have your feelings for me changed?" His voice was steady, yet pain flashed in his gaze.

"I still love Thomas, and at the same time, I hate him for what he did. And I love you but hate everything you've done to me. But you're… both of you. It's like I'm learning to get to know you, but I already have known you my whole life."

He sat next to her. "Tell me what you need."

"Time, explanations, and some space."

"I can grant one of those requests." His lips curled in a smile. "Before you were with child, I kept you secluded because it was the only way I knew how to protect you. I did not know what the consequences of being half-demon would do to a human, and so I distanced you from the rest of the world. I apologize for that."

Darkness filled the edges of her vision, and she took a shuddering breath as the room spun around her.

"Celina?" He took the cushion from her and placed his palm above her heart. "There is more essence than I thought." Without warning, he pushed her on her back against the sofa.

Her chest continued squeezing as though something was trying to crush it. Passing his hand over her, Celina trembled as black smoke rose from her, seeping into his fingertips. The tightness she'd felt since waking vanished, and her whole body relaxed.

He slid his fingers lower, brushing along her thigh, making her pulse race. His gaze flashed in desire, and she shivered. But all she saw were the lies. She pushed against him, but he didn't budge.

"Get off me."

His lips curled into a playful smile that didn't reach his eyes. "Do I repulse you now?"

"Does it matter? If you can't get it from me, I'm sure one of your old favorites would be willing. You know? The ones you used to keep in private rooms and all?"

He traced a pointed fingernail against her neck, and goosebumps crawled along her skin. "I am not interested in having anyone but you." He slid his hand between her breasts, making her heart beat faster.

"I said get off."

He gritted his teeth but leaned back, and she got to her feet, putting some distance between them. She paced, but grasped her chest, wincing at the renewed pressure pushing against it. Humans couldn't survive in this realm without withering to an empty husk. Darkness filled them like venom, latching into people like hooks in flesh. The only way to continue living here was to die.

"The essence has taken over you deeper than I thought possible," Kai said. "I will have to complete the end of our deal soon."

A lump formed in her throat, and as much as she tried swallowing, it wouldn't go away. Her lips trembled, desperate for the right words, but instead, she burst into tears. When he stood to go to her, she took several steps back and shook her head.

"No… I can't."

The floor shook, parts of the walls cracking. Celina glanced around, eyes wide. Well, at least she figured out why there were so many drafts in this place. When she met his gaze, she wasn't sure what to make of his expression.

"I know I no longer deserve your trust."

She rubbed her arms, her emotions flooding her like a tidal wave. Love and hate. Trust and doubt. She needed comfort from the man she loved, but how could she open herself to someone who'd broken her? She needed to change the subject, and fast. "The essence you took out just now. Is it the same thing you had done to me after you'd brought me back from Shiriki's laboratory from Hell?"

"Not quite. Mine is more potent."

"So, what now?"

He cocked his head. "What do you mean?"

She tried pushing the nagging voice from the back of her mind, telling her their relationship was doomed. "Will I be living here with you?"

"Of course."

Tears blurred her vision as a wave of energy surrounded her. Not the usual anger she felt from him, but love and care. "And what if I said I wanted to leave?"

His gaze searched her before his lips curled into a grin worthy of his title. "You do not want me to answer that question, dove."

She opened and closed her mouth, her hands curling into fists. Anger boiled her blood at his words. "You're really a condescending bastard, you know that?" Before shouting more obscenities at him, she marched away, needing time alone.

I wasn't ready to face him yet.

A crowd of demons blocked her way near the staircase, and her shoulders slumped. She wasn't willing to hold her head high through their judgemental stares right then. Instead, she opened the nearest door and stepped inside, bolting the doorknob behind her.

Floor to ceiling shelves filled with books seemed familiar, and her chest squeezed. It looked like Thomas's private room in her old house. A bitter smile curled her lips, realizing it was Kai's office.

Of course, it looks like his. He's the same person.

She strode to the desk, and focused on the papers scattered about, frowning at the symbols sketched on a few. She'd seen those same ones inside her mind before leaving her bedroom. A large black tablet had been anchored into the hard surface of the wooden desk, and she passed her fingers over it. With a gasp, she took a step back when a hologram floated above, a few pictures rotating. All were from the same scene. An alleyway with the message about a traitor within their midst.

Questions flew through her mind, but before she figured any of them out, the door opened. Kai walked into the room, and she swiped her hand across the screen, causing them to vanish once more. He glared at her, but she kept her head held high, refusing to back down.

"We were not finished with our discussion."

"I was." She crossed her arms, and his lips curled into a smile as though enjoying her fight.

He took a step closer, his irises turning a darker shade of red. "After everything you have gone through, you still try resisting me?"

She refused to take the bait, and instead, pointed at the desk. "Have you been planting images in my head?"

"I would never do that," he hissed, fury etched in his tone.

"Then why did I see the photos you have on your tablet inside my mind before I came downstairs?" She tapped the screen, and the image with the symbols appeared. "It says 'the traitor is within their midst.' What's going on?"

He frowned. "Where did you read that?"

"It's here." She pointed at the circular shapes.

"You can read this language?"

Memories flashed through her mind, but she closed it quickly, knowing he'd be looking inside. "I don't know what language it is, but yes, I can read and understand it." She wrung her hands together. "My father taught me lots of different languages. I guess this was one."

Her heart swelled at the memory of her stepfather, a kind man who'd loved her like she was his own flesh and blood.

"I see."

A knock at the door broke the heavy silence, and Kai's glower splintered the frame before it burst open.

Tess stepped inside and bowed. "Apologies, but there is a Sanguis with information about the potential location of your missing subjects." She shot Celina a disgusted glare before beaming at Kai.

Celina's chest tightened, and she wanted nothing better than to watch Tess die. She squeezed her eyes shut, trying to push away the comments the Viscus had said about her husband keeping favorites.

If I feel this jealousy, does it mean I still love him?

Kai approached the door and stopped near Tess. She stepped closer to him and leaned against the frame, lowering her voice.

"Your Majesty, I know you no longer keep us, but if you change your mind, you can order me to return to my duties."

She yelped when a cut ripped across both sides of her face, tearing open from her mouth to ears. Pressing her hands against the gushing wounds, her eyes widened at Kai's cold smile.

"Instigate my wife again, and the damage will be permanent," Kai said in a low voice, yet it vibrated through the whole room.

Tess clawed at her cheeks and ran out without a word. Not that she could've talked. A small part of Celina—a side of herself she hated—was filled with a sense of satisfaction at a maimed Tess. And Celina couldn't deny her doubts melted away when her husband defended her as he had. Yet his ease at using such violence was frightening.

Celina turned off the tablet, averting her gaze from him. She didn't want to talk about the lies, betrayal, or even the jealousy she felt. "What did you mean when you said you have to perform the end of our deal?"

"You owe me your life and soul." His tone had darkened, and she shivered.

He took everything away from me, and he wants more.

"It is necessary," he said.

She glared. "Is there any way to block you from my thoughts?"

"Why? Something you wish to hide from me?"

"I… never mind. I guess I assumed when you told me everything, it meant the deal was never real. That you wouldn't need to take anything else from me." She met his gaze as she ran her hand over her belly. "You don't want to do it?"

Although he was smirking, darkness lurked in his eyes. "What makes you think I am not looking forward to devouring you?"

"Because if you wanted to, you'd have done it already, and you'd hardly care to ask what my feelings are for you." She stiffened, fighting her instincts to go to him. "You... you're sure there's no other way? Am I going to find out later you bent the truth?"

A growl vibrated through his chest. "No. This is the only way, and it is not a lie."

She had to focus on her survival and that of their unborn son.

He took a step closer to her, and this time, she didn't move. "You have every right to be angry with me." He closed the gap between them but didn't touch her, his gaze pinning her to the spot. "But I will protect you and our son. By any means necessary."

A twinge of fear slithered into her mind at the darkness etched on her husband's face. As his pupils thinned, she glimpsed the monster within, ready to take what was his.

3

SECRETS

K ai paced his private study, each footstep echoing. Heat licked the dark wooden walls, burning into them. Celina had left the first opportunity she had when he moved away from the door. Knowing she didn't want to be in the same room as him boiled his blood, and he needed to destroy something soon or he'd lose control.

Shiriki entered the room and gave a small bow. "You wanted to see me?"

"Why can Celina read *Madka* symbols?" He pointed at the images floating above his tablet.

Shiriki remained silent as though choosing his words. "I am unsure."

"She said her stepfather taught her languages, but Madka is rare and used for ancient spells forbidden by most. Who was he?"

Shiriki's irises flashed in fury, and his jaw tightened. "He was no one."

Kai arched an eyebrow and smirked. "Well, well. Is this a delicate subject for you?"

"If Celina left you and someone else raised your son, would it not be for you as well?" Shiriki shot back. As though realizing what he'd said, he shook his head and chuckled, "I suppose it would not be the same."

Kai smelled the lie yet wasn't sure which part was true and which wasn't. Shiriki had a knack for being excellent at hiding himself and rarely did he lose control.

"I want his name."

"His name was Dean Perry, and you will not like the information I have about him."

Kai took a few steps closer, stopping a foot away from the Viscus. "I did not ask for a warning."

"He was a Venatore under the highest of the group's leaders, Jacob Mackenzy."

Kai felt another wave of anger flood his body. A few of the walls peeled and cracked under the heat. Shiriki glanced at his arm as his flesh blistered but didn't mutter any complaint.

Venatores. Lumen who were banished from the religious order because they practiced black magic. They could be threats if driven by one common goal, which didn't happen often as they were too power hungry, betraying one another for their own gratification.

"Why," Kai asked, grabbing Shiriki by the throat, digging his fingernails into his flesh, "did you not inform me years ago? He raised her for five years. Who knows what magic he may have implemented inside her mind?"

As soon as Kai released him, Shiriki rubbed his neck, the wounds closing. "Celina wore the pendant. We could harm none of them." Shiriki shrugged. "Besides, she can most likely read the language because he taught her. Not because she can use dark magic."

"Did Celina's mother ever mention anything about this?"

"After she birthed her, I visited them. But once you caught me, I did not—"

"Do not lie. I know you continued visiting Elizabeth without telling me. Even after I forbade it." He didn't hold a grudge against Shiriki's curiosity but admired his bravery for trying to deceive him.

Shiriki locked gazes with Kai, and white flames danced behind those silver irises. "Elizabeth did not share any information about the man she married." Shiriki glanced toward the door. "How is Celina faring?"

"Why? Do you care?" Kai scoffed, turning his back on his second in command. "I destroyed her entire world and told her so many truths that caused her pain. She is overwhelmed."

"She has been here for a month. When are you going to finish the process?" Though Shiriki asked innocently enough, Kai knew this demon better.

Kai released some of his power, and Shiriki winced as it pressed against him with a warning. "We are not discussing it. Do I make myself clear?" he said through gritted teeth.

The thought, usually desirable to any of his kind, brought him no joy. If he could, he'd postpone this forever, but it was inevitable. The longer he waited, the more he risked. He needed to destroy the one thing he loved soon.

His lips curled as he turned his attention on Shiriki. "We hurt everything we love… Inescapable, no?"

Shiriki averted his gaze. "Yes, and we spend the rest of our days trying to fix it." Before Kai asked about the unusual comment, Shiriki pointed to the door. "Did you want to see the finished product?"

Kai nodded and materialized near the gates leading out to the Inferno. The only place to enter and leave his realm… well, for other demons. *He* had a few places he could come and go as he pleased. The iron bent and twisted at the presence of the king, allowing him to walk through without slowing.

The guardian who was stationed outside the gate, Cameo, bowed. "My king."

Once out of the area of the dark realm where his dwelling

stood, the scenery changed. Corpses lay scattered as far as the eye could see, empty shells of their former selves, writhing in agony. Their souls remained trapped inside their painful flesh, blistering and peeling for eternity. None of them could be used at this stage. Hence Shiriki had come up with the idea to experiment while they were alive and in their own world.

Shiriki materialized next to his king, a smile curling his lips as he strode forward. A few hands reached out toward them in desperation but turned to ashes before they even came close to the king. Shiriki took a few outstretched hands, ripping off limbs, wanting to hear the screams he so adored. Kai's gaze swept the land as they strode through the carnage and guts. The strange earth beneath their feet squished where thousands of years' worth of life had soaked in.

Light came from the red vines growing within the corpses. The plant-like fauna didn't have leaves, but instead, bright flames sparked, the fires of Hell as described by humans for centuries, both in Demias—the human world—and the other world, Pyralis. Kai chuckled.

A demon talked about our realms, and the humans used it to put terror in the hearts of others. Keep them in line. Good. Let them fear us.

Eyeballs swiveled within the stone. They followed their king and Shiriki as they entered the cavern between worlds. One side led to the Silence realm, a place with many purposes. His kind ventured there to devour souls, and in his case, it was also somewhere he could unleash his spirit form without destroying his realm.

They took the tunnel as Kai's mind filled with... something. Worry? He didn't care for the feeling at all.

His mood turned darker than before, relieved slightly by the fresh claw marks on stone. Someone had dragged a victim through, adding to the broken fingernails scattered along the stalagmites. Beings fought hard when brought here.

His thirst for blood pulsed through his veins stronger than

ever. His urge to tend to a few subjects when he'd return to his dwelling, someone to quench his rage and frustration before he'd proceed with the ceremony, surged.

"How many prisoners do we have in the dungeon?" he asked.

Shiriki stopped near a nest of creatures, their bright yellow irises locked on the demons inside their lair. None of the black-winged creatures dared to approach. Their bodies had adapted, and though smaller than they once were, these predators were no less dangerous. Thin and rigid feathers created an oil-like substance they used to paralyze victims with so they fed on warm blood and flesh. Prey died from shock, but it took time. Shiriki had captured a few to develop useful paralyzing serums.

Focusing on his king, a knowing gleam sparked in his silver irises. "Five prisoners who need your personal attention."

"Always so gifted at reading me." Everything was frustrating him but knowing why didn't help in the least.

Spiders scuttled away as Shiriki leaned against the stone, and he stared at the stalactites hanging from the ceiling. "Since this will be the first time one of our kind will devour a soul without destroying the mind, I developed something that will help keep Celina unharmed during the process. However, since it has never been tested, there are… risks."

Bones crunched under Kai's feet as he took a step forward. "What kind of risks?" When he stayed silent too long, the wall next to him cracked, the loose rocks rolling into the darkness in repetitive echoes.

Shiriki arched an eyebrow, and his smile curled. "It will keep her intact and whole but devouring a being's soul will not be so simple. She will be terrorized at the thought, and it may shatter her mind."

"I know what I have to do." Kai's hands curled into fists. "Now show me the finished product."

Shiriki shrugged but turned and marched into one of the sacrificial chambers. Kai followed and slowed when his second in command stopped near a hole in the wall. Shiriki opened a small caged window, and inside, a glowing green orb pulsed with a faint light. Kai arched an eyebrow. Barely the size of an apple, he doubted it would do any good against his essence.

As Kai reached out toward it, the light brightened until his vitality recoiled from it. "Interesting."

"It will keep her safe during the transition when she will be most vulnerable." Shiriki glanced at the exit to the chambers. The only heartbeat in the whole realm belonged to Celina, making her a tempting target as the blood pumping through her veins could be sensed for miles.

Kai closed the caged window and glowered. "You are not to harm her. Do I make myself clear?"

"I learned my lesson from the last time."

Kai doubted his second in command would restrain his morbid fascination with Celina. Although Kai wasn't sure if it was because she was the first of her kind or because Celina was Shiriki's own flesh and blood.

Probably both.

The guardian to the gates stepped inside the sacrificial chamber, clearing his throat. "Apologies." He bowed in respect, his teal irises never leaving Kai's gaze.

"What is it?" Kai frowned. It was rare the guardian ever left his post unless it was important.

He straightened, his attention turning to Shiriki. "There seems to be a disturbance in the human world near your dwelling. Your caretaker, Hilda, has been requesting help."

"I suppose I should stop ignoring her calls." Shiriki grinned as he walked toward the door, glancing over his shoulder. "If you need any assistance with the orb before the ceremony, you know where to find me."

Kai gritted his teeth as he watched him leave.

Cameo stared at his king. "If I may… you look troubled."

Kai glowered, and his subject flinched. "I need to devour a soul and take a life."

"I am guessing your wife is the one you will rip apart and claim?"

"Yes."

And after I devour her, after she sees what I truly am, she will never let me near her again.

His hands curled into fists, puncturing his skin as he pushed the thought from his mind. All he thought of was pinning her down and loving her until she couldn't think of anyone but him. But he would have to be patient after he sealed their deal; he owed her that much. Besides, his contracts didn't come with an annulment clause.

He'd take what was his. Her soul. Her life.

4

———

A SCARE

Celina pushed the book she was reading into its place, taking deep breaths. Since waking up that morning, she couldn't seem to get rid of growing nausea threatening to make her retch anything she'd eaten. She patted her sweaty forehead and leaned against the shelf.

Shiriki walked in, and she kept her gaze fixed on him, ready to react if he tried anything. He reached into his pocket and pulled out a glowing green orb, letting it glide against his skin as he moved his hand to the sides of it.

"What's that?" She stared at the apple-sized orb.

"Curious? You rarely want to speak with me."

"I wonder why," she said through her teeth. He was the only demon she knew who didn't seem to care about being burned alive for hurting her.

"Always so much hate and fear for me. Good." He grinned as he stepped closer, holding out the orb. "I created a few of these so Mekaisto can proceed with the ceremony while keeping you whole."

Her stomach churned. "Oh."

He came closer. Before she scrambled away from him, he

grabbed her wrist and placed it in her palm. The green glow reflected in his irises, and she shivered. "Even Mekaisto's powers are no match for these. They burn demons who touch them. This will protect your mind as he takes your soul, pet."

All demons suffered… Her heart hammered against her ribs as she stared into Shiriki's gaze. "Then how can you hold it?"

"You catch on quickly. I am proud." When the thought of telling Kai about this crossed her mind, he chuckled. "No need to concern yourself. He has always been curious about my particular skills."

More questions than she could handle hung on the tip of her tongue. "Are you… the first Viscus like everyone told me? Is that why other demons fear you so much?" She swallowed hard, and his glower made her less brave. "And what does that make my husband exactly?"

His expression turned to stone, but something cold and furious rested behind his gaze. "I am feared because of my lovely methods of researching what I am passionate about."

"Is that all?"

A wave of energy fell against her so hard, she was sure Kai was nearby, but it wasn't her husband. It was Shiriki.

"It is all you need to know. As for Mekaisto, ask him yourself." He took the orb. "Now, run along."

Not wanting to press her luck, she rushed out of the room. Another pang shot inside her, and she slowed in the hallway.

Maybe I'm hungry.

A burning pain ripped through her and she cried out, pressing a hand against her belly. She fell to her knees, closing her eyelids tight as she hissed through her teeth. Warmth wet her leggings, and she stared as blood pooled underneath her, her clothes stained darker between her thighs.

"No…" She scrambled to her feet and screamed as her flesh tore, more blood soaking her clothes. "Please, no."

Kai.

Taking a few steps, she swallowed hard against the bile burning the back of her throat, but she gritted her teeth and pushed on. As soon as she built momentum, she didn't stop, ignoring the feel of her blood wet on her thighs and abdomen. She barely made it down the stairs when her legs gave out. Someone grabbed her before she fell, and her mouth dried.

Shiriki's cold gaze didn't match his smirk. "Seems like you are in some pain."

"Please, help me," she whispered, grabbing onto him.

Celina sat in the armchair near a table holding a tray of instruments. Nalie busied herself with checking Celina, muttering to herself from time to time.

Keeping her eyes averted, Celina tried her best not to meet anyone's gaze. Shiriki stood in the corner, arms crossed and watching her in silence. He had brought her to a private room, and Nalie arrived seconds later. Celina couldn't help her surprise when Shiriki didn't take advantage to hurt her in the weakened state she'd been in. She supposed having her husband inside the dwelling helped. Kai had been summoned, and although it looked like he was fighting himself to go to her, he respected her wish for space. Instead, he paced, his jaw clenched.

Nalie wiped a needle with a strong-smelling liquid, and Celina gripped the armrests. Nalie arched an eyebrow. "What is the matter?"

"She is afraid of needles," Kai said. He turned to Shiriki and motioned his head.

Celina's pulse sped as Shiriki approached, and she tried bolting to her feet to get away, but Nalie grabbed her wrist.

"Wait, what's going on?" Celina asked, hating how much her voice trembled.

Shiriki took the needle from Nalie. "I am better skilled with pointy objects."

"I know; I remember when you cut me open... twice." Celina continued tugging, her breath coming in faster.

"While I am skilled at causing an immense amount of suffering to any being, I can also make it painless. Although, I see little amusement in that." He crouched in front of her while Nalie kept her grip on Celina's wrist.

Celina shook her head, her eyes widening as she placed her hands over her belly. "Don't touch me. I want nothing near me. Please, I don't want—"

The lights flickered, and Celina focused her attention on her husband as his eyes glowed a brighter shade of red. Both Shiriki and Nalie stepped away, and as soon as her path was clear, she dashed to Kai. She buried her head in his chest, trying to regain her composure. It was hard considering she was trembling from head to toe. Kai had stiffened, but as seconds ticked by, he rubbed her back, silent as though terrified of breaking the sudden affectionate act on her part.

"Shiriki's skill in causing pain is only matched by his ability to use instruments with no one ever feeling it," Kai said in a low voice. "I would not let him harm you again, dove."

Shiriki chuckled, and Celina turned her head. She gaped as he held the needle up, the liquid inside gone. Glancing at her arm, she opened and closed her mouth, a small trickle of blood rolling along her skin. "You... I didn't feel... how is that even possible?"

"Useful for unsuspecting people who might be sleeping, no?"

She shuddered at the thought, pushing closer to her husband. "That doesn't make it sound better at all."

"It was not supposed to," he replied with a wink before

walking away. He returned the needle on the small table and left the room without another word.

Nalie left, and Celina backed away from Kai, her ears pounding in the heavy silence between them. He had held and reassured her while Shiriki injected the substance into her arm so she wouldn't realize it. Kai knew how much she hated needles ever since they'd been together when he was Thomas.

She met his gaze. "Thank you for doing that for me."

"Of course."

Her chest squeezed at the sorrow etched onto his features.

Grabbing the hem of her shirt, tears blurred her vision as she stared at the blood. "What happened?"

"Our kind will sometimes feed on their mothers while inside the womb." He ran his fingers through his hair, the dark silk flowing through his pale skin. "Usually, we can heal quickly, but in your case, only being half and with a soul…"

She twisted her fingers between the material, taking a step closer. "Is our son okay, though?" She took his hand and placed it over her abdomen. "Can you tell?"

"He is… weak. And so are you." He traced a finger along a blood streak. "I will have to go through the process sooner than expected."

"When?" she asked.

"I would do it now, but the risk is too great right after something like this happened to you. However, we cannot wait much longer and risk it happening again. Three days, at the most."

She took a few steps back and sat in the armchair. "I guess there's no other choice, then."

His hands curled into fists, and he gave her a curt nod before walking out. Celina wiped the tears rolling along her cheeks. His distance hurt, and yet she was the one who'd demanded it. But her mind hadn't accepted Kai was Thomas. And whenever she wrapped her brain around the truth, she remembered too well the video of him kidnapping those children.

She closed her eyes, the memory of Kai dropping to his knees, pleading for her to understand why he had done everything he had. To save her and their child. She had forgiven him at that moment.

Because I love him. Thomas. Kai. Whoever he is. I love him.

5

VULNERABLE

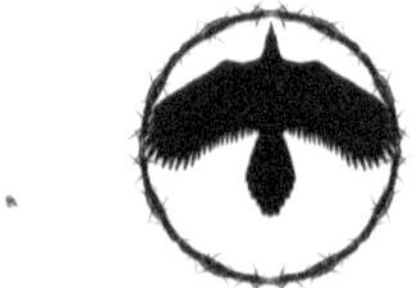

T he ceremony to claim Celina's soul would happen in a few hours, and she was anything but ready. She'd lingered for as long as possible inside one of the living areas but knew stalling wouldn't do any good. And so, pushing herself forward, Celina walked to her room, waiting for the end to come.

When she spotted Kai leaning against the wall near her bedroom, her steps slowed. He was in the lower demon form she'd gotten used to while seeking her revenge and wearing a tuxedo that fitted his muscular body. She swallowed hard as butterflies fluttered inside her stomach, stopping in front of him.

"It is time." He opened the door and motioned his head. "I have something for you before we leave."

Her heart hammered as she stepped inside, the corners of her eyes burning as she stared at her wedding dress.

Why does he want me to wear this? Some sick joke?

He grasped her shoulders and spun her, his irises glowing brightly. She held her breath, arching back.

"It will make the process easier for you." He pulled her closer until they were inches apart. "I may have lied and bent the truth, but my love for you has always been real. The day we married, when we said our vows to one another, those words held nothing but truth."

Tears filled her eyes, and she blinked fast, willing them not to fall. "You… hurt me so much."

"I know." He wrapped his arms around her, holding her close, and this time, she let him. "And nothing I can say or do will ever make it right. But you are my wife. If I have to start over with you and gain your trust once more, then so be it."

She narrowed her eyes and squirmed out of his grasp. "Don't make this sound like I don't have a choice again."

He clenched his jaw but said nothing. He didn't need to. His gaze spoke volumes.

You belong to me.

Running her hands across her belly, Celina turned away from him, her shoulders slumping. Neither of them had a choice in the matter of taking her soul. It was necessary to save their son.

But what about after?

She turned toward the dress and let the material run between her fingers. Her mind flew to when she had picked the dress months before her wedding day. They had agreed to marry with a justice of the peace instead of a traditional church wedding, but Thomas had insisted they dress for the occasion. A diamond white gown in a V-neck cut adorned with beads along the lace. The back was open, but delicate straps crisscrossed with beaded lines. She had always loved the bigger gowns, and so chose the chapel length train, making her feel like a princess on their special day.

He caressed her shoulders lightly as though terrified she'd flinch away from him. Shivers ran along her skin, and her breath caught inside her throat at the feel of his warmth.

"I had it altered, so it is not too tight." He leaned closer, his breath tickling her ear, and whispered. "Will you wear it?"

She reached behind her and grasped his hand, giving it a small squeeze, unable to say anything.

They stood in front of the gate, darkness slithering along the void. Celina couldn't look away as she tried to figure out the strange pull toward it. It looked like the strange liquid Kai had materialized at the bottom of the black tree in the woods where she used to live. The wind whistled in her ears, and she suppressed a shiver. Her wedding dress was sleeveless, and although it touched the ground, she felt vulnerable.

"Beyond this is the Hell humans speak of. We need to cross it to reach another area." He dangled a black cloth, a wicked grin on his face.

She took a step back, goosebumps crawling along her skin. "How many realms are there?"

Cameo straightened, pushing his forest-green hair behind his ear. "If I may, my king?" When Kai made a curt nod, Cameo turned his teal-color irises on Celina. "There is one realm, but within are different areas. The dark realm is where the king and you live, and then beyond this void is what we refer to as the Inferno, and then there is the Silence."

"So, we need to go to this place? Why?" She glanced between Kai and Cameo.

Kai waved his hand near the void, inviting the darkness to slither across his skin. "Because when I perform the ceremony, it reacts like an implosion. It will drain anything with dark essence, destroying this place. While the Silence is a part of the whole realm, powerful magic separates it. It offers a place for the many races to gather without draining too much life force."

She pointed at the blindfold. "And what's with that?" When his expression flashed with guilt, she took a deep breath. "You don't want me to see what humans call Hell."

"I do not wish to cause you further suffering." Without waiting, he wrapped the cloth over her eyes.

A knot formed in her throat, the memory of when Thomas had brought her to their dream house as a wedding present coming to mind. This time, there would be no gift. It would be her soul and life taken from her. She ran her palm over her abdomen, tracing the brand Kai had burned into her when they'd made the deal.

I have to do this. For our child.

He finished tying the blindfold, then hugged her tight, leaning in toward her ear. "I *am* sorry." His tone was strained like he was fighting two sides of himself. The king of the dark realm and her husband in a war against one another. "I will not wait until you and our son are on the edge of death."

She stiffened, her emotions continuing to fight at what she felt for him. Part of her loved him while another side could never trust him again. How could she when he'd made her whole life—the life they shared—a lie?

Kai lifted Celina off the ground and she yelped, clinging to him when he picked her up in his arms. Her pulse sped as a soft substance tickled her arms and legs. She held her breath, thinking she was submerged. Soon the silken touch vanished, replaced by scorching heat.

No, not heat. Pressure.

"It will be uncomfortable for a few minutes," he murmured, walking ahead.

Cries and moans vibrated through the air, and Celina squeezed her eyes tighter; she didn't want to take the chance the blindfold would slip. Her mind created a vivid enough picture with no help. A few times, the smell of what she imagined was burning flesh reached her nostrils. A pulsing in her ears muffled the screams, yet it wasn't in sync with her own heart.

What's going on?

Kai tightened his grip. "Your soul is connecting to the ones here."

She swallowed hard, but soon enough, cool air caressed her skin, and Kai put her on her feet. He slipped the blindfold off, and she rubbed her arms, staring around the dark cave.

Light filtered through cracks inside the cavern walls, and, ahead, darkness like she'd never seen beckoned.

"What's that?" she asked, pointing ahead.

"That is what I will use to perform the ceremony."

"It feels…" She clutched her chest, unable to finish the sentence. *Pure evil.*

He placed his hand on her back, staring at her with an unreadable expression. "It is."

Before she changed her mind and ran for the Hell outside the cave, Celina strode forward. It was now or never and never meant losing her son and dying herself. She refused to do that, so she continued, ready to face whatever this ceremony meant.

They walked through the tunnels but slowed at a fork. Celina halted, staring at a large body of water. Stretching farther than she could see, its surface remained unmoving. But she felt something there, swimming beneath, waiting.

"This way." He took her hand and led her down the second path, away from the eerie water. Up ahead, a few tunnels led to darkness, but the one they took was lit with torches anchored into the rocky walls. They stopped near a door in the stone. The dark wood added to the ominous look of the place.

Celina shrank as they approached, tugging against his grip. "Kai…"

He opened the door. "Your fear is normal." He pulled her inside, and it slammed behind them with an echo. She froze as he stood in front of her, blocking her view of the room. "I give you my word you will be all right. Let me prove you can trust me."

She nodded, unable to utter a single word as she stared ahead. He moved to the side and let her stare, silent. A stone altar stood in the middle of the space, chains anchored into the top block. Dried blood stained it, the haunting memories of eons of sacrifices. A history of the deaths.

She put her hands over her belly, holding on to her sanity as best she could. Her imagination ran wild, creating low-chanting acolytes dressed in robes. One hovered a dagger over a sacrifice, then cut out the heart and took a bite from the bloody organ. She pictured Kai devouring a victim as they screamed.

She shook her head, trying to force the ideas out of her mind.

"What is this place?" she asked quietly.

He was silent for a few seconds. "A sacrificial chamber."

Where a being was dragged inside, never to come out whole. Did they know what would happen? Had they been as terrified as I feel?

Glancing at Kai, she silently told him how scared she felt. His gaze softened, and he waved his hand toward the room. Ripples formed along the walls, warping everything in its path as the altar changed to a marble pedestal. A beautiful room replaced the morbid scene. The stone floor and walls changed to hardwood flooring and earth-toned walls.

She gaped, staring at the room where she'd gotten married to Thomas. "What—"

"This ceremony will be different. I told you. I have no wish to cause you any more suffering." He pulled her toward the altar but stopped when she dug her heels into the floor.

"I… can it wait? Just a bit longer?" Her voice shook. "I… I'm not ready."

He took a step toward her and kissed the top of her head. "We will go slowly."

After a few seconds, she took a deep breath and nodded.

Kai led her forward, and she stood near the pedestal, staring up at Kai like she had Thomas on the day they exchanged vows. Her throat tightened, and she drew a shuddering breath as he took her hands in his.

"Celina," he breathed, "the day we met, my world changed, and you became my everything. The world could stop, but so long as we are together, nothing else would ever matter. You are the light to my darkness, a breath of life within me. While I have little, what I give you is my being, all of me."

Tears burned the corner of her eyes as memories overwhelmed her. Those were the same vows Thomas had spoken the day they got married.

Does he remember?

A small smile touched his lips as he cupped her face. "Yes, I remember."

Her heart fluttered at the memory. Thomas brought her to this same room, just one more in the courthouse inside city hall. No church. Two witnesses: Celina's best friend, Namika, and her boyfriend, Terry.

Yet it had felt like they'd been alone that day. Just her handsome fiancé and herself ready to start their lives together as husband and wife. Thomas had spoken those vows then, his voice husky with emotions. She had answered, tears filling her eyes.

The justice of the peace smiled ear to ear as she spoke. "I, Justice Marlene Doyle, by virtue of the powers vested in me by the Marriage Act and the Province of Ontario, do hereby pronounce you, Thomas Leviet and Celina Tayen, to be married. I wish you long life, happiness, prosperity, and may the vows you made to each other today sustain you forever." She waved her hand, her smile widening. "You may celebrate your marriage with a kiss."

Even as Namika and Terry applauded and whooped in excitement, nothing else existed for Celina as Thomas's lips slanted over hers. Marrying the love of her life had made her happier than words could ever describe.

She looked at him now. So many years had passed. He wasn't her Thomas anymore. And yet he was.

"Kai, I loved Thomas." She met his gaze. "And I love you. You had a terrible decision to make when I became pregnant, and I understand you had to taint my soul while playing your part. I won't ever hate you for that, and I'm sorry it was something you were forced to do." She squeezed his hands tighter and swallowed hard. "I keep saying my life was built on a lie, and you made it crumble beneath me when you told me the truth, but the thing is you were always my life. Thomas, Kai, the devil I made a deal with—they're all you. And you're still here. My life is here." Tears ran down her cheeks and calm settled over her as she let go of her resentment.

He leaned his forehead against hers, his eyes closed as he inhaled. "I will spend the rest of eternity proving you can trust me."

The room undulated, this time transforming into a beautiful bedroom. A king-sized bed stood in the middle, the red satin sheets inviting.

"What—"

"I still have to take your soul," he said with a chuckle, "but I will make it so you are not aware it is happening. While I claim your body, you are mine, and I take what belongs to me."

"Only if you're mine, too."

"I am." He ran his fingers along her arm. "Now, undress."

She reached around her back, and pulled on the zipper, but slowed before finishing. Her body had changed in the past few weeks. She had stretch marks on her skin, and her breasts and hips were larger than before. What if he didn't want her anymore?

He growled, taking a step closer.

Quickly, she let the dress pool around her feet. She

removed her bra and slid down her panties, her breath coming faster.

She stood before him, naked and vulnerable.

His gaze raked over her body with a burning hunger. He took a few steps forward and reached out toward her belly, but hovered over her skin as though unsure.

She took his hand and placed it against her.

"He is growing faster than I expected." His fingers caressed her. "How are you feeling?"

She wrapped her arms around his neck and pulled him closer. "I'm fine."

"And how are you feeling about us?" he asked quietly.

"We have a lot to work on for the next while, but we'll do it together."

"We will do many things together," he said with a lewd grin.

In less than a second, Kai stood naked, his muscles rippling in the low lighting of the room. She ran her hands against his hard chest, her pulse racing as she stared at his pale skin.

Mine.

The word resonated inside her mind as she felt him invade her thoughts. He pressed her body against his, kissing along her neck as she closed her eyes. He felt so good, and he was hers as much as she belonged to him.

"Your body, soul, and life are mine." His tone darkened. "And although I never had a soul of my own, though my life is endless, you have all of me."

Before she responded, he took her mouth, thrusting his tongue inside. She moaned as he cupped her breasts, her nipples hardening under his touch. When he tugged at the hard peaks, their lips parted, and she let out a harsh breath.

"I want you." The words left her in a whisper, a plea from the need pulsing through her.

He lifted her in his arms and carried her to their bed,

sitting her on its edge. Despite his gentleness, an animalistic expression flashed across his face. He crouched and glided his hand along her thigh.

Heat filled her, and she licked her lips, parting her legs. Her throbbing increased when his gaze traveled to her sex. He stared with such carnal desire, she was sure she'd orgasm.

"You are so beautiful… and no one else will ever touch you." He kissed her inner thigh and trailed his tongue across her skin, nipping along the way as she gasped.

Letting herself fall onto the bed, her chest heaved as her stomach fluttered. He licked her swollen lips, and she trembled under the pleasure of his touch. He flicked her clit, and she whimpered. "Please."

His muffled groans against her wetness had her trembling, and she writhed as he sucked hard on her pink flesh. She grabbed hold of his hands where they held her hips, digging her fingernails into his flesh and crying out.

"Your screams are as delicious as you are, dove."

Running her fingers through his hair, she tugged so he'd look at her. He growled at being denied, his gaze darting to her sex as he licked his lips.

She panted. "I want you."

He stood and feathers flew around him, black as night. Within seconds, the feathers dissipated into smoke, leaving Kai in his true form. Her demon.

The horns on his head held red arcane symbols, glowing brightly. He folded his black wings as he took a step closer, the darkness behind his red irises sending a shiver down her spine. Her chest heaved as she crawled farther onto the mattress and reached her hand out to him. She wished she had the words to tell him how much she loved him but showing him would be better.

He chuckled as he got on the bed. Even kneeling he towered over her like a looming shadow waiting to pounce.

"You do not need to use words. I can feel it radiating off you as easily as I smell your lust."

She took shallow gasps trying to steady herself, but it didn't work. After a few seconds of suffocating as though someone pressed against her chest, she turned to her side and gasped. She rubbed her hand against her belly. "I guess he's grown so much he's pressing against my lungs or something." When he frowned, she grinned. "Yes, I'm okay. Now, please take me."

He lay next to her and held her against him. Pushing her hair to the side, he licked at her neck. His erections pressed against her ass, and she rubbed herself on them with a whimper.

"You drive my instincts out of control," he whispered in her ear as one of his wings curled over them. Sliding his hand between her thighs, his pointed fingernails glided along her skin. He lifted her knee, opening her legs, and heat rose in her cheeks as cool air caressed her soaked inner thighs.

"You are so wet for me."

He pressed his cock against her opening, pussy throbbed with need, and she moaned. When Kai's second cock rubbed between her ass cheeks, she held her breath. "Please, please, Kai."

In one hard push, he thrust both his cocks inside her, stretching her until she cried out, panting. He cupped her breast and squeezed it as he pulled out slowly, then pushed back inside. Over and over, he plunged her toward the edge.

Gripping her hair, he yanked it, forcing her head to the side. The shadows from his wings turned into something physical, slithering over her body. Wrapping around the hard peaks of her nipples, it suckled, and she moaned as it tugged harder at her sensitive nubs. At the same time, Kai slid his tongue between her lips, thrusting inside, fucking her mouth. His essence slid along her hip and licked at her clit, rubbing until she convulsed around his cocks. He muffled her screams with his ravaging mouth.

He pumped inside her harder, every thrust bringing her to the edge of another orgasm. Sweat cooled her, and their scents mixed as their wet skin slapped together. He slid his tongue along her jaw, then nipped at her neck as he kneaded her breast. His hand slid lower, and he nudged her clit with a pointed claw.

She came with a soul-shattering intensity, holding onto him like her life depended on it.

In a way, it does.

6

SOUL TO TAKE

K ai's hands curled into fists as he held back the urge to rip his victim into pieces. His wife. But the monster within wanted satisfaction, wanted her. Wanted deeper inside her.

All his other senses heightened, and his smile widened at the taste of her. His thoughts latched onto a memory of when she knew him as Thomas.

They had been lying naked in their bed inside the apartment they shared, and even back then, he smelled the fear coming off her. But there had been lust and excitement, too. Her first time. And he would claim her.

"Sorry, I'm nervous." With a small laugh, her gray irises twinkled, and her face grew flush.

Taking what was his, claiming something so innocent, had been a dangerous move. A few times, he was sure his eyes flashed red at something she said or, better yet, thought.

He pushed her hair behind her ear. "Relax. We'll take it slow." He brushed his lips over hers, and he groaned at the smell of her sex. Wet, and ready for him already.

He wanted to bend her over and take her hard. Make her scream and beg. But he'd promised to be gentle with her, and he wouldn't break his word. Not with Celina. His everything.

She slid her hand along his chest, then lower. He closed his eyes to keep his true nature from showing, letting out a hard breath. She wrapped her fingers around his erection.

"I want you," she whispered, her breath tickling against his mouth.

He slanted his lips over hers and thrust his tongue inside her mouth, exploring, taking. Celina belonged to him, so why was he waiting? A tiny whimper sounded in her throat, and he slowed.

That's why. I don't wish to hurt her.

He wrapped his arm around her, bringing her closer to him. Heat radiated from her, and his cock hardened at the desire flowing from her mind. He rolled her onto her back, spreading her legs apart, barely holding onto his control at the erotic scent of her body.

"I want to lick every inch of you." He lowered his head and lapped at her sex. Her taste was perfect. She tasted of... her. Of what was his.

He pushed a finger into her wetness, and she arched, moaning his name. A few curses left her lips, and he grinned as he thrust a second finger inside. He licked her clit, then sucked, pumping his fingers into her in a steady rhythm. She writhed under him, her toes curling as her pleasure came crashing in waves.

When he pulled back to lick at her juices, she cried out his name. "Thomas, I... please. Take me." Her chest heaved, her body covered in sweat.

Her gaze no longer held fear. No, it was filled with a lust that matched his own.

I'll most certainly oblige.

He spread her legs wider, wanting nothing more than to watch as he thrust inside her. But it would be too risky; he couldn't chance changing in front of her. He leaned forward and turned off their bedside lamp, plunging the room into darkness. The only illumination came filtered through their curtains.

He wouldn't be able to watch her reactions, but he'd feel them, sense her thoughts. That would be enough. Wrapping his hand around his cock, he placed the head at her glistening opening, holding back. He wanted to be inside her already; the monster within was impatient.

Slow.

Repeating the word inside his mind helped but not much. He pushed inside, ready for her discomfort. She hissed but pushed her heels into his ass.

That was all the encouragement he needed. He thrust inside, and she screamed before she stiffened.

He stopped, waiting. "Are you all right?" he asked. For the first time in his existence, it concerned him to hurt another being.

Such a strange feeling.

She cupped his face and nodded. "Yes. Please fuck me."

He slid out slowly, then slammed back into her in one hard thrust. She moaned, her fingers digging into his arms. But instead of going fast, he slowed, connecting to her mind so he could be everything she would need. Everything she deserved.

They explored each other in the darkness. His senses were heightened, and by how she reacted to him, the same could be said of her. He spread her legs wider apart, sheathing himself to the hilt and pumping harder until she climaxed around his cock. Her muscles squeezed around him and he groaned, spilling his seed inside her.

He kissed the top of her forehead as she panted. "I love you, Celina."

Her breath seemed to stop, her pulse racing faster than when they had sex. A strange feeling nestled inside his chest as he waited.

What is this? I'm... nervous?

"I love you, too, Thomas. Very much."

A shuddering gasp brought Kai to the present. Celina's breath hitched as he traced his pointed fingernail along her inner thigh, staring at her glistening sex. He lowered himself, careful not to hurt her with his horns, and lapped at his treasure. She tasted delectable, and he wanted more.

Without words, the blindfold appeared in his hand, and a lecherous smile curled his lips as he stared at Celina. Her cheeks flushed deeper, and he groaned, the urge to thrust into her surging through him.

"Trust me."

She nodded, and a deep feeling of pride filled him. He locked gazes with her, losing himself; Celina, the love of his existence, trusted him, and it was more than he could put into words. He vowed to nurture her gift and never break it again.

He placed the black material over her eyes and smiled at the blush creeping in her cheeks. He nibbled at her neck, sliding his tongue along her skin as he stretched her arms out at either side of her. Ropes materialized around the bedposts and around her wrists, keeping her still.

Her breath hitched. "Kai?"

"I will make you feel good." He pressed his thumb against her clit, circling faster as she arched, straining against her bonds as she cried out.

He suckled at her breast, his free hand pushing against her chest, urging what belonged to him to come forward. A filmy gold substance rose from beneath her skin, and she shuddered, riding the waves of her last orgasm.

Her soul scattered along her body, and he roared, the ravenous vibration shaking the room. Celina flinched, but he pressed the heads of his cocks against her openings and pushed inside in one hard thrust. She screamed, cursing his name as he sheathed himself deep. He clawed at the golden light, ripping parts as he pulled it into his mouth.

Will she still love me after this?

Her soul stirred atop her chest, desperate to find itself a place to hide, and he couldn't help but smile. There was no escape; it belonged to him.

He opened wider as he descended on his prey. His tongue latched on to the golden filament as it squirmed. She took a shuddering breath, a tiny whimper escaping her lips as he continued pumping into her faster. The sound of skin on skin grew louder amongst the cries and grunts of their pleasure.

He poured himself into her, groaning against her neck as he buried his cocks to their hilts inside her. She moaned, then passed out as he devoured the last of her humanity.

Mine, dove. All mine.

7

BEATING HEART

The dwelling was quiet. In Celina's state, Kai hadn't wanted any unnecessary witnesses. Her body needed time to adapt without a soul.

Another pang flowed through him at the thought of what he'd done. Guilt was a troublesome emotion, and he looked forward to when it would leave him. A whole day had passed, and every minute grated on his patience.

Will she truly forgive me after what I have done?

And there was no word about the subjects who had never answered their summons. One or two sometimes went rogue, and he dealt with those swiftly, but this many at once was unlikely. Adam had reported at least sixteen vanished without a trace. All from around the same area: downtown Ottawa near The CrowBar.

That couldn't be a coincidence.

Last Kai heard, two humans had disappeared nearby, and now the authorities of that world had their noses in his business.

With a heavy sigh, Kai sat on the edge of Celina's bed, watching as she slept with his black wings folded. Clenching his jaw, he ran his thumb over the back of her hand. Humans were so fragile. The memory of standing by as his wife had struggled through the woods behind their house, shot and dying, flew through his mind.

He focused on a thumping noise vibrating through his essence. Placing his hand over her chest, he frowned as her heartbeat under his palm.

"A heartbeat?" he whispered. Devouring her soul should have taken her life, yet… He glanced over at where Shiriki stood, silently asking the question.

His second in command shrugged. "She is the first of her kind. We did not know all the possible outcomes. Perhaps she needs to remain alive while carrying your son?" A slow smile curled his lips. "I can always do a few tests on her if you would like."

A few of the nearby mirrors cracked and shattered to the floor, and Kai glowered in their direction.

Shiriki glanced at the shards. "No need to take your anger out on innocent objects."

"Do not test me." He spat the words, sending a wave of energy against the Viscus. Turning to Celina, he ran his hand over her belly. Not for the first time he wondered what their son would look like.

"I rarely see you smile like that," Shiriki commented.

Her abdomen undulated as their son moved, and Kai frowned, unsure what to make of the feelings flooding him. "Had you ever wondered what Celina would look like?"

"No." He bit the word.

Kai didn't comment on the obvious lie. "She should wake soon."

Shiriki moved to the small hole inside the wall where one orb glowed. "These are not necessary since she no longer has her soul. I shall dispose of them shortly." His smile widened as the orb turned to smoke, and he closed the cage door to the hole. "Did she feel it when you ripped away her humanity?" Shiriki asked with amusement in his tone.

The glass shards rose into the air, hovering before impaling into the Viscus's chest and face. He hissed through his teeth, reaching to a large piece sticking inside his eye socket. Pulling it out, he grinned as he stared at his own eyeball impaled at the tip.

"Why are you provoking me?" Kai got to his feet, looming over his second in command as Shiriki put his eyeball back inside.

He blinked a few times, the gash in the eye closing, and returning to the cold silver irises. "Just curious to know if she suffered."

"Why does this matter to you?" He allowed his rage to burn out of him, careful not to affect any area near his wife. The glass melted into Shiriki's flesh, blistering the wounds. "You tortured her despite knowing the consequences. Why would it matter if she felt it when I devoured her soul?"

The shards cooled, and Shiriki wrenched it from his chest, ripping a large hole into his flesh and muscle. He coughed, blood spluttering from the wound as his body healed itself. Then he locked gazes with his king, an unreadable expression on his face. "When she nearly lost your son and died herself... when I found her... she looked so much like her mother... covered in blood." He glanced at Celina as she continued sleeping. "I suppose, for a second, I thought I could save her.

"And what do you mean by that?" When Shiriki didn't answer, he grabbed Shiriki's neck and slammed him against the wall. "You are hiding something. Ever since Celina removed her protective pendant all those years ago, you have grown restless, as though time could not go by fast enough. Your research became an obsession instead of a curiosity." He leaned in inches from Shiriki's face, gritting his teeth. "Why?"

"Time does not exist for us, yet it continues without waiting, and sometimes we need to run to catch up." He stared at the wall, his gaze unfocused as though seeing something that wasn't there. "There is only so far research can go."

Kai took a step back. "You are being cryptic."

"And it is why you tolerate me. I keep you curious enough not to murder me," he stated with a wink.

Celina gasped, and Kai rushed to her, sitting by her side. "You are safe, dove."

Tears filled her eyes. "Are you okay, Kai?"

"Am I…" He searched her mind, trying to understand what worried her. Her guilt slammed into him, and he raised his eyebrows.

She feels guilty about what I had to do.

"Leave us," Kai hissed. Without a word, Shiriki vanished, leaving Celina staring at her hands, tears dropping onto her skin.

He cupped her face, the red of his irises reflecting in her eyes. "I am all right but am worried about you."

"I'm… okay." She averted her gaze, but he turned her head so she'd look at him. "Kai, is it wrong of me to feel guilty about the people I killed to avenge Thomas… to avenge you?"

"No. It is what makes you human. Even without a soul, you are who you are." He inhaled her scent, wanting to taste her. She was so pure and innocent in some ways.

She ran her hand along her chest with a frown. "So… is my soul gone?"

"It is. This will allow you to stay in this realm and help our son grow." He smiled. "Because you are the first of your kind, it is difficult to say what abilities you may have. But considering your parentage, I expect you will develop hidden powers and talents you did not know you possessed."

"Powers?" She stared at her fingers. "As in magic? Like, I could finally kick Shiriki's ass when he tries to hurt me?"

Kai laughed, shaking his head. "I can barely put a mark on

him, so I doubt you could. But yes, it would give you a better chance at escaping, at least."

He took her hand and stood, pulling her to her feet. They strode out of the room in silence, Celina squeezing his hand whenever he glanced at her. He stopped in front of the large black doors leading to his bedroom.

With a silent command, the swirls etched into the doors slithered around. Black smoke seeped from them until an audible click sounded as they opened. He stepped inside and stood still so she took in her surroundings.

Decorated in black, dark reds, and silver, the whole room held his presence, preferring monotone colors. The four-poster bed stood against a wall, twice the size of the king-sized beds in her world. Silk curtains fluttered in the wind from the cathedral window. She shivered from the cool air, and he grinned.

"It would honor me if you shared my bedroom with me."

She nodded, wrapping her arms around his neck as a smile curled her lips.

He placed her on the large bed, and sat next to her, folding his wings behind him. He held her tight, kissing her forehead. A few minutes of silence passed, and he moved her hair behind her ear, his gaze boring into her. "Have you thought of a name?"

"What?" She smiled. "Well, no, not really, I guess. Why? Any thoughts?"

For a second, he remained silent, unsure she would care for the name. "Fenrir."

She closed her eyes and placed her hand against her belly. "I like it." Her smile widened. "Fenrir it is."

"I am glad you do," he said, then kissed her, his tongue licking at her lower lip. Rubbing her back, he traced his fingers along her spine. His shoulders relaxed, comfortable in his true form. The others were restrictive, but if he spent too much time in this one, it unbalanced his realm. He watched as his wife cuddled against him, and a smile curled his lips. Her hair fell past her shoulders in waves, colored like a beautiful fall sunset. Her smell teased his senses, but he resisted his urges. The last month had been torture, fighting between giving her time to adapt and desiring to be inside her. He burned for her.

He kissed her forehead. "You should get some sleep. I know you have been sleeping for some time, but your body needs more rest." He got to his feet. "I have a meeting with a subject."

"Now?" she blurted out, and her cheeks turned pink.

"I am meeting with Shiriki. A body was recently located, and I need to know if it is one of my missing subjects."

She stiffened. "Do you have to go now, though?" She placed her hand against him. "I love falling asleep next to you."

"If I stay, you will not be sleeping." A growl vibrated through his chest, and her breath hitched. She would be his undoing if she continued reacting to him like this. "I will return shortly. I promise."

He missed her warmth already, but he needed answers that would not wait. Once she was underneath the covers, he brushed the top of her head.

"Hurry back." Stretching out, she allowed her nightgown to ride up, exposing the curve of her ass. She grinned, her face flushing.

Oh, I'll definitely hurry back.

And awake or not, he would ravage his beautiful wife, reminding her that to taunt him was unwise.

8

———————

A STROLL

Afew days passed since Celina had started sharing Kai's bedroom, and although he tried spending more time with her, more Sanguis bodies were being found. With every new murder came a message in the language Celina deciphered for her husband.

That morning, he'd frightened her when he lost his patience.

He had grabbed a book from the shelves inside his office as Celina lingered, translating the newest message left behind along with four of Kai's subjects. "You won't like their last message."

Snapping the book shut, he glowered at her. "What did they write this time?"

"They're going to send a surprise in your realm." She hid part of what she translated, but when he thrust through her mind without mercy, she winced, and his body stiffened. She trembled at the pain he'd caused.

"I…" His aura sparked around him, and he strode to the door, pausing for a second. "I did not mean to hurt you. I am not good company, and I will leave before I do irreparable damage. I promise we will speak of this later."

And he'd left without another word. Celina had stayed longer, trying to decipher more of the message threatening to rip away anything that mattered to her husband, hoping she hadn't translated it correctly.

Not only were demons being found murdered, but humans as well. Never in the same location, but always with the same symbols left behind with cryptic messages. Some threatening and taunting.

With a sigh, she left the office and walked toward her favorite place; the living area with a large window looking onto the garden. The twilight turned the plants into eerie monsters. Most had teeth—she knew now—but they were beautiful.

She ran her hands along her chest and shivered. Kai had taken her soul, yet she hadn't felt it. Tears stung the corner of her eyes, and she smiled.

He promised he would make it painless.

"Oh, hello, Celina," Brihan said with a smile, stopping next to her. "How are you?"

She sighed. "I don't know."

"You seem preoccupied." He glanced over her shoulder as though expecting Kai to materialize out of nowhere. In all fairness, he could, so Brihan's fears were logical.

She shrugged. "Just thinking about the demons and humans found murdered. Whoever is killing them always leaves messages, but…"

"But what?"

She scratched her head, trying to explain her thoughts. "It feels like they use the human killings as a distraction. There are always fewer bodies, but it seems like they want the authorities to get involved. To make it difficult for us to find answers with police on high alert. The murders are about demons, and whoever is butchering them has to be strong. One body, maybe. But several at a time? I don't think so. Unless… they were killed individually then left behind together." She let out a sigh. "Wish I knew what was going on."

"Well, so far…"

His voice echoed away as though she was plunged underwater. Energy pulsed through her, and she closed her eyes as her body heated. Her mind numbed, yet she was aware of her feet moving forward.

What?

She wanted to say something, to stop and look around, but no matter how many times she gave the commands, nothing worked. Her heart hammered as energy coiled around her, suffocating her every breath. She gasped as her arm lifted on her own, and…

With a yelp, she opened her eyes and stared around, panting. A twinge of fear slid down her spine when she realized she was outside Kai's dwelling. She'd been outside with Kai once, before he'd taken her to the Silence, but she hadn't looked around much.

Brihan dashed out of the front doors, his eyes widening when he caught sight of her.

"Celina!" He ran to her and grabbed her shoulders. "Where the—what happened?"

She frowned. "I… don't know. It's like I had no control of my body."

"You vanished."

Arching an eyebrow, she crossed her arms. "Well, I didn't mean to." She recalled what Kai had told her after he'd taken her soul. "I guess I can't control my demon side yet. Apparently, it may come with some abilities, but I have no idea what kind." She almost scoffed at the thought; it seemed so strange.

He shook his head, and something in his expression turned to worry. "Even Viscus can't just vanish like that. I mean, if you're extremely powerful, maybe, and even then. We usually move faster than humans can see, but you…" He eyed her like he wasn't sure what she was anymore. "You vanished."

"Oh." Her shoulders slumped. Brihan mentioned only powerful demons could do that, and she would bet Shiriki could. It would explain why she might be more powerful even if she was half.

Rubbing her arms, she turned and looked around at the realm. Skeletal trees stood tall, their roots sticking out of old stones laid into pathways. In front of the dwelling, an old fountain had a familiar black tree standing in the middle. Black liquid moved around it despite the lack of any wind.

She walked toward it and stopped at the edge, her pulse speeding.

My tree.

The one she'd confided to all those years ago, where she'd first met Kai without even knowing it. How did it exist in both worlds?

Darkness slithered from the tree and shot straight to her. Celina raised her hand, and it slowed, hovering before wrapping around her wrist. Her breath came faster, unsure what was happening, but it felt the same as when she'd lost control of her body a few minutes ago.

Brihan grabbed her arm and tried pulling her away, but the darkness tightened, and she winced. "Oh, fuck. What's going on?"

The prickling in the back of her neck warned her to get inside, but her legs wouldn't move. Cracks formed within the trunk of the tree, and a void of darkness blurred her vision, shaking Celina to the core as shadows vanished into her body.

A second later, she staggered, clutching her chest. "What was… that darkness? All those shadows." She turned to Brihan who paled, his eyes wide.

"What shadows? What are you talking about?"

A figure materialized next to Celina, and she jumped,

backing away until she stood behind Brihan. By the amount of energy pulsing from the newcomer, she guessed the demon was a Viscus. His orangey hair ended at his chest, and his irises, although the same shade of orange, glowed so bright, the whites had a tint of red. He surveyed them both before smiling, revealing pointed teeth.

He gave Celina a curt nod. "I am Lokte, your husband's head of guards."

"Did he send you?"

"No. When I noticed you no longer were inside the dwelling, I followed your trail." He reached out his hand, his sharp fingernails bright red. "Return inside, and without resistance. I will report this to Mekaisto, but I am sure he will be lenient on you."

She narrowed her eyes. "I'm a few feet from the door. No need to make this a federal case." Grabbing hold of Brihan's arm, she dragged him toward Kai's dwelling and glanced over her shoulder. "And don't tell my husband anything. I can tell him myself."

He inclined his head, a grin spreading across his lips.

Once inside the dwelling, Celina returned to the room she'd been inside before taking her strange sleepwalking trip outside. She eyed the spot she had been standing in before it happened, wondering if a spell was left behind. But why would anyone bother just to get her outside?

Brihan huffed out a breath. "You really think Lokte will say nothing to Mekaisto?" He shook his head, a bitter smile curling his lips. "Better prepare to face the king's wrath with an explanation because the 'I don't know' and 'random shadows' won't cut it."

Protectiveness swelled inside her, and she drew herself straighter. "He's not—"

"Yes, yes." He waved his hand dismissively, his blond hair bouncing as he did. "I'm sure he'll be calm and collected as always."

Celina's mind worked fast, debating between telling him off and dropping it. Loyalty won. "I imagine you have your reasons for speaking like that about him, but my husband isn't all bad."

He stiffened. "I... I'm sorry. I shouldn't have said that. And don't get me wrong, I respect my king when he's the badass he usually is. But it's just... you're so gentle. I don't care for him hurting you."

"Like I said, he's not all bad," she said with a mock chastising look.

"It can't be easy for you being married to him. I mean," he cleared his throat, "being who and what he is."

"All marriages have their difficulties, but," she held her head high as she faced her friend, "I am Mekaisto's wife, and it's part of who I am. It's a part of my life."

"Do not butter me up, dove," Kai said, wrapping his arms around her from behind, "unless you are ready to receive my gratitude in a physical way."

Celina's cheeks heated as she looked at him. Pride shone in his eyes, and she couldn't help but smile. He kissed her cheek before focusing on Brihan.

"Mekaisto," he muttered, bowing his head.

"I heard a rumor you went out for a little stroll outside with my wife." If words could be laced with poison and kill someone, Kai had it down to an art form.

Celina pressed her lips together, mentally cursing Lokte. On the other hand, she didn't want to imagine what would happen to him if he didn't do his job and report it to his king.

"Kai, it's not what you think." She slid her hand along his arm, trying to soothe him. "I don't know what happened, but I guess I got distracted. Brihan came after me to make sure I was okay and was going to escort me inside when Lokte showed up." She turned in Kai's grasp to face him. "Both your subjects did their duty. Nothing more than that."

He stared at her in silence, glancing over her shoulder

every few seconds with a glower that could melt a volcano. "As long as you are safe." He kissed the top of her head, and she smiled.

She hadn't told him the whole story. Something had felt wrong when she saw the shadows, as though she had absorbed the realm's essence. Not in the way she had in the past when Kai had to take it out of her. This time, it was like the realm had wanted to merge with her. And ever since it happened, a tingling feeling of warmth flowed through Celina's veins with a power she'd never felt before.

It's fine. I'm overthinking it.

9

———

RIFTS

Kai stood on his balcony, watching the black liquid flowing below his dwelling as Celina slept. He glanced over his shoulder, slithering his energy into her to assure she was dreaming peacefully. At the thought, he grinned.

Peacefully contradicts being married to me.

His wife had lied about what happened today, but he wouldn't hold it against her. When he'd searched her mind, it turned blank as though something shielded what he wanted to know. But the way Lokte had described the situation, she walked out on her own, and Brihan came after her. Just like she said. Not for a second did he believe she stepped outside by accident, though. Something happened, and whether she was aware of what had or not, she was hiding it from him.

Not out of fear, but because she's concerned it'll make me worry.

He'd felt her energy and was pleased she was growing her powers. Not wanting to scare her, he hadn't pushed for what happened. He'd be patient… for now.

He moved to their bed and lay next to Celina, wrapping an arm around her to bring her close to him. Her scent had his energy surging through him, but he pushed his lust aside. She needed rest.

She yawned. "Is everything okay?" she asked with a sleepy voice.

The ground shook, and the realm's essence exploded around them in walls of darkness. Her eyes widened as she pressed her hands against her belly. Kai's own power encircled his bedroom, trying to shield Celina, but the blast was too strong. She opened her mouth in a silent scream, hands slipping as she trembled violently. Energy crushed against her until she fainted, and Kai let out a rage-filled roar.

Something… attacked the realm. Attacked Celina.

He raised the defenses around his chambers, keeping Celina safe as the rest of his realm lost some of its protection. Having to check on the energy left behind couldn't wait, but he wouldn't leave his wife without precautions.

His mind linked to the surroundings, and he vanished, following the spike. He found himself near the gates between worlds, staring out at the void. Layered rock in walls of dark grays towered over a massive and winding ravine, wind whistling over the stone. He focused on the realm's essence as it reacted to his presence. Running his hand along the power, he allowed it to slither along his arm, merging into him as he absorbed part of himself.

Memories of what occurred circled his mind, and he clenched his jaw. Powerful magic broke through his realm. He glanced at his feet, watching as the spiders from his world scatter. He connected to them, sending them a silent message.

Retrieve information as to who did this. I'll make them regret wanting to play with me.

He glided his hand over a tear through the void. The white light pulsed beneath his fingers and retreated as though fearing his touch.

Shiriki materialized nearby. "A few rifts have been appearing. They began around the same time as the disappearances in the human world."

"And you are informing me of this now?" Although Kai didn't raise his voice, darkness smashed next to his second in command like a lightning strike.

Shiriki glanced to where a crater smoked, pieces of rock and debris scattered. Kai's realm seemed to be screaming. He reached toward the rifts, the ground uneven underneath his boots, and ran his hand over the smooth stone worn by time. He gritted his teeth as he sought to understand the implications.

The threat wasn't aimed at just his subjects anymore. Whoever had attacked his realm targeted his wife. She couldn't stay here without being in further danger. He had to get her back to the human world. His hands curled into fists. "I am entrusting her to you." He grabbed Shiriki's throat, bringing him inches from his face. "She will stay in your highrise in Demias. Keep her safe."

"You trust me alone with your wife?" Shiriki arched an eyebrow.

Kai let go of him and smirked. "Your caretaker will look after her. Nalie will be present as often as possible, seeing to Celina's health, and monitoring you."

His second in command cocked his head and chuckled. "Will you not be there as well? To make sure I behave?"

"I need more information about those attacking us."

"I will make the arrangements."

Kai swept his gaze over Shiriki. "I have to see to Celina. Finish recording the energy attack and return to my chambers."

Without another word, Kai vanished, appearing outside the bedroom where Celina was, his chest squeezing. Two of his subjects stood by the door, guarding his wife.

Ancus cleared his throat, standing at the entrance alongside Nalie. "Is there anything we can help with, Your Majesty?"

"I will send her to Shiriki's dwelling in Demias for the time being. She cannot stay in this realm. It is too dangerous."

Ancus's eyebrows shot up. "Do you think it wise to trust Shiriki with this task? I know he is your second in command, but—"

"He is also Celina's father."

Silence hung heavy as both Viscus gawked.

"She… is Shiriki's daughter?" Nalie whispered.

"I trust he will not kill her. But he will hurt her if given the chance. That is why I want you," he glanced at Nalie, "with her. Shiriki's dwelling is the only place on Demias linked with our realm. She needs to be as close to it as possible while carrying my son." Glowering at them both, he stepped closer. "Now then, do you need any further explanation from your king?"

Both bowed.

"Apologies, Your Majesty. We are not questioning your orders. We are just concerned about your wife's safety." Ancus kept his head low, his dark red hair falling forward. Viscus often forgot their place, but this one had remained humble. A rare trait for his kind.

Kai stepped inside her room and stared at Celina. Her chest rose and fell, still passed out from the energy that attacked her moments earlier. Kai stood at the foot of the bed, watching. He cursed himself for feeling vulnerable and weak, emotions he deemed useless. He didn't care for the sensation.

Shiriki. Return. Now.

His second in command materialized inside the hallway and stepped into the room. He dusted off the long black coat he wore. "If you make it impossible to set foot inside this room, warn us *before* we *try* appearing inside. Almost cut myself in half—"

"Have you found out who is attacking us?" Kai interjected. He forced himself to reel in his anger, not wanting to destroy Shiriki before he got answers.

"I spoke to a ruler in Pyralis, and it is none of the races on his continent. No spikes in power from any other area and both dimensions are silent. That only leaves the one from our realm and Demias. It could be our kind, humans, reapers, fae, vampires, or Lumen." His smile widened to show his pointed teeth. "But there are none left of the latter."

Not any official ones. His mind flashed to Celina being able to read Madka. Rebels of the Lumen had learned the forbidden magic and grew into their own group. Could any Venatores be left? Their energy signatures had changed over the centuries.

Kai stared at his wife, running his fingers through her hair. Explaining to her Shiriki's dwelling was the safest place for her was out of the question. He scoffed at the thought, imagining her arguments.

His gaze traveled to her abdomen. There were no other choices. He had to protect them both. At least until he found out who or what attacked her. Then destroy them.

Kai held his unconscious wife in his arms as he entered Shiriki's dwelling. Nalie followed, rubbing her arms as though dreading the air in this place. He couldn't blame her; his second in command instilled a certain chill.

The lobby remained the same as always. Victorian-era style with light-red carpets contrasting against mahogany furniture. The blue and red wallpaper clashed with everything else, but it pulled together. It resembled Kai's own dwelling, but he supposed it was natural they'd have similar tastes. They'd gone through every human era alongside each other from the beginning.

The grandfather clock ticked through the heavy silence as

they waited. From behind the archway, footsteps echoed, and a woman strode inside. Hilda had been the caretaker for many years. Her dark-gray hair was tied in a tight bun, and she always wore the same old-fashioned dress.

She bowed low. "Mekaisto."

"Has Shiriki explained the situation?"

Her gaze fell on Celina, softening from her usual sternness. "Yes, poor thing. I'll ensure the master doesn't get carried away."

Kai grinned. Only Hilda could think she could stop Shiriki from doing what he wanted. Yet, throughout the years, he'd noticed a bond forming between the two. He supposed, after living here so long, some connection was inevitable.

"Report anything you believe excessive." He pressed Celina closer to him as she stirred. "I will not let him harm you if you speak out."

She waved her hand. "I'm not worried. He can't harm me until he claims my soul. Even if I was good all my life, I don't think he'll be compassionate when that time comes." For a second, her usual dull gaze sparked with life, and she grinned. "I have a few years, though. Leave her care to me. I'll make sure she's safe."

He gave a curt nod and marched up the stairs to the second floor.

The hearth fire jumped to a roar as Shiriki stepped inside. Nalie inched away from him in silence.

"Hilda is as spirited as ever," Kai said with a smile, putting his wife in bed, and covering her with a thick blanket.

Shiriki chuckled, glancing over his shoulder toward the door. "I regret making that deal every day. Never expected her to live this long." Amusement filled his tone.

Kai didn't comment. He knew his second in command was fond of the caretaker even if Shiriki would never admit to it. Instead, he turned to the healer. "Nalie, stay nearby."

"Of course." Nalie bowed and stepped from the room.

Shiriki crossed his arms, staring toward Celina as she slept. "I will ensure she stays within the dwelling and is kept safe." He chuckled and added, "Well, safe from the outside. I cannot guarantee anything while she is in here."

Kai stiffened to keep himself from throwing Shiriki into the flames. "I want the ones responsible for attacking my wife and the realm to be found."

"If you want me to hurry, it means leaving her alone." His smile widened, and Kai allowed his anger to coil around Shiriki.

"Whatever it takes." Kai stared at Celina, and although he didn't have a heart, he could've sworn his chest squeezed as though he did.

10

———

PREY

Celina opened her eyes, staring up at a pale-beige ceiling. She'd been awake for some time but feigned sleep in case anyone was nearby. For a while, she wracked her brain, piecing together what happened.

Terrible pressure. A force had entered her mind, wrapping around her core until something seemed to snap within. Then… nothing.

She swung her legs off the bed and frowned, not recognizing the room.

"Kai?" she called out, her voice cracking.

A hum of familiar energy throbbed through the floor. Where had she sensed this before? Her pulse quickened, and she grasped at the memory of the last time she'd felt the same eerie sensation.

No, it can't be.

Shiriki's dwelling had been the only place she'd felt this unease, but Kai wouldn't have brought her here. Unless…

"Okay, calm down," she muttered, running a hand through her tangled hair.

The door opened, and a familiar woman walked in. Celina

groaned when she recognized her. She'd been there both times Celina had come to Shiriki's high-rise.

"My name is Hilda."

Celina's eyebrows rose. It was the first time she heard the woman speak English. Hilda's dark-gray hair, tied in a tight bun, still reminded Celina of a teacher she'd had in elementary school.

"Please tell me this isn't Shiriki's dwelling."

Hilda hesitated but then answered, "It is. No harm will come to you while you're a guest here, but your husband needed you to be somewhere safe outside the dark realm."

Celina arched an eyebrow. "What happened?"

"There was an attack," Hilda mumbled.

"Where's Kai?"

"I believe he has research to conduct, but in the meantime, both Nalie and I will keep an eye on you."

Celina twisted her fingers together. Hilda was keeping secrets from her that was for sure. "I... don't understand. Why would Kai bring me to this place?" For a second, she imagined Shiriki having kidnapped her with plans of torture. Her pulse quickened as she shook her head. "I want to see my husband. I need to talk to Kai, please." She got to her feet, and walked a few steps toward the door, intending to leave and find Kai herself, but Shiriki materialized inches from where she stood.

Her heart leaped into her throat, and she shrank. The energy surrounding him crashed against Celina, and she pressed her lips together to keep from screaming. Memories of the first time she was in his dwelling resurfaced, and she trembled.

"No need to run off so quickly, pet. You only just arrived."

His amusement sparked her fury. "Why am I here?"

Hilda clucked her tongue but didn't repeat herself.

Instead, Shiriki took a step closer. "It is simple. You are here because it is the one safe place at the moment."

"When pigs fly." She pressed her back against the wall and started toward the fireplace, her gaze focused on a poker.

Shiriki glanced at it, his smile widening. "I dare you."

She gritted her teeth but stayed silent, knowing her words would be nothing but empty threats.

"Nalie will ensure you suffered no damage during the attack. She will be in shortly for a blood test." Shiriki's voice was like a bucket of icy water over her head.

Blood test?

He left, and Celina's shoulders sagged.

Hilda sighed, turning to her. "When Mekaisto returns, you can ask him questions. In the meantime—"

"I need to talk to him now," she said, staring at the opened door to the bedroom.

She smiled and placed her hand against Celina's arm. "I know you don't believe it, but Shiriki will not harm you."

Celina scoffed but stayed silent as Hilda took her leave.

She drew a few deep breaths to calm herself. She'd make sure Kai knew she was here, and if he did, she'd give him a piece of her mind.

Once Celina was calm enough, she grabbed the poker. They hadn't closed the bedroom door, and she took it as permission to leave. A long staircase greeted her. She eased down the steps, listening for anyone coming toward her. She glanced up, remembering what the seventh floor held, but the place was quiet.

Too quiet for her liking.

Once she reached the carpeted lobby, Celina tried the exterior door, but they bolted it shut. They hadn't made it easy for her to leave. It was just an illusion.

Something about this place felt unnatural. Whispers caught her attention, and she froze, staring around. The voices turned to sobs and screams, yet she strained to listen. She followed the sound, raising her weapon higher, ready to attack. She didn't believe Kai had sent her here, knowing what Shiriki had done to her.

And if he doesn't know, then I need to protect myself in the meantime. Find a way to escape.

Inching closer to a wooden staircase leading into a dark basement, she clenched her jaw as the sounds of crying grew louder.

"Of course," she muttered, running her hand along the wall for balance as she stepped down the stairs.

Maybe here, I'll find an exit.

Mildew and spiderwebs covered the cement floor, and she shivered. She continued onward, eyeing the shadowy corners behind piles of boxes up ahead. Childhood fears of monsters hiding in the dark flashed through her mind, and she stared at the pipes running across the open ceiling.

The first door she found was half-open. It creaked as she pushed against it, causing her to grimace. Her heart hammered as she lowered the poker and rushed into the room.

Someone had tied a woman to a chair, barbed wire cutting into her wrists and ankles. She was unconscious, her chest rising slowly, a large bloodstain soaking her top.

"Wake up," Celina whispered.

The woman didn't move an inch.

Celina stared. The area felt smaller because of the low lighting. Suction noises echoed from the floor drain, and she wrinkled her nose at the foul odor it emitted. She moved to the laundry tub, and her stomach lurched at the pile of bloodied rags left inside. The smell of bleach reached her nose, and she took a few steps back.

"Shit." The bare bulb buzzed overhead, and she stared at the ceiling.

A door slammed in the distance, footsteps accompanying

screams. Celina trembled as she stared around. She rushed between shelves and a workbench, trembling at the sight of bloodied saws, hammers, and drills. Pressing her back against the wall, she placed her hand over her mouth, holding back a scream. The furniture hid her well enough, and she could see through some trinkets on the shelves.

Shiriki appeared, dragging a man behind him who begged to let him go. Once he saw the woman though, the man sobbed. "No, Patricia. Please, don't hurt her. We made a deal!" He shrieked when Shiriki tied him to a similar chair, the metal bonds cutting into his limbs.

Shiriki smirked. "Make yourself comfortable while I take care of her. I will tend to you once I am finished."

A shiver crawled along Celina's skin as he fished inside a drawer near the chair.

"Wait, what are you going to do?" the man cried.

Shiriki pulled out a syringe and a small bottle filled with bright blue liquid. "If you are curious, you are welcome to watch." Once the syringe was full of the fluorescent substance, he plunged it through the woman's eyelid.

Celina turned away, her stomach churning as she gripped the fire poker harder. Then a gasp ripped through the air, and she looked back.

"Fred. What—" The woman shrank when Shiriki leaned toward her.

"Your fiancé made a deal and broke his end of the bargain." He rummaged inside the drawer. This time, he pulled out a strange contraption which he wrapped around Patricia's head.

Her gaze darted to Fred. "You said you didn't! You lied!"

"We need—"

"Yes, yes, but it no longer matters." Shiriki shrugged. He grabbed a long metal stick with the last six inches tapered to a point. He tightened a metal device on the woman's head-piece, then placed the thick needle into it.

"Wait. No. Stop. Stop!" she screamed, thrashing her head side to side, sweat covering her face.

Shiriki screwed on the long-pointed piece, leaving it touching Patricia's forehead. A small trickle of blood rolled down the bridge of her nose.

"Unless you want to suffer more, I suggest you stay still." He smiled. "I need to extract information, and it is no easy task without some pain. Moving will cause the agony to last longer." He licked his lips, and she froze. "Although, keep resisting and I will enjoy your screams."

The streak of blood mixed with her tears. "I never agreed to this deal!"

"No, but your fiancé included you." He pushed the metal farther against her skin.

Patricia screamed so loud, Celina thought her lungs might burst. She tugged at the restraints on her upper arms, and the wires tore into her flesh.

"Please, stop hurting her!" Fred cried over Patricia's screams.

She shrieked as he tugged the needle to the side so her forehead cracked and split open. Silence fell as her head drooped forward and she stilled.

Shiriki wrenched out the needle and placed a vial beneath the fatal wound as a green substance poured out. He moved to the man, still clutching the long metal spike. Blood dripped from its end, sinister and promising agony.

Celina held her breath, hand trembling over her mouth. If Shiriki heard her, there would be no escape from the pain he'd inflict. The way he'd killed Patricia... bile burned the back of her throat, and she swallowed hard.

"Was your fiancé's life worth breaking the rules, Frederick?" he asked.

Fred's shoulders shook as he sobbed. "Patricia... I'm sorry."

Shiriki shot him a disgusted look. "You are next. I will return shortly." And he left through another door.

Celina stared at Patricia's body, her stomach churning.

I couldn't save her.

She took several deep breaths, trying to calm down. There wouldn't be much time before Shiriki came back. She slid out of her hiding spot and strode to the table where Shiriki had found his supplies. The man gasped at her sudden appearance, but she ignored him, rummaging inside the drawers. She turned to Fred with pliers, cutting his bonds. Once he was free, she helped him up.

His gaze focused on her abdomen. "Who are you?" His voice was raw, and he cleared it.

She shook her head. "No time. We need to leave."

Grabbing his arm, she pulled him the way she had come. When they reached the stairs, she pointed up. "I don't know how to get out once you reach the ground floor, but I'll try giving you a head start and keep him busy."

Her stomach churned when a door slammed within the room, and she tightened her grip on the poker. She pushed Fred against his back. "Go."

She strode through the corridor, looking for somewhere else to hide, her neck prickling. Before she got anywhere, someone grabbed her hair and yanked.

She hissed through her teeth, her scalp burning. Clawing at a hand, she turned and stabbed Shiriki with the poker. Her eyes widened as she staggered and lost her footing, falling to the floor with a wince.

He stared at the object sticking out of him, arching an eyebrow. His irises glowed white in the dim lighting as he gazed at her. Yet he didn't move.

"I forgot since you no longer have a soul, you are better at hiding your presence. Even with a heartbeat." He pulled the weapon out and kneeled in front of her. "You set my prey loose."

A twinge of pain shot inside her abdomen, and she gasped. She pressed her hand against her belly as agony twisted her insides.

Why is this happening again?

Shiriki stared at her, unblinking. When she tried crawling away, he picked her up. She yelped, squirming to get out of his grasp. When the pain became unbearable, she screamed, stiffening.

She wanted Kai, needed him. The thought of losing her baby tore at her heart. Kai had taken her soul to stop another near-miscarriage like this from occurring a second time. So why was it happening? Her pulse thundered as Shiriki strode upstairs into the main lobby. Nalie joined them, arching an eyebrow in a silent question.

"Too much excitement." Although he grinned, there was no amusement in his tone.

He continued up the steps, two at a time as though he wasn't carrying a person. Demons were truly far more powerful than humans.

Once inside the room she'd been assigned, Nalie took Celina's hand and squeezed as Shiriki sat her on the bed.

Hilda strode in, and approached Celina, stacking the pillows higher behind her back. "Lay back."

Celina pressed against her abdomen as another wave of pain churned her stomach. Shiriki lingered, watching in silence as Nalie sat on the edge of the bed and ran her hand along Celina's belly.

Nalie glanced over her shoulder. "Hilda, fetch my bag."

The caretaker left in a hurry, dashing past Shiriki as quickly as possible.

"Is my baby okay?" Celina asked, her voice cracking.

"Seems to be fine."

Hilda returned and handed Nalie a leather bag.

Nalie rummaged inside and took out a device that looked like a baby thermometer. "He moved and may have torn a few places. I need to make sure though." Without waiting, she pressed the device against Celina's arm, causing a sting.

Celina flinched. "What was that?" She rubbed her arm, then stared at the tiny hole.

Nalie kept her eyes on the screen. "Blood test. You are already healing yourself. That is a good sign."

Hilda crossed her arms. "What were you doing in the basement? You shouldn't be wandering about in your state."

Celina pressed her lips together, the urge to tell them off strong. If she shouldn't be wandering in her state, then she shouldn't be anywhere near Shiriki.

Hilda shot a glare at her master. "I will report this to Mekaisto."

His silvery irises rested on Celina, cold and calculating before his lips curled into a cruel smile. "Of course."

Nalie walked past Shiriki, but he grabbed her arm and leaned closer to her ear. He whispered something, and Nalie flinched. Heavy tension rested between the two, but she lost her fighting stance. Nalie pulled out the blood test device and handed it to Shiriki before marching away.

With one last bone-chilling smile at Celina, he left.

After a few minutes of fussing over Celina, Hilda excused herself, this time, locking the door behind her.

"Where are you, Kai?" Celina whispered, letting her head fall against the pillows. Nightmares plagued even her waking moments, and she shivered, remembering what he'd told her during their deal. She had asked if she would have nightmares forever after she'd first felt his true form, and he'd answered that after their deal, she'd live inside the nightmares instead.

She ran her hand over her face. What Shiriki had done to his victim wouldn't leave her mind. Every horror she'd seen inside this place plagued her.

I need to get out of here.

11

───────

VALUABLE

After what felt like hours, Celina left the bedroom. It hadn't been easy, but she used a bathroom cabinet hinge to pop the pin from the hinges of the door. Her mother had taught her the trick when discussing fire safety years ago.

Celina rushed down the steps, hoping the exit from the lobby would be open this time. When she pushed against it, it didn't budge, and she cursed.

Running from one window to the next, she tugged, trying to wrench them open, but she might as well have been attempting to move the entire building. She strode down a corridor, searching for any kind of electronic device to call for help. With the antiquated architecture, she doubted she would be so lucky.

A door squeaked in the distance, and she dashed through an alcove to keep out of sight. The smell of copper churned her stomach, and she held her breath, waiting for the footsteps to echo away from where she hid. She exhaled as she leaned against the wall, but instead of the usual wallpaper texture, something squishy and wet pressed against her fingertips.

She staggered until she hit the opposing wall, her chest

heaving as she stared at what she'd touched. A body hung from a pillar, held by barbed wire cutting into its chest and abdomen. Celina wiped the gore from her trembling hand, squinting in the low lighting.

It was the man she'd freed from the basement. Fred.

His hands were outstretched as though having reached out for help, wires sticking out of his flesh, but nothing ever came to save him. Instead, Shiriki caught him in a deathly trap, and the man died screaming. Fred's mouth was opened wide, the metallic wire wrapped around his head, cutting into his cheeks. One eyeball hung loose, while part of the wire impaled the other.

"I'm sorry," Celina whispered as a lump appeared in her throat. She didn't know the man, and from what she knew of him, he'd included his own fiancé in a deal with Shiriki of all demons. That wasn't right, but no one deserved to die this way. She thought maybe, for once, she'd been able to save someone.

She left the alcove, more determined than ever to find a way out of this horror show. Although she was a lot more cautious now, looking out for potential traps.

One door at the other end opened, and Shiriki walked out, his gaze locking on her. She took a few steps back. When he appeared in front of her, grabbing her arm, she yelped.

"Well, since you seem to be well enough to escape, allow me to show you something."

She grabbed onto the door frame and dug her feet. Dried blood stained the surgical table. Patches of red and black puddled on the floor. A tray filled with rusted and bloodied instruments stood next to the table.

"Let her go now." Nalie strode into sight, accompanied by Hilda.

He loosened his grip, and Celina staggered into the corridor, panting.

Hilda narrowed her eyes. "I believe this is what Mekaisto

meant when he said not to cause her unnecessary harm."

"You two are no fun." A sadistic smile curled his lips over his pointed teeth. "I wanted to show her something interesting."

Without another word, he walked through a black door nestled at the back of the gruesome surgical room. Nalie rolled her eyes before disappearing in a blur of motion.

That was too close.

Hilda grasped Celina's elbow and led her down a corridor.

"So are there death traps all over this place or what?" Celina asked.

"They only activate if the person who walks into them is human. It is the way the master keeps escapees from running too far."

Celina arched an eyebrow, staring at the caretaker. "Isn't that dangerous for the both of us?"

"You are half-demon, so the traps won't set off, and as for me..." A small smile curled her lips. "I know where they are."

Celina followed Hilda in silence the rest of the way until they reached a sitting area. A dizzy spell hit Celina, and she sat by a window, closing her eyes. The grandfather clock in the lobby ticked away, gritting on Celina's nerves as she waited. She wanted out of this place yesterday.

Hilda cleared her throat. "I need to attend to a few guests. I won't be far but try not to wander... again."

Celina scoffed.

She grabbed a newspaper, reading the articles but not retaining any information. Until she caught her husband's name.

Thomas.

Her chest squeezed as she straightened, shaking the newspaper so she could get to the page. There was a continued investigation into Thomas Leviet's murder. His wife, Celina Leviet, had gone missing and was a suspect.

"Crap." A small giggle escaped her lips. Thomas never died, and if the police thought she had killed him—killed Kai—they had another thing coming.

Noise from a conversation carried to where she sat, and she frowned. She stepped out into the lobby and stared at a few demons near the entrance. Ancus, a demon Celina knew, stood near Hilda as the caretaker spoke in a language Celina recognized as Demos though she couldn't understand the words. The other demons muttered amongst one another in hushed tones. Ancus craned his neck as though trying to get a better view of the far door.

Celina's stomach churned as she noticed Tess—one of Kai's old favorites who took great pleasure in reminding Celina of that fact. Celina curled her hands into fists but held her ground even as the demon sneered at her. With Hilda busy, the caretaker didn't notice as Tess approached Celina.

"I hear Shiriki manhandled you, and your delicate human side couldn't handle it. Had to tell on him like some weak mortal." She scoffed, crossing her arms over her chest.

Celina couldn't help but hate her even more with the tight fitted clothes Tess wore, accentuating her large breasts and how tiny her waist was.

"If you've ever been targeted by him, then you'd know he does a lot more than just manhandle," Celina said through clenched teeth.

"The king's second in command rarely goes after my kind as we are superior and much stronger than—"

"Then I'll remind him Viscus are perfect for his experiments since, as you say, you're so resilient. You shouldn't have any trouble healing from him ripping you apart."

Tess narrowed her eyes, but a flicker of fear flashed through her expression. Before she could say anything else, smoke seeped around them. As it swirled in the middle of the room, Celina winced at the building pressure in her chest.

The demons and Hilda bowed, falling silent.

Black feathers fell from the ceiling above where they stood, turning to smoke before coming into contact with the floor. An aura of terrible silence pressed down, and it was like the shadows were swallowing any sound. Darkness moved, coiling against the walls and ceiling, slithering on the floor.

Celina's pulse hammered, and she smiled.

As though sensing her, Kai turned, his gaze locking with hers. Her emotions flooded through her, and she dashed to him, wrapping her arms around him. She buried her face against his chest, the corner of her eyes burning. His hands slid around her and held her tight.

"I am here, dove."

Her mind cleared of emotions, and resentment slammed into her with fury. She pushed away and glowered at him. "What the hell were you thinking, sending me here?"

His lips curled into a smile worthy of his title. "Feisty little thing," he muttered, grabbing her wrists just as the thought of punching him in the chest crossed her mind. "No need for violence."

The demons watching them muttered between one another, and Tess latched on the opportunity. "Human emotions are so troublesome," she said with an exaggerated sigh.

Celina's heart sped as most of the others agreed with the bitch's statement, but Ancus shot Tess an annoyed stare. "Can we talk somewhere in private?"

"Are you sure you want to be alone with me?" he asked with a wink as he pulled her harder against his body.

Heat crept into her cheeks as his erection pressed against her, and she swallowed hard, her pulse throbbing between her thighs. "We need to talk first."

"First?" The arcane symbols on his horns glowed brighter, matching the intensity of his gaze.

Tess let out another exaggerated sigh, and Celina locked gazes with her. Without turning away, Celina ran her hand along Kai's chest, a smug smile curling her lips with a clear message to the demon: *he's mine, bitch.*

Kai chuckled, placing his hand on hers, and giving a quick squeeze as Tess's face turned a darker shade of pink.

If looks could kill.

Hilda cleared her throat "Now that you seem in better shape, you should eat. I've prepared you a meal." She glanced at Celina's abdomen. "I suggest you don't make her wait too long. She's refused to eat anything since arriving, and it's not good to starve a pregnant woman."

A growl vibrated through Kai's throat, and Celina took a step back. Black mist swirled around him, and when her husband was visible again, he'd turned to his lower demon form. Still, the displeasure in his expression was unnerving.

"Why were you not eating?"

Celina averted her gaze. "I thought maybe I'd been taken without you knowing about it."

He took her hand and squeezed. "I brought you here after the attack on my realm. This is the safest place—"

"After what Shiriki has done to me, you really think that?" she shouted, but quickly pressed her lips tight, glancing over to the demons watching. Tess's sneer was enough to make Celina want to cave in the Viscus demon's face. "Can we please speak in private?"

With a curt nod, they walked away from the curious subjects, and into the dining room. Hilda closed the French doors, and curtains fell, hiding them from view so they could have privacy. Kai pulled out the chair next to the head of the table, and Celina sat, watching as he took his seat. Hilda had laid assortments of food upon the surface, and so far, nothing seemed out of the ordinary.

"Why weren't you here when I woke up?" she asked in a whisper, her throat tight. "Do you know how terrified I was, thinking I'd be tortured by him?"

He placed his hand on her arm. "I am sorry, Celina. After

the attack, it left the realm bleeding, and a few of my subjects were destroyed. It created such a rift, a few of the condemned souls in the Inferno escaped."

"I'm sorry about your subjects." She meant it. Although some didn't like her, she'd grown fond of others. "I heard they found more bodies near The CrowBar. Is the attack on your realm related to whoever is killing demons?"

His jaw clenched. "And who told you something they should not have?"

"You seem angry." She pulled away and twisted her fingers. She had overheard Nalie talking about the latest murders with Hilda. Celina refused to have either of them suffer because of what she'd heard.

"I am."

She sighed and shook her head. "I know you want to protect me, but please don't shut me out. You can talk to me about these things."

"You should not get involved in my business. These matters do not concern you."

"You brought me to your realm so we could live there together while raising our child. So, if it's supposed to be my home, I have every right to get involved."

"It—"

"Our son will grow up there once he's born, so this concerns me." Placing her hand over his, she squeezed. "Don't push me away."

"These beings are dangerous and powerful."

"Unlike you?" she muttered with a grin.

He ignored her comment but glared. "They dared murder my subjects, and attack my realm, and you." His shoulders tensed, and he rolled them a few times. "It might mean they know who you are. Or they attacked anyone near me at that moment. If they ever found out who you are to me, they would hold you hostage knowing I would give them anything they want."

"So you plan on locking me up? And for how long this time?" When she lifted her gaze, she stiffened to keep from flinching.

An aura of darkness surrounded Kai as he stood, and he leaned forward against the hard, stone surface of the table. "Do not tempt me to lock you away, dove. I have cages I would enjoy putting you inside."

She narrowed her eyes. "Did you keep the one David Corval threw me in?" She gritted her teeth, the memory of the murder still too fresh in her mind.

David Corval—the man who had blackmailed her husband into kidnapping children for him. The asshole who caged Celina and summoned a demon as she watched, too numb to care after he had shown her evidence that Thomas—no, Kai—had been the kidnapper.

His grip on the table tightened, and a large crack split along the surface. "I do not need to take what belongs to others. Mine are much more... entertaining for what I would use them for."

She got to her feet, her hands curling into fists. "Stop threatening me. You're not the demon I made a deal with anymore. You can stop playing the part."

He stalked toward her, and she grabbed onto the edge of the table, willing herself not to back away. When he stopped inches away, he leaned to be at eye-level with her, and the smirk curling his lips sent a shiver down her spine.

"The part I played was always Thomas. Not the other way around."

The words were like a slap to her face, and tears blurred her vision. "You really are a monster sometimes," she said with a cracking voice.

His jaw tightened. After silence passed between them, he cupped her cheek. "I should not have said that."

"You're used to being ruthless. You command fear. It's who you are. But you shouldn't have to be like that with me."

"The first demons I created were twisted beings who turned on me and Shiriki. They were easy to dispose of, but the others were clever and sought to challenge and betray me at every turn. It became clear keeping them in their place required pain and agony."

"But I won't betray or challenge you. Ever." She placed her hand over his. "You've gone through millennia living a certain way, and I don't expect you to change overnight. But I need you to make an effort not to use fear against me. I'm your wife, and after everything, I deserve to be trusted and loved."

He traced his thumb along her cheek, sending goosebumps through her body. "You are right. You deserve all that and respect. I am sorry."

"And you'll let me help with what's going on? I don't know why, but sometimes I see what happened. I can be valuable to you."

His expression flashed as though in pain. "You are invaluable as you are."

"I still want to help." She ran her fingers along his knuckles. "Please."

He sighed but nodded. "Only if it does not place you or our son in harm's way."

She scoffed, poking him in the chest. "In that case, force Shiriki to move to another world."

"While I understand you do not care for your father—"

"He's not my father." The words came out louder than she'd expected, and her shoulders slumped. "I'm sorry."

"Shiriki is my second in command, and a powerful Viscus."

"So that makes me a powerful half-demon, no? I can help. Tell me, who are the ones attacking us?"

An aura of darkness surrounded him, pressing against her as his pupils thinned. His cruel smile didn't help calm her nerves. "Rebel Lumen. They are known as Venatores.

Members who were exiled for using forbidden magic who formed their own group. I believe David Corval was a part of that rebellion."

She gaped at him, wrapping her mind around the new information.

Didn't you kill us all?

The ghost of a smile touched his lips at her silent question.

"They are no longer considered the same as they barely possess any skills worthy to be called a Lumen. Well, if that bloodline still existed."

She narrowed her eyes, hating how lightly he spoke of what was part of her own heritage, but stuck to the point. "So, they're a separate group now? What makes them different?"

"They used too much black magic and are now considered tainted, in a way." He scoffed as though remembering something. "They cannot even recognize demons. Because of this, I did not consider them a threat, but it seems they have grown in both number and power."

"Why are they attacking, though? Why so suddenly?"

"I suppose with a higher number of members, they may think there is a chance. And if they have a common goal, it keeps them focused. Especially now they have something they can use against me. I had been hiding you away for your own protection, but also to keep others away from you. Discovering who you are, what you mean to me..." He moved to his chair, and sat, staring into the empty hearth until flames blasted within.

She flinched, but her chest squeezed as she took her seat. "The name rings a bell. Weren't Lumen called Venatores at some point?" She picked up her fork, and stabbed it into the Brussels sprouts, then popped a bite into her mouth.

"Yes. Once the rebel members were banished, they returned to the original name. A way to separate themselves, yet maintain their history."

"My aunt's box, the one the lawyer brought at the hotel we were staying in during…" Her heart sped at the thought of what he was to her before she found out the truth. The last time they'd been inside the rented room was after she'd attacked him, and his reaction had been terrifying. "What happened to the box?"

"I left it where it was after I discovered your mother's note and realized you knew of your parentage."

She swallowed hard, willing the memory from her mind. "I should go back and see if they have it in lost and found. There was a lot of useful information in there. Maybe there's something about the rebels, and—"

"No."

"We agreed you'd let me help."

He chuckled and shook his head. "I agreed if it did not put you or our son in harm's way. You cannot leave Shiriki's dwelling—"

"You can't keep me locked in here. It's not fair."

He flashed another charming smile laced with poison. "I can, and I will, dove. You will stay here."

"Make me."

He grabbed her wrist, pulling her to her feet. "If that is what you want." In one fluid motion, he grasped her hips, sat her on the edge of the table, and pushed their dinner to the floor with a crash. Before she could say anything about it, he leaned her back, kissing her knee, and sliding his tongue along her inner thigh.

She panted as he slipped off her panties, her cheeks warming. "We're not finished… discussing this."

"That pleases me."

Her toes curled as his hot breath tickled her sex.

"Your subjects are right outside the door," she said in a breathless whisper.

"They can wait. I am not finished eating yet," he said with a wolfish grin as he lowered his head between her legs.

12

INSIDE THE BOX

Celina settled in the library within Shiriki's dwelling. For the last couple of days, she spent her time trying to find answers to her questions. She read a few books containing symbols she understood, but nothing pointed toward stopping the Venatores.

Kai walked in, and her heart sped. But when Shiriki followed, she clenched her jaw, wanting to kick him into whatever room he spent most of his days hiding away in.

Probably his laboratory from Hell.

Shiriki reached inside the pockets of his coat and pulled out a pendant. A black stone within pulsated as he held it out to her. It looked like part of the dark realm's essence lived within.

Celina stared at him, then moved around the table. She took the jewelry from him and backed away, wanting distance between them. "What is this?"

"It keeps you protected."

"I doubt this keeps you away from me," she muttered.

She jumped when Kai stood in front of her and grasped the pendant. Their fingers touched as he slipped the chain out of her hand, and she shivered. "While the rebels are attacking,

I need to keep you safe." Slipping the chain around her neck, he secured the clasp and let it slide to her cleavage. "It has a tracker inside—"

"You're tracking me?"

"After what happened, I have to ensure I know where you are."

She placed her hands against her hips. "But I'm always here, remember? My own little prison whether or not I like it."

His irises glowed so bright, she had trouble keeping eye contact with him, but she didn't dare look away. She couldn't look weak or he'd call her bluff.

Shiriki chuckled. "If it is not with a pendant, we could find another way to monitor you, pet. Perhaps spending every waking moment with me?"

She threw him a dark stare. "If it gets me close enough to kill you."

The baby kicked, and she pressed her palms against her abdomen. He moved a lot more every day, and every time, it filled her with excitement and terror at the thought of being a mother.

She stared at Kai, but he was transfixed at the spot where her hands rested. An unreadable expression softened his gaze. She held his palm, placed it against her belly, and grinned when his eyes widened when their son moved again.

He brought her closer. "I want to keep you both safe. I understand you want independence, but until I deal with these rebels, please wear it."

"If you insist," she said with a grin.

Shiriki cleared his throat. "There is a certain amount of dark essence within. Your child needs this since he is more demon than human. Without being able to live in the dark realm at the moment, this should keep him healthy."

She nodded, turning to Kai. If it kept her baby safe, too, then she'd keep it on. Tracker or no.

"I am returning to my realm. A few of my subjects had been looking into the Venatore's location, and I need to know if they found it. Or any information for that matter." He took her hands in his and squeezed. "Stay safe."

She nodded, and once he left, she turned toward Shiriki.

He smirked. "Well?"

"Well, what?" She clutched the pendant.

"No thank-you hug?" he asked in a mock pout.

All the insults she knew rolled through her mind. "Leave me alone."

He shrugged and turned to leave but glanced over his shoulder. "Magical pendants are fickle things, are they not? Tamper with one, and instead of protecting you, they get you killed."

Her mouth opened and closed as he rounded the corner and disappeared. Her mother had borrowed the pendant Celina used to wear for as long as she could remember. That same day, her parents died in a car accident. She knew something deeper related Shiriki to her family in a twisted way, but more and more, she was certain he'd murdered her mother and stepfather.

So why won't he admit to it?

Celina lingered in front of the lobby doors. Hilda placed three pieces of luggage near the entrance. One fell to its side, spilling its contents with an echoing clanging of objects, and the caretaker muttered something under her breath.

With a grin, Celina made her way forward, doing her best to crouch and help her pick up the escaped items. It was much harder to bend with her belly so big.

"You shouldn't be—"

"So close to Shiriki in my condition? Yes, I agree," Celina said with a wink.

Hilda pressed her lips together but didn't argue further as they put the trinkets into the suitcase. Celina paused on one. A talisman with a white quartz stone shaped in a half-moon encircling a ruby that looked like a drop of blood. It pulsed in her palm, and she frowned.

"What are these things?"

Hilda took the talisman from her and put it away before latching the bag closed. "With the attacks, Shiriki ordered I bring the valuable artifacts to his storage outside the city. Some demons who were found dead were traveling from different parts of the province, gathering these rare items to return them to the Sanguis leader. Their bodies were found, but the objects are gone."

"Artifacts?"

"From the Lumen churches. Some objects remained hidden, but your husband's subjects located a few. Shiriki thought it best to bring what he already has to his storage."

Celina didn't like the idea of magic objects that once belonged to her mother's group ending up elsewhere, but demons were more her people than the Lumen had ever been.

"I'm picturing a place that holds body parts and objects," Celina said with a shudder.

"Nonsense. It is a normal cottage inside the Kemptville area."

Celina was about to ask about this place in greater detail but stopped.

She's leaving. Kai is in the dark realm. Shiriki is always inside that room in the back of the surgery.

"Are you seriously leaving me alone with Shiriki?"

Hilda nodded. "I won't be long, and Nalie should arrive shortly to guard you in case he gets... well, the way he is sometimes."

"You mean monstrous?" Celina waved her hand in dismissal when Hilda opened her mouth. "Never mind. It's fine. Like you said, Nalie will be here soon." She grabbed a suitcase and rolled it toward the door.

Hilda grabbed her wrist. "You can't go out there. I was—"

"I'm taking two steps outside to help. If I'm not safe doing that, then leaving me alone here for even two seconds is even more dangerous." Celina grinned, tugging against the luggage. "I'm so cooped up in here. I need to get some fresh air even if it's for a minute or two. Please."

Hilda let out a sigh. "Very well."

The doors opened, and Celina squinted against the sunlight. A fresh summer breeze brushed against her skin, and she smiled. Vehicles rushed by in front of her prison, and she formulated a quick plan. The guard near the entrance took a suitcase, helping Hilda with her task, then walked to the car.

As they shoved the last luggage into the vehicle, Celina waved at Hilda. "Have a safe trip."

Hilda gave a curt nod and ducked into the passenger seat. There was no driver, and Celina assumed it was because the guard was driving the caretaker to the location.

He turned to Celina and strode to the door. "Please step inside the building, miss."

Celina stared at him.

Is he human or something else?

She shoved her hand into her pocket, grabbing hold of the metal piece she'd used to break out of her room. Taking a few steps back, she waited for her chance. Her heart hammered against her ribs. The guard turned around as the doors closed. Celina rushed forward, shoved piece between the door and frame near the lock, and held her breath.

She stood still, unmoving as she listened. A few seconds passed, and she moved closer, reaching for the handle with a trembling hand. And… opened it.

The metal fell to the floor, and she picked it up, smiling ear to ear.

Freedom.

Kai had returned to his realm to fix the rifts, but while he was gone, he couldn't sense her. This was her opportunity to help and retrieve the box her Aunt Marie had left her. Although the pendant was a tracker, she'd be back before Kai returned here. Besides, by the time she told him the truth, it would already be done.

I won't be gone long.

She stared down the street, getting her bearings, and hurried onward. The hotel she had stayed in with Kai wasn't too far, and she could make it on foot in around thirty minutes.

Hot concrete burned through her flats, and her feet throbbed at being on them too long already. Still, she pressed on against her screaming legs as she approached her destination.

The Hotel Fairmont Château Laurier looked like a castle, beautiful and well maintained. Valets drove clients' vehicles away from the entrance called out to rich people, and Celina couldn't help grin. Kai was rich all right. Millennia of collecting money made that possible.

She stepped inside the lobby, enjoying the sudden cooler air. The marble white floors reflected the chandeliers and anchored candelabra, the illumination providing a sunny feel. She stared down at herself.

I don't fit in now any more than the first time I came here.

The hairs on the back of her neck rose, and she kept still, her gaze sweeping around her without moving her head. A few people stared at her, but maybe she was being paranoid.

Bellhops pushed golden metal carts around, filled with luggage, and Celina trudged behind them as she approached the front desk. The woman smiled, but it was the customer-service of forced friendliness. "Good morning. How can I help you today?" Her makeup was applied perfectly, and she could have passed for a model with her flawless skin and straight blonde hair.

Celina patted her top feeling dumpy with her baggy clothes. "I stayed here with a friend a few months ago, but it was during a difficult time." She leaned forward to get closer to the woman so fewer people would overhear. "I'd just lost my husband and my aunt a few weeks apart. While I was here, my aunt's lawyer brought me a box of her belongings, but I accidentally left it in the penthouse when I left." She straightened. "Do you have it by chance?"

"The penthouse? Whose name was it under?"

"Kai..." Celina bit the inside of her cheek, unsure what name he used. He wouldn't have used Leviet or the police would find that suspicious. She focused on any information she remembered of Kai when she'd made her deal with him, and something sprang to mind. "Maybe Markham?"

"Yes, I see he registered here." She smiled up at her. "And your name?"

"Celina Leviet."

She nodded as she clicked on the computer mouse a few times. Celina inhaled deeply. Thomas had mentioned his last name, Leviet, could have been Markham. He'd told her it had been for generations until his great-grandfather was left with the one daughter, who married, and so the name died. Fake story, but she wondered if there was any truth behind it.

"Yes, we registered you in the penthouse." Her blue eyes stared at Celina. "Can I see identification please?"

Shit.

"Actually, I left my hand purse with most of my possessions inside the box." She ran her hands over her abdomen. "I found a letter inside that brought back... difficult memories and left after. Had a bit of a nervous breakdown, and—"

"No, no. Don't worry, I understand." She tapped a few things on her keyboard and gave a sympathetic smile. "We have a lost and found. If you'd follow me, please?"

Celina nodded and waited near the counter as the employee strode around. The three people who had been staring at Celina when she'd walked in kept their gazes on her, and she swallowed hard.

The woman stopped near her. "This way please."

Pushing the nagging warning to the back of her mind, Celina followed toward another desk where a security guard sat. A label stuck to the door, and her heart sped, crossing her fingers that leaving Shiriki's dwelling wasn't for nothing.

The guard smiled. "Do you have any identification?"

The employee leaned closer to the security guard. "It was during a difficult time. If you could check the lost and found, there should be a card with a photo ID we could verify."

He gave a quick nod and unlocked the door. Once he disappeared inside, Celina turned to the woman, glancing at her nametag. "Thank you for your help, Melanie."

"Of course. I'm very sorry for your loss."

Her stomach churned. While her husband didn't die, her aunt had, and no matter how much time passed, guilt for her death never vanished.

"Thank you."

The guard returned with a familiar box and set it on his desk. "I found a wallet inside with a provincial identification card with a photo." He glanced at her and smiled. "You match the photo. Anything found within the room was put into this box, but if anything is missing, please let us know and we'll look into further."

"Thank you so much." Her voice cracked. "These were my aunt's last possessions before she passed. I can't believe I left them behind like that."

The woman pointed at the box. "I can get an employee to help you with this."

Celina was about to refuse, but her pulse quickened as the three people who'd stared at her since she walked in got to their feet. One walked out while the others continued watching.

"I've got a friend who's picking me up here, but I wouldn't say no to help getting this thing outside," she said with a nervous laugh.

The woman beckoned to a bellhop who strode to them. "Please bring this out into the valet area."

"Of course." He smiled as he took the box.

With a final thank you, Celina followed the man outside, keeping alert as they walked near two of the men watching her.

Once outside, Celina pointed toward the side of the hotel. "My friend is picking me up in the alleyway to avoid traffic. Would you mind putting it near the wall there?"

"Are you sure?" He arched an eyebrow, but when she nodded, he shrugged and did as she asked.

Celina waited until the man returned inside, peeking her head around the corner. The person stalking her stood at the entrance looking around. He seemed to have lost something.

Me.

She pushed the box with her foot closer to the garbage bin to keep out of sight. Crouching to pick it up took more effort than she wanted to admit, but she managed. She rummaged to the bottom, pushing aside papers, then froze. Her hand brushed against a scrunched-up letter, and tears burned the corners of her eyes.

Her mother's letter.

Taking a deep breath, she continued rummaging inside. She grabbed Father Robert's journal and frowned when she found a key. The etching on the silver was familiar, and she wracked her brain trying to recall.

Her days at Yonah Church came to mind, and she recalled the safe near the altar with the same symbol: a sun with wings inside. She pocketed it and left, holding the journal close to her chest.

The man who'd been looking for her wasn't in front of the hotel anymore, and her shoulders relaxed. Kai usually returned around dusk, and with the sun still high in the sky, she headed to the church Kai had burned. She had time to find out what was inside the safe before getting back to Shiriki's dwelling.

A shiver ran through Celina at the prospect of admitting to Kai where she had gone. He would be so pissed. She held her head higher at the thought.

Too bad. I'm half-demon, and his wife. He has to let me help.

13

———

VISION

The ping of the crosswalk lights started, and a few brakes squealed as impatient drivers revved their motors.

As Celina approached Yonah Church, she picked up her pace. Although she had been there when it happened, the destruction still sent goosebumps crawling along her skin. The church was burned, nothing but its outer walls left behind. They'd boarded a few places up to keep people out. The thick wooden doors to the sanctuary blocked her way inside. The building next to the ruins was blown to bits, part of the structure collapsed.

She approached a boarded up side entrance and spotted a graffiti-covered panel that opened to allow workers to come and go. She frowned at a few familiar symbols on one wall: The angel is guarding you.

What?

Shaking her head, she made her way through the small entrance, rolling her eyes at how difficult it was with her abdomen bigger than usual.

The inside looked eerie. Fire had burned the wood and cracked the stone. Her footsteps crunched over debris, and she stopped in what used to be the sanctuary. A horrific flash-back flew through her mind. She saw her Aunt Marie clawing her way out of the burning room at the back. Celina shook her head, and the memory vanished, leaving her shaken. Tears blurred her vision, but she pressed her lips together, refusing to cry.

She walked deeper into the ruins of the church, needing to get to where the safe used to be. Metal beams were left twisted, and a shiver ran down her spine. She ran her hands against the cool metal, and a surge of familiar energy zapped through her fingers.

Kai.

Most of the stained-glass windows she remembered had shattered, pieces glowing in beautiful colors on top of what was left of the confessionals. She rushed to the wooden door and pushed against the pieces. The safe stood anchored to the wall, the etching of the sun with wings identical to the one on the key she pulled from her pocket.

She inserted the key, and opened it. Hundreds of smaller safes stood in front of her. "Can't ever be simple, can it?"

Celina spun the key and stared at the number thirty-five etched on the back. If this didn't work, she'd run out of time. She pushed it into the fifth box of the fourth row and smiled when it opened.

She grabbed a gray box, then rummaged inside. A few objects were left, and she took anything that looked valuable. She emptied the remains and frowned. Inside a tiny glass casing, a small obsidian shard floated mid-air. It was as though no light could penetrate it, and all the darkness of the world lived within. She pocketed the shard with the other things she'd taken.

Leaning against the wall, she inhaled, trying to push her fears from her mind and focus on what she needed to do next. She closed both doors and locked them, not wanting anyone to discover what she'd taken. A whistling noise filled her ears as a breeze fluttered in from a window.

Her vision blurred, the edges darkening, and a force threw her back as though going through time itself. Her breathing sped, and she looked around the main room of the church.

Wasn't it daylight a few seconds ago? Why is it night?

Illumination from the outside lamps filtered through the boards and cracks, plunging the area into near-darkness. Debris crunched nearby, and she spun, squinting in the darkness as a figure dragged someone into the sanctuary. Taking a few steps closer, her stomach churned as she spotted a Sanguis, her arms flailing, trying to get away from the figure pulling her deeper through the ruins. Someone had ripped the lower half of her face off, silencing her, and bile burned the back of Celina's throat at the sight.

Celina staggered as a wave of energy pushed against her again, and she gasped. Daylight filtered through the church once more. Her heart throbbed inside her ears as she glanced at the safe next to her. She hadn't moved from her spot, so what the hell had just happened?

Why am I getting visions?

A sinking feeling crept through her as she headed toward the exit but slowed. What she'd seen was deeper within the sanctuary. What if there was something important there? Information she could bring to Kai.

Taking a deep breath, she changed direction, needing to check. Energy prickled at her neck, and a blast shook the ruins. She yelped, grabbing onto a piece of wood to keep from falling. Dust rose, and she coughed, waving her hand through the air, trying to clear her surroundings.

She froze, staring at the scattered bodies lying near what was left of the benches, dirt and maggots covering them. All of them had their jaws ripped out, their eyes wide with fear and pain, like the way they looked when each was murdered.

Celina pressed the journal tighter against her chest. More murdered demons. Her heartbeat pulsed in her ears, and she took a step back. A heavy silence fell inside the ruins, and she shivered as the temperature dropped. White feathers fell, and Celina looked up, her eyes widening as she caught one mid-air.

"Is… someone here?" she called out, her voice shaking.

Silence.

Something fell, and the sound echoed within what was left of the church. She froze, fearing whoever had killed these demons was nearby.

Shiriki walked in through the opening, surveying the bodies.

"What did you do, pet?" he asked in an amused tone as though finding the whole situation funny.

She kept her mouth shut, unable to explain anything. When he drew a step closer to her, she forced herself to speak. "I did nothing. They… I don't know what happened."

"And why did you run away?" He cocked his head.

"I didn't run away. I needed to get—"

"Is this what you will tell Mekaisto?" His smile widened, and she flinched. "Having realized you left has made his mood… sour. I suggest you come up with a better explanation as to why you disobeyed orders while I drag you home."

She swallowed hard, grasping the pendant and hoping it would keep Shiriki from murdering her where she stood.

AN INSIDE SOURCE

Celina stared at Father Robert's journal, but after reading the same sentence a dozen times, gave up. She could feel Kai's glare from where he sat across from her, silent. He hadn't spoken a word to her since Shiriki brought her back to his dwelling. It was worse than yelling or scolding her.

Slowly, she closed the journal and met his gaze, lifting her head higher. "I know you're angry with me for leaving, but—"

"I am not angry." His voice expression turned to stone, and it sent a shiver down her spine.

"You—"

"I am furious." His tone darkened, the glow of his eyes brightening. "I returned to find you gone, and out in the open after I explained why I am keeping you here." He shook his head. "If this is the way you want to take your revenge against what I did to you, please wait until our son is born."

She narrowed her eyes. "I make revenge deals *for* people I love. Not against them."

"Why would you put yourself and our child at risk? After I told you who is attacking us."

Guilt filled her, knowing she shouldn't have run off. She got to her feet and moved around the sofa, her gaze focused on the journal. Had it been worth it to worry Kai?

She stiffened as he approached, willing herself not to show fear. At the thought, the corners of her eyes burned, and she blinked several times. He stopped inches from her, his breath tickling her skin as he seemed to struggle with his own emotions. She lowered her head, trembling.

Why am I scared if I love him?

He placed his finger under her chin, forcing her to look at him. "Because you know what I am capable of." Cupping her cheek, his gaze searched hers. "Were you hurt out there?"

"No. I'm… okay."

"What happened?"

Her mind filled with darkness, and she shook her head. "Please stop doing that. I'm allowed to share when I'm ready, and not because you invade my personal space."

"Are you going to tell me or hide it?" His presence left her, and she sagged in relief.

She decided on the truth. Honesty was important to her, so she told him about how she left the dwelling and got what she needed inside her aunt's box. Once she got to the vision, though, she picked her words carefully. "I saw someone dragging a Sanguis who was alive, but when I… walked deeper into the sanctuary at Yonah Church, there were more Sanguis demons. They'd been dead for a while from how their bodies were decayed."

His expression turned blank. "Did you see the one who did it?"

"No." Her shoulders relaxed, hoping if he asked, it meant he believed her. "Why is this happening?"

He glowered over her shoulder toward the door. "I do not know for certain."

"And will you tell me when you find out, or do you plan

on keeping the information from me?" she asked, not hiding the frustration from her tone. "Unlike you, I can't fish inside your mind."

He took a few steps forward. "Celina—"

"If you included me, I wouldn't have to go behind your back." She marched away from him and stared at the bookshelf. It looked suddenly so interesting. "You always push me away unless you need something from me. I'm useful to carry your children and have sex, but for anything else, I don't matter."

He spun her, and her breath caught at his strained expression. Like she had ripped him apart.

"Do you truly believe that is all you mean to me?" he asked in a hushed voice.

Her heart squeezed at the unexpected emotion in his voice. "I… no. I'm sorry. It's just… sometimes I feel like I'm not allowed to do anything. You're locking me away again, and I don't like it."

"It is for your protection. Just like last time." He shook his head as though lost in thought. "But I understand why you no longer want that kind of life. I will try to give you more freedom. I promise."

He held her close, and she relaxed, sliding her hands along his waist. "I'm sorry I ran off. I shouldn't have gone behind your back."

"When I found out you were gone, I was ready to burn everything if it meant finding you," he whispered.

"I didn't mean to worry you."

He pulled her away and smirked. "Do you know what the consequence is for disobeying a direct order from me is?"

"No, I don't." But she was curious.

He slid his hand behind her back, lifting her shirt so his sharp fingernails glided along her skin. "I would whip you. Your soft flesh would mark so easily. Redder with each lash."

Leaning toward her ear, he lowered his voice. "I would strip you bare, your wrists tied above your head. Your moans and cries would drive my desire to claim you where you stand, mine to take."

Her breath hitched.

Why does that turn me on?

"I am pleased it does." He chuckled as he pulled back. "We will have many new things to explore together."

"You'll hurt me because I don't obey you?" She didn't bother hiding the hurt from her tone.

He shook his head. "No. Anyone else would have suffered lashes until their skin peeled from their bones, but not you. You are mine to protect."

"So, no punishment for me?" she asked, running a finger along his chest.

His grin turned predatory, and a shiver shot down her spine. "Who said anything about not punishing you?" He slid his hand to her ass and squeezed. "Now then... bend over, wife."

Celina sat by the window looking out onto the busy street. Ancus sat nearby, reading a book, but she had a feeling he was just staring at it and keeping his focus on her.

A familiar man walked toward the building, and she arched an eyebrow, trying to figure out who it was. When she realized it was Brihan in his human form, she got to her feet and dashed to the lobby.

She joined Hilda as the Sanguis stepped inside. "Celina, it's good to see you." He grasped her hands, but she pulled him into a hug.

Brihan stiffened, then backed away several steps, bowing his head low. Celina arched an eyebrow, then glanced over her shoulder, heart pounding as she caught Kai and Shiriki staring at them. While Shiriki looked amused, as usual, her husband looked like he was holding back on killing her friend where he stood.

She wanted to tell him off about jealousy, but the memory of Tess baiting her rolled around in her head. Instead, she turned to Brihan and smiled.

"How have you been?"

Brihan glanced up. "Better now since I can bring news."

Kai stepped next to Celina, and she slid her hand into the crook of his arm. His gaze bored into her, gentling.

By the time he looked at his subject, he seemed in a better mood. "What news?"

"I know where the Venatores are."

Shiriki approached Brihan, and he stiffened, his green eyes darting from him to his king. Celina couldn't help but sympathize with her friend. No one wanted Shiriki to get too close. Or close at all.

"And how did you find them?" he asked. His usual smile had vanished, replaced by a cold expression that sent a shiver crawling along Celina's skin.

Hilda frowned. "Perhaps you would care to sit and discuss this while I serve lunch?" She shot a pointed look at Celina.

Ever since having arrived here, the caretaker took her duties to feed Celina seriously. Kai placed his hand over Celina's and squeezed.

"Have you not eaten since breakfast?" he asked with a note of annoyance in his tone.

It was Celina's turn to shoot a glare at Hilda. "I wasn't hungry." She pulled her hand away and trudged toward the dining room. "Besides, I thought the whole thing with taking my soul got rid of my humanity. Aren't I considered dead or something? Why am I eating constantly?" By the time she finished venting, she sat in her usual seat, drumming her fingers against the surface.

Kai joined her at the head of the table and sat. "You are a unique case. Your heart still beats, and so you are very much alive. Even if you were fully demon, our kind needs to consume food while with child. It is a rare occurrence, but Nalie has enough experience, and she insists you need food."

"I offered my services as an expert, but they refused it," Shiriki said with a grin.

Her stomach churned at the thought, but she didn't take the bait. Instead, she turned to Brihan as he hesitated at the door, and patted the chair next to her, but his face paled. Darkness slithered across the surface, shooting at the Sanguis as though to impale him. Celina bolted to her feet and spun to her husband.

"Kai. Stop."

The darkness rose to the ceiling and crashed against the beams. Her eyes widened, and she gripped edges to keep from falling as debris and wood crashed onto the table.

She coughed. "That's excessive, even for you." She froze at the icy stare her husband gave her. "Kai?"

Shiriki chuckled. "That was not Mekaisto who sent the energy up to blow up my ceiling, pet." His gaze swept her, an unreadable expression turning his features cold and almost... calculating. "And a Sanguis could not have done that either. This leaves one other person in the room."

"So why did *you* do it?" Celina shot, knowing where he was going with this. "It wasn't me if that's what you're trying to say."

Shiriki's eyes flashed brighter. "How would you know? You do not have control over any powers yet; you are not even aware of what you can or cannot do."

The blast had been so strong. How could it have been her who caused it?

"Well, I didn't mean to—"

"Stop your husband from attacking your friend?" He stared at the ceiling with a glare.

Kai straightened, but his shoulders were tense. "We will discuss this later."

"And in the meantime," Shiriki waved his hand, and the destruction fixed itself in the blink of an eye, "try to keep from destroying my property."

She sat, and Kai turned his attention to Brihan. "How did you find the rebels?"

"I watched Yonah Church for any signs of the culprit, and after a few hours, someone came into the sanctuary." He leaned his elbows on the table, a slow smile curling his lips. "A Venatore, as you guessed."

Shiriki rested his chin against his knuckles. "Are you certain? They are crafty at hiding their presence from us."

"I'm sure. I grabbed the man and dragged him underground to… ask him a few questions."

Celina's stomach churned. Brihan had always been a kind friend to her. It was a harsh reality to remember what he was.

And remember who your husband is? Idiot.

She turned to her friend. "And so he told you where they are?" She almost added "just like that?" but knew he had tortured the Venatore. Not something she was interested in hearing about.

"It's the only thing I got out of him. He was one stubborn bastard until his last breath."

"You should have brought him to me," Shiriki said, his eyes flashing whiter. "I could have extracted the rest."

Brihan shrugged. "I didn't kill him. He killed himself."

Shiriki's expression changed, but Celina pushed the unease in the back of her mind when his smile returned. That couldn't have been pain she'd seen.

Kai placed his hand over hers and squeezed. "Lumen and Venatores have taken their own lives if it means protecting secrets from us."

"They cloaked their headquarters within a café down-town, so I checked it out. So far, I've noticed a few Venatores, but it's the right place." He leaned back in his chair. "When the Venatore was dying, he mentioned a woman's name, and someone with the same name works at the café."

Celina arched an eyebrow. "Some names are common, though."

"True, but how many people do you know are named Namika?"

Her pulse quickened, and a cold sweat sent goosebumps crawling along her skin. She jumped to her feet. "What's her last name?"

"I don't know. He didn't—"

"Then what was *his* name?" When he continued staring at her like she'd gone insane, she grabbed the front of his shirt. "His name!"

"Yasuo."

She let him go, tears blurring her vision. Namika, her best friend from childhood, had brought Yasuo to visit Celina at the hotel, and they had talked and laughed. They had done their best to keep her mind off of her husband's death. And now Yasuo had killed himself…

Her mind caught up like she hit a brick wall. Yasuo was a Venatore? Did this mean Namika was one, too? And now they would go after her friend, and…

"I… need air." And without waiting, she dashed from the room.

Hilda straightened as Celina walked past her, following behind in silence. Not knowing where to go, she stopped in the lobby and stared outside the window. A part of her wanted to warn Namika about what was coming, but if the rebels were the ones killing demons and attacking Kai's realm…

"It's difficult being in the middle of everything," Hilda said.

Celina glanced at her. "No, it's not. I mean, she's my friend. But I didn't know she was... She's not." Her breath came in faster, black spots obscuring her vision until the room spun.

Strong arms slid around her chest. "Breathe, dove."

She closed her eyes, focusing on her heartbeat as it slowed. "I'm okay." Ideas flew through her head faster than she could keep up. She was so focused on planning everything, she didn't even feel Kai slide into her mind.

"Do not even think about it," Kai growled in her ear.

He let her go when she squirmed, and she paced the lobby under everyone's watchful gaze. Even Ancus came to see what the fuss was about. She gritted her teeth, running her fingers through her hair.

Why did they leave the dining room? We don't want witnesses to yet another disagreement.

"It's a good idea." She slowed and glanced at Kai. "You know it is. We could find out what they want, and how they plan on doing it so we can stop them."

"I would rather annihilate them all," he said in a dark tone.

Brihan shook his head. "The Venatore..." He shot Celina a pitiful glance. "He mentioned they..."

Kai's essence slithered around Brihan's body, burning parts of his flesh when Brihan trailed off. Celina opened her mouth to tell him to stop, but Shiriki raised his hand, and she pressed her lips together.

"They what?" Kai hissed. "Or would you prefer I find out myself?" Darkness coiled around his head, and Brihan's eyes widened.

"They have an inside source!"

Kai's muscles tensed, but the essence vanished, and Brihan fell to the floor, trembling violently. As much as she wanted to go to her friend, she stood by Kai's side, putting her hand on his arm.

"Any idea who this source is?" Kai asked, ice lacing every word.

Brihan shook his head, still kneeling. "No, but he said the source would make it possible to achieve their goal."

Celina ran her palm over her abdomen and sighed. "Kai, please consider my idea."

"No." He spoke the single word with such force, she took a step back. His expression softened, and he took her hand in his. "It is not—"

"I'm getting tired of this. You promised you would let me help."

"And I agreed only if it did not put you or our child in harm's way."

She motioned toward Shiriki. "Because we're not in danger every day?"

"I am standing right here, pet. Hurtful words if I had a heart to care," Shiriki said with a smirk.

Celina ignored the comment, moving to Kai. "Please hear my plan out." She swept her gaze from Brihan to Shiriki, and then Hilda. "Hear it out, and then we vote."

"This is not a democracy." Kai's lips curled over his pointed teeth. "It is a tyranny."

"In which I am the queen and have a say." When he opened his mouth to counter, she raised her hand. "You also said I deserved love and respect. That includes deciding *with* me, not *for* me."

His jaw clenched, his gaze focused on nothing as his pupils thinned. "Very well. We will hear your plan."

"And you're not allowed to punish or threaten anyone who agrees with me."

Shiriki burst out laughing as Kai's murderous glare landed on him. "Apparently, she knows your tricks better than you thought."

After Hilda brought Celina's meal and insisted she eat,

they settled at the dining room table. This time, Nalie joined them.

Celina took a deep breath and explained her plan. She'd never enjoyed speaking in public, and this was worse. By the smiles everyone gave her though, she was sure they'd vote for her idea.

Now if her husband would only stop glaring.

15

INTO THE DEN

The café was bustling with customers, and Celina bit her lower lip, giving a sideways glance at Kai. He stood rigid beside her in his human form, and a part of her tingled at seeing him like that. His hair ended below his ears, and he wore black jeans and a dress shirt. After the deal was over, after everything, she didn't think she'd see him look so human ever again.

"I know you don't like my plan."

He cocked his head, his smile bordering on evil. "Whatever gave you that idea?"

"Just the feeling I got when you were the only one who voted against it." She was still shocked Hilda and Nalie had voted yes. "Look, it's a good plan. It gets us in, we find out what they're planning, who's their source, and then we stop them. Simple."

He started toward the café. "Nothing is ever simple. And as soon as I find the source, nothing in any realm or world will stop me from twisting them from the inside out until they're a pile of organs and bones at my feet. Then I'll start over… slowly."

"I love when you talk about things you're passionate

about," she said with a grin, then clapped her hands together. "Now, then. Let's go inside. And remember: I do the talking."

He rolled his eyes, the maroon color flashing red in the sunlight. They stepped inside the building, the blast of air conditioning cooling her sweaty clothes. She shivered, and Kai rubbed her back absent mindedly.

She caught sight of Namika, her pulse quickening, and tapped Kai's shoulder. "There she is. I'll be right back."

He gave a curt nod, sweeping his gaze across the room at the customers sitting at the tables. Some stood in line, waiting to order, and more entered the shop every few minutes.

Celina walked toward the small corridor leading to the public washrooms where Namika was slipping off her apron. Her black hair was longer, but apart from that, she never seemed to change. Still as beautiful as ever.

"Namika."

She turned, and her eyes widened. "Celina?" Pulling her into a hug, Namika squeezed tight. "Where have you been? What happened?" She pulled away, and she gaped at Celina's abdomen. "What…"

"Can we talk somewhere in private?" Celina grinned. "A lot's happened."

Her friend's eyebrows shot up. "You're telling me?" She lowered her voice, glancing around. "Do you know the cops are looking for you? They came to my place asking about you. When was the last time I saw you and all that."

Namika motioned with her head, and they walked to the employees' only door, and into a break room. Instead of stopping inside, Namika continued until they reached a smaller room with a table and chairs.

"What did you tell the police?"

"The truth. At your hotel room with Yasuo…" Namika's shoulders slumped, and she stared at the wall. But she shook her head. "Sorry, I'm worried about him. He left two days ago and should be back."

Celina's stomach churned, knowing Yasuo's fate. She pressed her hand over her abdomen, lost in thought.

"So, what happened?" she asked, pointing at Celina's baby bump.

"Well, when a man and a woman love each other—"

"Oh, shut up!" Namika said with a giggle before sobering. Her gaze softened and tears filled her eyes. "Did you know you were pregnant before… your husband passed away?"

She shook her head. "No. I found out after. It was a shock, to say the least." And her friend had no idea how much of a shock it was. "But it's okay. I'm coping."

"Listen, about what I had said at the funeral about Thomas… I'm sorry. It was insensitive of me, and not my place. I didn't know him and had no right to judge your situation." She took Celina's hand. "I'm so, so sorry."

Part of her wished she could tell her friend the baby's father—her husband—was alive and well, but it was impossible. Instead, she followed the plan.

"I need your help." When Namika nodded, Celina released the breath she was holding. "It's a lot to ask, especially since the police are looking for me."

"Why are they? I mean, I know you didn't murder your husband, so what's the deal?"

She pressed her lips together to stop from scoffing at her friend's choice of word. "I'm being chased, and I can't go to the cops for help, so I've been hiding. Problem is, they think I'm being uncooperative, and without a suspect in Thomas's case, they think I have something to do with it."

"Don't worry. I've got somewhere no one will find you."

"Thank you. I…" She squeezed her friend's hand. "You know I was part of the Lumen, right?"

She arched an eyebrow. "I knew your aunt was, but…" She averted her gaze. "I'm sorry about her, too. I heard she was inside the church when it burned."

"My mother left the Lumen when I was around ten years

old. I never officially renounced, but something happened recently. I found out my friend Kai, the one you met, is part of a… well, this sub-group of Lumen. Anyway, that's not what's important, but—"

She raised her hand. "Wait, what? Are you telling me he's a Venatore?"

"Yes, he is. But he's from an underground group in western Canada near the Alberta and British Columbia border."

Namika smiled ear to ear, clapping her hands together a few times. "Oh, angels above, this is a sign! Celina, if your friend is one of us—"

"Us?"

She leaned forward. "I have a confession to make. I'm a Venatore. I was also a spy of sorts, pretending to be a Lumen to gather information for a while. It's how I met your aunt again, and it's when she told me about what happened to your husband."

Celina had her doubts when Brihan told them about what he'd gotten out of Yasuo, but to hear Namika admit it weighed on her. Namika had been her best friend for years and for her to have hidden such a big secret for so long felt like a stab of betrayal. A feeling Celina experienced too many times in a short span.

"So it's true…"

"What is?"

"Kai said they sent him to this café to find a contact within the Venatores because something big will happen soon. He said, as a former Lumen, I would be safer joining this group to help protect my baby."

"From what?"

"Demons. They're after me and my baby. Apparently, they need something from us both to stop an attack or something like that."

"I have to take you to Jacob Mackenzy. He's the leader of

the group here. He has to meet your friend, too, so they can discuss the plans."

Namika stood, and Celina stared at her. "Why didn't you ever tell me you were a Venatore? We've known each other for years."

"I'm sorry. It's a secretive group, and I was never allowed. But since you seem to be right in the middle, I thought you should know now. Besides, your friend is right. The safest place to be is with us." She bit her lower lip and then added, "Members have been disappearing more and more every day. Recently, Fred and Patricia vanished."

Celina's heart jolted at the names. They had been Shiriki's victims in the basement at his dwelling. The woman was dead, and Celina had discovered Fred in one of Shiriki's twisted traps. She still cringed at what was left of the two after Shiriki had killed them in brutal ways. Yet they were from the very group set on attacking her husband, threatening her family's existence. She despised the part of her that was relieved neither of the Venatores ever made it out.

They returned to the customer area of the café, and Celina spotted Kai chatting with a stranger. The man had light blond hair with silver highlights, catching the fluorescent lights. When Kai spotted her, he waved, and both Celina and Namika approached them.

"Kai, you remember my friend, Namika?" Celina waved toward her.

Her husband smiled and shook her hand. "It's good to see you again."

"And you." Namika motioned toward the man. "I see you've met Terrin."

Celina guessed if Kai was speaking with him, then the man must be a Venatore.

Terrin locked gazes with Celina, and she couldn't help dislike him right away. His smile didn't reach his eyes, and the way he looked at her raised red flags.

"It's nice to meet you, Terrin. I'm Celina."

Namika leaned closer to the man. "We need to bring them inside so they can settle in and then talk with Jacob."

He nodded. "All right. Follow me."

The four strode to the employee only door. This time, instead of stopping inside the small room, they walked past it and through double doors covered with a large curtain.

Except it wasn't a curtain.

Celina grasped Kai's arm as they passed through a veil, the eerie liquid soft and dry against her skin. Once through, it revealed a mansion hidden beyond. Venatore headquarters.

Terrin motioned his head. "This way."

They moved through multiple corridors. The place looked like an ancient museum. Every few feet statues or artifacts stood amongst paintings hanging on the walls. The white marble brightened the space since most of the lights were dimmed, and Celina couldn't help holding on tighter to Kai.

He stared at her but stayed silent as they continued forward. Namika stopped near a door and glanced from Celina to Kai.

"Do you want separate rooms or…" The question hung in the air.

Terrin crossed his arms as though curious himself.

She cleared her throat. "I'd prefer we share a room. Kai's been a great support, and I need someone familiar to stay with me." She glanced at her belly and smiled. "Helps with the stress."

"Is there a sofa or armchair?" Kai asked. When Namika nodded, he smiled. "Good. I'd hate to sleep on the floor."

They laughed, and the tension faded between them. Still, Kai gave Celina a quick wink no one else noticed, and she averted her gaze to keep from blushing.

Terrin pulled out a cellphone. "I'll let Jacob know we've got guests, but in the meantime, make yourselves comfortable."

Once alone in their bedroom, Celina turned to Kai and crossed her arms.

He arched an eyebrow. "What?"

"I told you my plan would work. We got in!"

He swept his gaze along her body, approaching her with slow steps. Once he reached her, he leaned his hands against the wall behind her, and a red glow shone across the surface. Her breath hitched, remembering he'd done the same thing at their hotel in Montreal. It was to cover any noise within a space.

She swallowed hard, trapped between his body and the wall. "Kai?"

His lips brushed against hers. "Yes, dove?"

"What are you doing?"

"We have a while before we're fetched. Why not enjoy some alone time?"

Her pulse throbbed south, and she smiled.

16

THE TRAITOR

Celina glared at her hands. "It's not working."

"You're overthinking it," Kai said with a smile. He stretched on the sofa, his human form no less intimidating as he gazed at her. "With natural power suppressed for years, it won't just work at full capacity. It'll take time and practice."

"Well, that's nice and all, but I need it to work now." She wiggled her fingers, but nothing happened. "I feel warmth pulsing through my veins, but—"

"Between your legs?" he asked with a lewd grin.

She turned toward the door to hide the heat scorching her cheeks, but knew the act gave away her guilt. Still, she had to focus. "It starts inside my chest, and flows out toward my extremities. Especially through my hands, though."

Kai wrapped his arms around her, and she turned her head to look at him.

"Power stems from emotions when a demon is young. While you're no longer a child, using your abilities is new." He brushed his lips against her neck, and she shivered. "So far, when you've felt your power at its strongest, what were you feeling in those moments?"

She tried recalling the times. "Frustration, pain, fear…"

"Negative emotions are our strongest sources." He nipped at her skin, and she yelped. "We should practice using those kinds. At least for the first few times." He let her go, and she spun around to face him.

"What do you mean?"

He crooked his finger, a sly smile curling his lips. For a second, she forgot he wasn't in his demon form because she could've sworn he looked as evil. "Attack me."

"Excuse me?" Her eyebrows shot up. "You want me to attack you? Are you kidding?"

"Well, I should've said *try* to attack me."

"That's not the part I misheard," she said, rolling her eyes. "In case you need a refresher, the last time I attacked you, it didn't end too well for me. You're the one who told me about not being able to control your instincts when provoked. And now you want me to try?"

"I won't hurt you."

"We don't always agree on what you consider not hurting me," she muttered but regretted her words as his smile vanished.

"I suppose I deserve that," he said with a sigh. "Well, if you won't attack on command, let's see if out of fear will work."

All but one light flickered off, setting a bright spotlight in the middle of the room. The shadows darkened, and Celina's eyes widened as they formed into tentacle-like arms, each one adorned with clawed hands.

She took a step back, her pulse throbbing in her ears as the warmth in her veins turned to fury to protect not only herself but her baby. The darkness shot out, and she raised her hands, pushing against the pressure and keeping the shadows away from her. She ducked as a claw swiped toward her, and she clenched her jaw, focusing her energy at the attacker. The light between her fingers flickered from white to gray, but she barely paid any attention to it until…

Kai stood in front of her, his vertical pupils thinning as they contrasted against the glowing red irises. The shadows vanished, and in the blink of an eye, the room was alight as though nothing had happened. Slowly, he took her outstretched hands into his and grinned.

"You did well, dove."

She gave him what she hoped was a poisonous smile. "Don't. Ever. Do. That. Again." When he laughed, she wrenched her hands away. "What the hell was that?"

"Again, the answer is somewhere in your question," he said with a wink.

She leaned her forehead against his chest and let out a quiet laugh. "You are impossible."

"And yet I'm here," he said, rubbing her back. "No need to worry. Those were nothing but simple illusions, nothing that could hurt you."

An hour passed as they discussed ways for Celina to practice without having to react out of fear, but no one came to fetch them for a meeting with whoever this Jacob was.

"Let's go explore," Celina said, walking to the door. "Maybe I can find Namika and get information about—"

Kai moved in front of her, blocking the path. "If we're caught snooping around—"

"We won't be doing any kind of snooping. I want to find and talk to my friend. Find out if she knows more about what's going on. Let's face it, this Jacob won't tell us much. But Namika? We've been friends for years, and although she kept this secret from me, I'm sure she's excited to finally share it."

He crossed his arms. "I already don't like this plan. Don't make it more dangerous for yourself."

She placed her hand on his chest. "But we *are* following my plan. You remember what happens if they discover one of us? We play the part. No matter what it takes, one of us has to stay behind to find out who's the inside source."

He stayed silent but gave a curt nod. Celina's heart swelled; he was trying, fighting millennia of instincts not to do things his way. She pressed herself closer to him, and he arched an eyebrow. "I know you could've easily locked me up, and not even bothered listening to me. Thank you for trusting me and giving my plan a chance."

Standing on her tippy-toes, she kissed him, and a flutter settled into her stomach as he slid his arms around her. He kissed her back, gentle and soft, and for a second, he was Thomas again.

They withdrew, and she smiled against his lips. "I love you."

"And I love you. Very much." His gaze bore into her.

A knock sounded, and he chuckled. "Speak of the devils…"

"You're one to talk," she muttered with a grin.

He opened the door, revealing Namika standing at the threshold. "Hey, sorry it's taking so long. Jacob is busy with a few things, but I thought I'd drop in. See how you're doing."

Celina pressed her hand against her belly and smiled. "I'm a bit hungry. Do you have anything I could eat? I'm not picky."

She could feel Kai's essence slithering around her to see if she was all right, and she flinched. It wasn't a lie—she was hungry—but it was more of an excuse to explore and talk to her friend.

"I can take you to the kitchens." Namika motioned, and both Celina and Kai followed.

If Celina thought the basement part of The CrowBar was a maze, this place was worse. Every corridor had nooks that looked like it may lead to other places, but stopped halfway.

They arrived in the kitchens, and it surprised Celina at how small it was for a place as big as this. A woman cutting up vegetables at the counter looked up and gave a shy smile. She looked younger than Celina, with light brown curly hair, and pale green eyes. There was an innocence to her, making her look like she didn't belong in any kind of group going up against demons.

"Hello."

Namika strode forward. "This is Faustina. She's a great cook!"

Celina smiled. "Hi. I'm Celina, and this is Kai."

The woman paled as she stared at Kai, and Celina had to stop herself from nudging him in the ribs. He was likely giving a signature smile that could have the toughest biker run for the hills. She made a mental note to remind him to play nice.

Play nice? Ha!

Namika didn't seem to notice anything. "Do we have anything Celina could eat right now?" She pointed at Celina's abdomen with a giggle. "And for two?"

Terrin walked into the kitchens, an annoyed expression etched on his face. "Ah, there you are." He motioned at Kai. "A few members have questions about the Venatores where you're from. Follow me."

Celina stared longingly at the food Faustina was taking out of the refrigerator. "You go ahead without me."

Kai narrowed his eyes, but she could tell he was debating between leaving her alone and the need for her to eat.

Celina pointed from Namika to Faustina. "I'm in good company. I'll eat, we'll chat…" She hoped he caught on. There was a better chance of her friend opening up if they were alone. And Faustina looked like the kind of person who knew a lot and would let information slip.

He sighed. "I'll meet you back in the room, then?"

"Definitely," she said with a smile.

As soon as he left, Celina grabbed the food offered to her and shoved it into her mouth. She was hungrier than she'd realized, and her stomach settled with the first few bites.

Celina turned to Namika as Faustina busied herself with

the dishes. "Do you have a library here? I'd love to read more about Lumen and Venatores. I'm hoping to find out what the demons want with me so I can avoid them better."

"We have quite the collection," she said with a smile. "But you'll have to ask Jacob if it's okay for you to wander around. I'm sure once he talks to you, he won't mind."

Her heart sank. "That makes sense." She grabbed onto the counter to stop herself from drumming her fingers in frustration. How would she be able to get information on her own?

She fidgeted, shifting from foot to foot.

Namika arched an eyebrow. "Are you all right?"

"In the last few weeks, I've had to use the washroom more." Celina grinned as she ran her hand across her belly. "I guess he's pushing against my bladder."

"I can show you to the washrooms," Namika said, bolting to her feet. "Come on."

They stopped in front of a wooden door left ajar. A clean washroom made of white marble sparkled as Namika turned on the lights, forcing Celina to squint.

"Wow. Pretty nice."

Namika nodded. "Go ahead."

"Thanks." Celina glimpsed a large archway farther down the corridor, and her pulse sped. "I might be longer than I thought."

"Oh." She shrugged. "I can wait if—"

"And die of embarrassment? Sure, stay right here. No pressure," Celina said with a laugh.

Namika grinned. "You remember how to get back?"

Celina pointed toward where they'd come from. "Straight, then turn left for the kitchen. Think I'll manage," she finished with a wink.

Celina closed the door and used the washroom. She had no idea when her next opportunity would come along, and she hadn't lied about her unborn baby pressing against her bladder, but what she had exaggerated was how much it bothered her. Being half-demon, having to relieve herself wasn't as necessary as it used to be.

Once she was done, she opened the door a few inches and peeked out, checking to make sure the corridor was empty. The way was clear, so she strode to the archway ahead. Glass doors were built into the arch and covered with blue curtains, so she couldn't see what was on the other side. Slowly, she opened a door and gaped at what was in front of her.

Celina stepped inside, her footsteps echoing in the vast room as she walked toward the center. Light polished wood shone under the white frosted lamps lighting the area, giving it a bright glow. Thousands of books stood in shelves lined up in rows, creating hundreds of aisles. Near the ceiling, a gigantic circular window made up most of the dome.

She moved to the first section of books, but after reading a few of the spines, approached a computer station, staring at the search bar. She typed the words "Lumen" and "Venatores" and over two thousand results popped-up.

Gritting her teeth, her fingers hovered over the keyboard. Following an instinct, she typed the word "angel," and one book appeared in the result. It didn't take long for her to figure out the coding system, and soon enough, she stood between the aisles.

Pulling out the large tome with glowing golden letters, she flipped through the yellowing pages and read.

We, the guardians, were a neutral race. We were often sought for advice on disputes worldwide. The angels were a quiet race who kept to themselves. Although they often bent rules for the greater good, we deemed one deed unforgivable: one of the angel leaders shared his powers with a few humans. Through generations afterward, those humans called themselves Venatores. Charged with hunting dark beings, they had longer lifespans than most humans.

When the two leaders of the angel race waged war with one another, it forced us to intervene. We imprisoned the leaders and destroyed the rest of the angels. Still fearing these two angels, we took matters into our own hands. We mixed our own blood with theirs, creating a race called drakin, but the newly created race was too powerful. And so, we forced them into an eternal slumber.

Years passed, and the two angels escaped and attacked us, killing most of our brethren.

In the end, we cursed one angel using a rare obsidian shard while the other was lost to time.

The guardians destroyed angels, then murdered them save for the two leaders? Not only had those leaders lost everything, but they were used to create a new race of beings so powerful, their own creators had to put them in a permanent slumber. It seemed so... fictional. And yet, here Celina was, carrying the demon king's son while being half-demon herself.

She flipped through a few pages, trying to wrap her mind around what she'd read. A few sketches caught her attention, and she frowned. Artifacts rumored to be powerful weapons but also used to suppress magic. One object, the obsidian shard, looked familiar.

She patted her pants and took out the dark shard she'd found in her aunt's safe deposit box inside Yonah Church.

Is this the same artifact?

Putting it inside her pocket, she stared at the page, trying to memorize the rest of the artifacts. She held her breath before tearing it out of the book. Her heart hammered as she folded the page and shoved it into her pocket along with the shard. She shut the tome and slid it to its place.

Her pulse was already throbbing too quickly as she walked out of the aisle, but it picked up further when she spotted a man standing near a table, his sky-blue eyes locking on Celina. His long blond hair matched the light tones of the room, the white highlights shimmering in the lighting filtering through the bookshelves.

"You must be Celina Leviet."

"I am." She approached him. "And you're Jacob Mackenzy?"

"Yes," he said with a polite smile. "Wanted to do a bit of light reading?"

She shrugged but gave the best sheepish smile she could muster. "I got curious, and couldn't believe how many books there are here. Sorry about that."

"No need to apologize. I have to say, I'm pleased you came to us. We've been looking for you for a while. Had we known you had demons hunting you, we would have acted faster."

"And what do the Venatores want with me?"

"We've worked at gaining entrance to the dark realm for some time, trying to vanquish Mekaisto. A few years ago, a powerful being with access to the realm contacted us and has been helping us gain power since then."

She tried keeping her expression neutral. "A being more powerful than Mekaisto?"

"Yes. An angel," Jacob whispered the word. "He told me we'd need you to succeed in our plan. Although, before you ask, I don't know what that part is."

"So, you believe angels are real? Have you seen one?"

"You've been around demons and Venatores while the group you used to belong to hunt paranormal beings... but you don't believe in angels?"

"Considering you didn't answer my second question, I can guess you haven't seen any." Deep down, she knew at least one was real; she remembered the white feathers falling from above in Yonah Church after she'd had another vision and found the maimed bodies.

"Or maybe it's harder to believe in good beings after you've had so many terrible things happen in your life."

She leaned against the table and crossed her arms. "What do you mean?"

His gaze bore into her, and she shifted. "I know who you are."

Her eyebrows shot up. "Oh?"

"Your mother was Elizabeth Tayen, a well-known Lumen. Exiled a few of my own brethren herself."

My mother.

She raised her hand as her pulse quickened. "Okay, one thing at a time. So, Venatores are working with an angel to overthrow the demon king?" Part of her was relieved Kai wasn't with her during this conversation or Jacob might not have a head attached to his neck much longer. "And the angel needs me for something, but you don't know for what?"

"He instructed us to bring you here. As I said, I'm pleased you came on your own." He stared over her shoulder and smiled.

Celina turned, and her shoulders sagged in relief when Namika walked toward them. "Celina! There you are. I was getting worried. And, Jacob. You're here, too." She glanced from one to the other. "I'm glad you two met."

Celina was still trying to come to terms with the new information, her mind numb. Namika was talking to Jacob, but Celina half-listened, too preoccupied with what would happen next. The plan had been to find out who the inside source was, but now, they were up against a traitor and a powerful being.

An angel? This makes it way more complicated.

Namika put out her hand, and Celina arched an eyebrow. "What?"

She grinned. "We'll perform a quick spell to make sure demons can't trace you anymore. It'll keep you safe."

Cold sweat trickled down her spine. If they did this spell, would it hurt her or her baby since they were both part demon? How would Kai react if the link between them was severed? When she'd left Shiriki's dwelling, he was prepared to burn everything to find her. Losing their connection inside this place could result in nothing less than a full attack on Kai's part. But to refuse their help would look too suspicious.

She bit her lower lip. "Will it… do anything to hurt my baby?"

"No, of course not," Jacob said, putting out his hand.

Taking a deep breath, she took Namika's hand, then Jacob's, and waited. She couldn't help the slight trembling and the way her stomach churned as they muttered words she didn't understand. Thin white lines glowed beneath her skin in symbols she recognized, the same left behind where the demons' bodies were found.

Once it was over, the markings vanished, and she tried relaxing her shoulders. "Is… is it done?"

Namika nodded. "Yes, this should keep you safe."

"Thank you," Celina said, nodded at both of them.

Jacob smiled. "You're one of us, Celina. We've been waiting a long time for you, and with your help, we'll be able to overtake the dark realm."

"My help?" She raised her hand. "Hang on. You said you didn't know what the angel needed me for."

"We don't know exactly how he plans to use you, no," he said, shaking his head. "But our source said Mekaisto took an interest in you. You're our way into the realm."

The message left behind from the first vision she'd seen suddenly made sense. The traitor is within their midst.

I'm the traitor.

All they had to do was get to Celina, and use her to get in. Her chest squeezed at the thought, knowing all too well the sting of betrayal. But she'd never meant to. It wasn't her fault. Would Kai see it that way? Or his subjects? They already despised Celina… could they convince their king she was a danger to have around? Clearly, she was.

The doors to the archives opened, and Kai walked inside, accompanied by Terrin and someone she hadn't met. The younger man pressed his lips together as though to keep from laughing and Celina's heart sped. He had been one of the people watching her at the hotel when she had been retrieving her aunt's belongings.

Jacob crossed his arms. "How good to meet you." The walls glowed white, familiar symbols appearing against the wood. More people ran inside the archives from different directions, their hands held high, light sparking between their fingers. Jacob took a step closer. "Mekaisto."

Namika gasped, grabbing Celina's hand.

What…

Celina's heart hammered as she stared at her husband. Terrin and the other man stepped aside as white flames burned in a circle around him. She couldn't help remembering when the Lumen had tried something similar with Kai, and that hadn't ended well for any of them.

Celina crossed her fingers he'd stick to the plan. One of them had to stay to find out who the source was, and it looked like it would be her. With the murderous look in Kai's eyes, she wasn't counting on him playing along nicely.

17

MONSTERS

C elina swallowed hard, the sound of the white fire and breathing the only sounds in the room. Kai stayed silent, remaining in his human form. It was time for her to play her part.

She turned to Jacob. "What's going on? Why have you trapped my friend?"

The Venatore who'd come in with Kai stepped closer to Celina, ruffling his brown hair. "We have a little surprise for you," he said playfully.

She threw every curse word inside her mind, hoping her glare was enough. He smirked, but when he looked over her shoulder, fell silent.

"This isn't funny, Rupert," Jacob said in a dark tone. "Celina, you trusted the wrong friend. He's not who you think he is."

Rupert snickered. "He's not *what* you think either."

Kai's gaze swept across the room, and a few of the Venatores took several steps back. Jacob however, approached.

"I contacted all the members of our group in the Western area, and none have ever heard of you, *Kai.*"

Namika's grip tightened. "Wait. Are you saying that's...

Mekaisto?" She glanced at Celina, tears flooding her eyes. "Oh God, are you okay? Did he do anything to you?"

Celina shook her head. "No, there has to be a mistake. He's my friend and a Venatore. Please—"

"No, he's been tricking you," Jacob said, shaking his head. "He needed a way inside our headquarters and used you to get in."

"If you knew, then why let us in? It doesn't make sense." Celina turned to Namika. "Please, you've met Kai before. Tell them they're wrong."

"We let him in," Rupert said pointing toward her husband, "because we had a trap waiting."

Jacob placed his hand on Celina's shoulder. "He's lied to you, hasn't he? I can see the pain in your eyes. But you wanted to believe there were good reasons. Because he cared. Am I right?"

Her breath hitched at the truth behind his words although the Venatore leader had no idea how close he'd hit home. "No… I mean, yes. It was to keep me safe from the demons chasing us, and—"

He raised his hand, then focused on Kai. "I'll tell her something, and I want you to stop me if this sounds familiar to you, demon king,"

The lights flickered, and goosebumps crawled along her skin. Despite his irises being a dark maroon, hatred burned behind them as Kai stared at Jacob.

She hoped he'd look inside her mind.

Please act your part. One of us has to remain behind. Don't kill them.

Kai cocked his head as the few shadows around them twisted in eerie shapes. "If you're so sure I am who you say, why take the chance your little trap here doesn't work?" he asked in a growl.

Terrin crossed his arms. "Don't fuck with us. If you weren't a demon, the flames wouldn't have lit."

"Who said I was human in the first place?" He opened his palm and shadows danced within, black feathers floating above his hand.

Jacob frowned. "Our source says you knew Venatores would come after her." His words lingered in the air like a poison.

Celina's chest tightened.

He knew? Why didn't he tell me?

Kai closed his hand, the feathers vanishing. "And what source would that be?"

Jacob crossed his arms. "Do you think I'd tell you?" He leaned against the table. "You've had your second in command looking for me." He grinned. "And I mean this with all offense, I have no desire of being anywhere near that monster."

Celina took a step forward. "I don't understand what's going on. Please—"

"You seem to have an interest in history," Jacob began with a pointed stare at her. "We've had powerful Venatores throughout the years. One who served under me was one of the greatest. He was determined to find a way into the dark realm, so much so he tortured his own child for the greater good." With a sigh, he shook his head. "He and his closest friend— my brother, Zachary—wanted a better world for us. A world away from the threat of monsters."

The edges of her vision blurred. "And what happened to them?"

Kai growled. "Enough."

Jacob ignored him despite the white flames sparking. "One died, and my brother is gathering more members to help in the fight against the demon king."

Namika shook her head. "Jacob, please wait. You said I could tell her in private. This isn't something that needs to be said in front of everyone."

Celina's eyebrows shot up. "Tell me what?" She swept her gaze across the room but locked on Kai.

Jacob let out a sigh. "Before Dean Perry was killed in a car crash with your mother, he told us something." When Celina turned to him, he gave her a sympathetic look. "Your mother told your stepfather about Mekaisto's plans for you, and so, he took it upon himself to act. To use you as a tool. You were the one he and Zachary experimented on, Celina."

Her chest tightened, and she shook her head as the pressure increased against her. Dean Perry… her stepfather. The Venatore who'd experimented on his daughter.

Her vision blurred as tears ran down her cheeks. "No. It can't be true."

He was a good man. It's a lie.

She remembered how he'd taught her languages, read to her every night before bed.

He had conducted experiments on her.

I can't remember him doing that. It can't be true.

Jacob continued talking, Namika adding pieces of information, but Celina wasn't listening. Until…

"And you knew about this, didn't you, Mekaisto?" His voice seemed to echo around the room as she stared at her husband. "You knew her stepfather was a Venatore."

"You… lied? Again?" Her voice came out hushed.

She had to act hurt and surprised to stay on the Venatores' side, but with this new discovery, it wasn't too hard to pretend.

Namika wrapped her arm around Celina's shoulder. "I'm sorry. I didn't know until recently, but you're safe now. This demon or any other can't hurt you anymore."

Jacob arched an eyebrow, and Celina stiffened.

I need to react more.

She took a few steps toward Kai. "Tell me the truth. Did you know my stepfather was a Venatore?"

The white flames danced around him as he stared at her in

silence. Anger filled her at his refusal to answer. They were supposed to play their parts, but she still wanted the truth.

"Tell me!" She curled her hands into fists. "Did you lie to me again? Why? After everything, you—"

"I said enough." His words echoed inside the room, and she froze at the menacing expression etched on his face.

Black feathers flew around him, smoke billowing to the ceiling as the white fire lowered. The Venatores took a few steps back, muttering between one another, but Celina stayed still. His true form was familiar, but the burning glare in his eyes wasn't. She hadn't even seen him this angry when she had attacked him. Her heart sped, and she slid her foot back an inch.

"Poor little Celina," he said with a voice laced with iciness. "So trusting. Believing if I showed any hint of care, it meant I was good. If I expressed remorse, you forgave me." His lips twisted into a cruel smile. "How naïve."

The corners of her eyes burned. "Stop."

He cocked his head. "One plea and you think I will listen?" He bared his pointed teeth. "Beg for me, and perhaps I will be merciful… one more time for you."

Someone grabbed her arm and pulled her back a few steps. By the erratic breathing, she guessed it was Namika.

Kai raised his hand, and the flames turned into regular fire, the reds and oranges dancing in his irises. "I have taken souls and destroyed lives for eons, and not once have you questioned why, why I would show any kindness to you."

The lump in her throat wouldn't vanish. "I thought you… cared about me."

His chuckle was enough to freeze the blood in her veins. "I am a master of deceit. Playing a part is what I do best. Lulling my victims into a sense of ease, making them feel safe." The flames exploded around him, and Celina winced at the heat, squinting through the brightness.

Jacob shouted orders while the members raised their

hands, creating barriers of white lights to protect themselves. The fire turned to smoke, falling in curtains of black velvety essence, plunging the room into dim lighting.

"Oh my God," Namika whispered, her eyes widening.

Goosebumps crawled along Celina's skin.

Kai—no, Mekaisto—hovered above swirling red flames, darkness coiling around his opened black wings. Screams echoed throughout the room as humanoid creatures with large opened mouths slithered from the essence, gathering around their king.

"Now then, Celina," Kai hissed her name, and she flinched. "Do you still feel safe?"

Tears rolled down her cheeks. "No. I don't."

His smile widened, curling over his gleaming teeth. "Good."

He whispered the same twisted prayer as when she'd attacked him, and shivers crawled along her skin.

Now I rise up to relive,

I pray the Devil my soul to give,

If I should fall before I wake,

I pray the Devil my soul to take.

Kai's voice was low, yet it resonated through the whole space. "Or should it be 'I pray the Devil my life to take'?" He turned his focus on Jacob and sat still hovering in the air as though there was an invisible seat. He leaned his chin against his knuckles, his red eyes glowing brighter. "Now then, Venatore. You have massacred my subjects. I will not ignore such a blatant attack on my kind. What makes you so readily declare war with me?"

Jacob paled but glared. "It looked like murder when I saw the report on the car accident that killed Dean Perry and his wife. If you want to talk about declaring war so easily, then take a closer look at the past. I'm sure one of your own murdered them."

It was Celina's turn to grab hold of Namika's arm for support.

The fire beneath Kai roared as though alive. "You would have to ask my second in command about that."

Shiriki materialized next to his king, his white hair fluttering in the heat of the flames.

Jacob gaped. "Fucking hell!"

"I am unsure you can do that, to be honest," Shiriki said with an amused chuckle, "but we could find a way."

Celina took a few steps back, dragging Namika with her.

"Why would you summon him here?" Jacob stared at Shiriki with horror. The feeling seemed to be shared with the rest of the Venatores as their magic trembled and cracked.

"I summoned him here because he was the last being to see Dean Perry alive." He shrugged. "You said you had the feeling someone murdered your powerful little disciple. Well, now is your chance to find out."

Jacob stiffened, but Celina's pulse throbbed into her ears. Shiriki remained silent, his gaze locked on his king, as though daring him to ask the question.

"Well?" Kai asked with a smirk.

Shiriki chuckled. "I murdered Dean Perry if that is what you want to hear."

A boiling feeling burned through Celina's veins as she stared at the demon who'd caused her pain. He'd murdered her parents. Their deaths weren't accidents, and she would make him pay.

"Kill him." Her voice was so dark, she didn't recognize it. "I'll do whatever you want if you kill this fucking monster. Use one of your traps or spells, I don't care, but just destroy him."

Shiriki chuckled, but his amusement didn't reach his glare. "If it were easy to kill me, I would have been dead ages ago." He leaned forward, and his lips curled into a wicked smile. "Get in line, pet."

Jacob went to Celina. "We will destroy them all in good time. We're still safe right now because of the spell. They can't trace or touch you."

Kai placed his hand against the barrier, but it sparked and his skin turned black. He frowned, his jaw clenching. "Well, well, well. Your magic seems to have gotten stronger throughout the years."

Rupert raised his head higher. "Did you think we'd let you in here without being prepared?"

Shiriki stared at the magic wall separating them, and although it sparked, nothing happened.

Laughter shook from Kai, and the whole room went still as they turned to him. "Your mistake was assuming I would not use other methods to take your pitiful lives." He motioned his head, and with a small bow, Shiriki vanished. "I cannot touch you, but fire can burn through markings." He licked his lips. "And flesh."

"Hold your ground," Jacob said, raising his voice.

"I will return for all of you." Smoke surrounded him until he exploded into thousands of crows, the flames licking their feathers and sending them alight. Celina's eyes widened, and she screamed, but the Venatores covered the noise when they shouted spells.

Kai. Be okay. Please.

"Run!" Jacob's shout resonated through the room.

While Celina hesitated, her friend didn't give her the choice. Grabbing Celina's hand, Namika dashed away in a crowd of people scrambling to escape. Lights flashed down the corridor.

"This way," Namika said, pulling her down a hallway.

The cool night air brushed against her skin, and before she knew it, they stood in an alleyway behind a few buildings. Every instinct urged Celina to call out to Kai, but she pressed her lips together. The plan had to continue.

18

BLOOD AND FLESH

Celina twisted her fingers together as she and Namika walked through the downtown area in darkness. The moon was high in the sky, and a chill had settled in the air.

"Any idea where to go?" Celina asked.

Namika shook her head. "I thought maybe going to Yasuo's place, but..." She slowed her steps and burst into tears. "He hasn't come back, and now with Mekaisto involved like this... what if he's dead?"

Celina opened her mouth, but she didn't know what to say. Everything would be a lie because she knew Yasuo had killed himself rather than give away more secrets about the Venatores. Her own friend, Brihan, was the reason Namika had lost someone she cared about. And didn't even know it yet.

Her neck prickled, and she grabbed Namika's arm, pulling her forward as she picked up her pace. Namika arched an eyebrow, her cheeks shining with tears in the streetlamps.

"Someone is following us," she whispered without stopping. And she would bet it wasn't human.

A familiar demon stepped in front of them, and they both stopped in their tracks.

Ancus.

"He is coming for you," he whispered. His long dark red hair stood out as though glowing. There was something in the way he stared at them like he was in a daze.

"Stay away from us," Celina said, energy prickling against her skin.

He was a close subject to Kai and powerful from what she'd heard. Water poured from his mouth, black but shimmering as though made of silver. She staggered as the sidewalk faded away, pulling Namika with her, and they both gasped. Their surroundings changed into a twisted image of what the human world was supposed to be.

People walked by, continuing on their way, unaware of the shift, but a few turned toward Celina and Namika, their eyes glowing white. Their mouths curled into wide smiles, empty holes stretching.

She bit her lower lip to keep from screaming as a wave of power brushed against her. Pressing her hands against her abdomen, a sharp pain pushed its way through her body. Namika tightened her grip on Celina's hand, and they dashed away.

"Celina?"

Inhaling deep breaths through the agony, she shuddered.

What the hell is going on?

Ancus materialized in front of them again, his brown eyes glazed over. Before they could run, he grabbed Namika by the neck, lifting her like she weighed nothing.

"Let her go!"

He threw her to the side, and she rolled a few times before coming to a stop, lying still amongst pooling darkness. Celina ran toward her friend, but Ancus grabbed her, pressing his hand against her mouth. She kicked and tried screaming, but it did nothing. She dug her heels against the ground as he pushed her toward a hole forming in the street. Reflections warped the buildings as creatures slithered in the shadows. With a last effort, she rammed her elbow into his ribs, and he grunted.

She fell forward as soon as he released her. Plunged in darkness, she felt around the asphalt. The lights from her world shimmered against the shadows, illuminating the molded surface. It glistened with humidity, and a few centipedes and spiders scattered into cracks. Her gaze fell on Namika, and her heart hammered.

Ancus crouched in front of her, and her eyes widened.

"Stay quiet, and he will take you to a safe place," he whispered.

She jumped to her feet and backed away, pressing her hand against her abdomen. "Who—"

"You will see soon." He closed his eyes and frowned. "It is strange. You smell… so good."

Black spots obscured her vision, and she fought for air, glancing toward an unconscious Namika. "Ancus, listen—"

"There is something flowing beneath your skin. It smells…" He cocked his head as his irises glowed brighter.

He lunged at her, and she screamed. A slicing pain ripped through her neck, and she staggered. She pressed her hand against her wound. Warm blood wet her fingers. She trembled, staring at the demon as he focused on his bloodied fingernails.

"Your blood smells delicious." He sucked on his fingertips, his sharp fangs protruding as he panted. "I… need more."

Celina stood helpless as he strode to her, frozen in fear. He grabbed a fistful of hair and wrenched her head back, sinking his fangs into the wounds. She clawed anywhere she could, yet he remained unfazed. Soon she had no energy left, and her knees buckled. He held her as he guzzled, swallowing her blood. Her eyelids became heavy, and he wrenched his mouth away, then dropped her to the ground.

"Please, stop," she whispered

Terror filled her core as he crouched in front of her, blood smeared across his mouth. "Oh, I am so sorry. I took too much. It is so delectable. I have to wait before taking more or you will die. I… I cannot let that happen." His smile widened as tears blurred her vision. "You have enough flesh, though."

She gasped, unable to stop him as he rolled her to her side. He pulled up the back of her top. Searing pain burned into her skin, and she kicked at him, but he pressed his knee against her legs, pinning her. She screamed as he dug into her back, tugging against her skin, sending waves of anguish through her body.

The world spun, and she closed her eyes, feeling sick. Something crawled along her arm, and she pushed it away, desperate not to picture eerie insects scurrying around.

The pain lessened, and she spun her head, gagging as he ate a long strip of her flesh.

"So good." He closed his eyes as though savoring. "I am still… so hungry. But, I need to make you feel good too. Need to taste your pleasure."

He gripped the waistband of her leggings, tugging them down.

She whimpered. "Stop."

"If you fight me, I will rip your unborn baby from you, and tear him apart in front of your eyes." His tone changed, fury lacing his every word as he panted.

Something sharp pressed against her throat, and she gasped. A flash of light threw Ancus to the side, and she crawled away with the remaining strength she had. She got to her feet, pulling her pants up as her vision blurred.

Someone had helped her? Who?

No one else is here.

Silver gleamed in the dim light and she staggered as

Ancus lashed out with a dagger. She hissed through her teeth as hot pain shot through her arm.

He wrapped his hand around her throat, and she grasped his weapon hand, ramming the dagger into his own neck, plunging it deep. Blood spluttered from his mouth. Symbols glowed along his face and flashes of light ran underneath the surface of his skin. His irises turned white, and he opened his mouth wide in a silent scream. He fell to the ground, his body twitching. The etchings in his flesh became clear, and his body combusted, the smell of burned flesh strong.

Celina backed away, shivering as she watched the fire turn black.

Her skin tingled along her neck, and her hand shot to the wound. "What?" Her back numbed, and she hissed through her teeth as the same feeling throbbed against her arm. Even in the semi-darkness, the flesh mending was obvious. She wasn't sure how to feel about being able to heal that quickly.

I really am half-demon.

Celina pushed the surreal feeling from her mind and looked around until she found Namika.

"Namika, wake up. Come on." She shook her, wincing as pain shot from her abdomen. "Please, Namika."

She stirred, coughing as she rose to a sitting position, and rubbing her neck. It still bled, and she seemed to have trouble breathing. Placing Namika's arm over her shoulder, Celina helped her up, and they staggered forward.

"I'm okay," Namika said, pulling away from Celina. "Are you?"

Celina nodded, more preoccupied with finding a way out of this twisted world. Namika screamed, and then in a blur of motion, her friend vanished.

"Namika? Namika!" She spotted her friend standing in the alleyway beyond the undulating wall of darkness, staring around and calling out to someone, but Celina couldn't hear.

White feathers fell around Celina, and she trembled,

staring at the darkness above. She stiffened as a hand reached out from behind her, pressing against the barrier separating her world and the void she was trapped inside. Pointed fingernails etched along the darkness as energy pressed against her. She held her breath, waiting. For what, she didn't know, but she couldn't move.

Images of the writing on the outer walls of Yonah Church flew across her mind.

The angel is guarding you.

A crack formed in the shadows, wide enough for her to pass through. She turned toward whoever was behind her, but the hand pushed her through, and she yelped. Trembling from head to toe, she stared around. She was in her world again, and everything seemed normal.

"Celina!" Namika ran to her, and hugged her tight, crying. "What happened?"

"I… don't know. I'm not sure."

She winced at another wave of pain, and Namika took a step back. Symbols glowed beneath Celina's skin, and she staggered as though she could escape her own arms.

These weren't the markings from the Venatore spell.

They looked like the same ones on the demon before he combusted. Her chest heaved as she looked at her skin, waiting for the agony to start, but nothing happened.

Then, another tightening throb shot from her abdomen to her lower back, and she gasped.

"I…" She took a deep breath and stared at her friend. "I think I'm having contractions."

Namika's eyes widened. "Oh, God. What… tell me what to do."

The sound of footsteps caught their attention, and they both turned toward the end of the alleyway as a figure appeared. The woman squinted, her light brown hair cut short around her ears while the bangs fell in front of her eyes.

"Are you Celina?"

Celina pressed her hand against her neck where blood still flowed. She didn't know this stranger but felt prickling energy coming from her. Before Celina could ask who this was, she fell to her knees as pain flooded her body. She cried out as darkness surrounded her, and then Celina passed out.

19

THE START

Celina pulled against the metal latch of the wooden door, but it wouldn't budge. She cursed, pacing the room again as her pain shot through her abdomen.

Namika stopped her in her tracks. "You need to lie down." She pointed at the bed.

"No." She continued pacing, her heart hammering against her ribs.

She recognized the room she was locked inside. Somewhere in the CrowBar's basement. Having been in two different rooms here and all of them identical with their cracked stone walls, there was no doubt. This one was only a bit different because of the chairs, drawers, and bed tucked into a corner.

When Celina woke up, Namika explained the woman who found them had a few other people with her, and that together, they brought them back to a nightclub. Namika guessed they were demons, but with wounds of her own, she didn't have a fighting chance when one grabbed her.

Upstairs was buzzing, so it was likely still night. Celina winced at another contraction, sweat sticking hair to her face.

She went back to the door and pounded against it. "Let us out!"

It opened, and she faced a familiar demon. The Sanguis leader, Adam. His irises glowed red, then returned to their usual brown. He'd combed his hair back, looking more like a businessman than ever.

"Well, well. Awake now?" He clicked his fingers, and two other demons she didn't know appeared next to him.

Without a word, they walked past her and grabbed Namika.

"Hey, stop it!" Namika squirmed, but their grip tightened, and she whimpered.

Celina shot a glare at Adam. "Don't you dare touch her. She's my friend."

His eyebrows shot up, but he nodded. "You have my word; she won't be harmed."

When the demons tried leaving, Celina blocked their path. "Leave her right where she is."

Adam grasped Celina's shoulder, pushing her farther into the room as his subjects pulled Namika out of sight. Celina tried fighting back, but another pain shot through her, and she nearly fell to the floor.

"Don't worry about your friend. She's quite the fighter. Gave me a good punch in the face when I first walked in."

Celina gaped at him, trying to picture her friend doing that. Did she know who Adam was? Still, her heart squeezed knowing her friend had tried protecting her despite being wounded.

"What happened? Why are you taking Namika away? Where's Kai? What happened to Ancus?"

He tsked. "So many questions, as usual, Mrs. Leviet." He straightened his suit jacket and winked. "Or have you stopped using that last name considering it was Mekaisto all along?"

She glared. "Did you know?"

"No, I didn't. Mekaisto told me when he came to my club asking about the first disappearances." His gaze swept her from head to toe. "Have to admit, I'm surprised you're half-demon. And even more so you've been married to him this whole time without knowing." His grin faded when she blinked fast to keep her tears at bay. Placing his hand on her shoulder, he smiled, but it wasn't smug this time. "Don't be too hard on yourself. He's the tyrant of Hell. If he doesn't want others to know something, there's no way they'll find out. I made a deal with him thinking he was just a normal human ready to trade secrets for his blood."

She studied Adam. Trying to make her feel better seemed out of character, yet she didn't really know him. With no tricks, he'd held his end of the contract when she had rescued Kai. Maybe he wasn't so terrible.

"I... why was I brought here?"

He arched an eyebrow. "One of my children found you and your friend, both wounded. She brought you here so you can deliver your child. I have let Mekaisto know. He should be here any minute."

"Is Nalie here?"

"I sent for her, but in the meantime, the one who found you will tend to your needs." Right as he finished, the woman who had found Celina and Namika in the alleyway strode through the open door.

She bowed. "Celina, it is an honor to make your acquaintance."

Celina's eyebrows rose. No one had ever shown her respect like this. She wasn't sure how to react. "Er, thank you for the help earlier. What's your name?"

She straightened. "Eire." Glancing at Adam she motioned to the door. "If you wouldn't mind, master, I would like to have her change into something more comfortable. I doubt Mekaisto would approve of you seeing his wife's naked body."

Adam chuckled but shot a lewd stare at Celina before waving his hand in farewell and closing the door behind him.

"I don't think I've ever heard any of Adam's children talk to him like that," Celina muttered with a grin.

Eire opened the drawers and pulled out a silver nightgown. "He's not the one who made me, so maybe that's why. I respect him, but there are times he's oblivious to what is common courtesy for humans."

"Do you spend a lot of time with my kind?" Celina slipped off her bloodied top, sucking in air as it brushed against her wounds. The Sanguis had healed them, but they were still raw.

Eire helped her unhook her bra, then slipped the nightgown over her head. Celina froze as she tugged on her pants; the memory of what Ancus had tried doing flashing through her mind. Bile burned the back of her throat, and Eire frowned.

"Are you okay?" she asked, placing her hand against hers. "Take a deep breath."

Celina nodded, shutting her eyelids tight before Eire pushed her pants the rest of the way. Once around her ankles, Eire helped her out, not commenting as Celina cried.

Eire took her hand and squeezed. "Walk. It'll help."

Celina nodded, but as another pang ripped through her, she grasped the drawer, her fingers digging into the wood.

Energy swept the air, and she felt Kai before his footsteps approached. The door opened, but she didn't turn around, instead concentrating on her breathing.

"Mekaisto," Eire's voice was filled with awe, and Celina couldn't help a smirk. This Sanguis was different, but Celina liked her.

"I want to speak to you later. Leave us." Kai's voice was hushed but also laced with anger.

The sound of the door closed with a snap, and silence fell in the room.

"Did you… find Ancus?" she asked quietly, still keeping her focus on the wall.

"He is in my private dungeon."

She shook her head and smiled. "That sounds morbid."

Another contraction surged through Celina, and she cried out, gripping the desk so hard, the wood splintered. She burst into laughter, tears blurring her vision as she turned to face him. "Oh, I really, really hate you right now."

"Is that so?" He closed the distance between them, the ghost of a smile touching his lips.

She pointed at her belly. "You did this. And because I'm in pain, and need to blame someone, it's you."

After another wave passed, she leaned her head against his chest and sighed. "I know I'm an open book, so it's why you had to say those things… to make my reactions natural."

"Celina, I—"

She lifted her head and smiled. "Thank you, for trusting me with the plan, and following it through."

He laughed, his expression softening. "I was concerned you would hate me after what happened with the Venatores."

"Hate? No. Terrified? Yes. You play your part well because you're not acting. I know what you are. You're the Devil, and I have no illusion you're not, but you're also my husband." Another contraction, and this time, she gripped his arm. "We will talk about you hiding the fact you knew who and what my stepfather was… but not now."

He chuckled, cupping her cheek. "You are perfect, Celina. Absolutely perfect."

She smiled as he pushed her sweaty hair from her face. It fell behind her shoulder, revealing the wound on her neck. A growl vibrated through his chest as his gaze focused on her skin.

Darkness thickened around him as though trying to smother any living creature in proximity. As pressure increased in her mind, she went numb. She didn't flinch as she felt him inside her head, his glower burning through her. He saw what happened, and her heart squeezed at the pain flashing across his features.

"Please, I don't want to talk about it." She turned her back on him, grabbing hold of the drawers and leaning forward, trying to take the pain out of her lower back.

He grabbed her hips, pressing his thumbs along the sore spot, and she relaxed.

"I will not talk about what happened with Ancus but just like the subject of your stepfather, we will talk about it later."

She closed her eyes and nodded. "Fine."

He massaged her shoulders and rubbed her abdomen. "Would you be up for some quick traveling?"

"Where and why?" Her eyelids grew heavier.

"I would rather take you back to Shiriki's dwelling since he has the best protection. Hilda is there as well and used to be a midwife. It would not be a bad idea to have her there for the birth."

The thought of returning there churned her stomach. "Can we stay here? Please? Not that I don't want Hilda; could we send for her?"

"Anything you need. But we will move into a more comfortable bedroom."

She nodded, barely registering anything as he picked her up and left the room.

20

PRINCE FENRIR

Inside the new bedroom, Celina could better relax. It looked nothing like the rest of the rooms in the CrowBar's basement. With its hearth warming the place with a large fire, and the decorations of dark greens, it helped put her at ease. It helped as well that Kai had assured her Namika was safest with Adam; with the war on Venatores, she was at risk of being killed if caught alone.

Her contractions came and went, but when they came, they sent her to the floor, screaming. Kai looked like he was ready to burn something down, and more than once, she'd begged him to stop the agony.

"Try to hold on."

She gritted her teeth, glaring at him. "Hold on? You better hold on to your cocks because I'm about to rip them off and shove them down your throat at the same time."

He pressed his lips together as though trying to stop himself from laughing. He was saved from her anger when Hilda walked into the room, placing her hands on her hips.

"Have the death threats started already?"

"Just the ones on my cocks," Kai replied in an amused tone.

"Well, I brought experts. I have delivered many babies in my day, but they were human." She rolled her sleeves, and went to Celina, helping her to her feet. "Let's get you walking while your husband has a chat."

Celina arched an eyebrow, but a shiver shot down her spine when Shiriki walked inside, followed by Nalie.

"How the fuck is he an expert? The only thing he can do is cause pain, and I'm here to report, I've already got plenty of that."

Shiriki's gaze narrowed. "Do you think your mother birthed you alone?"

She gawked at him, the room falling silent as though someone had frozen time. Kai shot him a dangerous stare, but Shiriki shrugged. "A story for another time."

Celina opened and closed her mouth, but another contraction hit, and she screamed. Hilda helped her forward, and Celina gripped the edge of the mattress. "I swear, if it's the last thing I do, I promise to make you feel this same amount of pain one day."

Kai chuckled. "Are you talking to me, dove?"

"It doesn't matter. Any of you can die right now if it takes this agony away."

"Speaking of which," Nalie said, and Celina tried listening, wanting to distract herself from the pain, "have you ever seen one of our kind during birthing?"

"I never had a reason, no," Kai said darkly, as though her assumption that he would have been anywhere near a birthing demon was insulting.

"We become aggressive and violent. Celina may very well try to kill someone."

Celina sat on the side of the bed, taking deep breaths. "Okay, then everyone leaves to make sure I don't kill you." She gave her nastiest smile at Shiriki. "You can stay."

Hilda scoffed. "Don't get yourself in a tizzy."

Kai and Shiriki snickered, but Nalie frowned. "The best

way to stop this from escalating is when the female attacks, her male must subdue her with dominance."

Celina burst into laughter, half-crying as another wave of burning pain settled around her waist. "I'm not an animal, but I'll become one and rip your throats out if you don't all leave now."

"Need I say more?" Nalie said with an exasperated sigh.

Celina let herself slide down along the bed and sat on the floor. The contractions diminished, and she breathed in deep.

"Please, just… everyone needs to leave. I'm a danger. I don't want blood on my hands." She couldn't help grinning. "More blood."

Nalie approached. "Hilda, you should not be here. If she lashes out, you could die."

"I highly doubt Shiriki would allow for such a quick death," Hilda said, glancing over her shoulder at him. He grinned but said nothing.

Celina shook her head as another wave squeezed. It was as though someone was tightening a waistband with spikes around her. She screamed, grabbing the sheets hanging from the bed, and they ripped.

Kai stared at her, fury burning behind his stare. "Nalie, is there nothing we can do for her pain?"

"Because she is half, I would not chance it. Usually, we need to wait until the last few minutes."

Shiriki beckoned to Hilda and Nalie, and all three left the room, giving privacy to Celina and Kai.

Kai pulled Celina to her feet and helped her walk around the room, rubbing her back. "Neither of you will come to harm."

"And what about you?" she asked. "I'll be honest. From time to time, I really want to destroy something."

She sat on the armchair, staring at her husband as black feathers circled around him. Her pulse sped when he stepped out, smoke vanishing, and leaving him in his true form. His irises glowed red, adding an eerie hue to their surroundings. He was a sight of dominance and power that shook her core. But even more so than usual in her current state. As though she was more animal than human.

She got to her feet, wincing as the pressure increased, shooting from her belly to her lower back. He approached her, but she staggered back, shaking her head.

"No. You should go."

He wrapped his arms around her and brought her close. "And why is that?"

She stared up at him, lost in his intense gaze. "I don't want you to die."

He leaned forward, his breath warm against her lips. "Do you believe you could destroy me?" When he withdrew, something dark hovered on the edge of his gaze.

Her hands curled into fists. One thought circling her mind.

Kill.

His lips curled into a cruel grin. "Is something wrong?"

"No. Just suddenly hungry…" She headed to the hearth and lifted the poker with the sharpest end as heat flooded her core.

"Plan on killing your supper?" Kai's voice was quiet, despite it coming from right behind her.

In one swift movement, she turned and slashed. He caught her wrist, his expression unreadable, yet something dark swirled behind those red irises.

"Let. Go." She gritted her teeth, trying to reach toward her weapon with her free hand. He grasped her other wrist and pinned her against the wall.

"How interesting." He cocked his head, and his sadistic grin sent a shiver down her spine. "Your mind is not your own right now. However, instincts," his lips parted, revealing his fangs, "are so difficult to control."

She tried to wrench away, but he didn't slacken his grip

and squeezed harder. With a wince, she dropped her weapon, the sound of metal clattering against the floor.

His wings opened wide, and her heart hammered as he wrapped them around them both, forming a cocoon plunged in darkness. The glow of his irises and arcane symbols on his horns were the only sources of illumination within their small space. "How should I subdue you, dove?"

His feathers turned to black goo, dripping onto them. Celina squirmed, desperate to get away, and screamed when the essence coiling around him plunged into her chest. The pain in her abdomen diminished, and her knees buckled, but he kept his grip on her wrists before wrapping his arms around her waist.

"I…" She pushed him away but didn't get far as he kept a hold on her. "You shouldn't be here."

The cruel smirk didn't leave his features. "And what makes you say that?"

"What makes me…" Her eyes widened. "I tried to kill you! But… wait. No. You have to stay. You need to take Fenrir from me, so I won't hurt him. I don't want to hurt him." At the thought, she burst into tears, pounding against Kai's chest to let her go.

He took her hands in his. "Trust me. I will keep you both safe. The instinct to kill will vanish once you birth our son." He folded his wings back, and she squinted at the light.

The door burst open, and Celina yelped. Kai glowered at Adam and Shiriki standing in the doorway.

"Ah, perfect timing. My wife is still feeling murderous and needs sacrifices," he said in a growl.

While Adam flinched, Shiriki bowed his head. "There has been another attack on the realm, and it is bleeding out. A few of your subjects have perished at the hands of the damned escaping from the Inferno."

Celina was about to grab onto Kai's shirt and beg him not to leave, but she sighed. "You need to go."

"Out of the question."

She held his gaze and smiled. "You're their king and the only one who can stop further damage. Don't abandon your subjects when they need you most."

"You are my priority, and—"

"And that's all I need. Knowing I'm your priority is everything." She cupped his cheek. "If you go now, I'm sure you'll return in no time. I'll hold on as long as I can, okay?" She glanced toward Shiriki and Adam. "Nalie and Hilda can help me in the meantime."

His irises glowed bright red, his expression torn. "I am not leaving you."

"You're right, you're not. You'll be back as soon as you act like their king and go fix this mess." She pushed against his chest and grinned. "Or do I have to threaten to rip your cocks off again?"

He brought her in for a tight hug. "You are nothing short of amazing." He stared down at her. "I will return shortly."

He strode toward the door as Shiriki and Adam left, then glanced back at her one final time before vanishing.

Footsteps approached, and Celina pressed her lips together.

Deep breaths.

Nalie and Hilda walked inside and closed the door just as pain shot through Celina's abdomen, stabbing in her lower back, and she hissed. The agony wasn't stopping this time. She leaned against the armchair, and her eyes widened as a gush of warm fluids streamed down her legs and onto the floor.

"Oh, er... crap."

Her waist contracted in paralyzing spasms, and she cried out. It took all her strength not to collapse. Nalie helped her onto the bed, and Celina crawled onto the soft mattress.

Hilda sat at the end. "Your son picked now to come into the world while his father needs to be away? He'll be a handful." She winked, and Celina relaxed at Hilda's lighthearted comment.

Nalie sat on the other side and brushed a stray hair from Celina's face. "I can help with the pain."

"If Shiriki said that, I'd assume he'd mean making it worse," Celina said with a scoff, and the three of them laughed.

Celina clenched her jaw as another wave of agony tightened her muscles, and she cried out, arching her back to ease the pain. "It feels… wrong."

Hilda moved to the end of the bed. "Birthing is difficult even when it's a regular human babe, but being more half…" She frowned but motioned her head at Nalie. "Do what you can for the pain."

Tears blurred Celina's vision, the lower half of her body feeling like it was twisting. Hilda spread Celina's legs apart, and she whimpered.

Nalie moved the heavier quilt under Celina's back to lift her hips. "I can reduce the pain, but I have to touch your belly. Is that all right?"

Celina nodded. As soon as Nalie draped a hand over her swollen stomach, numbness spread through her, and she went limp. "Thank you."

The ghost of a smile touched her lips. "Having the ability to numb away pain has its benefits."

Hilda raised Celina's legs up. "I need you to push, okay?"

With the little strength left in her, Celina doubted it would be possible, but she tried her best. After what seemed like an eternity, a shiver ran through her, and Celina let herself drop.

"There we go," Hilda muttered. Pressure built until something slid out, but there was no pain, and soon, the tightness vanished.

Nalie moved away and grabbed a small blanket, then joined Hilda at the foot of the bed.

"Your son is fine."

"Wait, what?" Celina lifted her head, and she gaped when Nalie placed a pale baby on her chest, his eyelids closed. "He's not crying. Why isn't he crying? What's wrong?"

Nalie grinned. "Demon babies do not cry. The prince is fine."

Celina held her baby against her, watching him. He let out a tiny hiccup. Fuzz covered his tiny body, and she smiled. Her baby. He was so quiet.

Are some really silent like this?

Celina pressed her baby to her skin, her heart beating faster. "Hi, Fenrir."

Hilda got to her feet, wiping the blood and fluids from her hands.

Celina swallowed hard. "Thank you, both of you. I wouldn't have made it without your help."

Tears ran down Celina's cheeks, and Hilda turned to Nalie. "Will you please let Mekaisto know about the birth of his son?"

Nalie gave a nod and dashed out of the room. Hilda placed her hand on Celina's arm and smiled. "You did well, Celina."

"Thank you," she said between sobs.

21

FAMILY

Celina sat in the cleaned bed, holding Fenrir against her. His tiny eyelids opened, and she locked gazes with him. Yellow irises bright against his vertical pupils stared. His mouth opened, tiny fangs protruding, and he reached out to her, a small cry leaving his lips.

Propping herself better against the headboard, she unbuttoned her nightgown. She stared into his gaze as he latched on to her breast, then whimpered when he sank his tiny fangs into her flesh. She closed her eyes, willing herself not to wrench him away. Her son suckled and she felt the pressure, her blood mixing with the milk he swallowed.

Once he finished, he let go, and Celina winced at the blood streaming from the lacerations. He stared at her, his legs kicking as he made a few babbling noises, and she smiled.

Time passed, and she closed her eyes, the warmth from her son lulling her into sleep.

She jerked awake after a while, and stared at Fenrir, his eyelids were closed, dreaming peacefully. She'd left two table lamps on, too scared of being in the dark, but she wanted him to sleep without too many lights.

The door to the chambers opened, and Kai walked in. Darkness encircled him, his eyes filled with an evil she couldn't put a name to. At the thought she'd displeased him, a lump formed in her throat, and she held Fenrir closer to her.

Tears blurred her vision, and she pressed her lips together to keep from bursting into sobs. In less than three steps, he strode across the room, and sat on the edge of the bed, cupping her face. Kai's stare seemed to reach into her core, and she smiled at the tender act.

"I am sorry I was not here for you both." His voice was husky, and darkness coiled around him thicker than before.

Her eyebrows shot up, her heart speeding. "You were out there to keep us safe. You have nothing to apologize for."

She buried her face against his chest, and inhaled, relaxing under the touch of his fingers tracing along her arm.

When he pulled away, Fenrir's blanket loosened, and as soon as their son came into view, Kai stiffened. A mixture of emotions flashed through his gaze as he reached out toward him. His hand hovered mid-air, then dropped, his expression unreadable.

"What's wrong?" she asked quietly.

"I…" He stared at her, sorrow etched on his face. "He looks so fragile. I do not want to hurt him."

She smiled, shaking her head. "You won't." She shifted, and their son woke with a tiny gasp. In the few hours since he'd been born, Fenrir seemed to need nourishment every thirty minutes.

"Is it normal he needs to eat so much?" She unbuttoned her nightgown, her fingers trembling.

When she missed the same button a third time, Kai placed his hand over hers, pushing it aside as he took his time unbuttoning them for her. His gaze never left her, and when he finished, he pulled back.

"Infants are famished when they are born, and I suppose it is the same for a being who is only three-fourths demon."

She moved the clothing to the side, wincing as it rubbed against the wounds her son had caused when feeding. Kai's irises flashed as he stared at her maimed breast. Fenrir sank his teeth into her flesh, and she muffled a cry. Tears rolled down her cheeks as she cradled him tighter so he could feed easier.

"This may not be a good moment to bring it up, but I wanted to let you know Ancus' fate is sealed. After searching what I left of his mind, I have sentenced him to a permanent end."

She averted her gaze. "I… I'll be honest. He was one of the few subjects in your realm kind to me. What he did…" She caressed Fenrir's head. "Maybe that's why I was so weak…"

"What do you mean?"

"It's nothing." That part, she had blocked out, refusing to admit even to herself.

"Celina." He growled her name, and her heart skipped a beat.

"When Ancus… when he dragged me through that horrible twisted world. He…"

Fenrir yawned, his pointed teeth letting go of her tender flesh, and her temporary numbness vanished.

She got to her feet and patted Fenrir on his back as she continued her aimless walk. With a sigh, she laid her son in the basket at the side of the bed, then gripped the edge. She stiffened when Kai grasped the edges on either side of her, his body pressing against hers.

"Talk to me. Please."

"I… didn't fight. He said he would rip our son out of me if I fought against him. But what if he had hurt him either way? I should have fought, but I was so scared…" She burst into sobs.

He spun her to face him, then wrapped his arms around her. Pressure filled within her mind, and she opened it to what had happened for the first time. A growl vibrated through his chest, the room shaking under his anger.

Kai cupped her face with both hands, wiping her cheeks. He leaned forward, pressing his forehead against hers. "None of what happened is your fault. Say and mean it. You did nothing wrong."

"I... did nothing wrong."

"Say it again," he whispered in her ear.

"I did nothing wrong," she repeated, this time less hesitant. Her breasts pressed against his body, and she winced.

"Let me heal you." He put out his hand, and she took it, following him to the bed.

He wrapped his arms around her, lifting her so she'd sit over his legs. She buried her face in his neck, taking comfort in his scent, but also in his understanding. The words he'd made her repeat helped to let go.

He slid his fingers underneath her shirt, tracing over her wounds. She blinked a few times, unable to look away from him as the throbbing pain vanished.

Once healed, he put her to bed, underneath the covers to keep her warm as he slipped in next to her. "Sleep, dove. I am here."

Celina stretched on the bed, the silky blankets smooth against her skin. She listened to Kai's voice as he whispered words in the Demos language. It stirred something within her, and she kept her eyelids closed, needing to hear. From time to time, he'd switch to English, and she smiled.

"All I want to do is protect you, Fenrir." His voice was hushed, and an emotion she hadn't heard from him gentled his tone.

She opened her eyes and stared. The arcane symbols

etched into his horns pulsed red, his gaze focused on the tiny form he held in his arms.

Fenrir stared at his father, reaching out. Her son's head fit within Kai's palm, his claw-like fingernails pointing up as to not hurt him. Fenrir wrapped his whole hand around Kai's finger, staring into the red irises.

With a smile, Kai leaned his forehead against Fenrir's and whispered something. The darkness seemed to pool thicker every time he spoke the demon language.

"I wanted you to rest longer. He needed nothing, just attention." He straightened and laid Fenrir inside his basket.

She propped herself on her elbow. "Thank you."

A knock at the door broke the comfort in the air as Shiriki stepped inside.

"This better be an emergency," Kai growled.

He shrugged. "You ordered me to inform you if I discovered any new massacres."

Celina's skin tingled, and she drew the covers higher. Kai glanced at her, then at his second in command.

Kai ran his fingers through his hair. "Where?"

"Near here."

Fenrir made babbling noises, and Celina turned to him, her heart skipping a few beats when Shiriki materialized next to his basket. His expression was unreadable as he stared at her son. She crawled across the bed to get between them, but Kai reached him faster.

Shiriki cocked his head. "He is so small."

"All babies are," she said, inching her way closer.

Shiriki's smirk returned when his gaze settled on her. "You were not as small. Although you fit in my hands well."

"Shiriki, enough," Kai warned.

Her pulse echoed in her ears as she stared at him. She still didn't believe her mother had ever let him near Celina as an infant. Unless he'd gotten to her in secret. She shivered at the thought.

"I will meet you at the location." With a small bow to Kai, Shiriki left the room.

"You should get more sleep. I need to go for a few hours."

"Please stay safe." She knew how ridiculous it sounded, considering who and what he was.

"I always am." He pulled her to him and kissed her.

22

A MESSAGE

The wind vanished, and an unnatural hush fell between the buildings. The scent of blood wavered in the air as a crow flew lower. Its wings flapped open, and boots touched the ground, silent.

Kai's gaze swept the darkness, picking up every sound. "Report."

"Not much more than what you see," Shiriki said, peering through the shadows. He stepped next to his king, litter crunching under his feet.

To the human eye, nothing unusual stuck out in the alley, but some things could only be seen by otherworldly beings. Bodies lay anchored to the walls, limbs ripped off and placed at strange angles. Four heads lined the wall, side by side, near a dumpster. The smell of garbage mixed with rotted flesh. Human body odors tickled his nose, but his thirst for bloodshed pushed aside his instincts to kill.

Kai moved amongst the corpses of his subjects—all Sanguis demons. Venatores would pay, and he relished in the thought of delivering the sentence.

A faint scent of life flitted in the air, and Kai ignored it. Probably humans nearby.

Shiriki prodded an arm hanging from a thin wire. The blood had turned black, leaving a puddle of foul liquid beneath the limb. "They're getting more violent."

"Yes." He leaned forward, inspecting one of the severed heads. Its face was twisted in pain. A wave of energy rolled off from Kai and pressed between the walls. A few street-lamps flickered.

Shiriki's focus shifted to the chain link fence at the alley's end. "There are several Sanguis, as though the Venatores knew they would be here."

Kai stared as a few people staggered past the alleyway. Part of him wished they would get curious, but none of them stopped. He needed to take his rage out on someone, and soon.

A few spiders crawled along the stacks of crates, and Kai listened to their whispers. They brought only webs of stories filled with gaps and holes, never complete. When they fell silent, and the wind picked up, he turned his attention to Shiriki.

Kai motioned toward the bloody scene. "They've sent plenty of messages, and I'll oblige by answering them all at once."

He glanced at the brick wall where Madka symbols were left behind but was distracted by a sound. Someone stirred in the pile of garbage tucked against the chain link fence at the end of the alleyway. Kai approached the survivor, a Sanguis maimed beyond recognition, his skin flayed. "They… said…" Blood spluttered from his mouth, and Kai crouched… to better hear him.

Shiriki chuckled. "Oh, they're creative." He pointed at the demon's chest, two arrows cut into the muscles. "A message on his ribs."

Kai scoffed, but as he reached toward his subject, the Sanguis jerked. "Please… not… again." Each movement seemed like it caused him agony.

Shiriki glanced around. "We shouldn't do this here. It'll attract curious little humans. And as much as I need to resupply my stocks, now is not a good time."

"Let them come and get rid of them if the sounds don't scare them away. Unwise humans shouldn't survive."

"Such a waste of good souls." Shiriki strode to the edge of the alley, waiting.

Kai's glowing irises reflected in his subject's fearful eyes. With one hand, he pressed against his subject's head to numb the pain, then rammed his other hand through his chest. Blood pooled around Kai's hand as he pulled the muscles apart, tearing through as the Sanguis hissed through his teeth.

His subject went limp as Kai stared at the ribs, reading the message carved into the bones.

She is ours.

The lights in the vicinity sparked and burst.

"I take it, you didn't like the message?" Shiriki called out in amusement.

Kai straightened and frowned. "They used something that won't let him heal."

"Permission to extract the substance for research?" He stepped closer, smiling at the maimed body.

Kai glowered at his second in command, and in a rare moment, Shiriki lost his smirk. "I will have the guards bring him to your laboratory. Heal him after and send him to court as soon as he's well. I need to know if he has information we could use."

Shiriki motioned to one side, and whispers accompanied a gray hand extending from the ripples of darkness he'd summoned. Screams rang through the air as its fingers wrapped around the Sanguis's ankle, pulling him into the void. In a second, the maimed body was gone.

Shiriki took a few steps back, staring along the wall covered in Madka, tilting his head to the side, looking for another angle.

Kai's gaze narrowed on the symbols. "Let's go back."

He placed his hand against the mildew-stained brick wall, and black shadows formed. They twisted until it opened a large hole, and both stepped through.

"Have you noticed Celina has gotten weaker since she birthed your son? Perhaps it is because of the spell the Venatores cast on her."

"It is a tracing spell, nothing more. Unless you know something?" When he stayed silent too long, Kai stopped and stared at Shiriki.

Shiriki shrugged. "What if it is more than that?"

"We still have my wife's friend as a guest at Adam's club. I will send a message to him so he may ask her about it."

Once inside his dwelling in the dark realm, Kai's advisor approached. Maili bowed, her jet-black hair brushing past her shoulders, but her black eyes never left her king. "The Viscus would like to report their findings. Permission to call a meeting?"

"Yes. Now." He marched toward the hall, summoning his subjects with a simple command, never uttering a single word.

The meeting hall was already filled with the Viscus inside his realm when Kai arrived. Built in the middle of the outside garden, it looked out on the black skeletal trees with white leaves. A few of the flowers wavered without the slightest wind, and his mind wandered to his wife. Celina found the flora beautiful.

"I have news." Wyla tossed her brown hair to the side. One side was shaven, and the way she dressed made her look like she lived in the aftermath of an apocalypse. "I traced the energy signature of the first attack on the realm and your wife," she said. "It occurred from within."

"Within?" Kai repeated in a tone so low, he wasn't sure if his subjects heard. Every inch of him demanded pain.

She nodded. "My source in the Venatores will help

again… for a price. She wants a guarantee after everything, she'll be left alone and not hunted."

He stared at her, still thinking of what she'd said. "I want to learn where they are keeping their weakest members. Obviously, they are no longer staying at their headquarters since I know where it is located." His lips curled into a smile, and most of his subjects stiffened. "Inform your source she will get her wish if she gives up the weakest links."

With a bow, Wyla vanished.

Within.

23

THE SOURCE WITHIN

The hall buzzed as demons spoke amongst one another, a mingling crowd summoned by Kai. A week had passed since Celina had given birth to Fenrir, and since the Venatores were attacking more and more within the human world, Kai had brought Celina and their son home to his realm.

And now, the hunt for the Venatores would begin.

Celina strode inside the hall followed by her husband's head of guards, Lokte. A painting of distorted, wolf-like creatures tearing humans apart decorated the vaulted ceiling. The murmur of many voices carried from the curved observation balcony on the upper level. Her gaze focused on the tiered crystal chandeliers as they glittered. As she inspected it, she couldn't help grin; each of them was a tiny crystal skull.

She wished she could enjoy the meeting but leaving Fenrir with Nalie caused her chest to tighten. Even though the demon had helped deliver her son, Celina wasn't quick to trust. But Kai had ordered it, despite her protests.

She glanced over her shoulder at Lokte. "I'll be fine alone if you want to, I don't know, go talk to the others?"

He gave a curt nod, but his grin told her he'd be watching her from a distance.

As soon as he left, Tess sidled up next to Celina, and an icy smile curled over her pointed teeth. Celina's hands curled into fists; just this woman's presence was enough to send her into a boiling rage.

"It must be terrifying for someone like you to be surrounded by so many of my kind. No need to worry. No physical harm will come to such a weak half-breed."

"You know how to fuck with people's minds as much as their bodies. And considering who my husband is, I fear little anymore," she shot, crossing her arms.

The Viscus' eyebrows shot up, but before she could add anything more, Kai walked into the room. A hush fell over the crowd before he even raised his hand. "The Venatores have declared war," he said, his tone serious. "If you find any, you will not kill them. Bring them to my private dungeons. I want their location. Now."

Most vanished, but a few spoke amongst themselves, making plans.

Without another word, Celina walked away from Tess, needing to be alone. Difficult when she was surrounded by demons, but most left her alone even if they shot curious stares toward her. Kai walked over to Celina, and she averted her gaze. He stayed silent, and her shoulders tensed as she spotted Tess straightening so her breasts were impossible to avoid. To Celina's annoyance, Kai's half-grin while staring at his old favorite didn't help.

"By all means, ogle your ex fuck-friend so obviously," Celina muttered while crossing her arms.

Her husband chuckled. "Is it wrong of me to find it amusing when someone tries so hard when they know they have no chances of succeeding?"

"If I gave that kind of smile to Brihan, you'd be pissed off."

He turned to her, his pupils thinning into slits. "Actually, I would peel his flesh off one layer at a time, then set him on fire." By his tone, Celina guessed he wasn't joking.

"There's a big difference. For one, he's my friend, and second, we've never slept together."

He cupped her cheek, but the look in his gaze was anything but gentle. It was possessive. "You have lived a little over two decades while I have existed for millennia. Do you not think there might be a bit of difference in experience between us?"

She couldn't help scoff. "A bit? You've lived several lifetimes over me."

"Exactly. It is normal I have ex-lovers after all this time. But as I have said before, since I met you when you were sixteen years old, I have never so much as looked at anyone else in lust."

The wall around his mind vanished, allowing her to feel the truth of his words. Calm settled through her body; he only had eyes for her. No one else. Tess was no more important to him than another of his subjects.

She smiled. "I trust you." She motioned toward the demons who'd stayed behind to discuss how to lure out Venatores. "I'm sure your subjects will bring a few innocent members, too. Planning on giving those over to Shiriki?"

He chuckled. "If you are referring to children, I assure you, I will not torture or kill them. I know you would never stand for it. No, for them, I have less painful plans."

"Care to share?"

He took a step closer, and she could feel the heat radiating off his body. "Leave the details to me."

"Fine," she muttered.

"Are you angry with me? I thought we settled the whole jealousy issue." He wrapped his arm around her waist, pulling her closer.

"It's not that." When she refused to look at him, Kai took

her chin, turning her head to the side so they locked gazes. "You… you ordered me to leave Fenrir with someone I don't trust fully. We talked about this before, about me not being your subject, but now we're back to square one." She swallowed hard, determined to discuss this calmly.

"There will still be times when I order something. It is not because I think less of you, but because I have important reasons. Our son is safe with her. If he was not, do you think I would have left him?"

"No. I know you trust her, and I do, too, to some extent." She leaned against him. "But you don't get to snap your fingers and get everything you want. Not without me having something to say about it."

He kissed the top of her head. "I make no apologies for giving orders when we are in bed."

She slapped his arm as heat burned her cheeks.

Another Viscus came forward and bowed, his dark-blue hair falling forward. "May I interrupt?"

"Sorry." Celina pulled back. "We shouldn't be discussing private matters during a gathering." She shot a warning glare at Kai, daring him to comment.

He took the invitation. "I suppose this means we will discuss more later? Hopefully while in bed?" He licked his lips, and the demons standing close by chuckled.

She rolled her eyes. "You're the one being inappropriate now."

The Viscus with dark-blue hair laughed but didn't comment. "Your Majesty, did you want us to question any Venatores before bringing them to the realm? Rumors have it they kill themselves as quickly as possible."

Kai glanced at Celina. "My advisor, Maili, is nearby. Stay with her while I discuss a few details. Please."

She stood on her tippy-toes and kissed his cheek, smiling ear to ear. "Come find me later, okay?" And without waiting for a reply, she walked away.

A few demons stood near the living area, waiting their turn to speak with their king about their plans to capture Venatores. Celina couldn't help being relieved Namika was still at Adam's club. Although, she was sure her friend wasn't pleased with it, at least no one would harm her.

Celina strode across the room, trying to find Maili, but ended up spotting Brihan. Then Adam blocked her path, smiling. "I hear congratulations are in order. Fenrir, is it?"

She nodded with a smile. "I never thanked you when Eire brought me to your club. I'm also sorry I caused a mess in your basement of death," she said with a grin.

He burst out laughing, a charming smile curling his lips. "I'm pleased you found it comfortable."

"How's Namika?"

He smirked. "She's adapting. Many of my children are making sure she doesn't leave the room I so graciously provided her. I can't understand why she's not grateful about being locked up in such a beautiful cage."

"Funny," she said with a mock glare.

"Well, when Mekaisto ordered me to question her about what she knew about your stepfather—"

"Wait, what?" She almost winced as she raised her voice, a few people turning their heads in her direction. Kai stared at her for a few seconds before returning to his conversation.

Oh, we'll be conversing *about this later.*

Adam adjusted his cuff. "By your reaction, I'm guessing he didn't tell you." When she shook her head, he shrugged. "Perhaps he forgot."

"I bet." Yet, there was no anger in her voice. Kai had been so occupied, she didn't want to assume he had purposely not told her. "So, did Namika have anything to say about my… about Dean?"

"No. She was never close to the leader. Apparently, it was a close-knit circle." He grinned. "And before you ask, since you adore questions, no, I didn't harm your friend. I asked, she told me to fuck off, and after I threw empty threats, she answered."

Celina narrowed her eyes, and at the same time, pride swelled at how brave Namika was to stand up to the Sanguis leader. She wondered if she'd ever be able to see her friend again. Their worlds were different now. Could they stay friends?

Adam's gaze sobered. "How have you been feeling since… everything?"

Linda strode forward, followed by Haku. Flicking her blonde curly waves off her shoulder, she stared at Celina. "I wouldn't worry too much, Master. She can take care of herself."

The last time Celina had seen the demon was at The CrowBar when she got Wayne out and… shot Linda. Biting her lower lip, Celina met her intense stare. "I tried to leave with Wayne Pierce with no one knowing. I didn't want to hurt anyone."

"I'm sure Emily Pierce would disagree," she said with a smug expression.

A shiver ran down Celina's spine; she tried her best not to think of those who'd died at her hands. Celina had gotten revenge against Emily, one of the people responsible for Thomas's murder. The memory of shooting Emily in the back of the head haunted her every nightmare. When Celina returned to The CrowBar to get Wayne out, Linda had tried to stop them from leaving. That left Celina with one choice: shoot the Sanguis to escape.

Before Celina could say anything, Adam cleared his throat. "Linda is fine." He stared at Celina, something like anger and admiration flashing across his features. "She healed, though not so much after your husband showed up and found out what hap—"

"But it wasn't your fault," Celina interjected, gawking at Linda.

Haku's eyebrows shot up, and he shook his head. "Still don't get it, do you? Mekaisto wasn't angry at Linda. He just took out his rage on whoever was nearby."

Celina's hands curled into fists. "Considering when we first met you tricked me into following you into the basement of demon club central and tried draining me, you have no right to pretend to be any better. I'm not an idiot, you know."

Linda scoffed. "Oh, but rescuing Mekaisto was a smart move, sure. Just needed information from—"

Adam sighed. "That's enough."

Haku glanced around as though nervous about being overheard.

Linda sneered, ignoring her master's order to stop. "I heard you gave birth to a child you're saying is Mekaisto's. Is it true, or is it someone else's since you've been here surrounded by powerful Viscus?"

Adam glowered at her, but Linda didn't seem to notice.

Celina clenched her jaw, not regretting having shot this bitch in the face. "Listen, Demon Barbie. Unlike some, I'm not interested in power."

A few of the other demons listening in chuckled at her comment, and Linda's glare could've burned a hole through a concrete wall.

Hopefully, she doesn't have those kinds of powers.

"Now, now," Adam said, the ghost of a smile touching his lips, "there's no need for that."

Linda scoffed. "Don't worry. She can't do anything, unless she brought a gun with her."

"No need." Her tone darkened. "I'm sure I could ask Shiriki for a favor. He'd do some permanent damage."

The demons took a few steps back, their faces paling. Haku dashed through the crowd, a few following him.

"My ears are burning," Shiriki said in an amused tone from behind Celina.

She spun, coming face-to-face with him, stiffening to keep

herself from backing away. Her threat would hardly hold if she showed fear… though standing this close seemed idiotic.

She raised her head higher. "I was using your love for torture as a threat."

What. The fuck. Am I doing?

He stared at her, his smile curling wider and wider until his teeth were visible. Something Kai had told her when they'd first met shot through her mind.

"I believe you are supposed to say, 'My, what big teeth you have!'"

Brihan appeared next to Celina, staring at her with bright green eyes. "Hi."

Celina smiled, ignoring the strange expression on Shiriki's face. "I haven't seen you in a while. I was heading to see my son. Did you want to come along?"

He paled, staring from Shiriki to Adam. "I can escort you there, yes, but staying would be out of the question. My status is not high enough to—"

"You're my friend. That's all the status you need."

And without another word, she grabbed Brihan's arm, and pulled him away.

As soon as they approached Celina and Kai's chambers, Brihan glanced at the end of the corridor. "If Mekaisto finds out, he'll skin me alive."

She shook her head. "I'll make sure he doesn't. He knows we're friends, and he has to respect that."

They stepped inside and Nalie frowned, getting up from the sofa.

Celina looked around. "Where's Fenrir?"

"He is sleeping." She stared over Celina's shoulder and gave a curt nod. "Brihan."

The door burst open, and Celina's eyes widened as Lokte and another demon Celina didn't recognize marched into the chambers. Nalie's icy-blue stare could have frozen anyone in place, and it seemed to work on the stranger and Brihan.

"What rights do you have coming in here unannounced, Wyla?" she asked in a cool tone.

The woman, Wyla, raised her head, although she peered around as though scared Kai might be nearby. "The king tasked me with finding whose energy matched the one who struck this place."

Celina's eyebrows rose as she glanced from Nalie to Brihan. It couldn't be either of them. They were her friends; she trusted them.

Wyla scratched the side of her shaved head. "I traced the signature to the front of the king's dwelling mere hours before the same power attacked the realm. Only three subjects were outside when this energy first appeared." She swept her gaze across the room. "Lokte, Brihan, and you, Celina."

Nalie narrowed her eyes. "Have you—"

"Yes, I had tested Brihan a few days ago and confirmed with Lokte neither of them carries this energy. And so, this only leaves Celina."

Celina took a step back. "That's ridiculous. My powers aren't strong enough to cause damage to the realm. And besides, why would I have attacked myself?"

Lokte shook his head. "It is not impossible. You had lost your soul and were adapting to everything. If the energy came from within, it may have overpowered you. So, what seemed like an attack stemmed from yourself."

"I… I'm the one who attacked the realm?" she asked quietly. "But what about the ones after? I wasn't even here."

"The other times there was less destruction, and it was definitely the Venatores. But that first attack," Wyla took a step forward, "was definitely you."

"No, this is ridiculous." Celina paced, averting her gaze.

Memories of Kai telling her about the attack flooded her mind. He'd been so distraught as his realm bled out, destroying his subjects as he tried to protect his home. Was she the cause of his pain?

Wyla grabbed Celina's arm, and she gasped when it glowed white, symbols flashing beneath her skin for a second before vanishing once more.

Celina met her gaze. "The Venatores put a spell on me to prevent tracing. But this was *after* the first attack."

Wyla's jaw clenched, and she raised her hand. White filaments floated from Celina's skin, and her eyes widened. Without a word, the demon motioned her head at Lokte, and he stepped forward. He took out a tablet, tapped it with a pointed fingernail, and what looked like a hologram appeared in the room. It was the same white filament hovering above Celina's skin.

"The same signature," Wyla whispered.

Brihan frowned. "Right before the attack, you vanished, remember? The shadows only you saw… could it have been coming from within you?"

Lokte nodded, putting away the tablet. "You being here is a danger to the realm. You may end up destroying it without ever meaning to."

Celina swallowed hard as Wyla let go of her arm, and the filament vanished. "Don't tell Kai. Please." She stared at everyone inside the room. "I'll tell him myself."

Wyla's eyebrows shot up. "My task is to report my findings. I cannot lie to—"

"I'm not asking you to lie. Just don't report it. Stay far away from him so he can't ask. I want to be the one to tell him." Tears rolled down her cheeks, and she wiped them away fast. "It means I can't remain in the realm, but my son… Fenrir can't stay in the human world too long. I… I need to talk to my husband about this. Please give me time."

Wyla's shoulders slumped when Lokte gave her a dark look. "I will give you until the end of today, and if you have not by then…" She didn't finish her sentence.

Celina nodded, her stomach churning. She had been the

one to attack the realm and wouldn't be able to stay here anymore. She would have to be away from Fenrir for long periods of time. The thought tightened her chest to the point she was sure her heart would stop.

CONFESSION

Celina sat in silence at the dining room table, holding her son on her lap as Kai ate. In only a few days, Fenrir was strong enough to hold his head up. His dark-brown hair had grown longer, and his irises glowed a more vivid yellow as though more alert.

Her food sat untouched. She wrapped her arms around him, needing to grasp these small moments. It was the end of the day, and her last chance to tell Kai before Wyla would report it to him.

She had gone to bed for a nap and kept a wall of distance between them. She hated herself for being weak but was terrified of what it could mean once she told him the truth.

"Celina?" Kai's voice shook her from her daze.

"Yes?"

"You have not been eating. What is going on?" He picked at his food, allowing her to compose herself before answering.

The lump in her throat grew unbearable. "Nothing. I'm just not hungry."

"Do not lie." His gaze lacked amusement or curiosity, making her swallow hard.

She got to her feet. "I should give Fenrir his bath—"

"Celina," he growled her name as he straightened. "Do not make me ask you again."

"Don't threaten me." She clenched her jaw, but her chest squeezed, and her shoulders slumped. "I... please, let it go. Okay?" She stood, headed for the bath.

He blocked her way. "Give him to me."

"Why?"

"Am I not allowed to hold our son?" He took a step closer. "Have I done something wrong?"

Tears blurred her vision. "Of course not." Her voice cracked. She handed him Fenrir, and Kai walked to the other side of the table, murmuring words in the Demos language.

Shiriki strode into the room, making Celina's stomach clench.

"Ah," Kai grinned. "Such good timing." He handed Fenrir to Shiriki.

Celina's instincts went into overdrive. She dashed toward him, wanting to get her son the hell away from the monster.

Kai wrapped his arm around her waist, holding her.

"What the hell are you doing?" She squirmed, trying to lunge at Shiriki, but Kai's grip was strong.

"He will not harm him."

Shiriki grinned, then stared at Fenrir with a smile Celina had never seen before. It was... real. "Well, you are a small thing. Do you have a soul in there somewhere? Shall we check and see?" He rested a pointed fingernail against her son's chest but then chuckled. "No. Grandpa would never do that."

Celina shuddered. "This is so fucking disturbing."

Shiriki laughed. A true laugh, not something sinister or morbid. Making his way to the nearest chair, he sat, holding Fenrir against him. He placed his hand in front of her son's face, and a tiny white hummingbird flew in wisps of bright light. Celina gaped at the scene, unsure what to think or feel about it. Shiriki stared at her, his usual smirk returning.

Patting his thigh, he winked. "You can have a turn after."

She lunged. "You fucking—"

"Celina." Kai spun her to face him. "Tell me."

"Not until you get our son the hell away from that monster."

He leaned closer. "He will hold him until you explain, so the faster you do, the faster Fenrir comes back to you."

She curled her hands into fists. "You're using our child against me?"

"No. As I said, Shiriki will not harm him, so he is in no danger. But you need to tell me what is going on. After the meeting was over, you started acting—"

"After the meeting?" Shiriki said with amusement in his voice. "Around the same time Wyla was escorted by your head of guards heading for your chambers? Seems to be a bit of a coincidence Celina was heading there herself just before, accompanied by Brihan."

I'm going to fucking kill him.

Kai's eyes narrowed, and he grabbed her wrists. "You either tell me or I find out through Brihan." He pinned her between his body and the table.

She raised her head, holding his glare. "Brihan is a friend, and he's done nothing wrong."

He took a step back, the surrounding energy sparking. Shiriki sighed and stood, coming closer to his king. Without a word, he handed him Fenrir and stood in front of Celina.

She leaned back.

"Tell me," Shiriki said.

She arched an eyebrow. "What makes you think I'd tell you anything?"

"If you do, I will share a secret."

"Leave me alone." She gritted her teeth. No way would she play along with his games.

He leaned toward her ear, and she fought to keep from running or attacking. "You do not want to know what your mother's last words were?" He straightened, his irises glowing in such a bright white, she could barely hold his gaze.

Heat rose through her body, and she trembled. "Did… you kill her?"

"Well, that would be a secret now, would it not?"

She lunged at him and gripped the front of his shirt. "Did you murder my mother? Are you the reason I lost her?"

"Such harsh words." He grasped her wrists.

Her mouth dried as white filaments rose from her skin.

It happens when I get mad?

"How interesting. Wyla showed me the signature of the first assault on the realm… the one who attacked you." His smile curled over his pointed teeth. "Why do you have the same energy, pet?"

Kai's expression was unreadable as he came closer and placed his hand over her arm, tracing his thumb over her skin. Fenrir squirmed, reaching toward Shiriki. She wrenched free and took her son in her arms, holding him close.

Kai stared at her as his eyes darkened. "Celina?"

"I… Apparently I'm the one who attacked the realm. I didn't know I did…" She met his gaze. "I didn't mean to, I swear."

"And who told you of this?" he asked in a growl.

She swallowed hard. "I begged Wyla to let me tell you myself. She gave me until the rest of the day, and this was my last chance. I wanted to before, so many times, but it terrified me."

"You believe I would—"

"No." She shook her head. "I just… it means I can't stay in your realm, but Fenrir has to stay here most of the time because he's young and needs this place." She took a shuddering breath. "I have to be away from you both, and I don't even know why."

Shiriki clapped his hands together. "Well, my news comes

at a good time." He turned to Kai. "I have located and… secured Oliver. He was a disciple of Dean Perry and Jacob's brother, Zachary."

Celina arched an eyebrow. "And what good does that do?"

"I have the feeling your little accidental attack may have something to do with the experiments done on you as a child," he said in an icy tone. "If we find out what, perhaps the spell can be broken so you stop poisoning this realm."

Hope filled Celina. "Can we talk to him?"

"I extracted information about the whereabouts of the more powerful Venatores, and he is now in a coma of sorts. Once I am finished, I do not see any issue preventing talking to him." Shiriki grinned, something in his gaze gleaming. "In the meantime, I came to inform you there has been yet another slaughter."

Her throat tightened as she met Kai's gaze. Without a word, he left, followed by Shiriki.

She held Fenrir closer, staring at the door where her husband had left. She'd wanted to tell him sooner, but knowing it meant being separated from her family had torn her apart. "I'm sorry, Kai."

25

—————

WRATH

Kai hated himself for leaving his wife as he had, but he needed to get away before he destroyed the realm. Rage surged beneath the surface, threatening to annihilate his home if he released it. Kai was as much a part of this place's essence as it was a part of him; if he unleashed Hell, it would drain the Dark Realm.

Cameo frowned as Kai appeared near the gates. But Kai didn't utter a single word, not wanting to chance major destruction. Striding through the Inferno, he released some of his fury, turning the damned into piles of ashes. Others blistered and exploded as he passed. Their bodies reformed, tendons, muscles, and flesh knitting together around the white filaments of their souls. Then the agony would start over. Pain for eternity.

As soon as he crossed into the Silence, Kai unleashed his wrath. The ferocity slammed against the cavern walls, carving into the stone. As he marched down the corridor, the violence surging through him ripped everything in its path. He plunged the whole area into darkness. The glowing of his irises lit the main room in crimson, the furniture disintegrating as he approached.

"We knew there were risks, being the first of her kind." Shiriki's voice echoed in the emptiness, and Kai turned. His second in command walked forward, focusing on a pile of ashes on the floor. "Now where are we supposed to sit?" he muttered.

Another wave of fury crashed against Shiriki. Though he brought his hands to his face as his flesh melted away, he remained silent.

"She cannot stay in the realm, but my son cannot be in Demias for long. No demon infant can. Fenrir needs her to share energy while he grows, or he will die." Saying it out loud created a suffocating sense of loss in his chest, and he unleashed more dark energy. Those shadows took form, teeth snapping as it stalked inside the room, growls vibrating against the walls.

Shiriki glanced from one to another. "Whichever spell Dean Perry cast was meant to destroy this realm. Jacob said he knew you would come for Celina, so they must have used a Madka spell that would only take effect once you took her soul."

"And how do you propose we find out which spell it is since you killed Dean Perry?" Kai took a step toward Shiriki, grinding his teeth. "The only ones close enough to him seem to have gone into hiding."

"Oliver will regain consciousness, and we will question him. Once he gives us the new location for their headquarters, I am certain one of them will know where to find Zachary. He will know the spell, and then we can break it."

The energy diminished, and with a wave of Kai's hand, new furniture appeared in the room. Lights flickered to life, illuminating the space, reflecting against the large marble table. "I need to question Oliver." Kai relished the idea of breaking this Venatore himself.

"Not yet. Poor thing is under the weather," he said with a smirk. "But the good news is Wyla informed me her source within the Venatore gave her the location where they hid the weakest members." Shiriki's eyes gleamed of malice.

"I will meet you at your dwelling by the end of the day, and we will pay them a little visit." He walked past and strode out of the cavern, needing to see Celina.

The trip back seemed to take longer, and his gaze swept over the destruction he'd caused to the Inferno realm. As they were condemned souls, he felt no regret at their pain. He swept his focus over his dwelling and found his wife and son in the garden, accompanied by Brihan and Nalie. Even Lokte stood nearby, hidden in the shadows.

Kai strode into the garden, and his subjects bowed. Nalie had been holding Fenrir in her arms, Celina standing in front of a tree.

"Leave us."

Nalie approached. "Your son?"

"Take him to my private chambers. Stay with him."

Brihan left without a word as Nalie walked away, followed by Lokte.

As Kai neared Celina, she glanced over her shoulder at him, then to the crow she was petting. A few of them flew from the trees, landing near her.

"You have a large group of crows," he said, trying to break through the heavy silence.

She turned to him. "A murder."

"Oh?" He arched an eyebrow.

She let her fingers glide along its feathers. "A group of crows is called a murder," she said with amusement in her tone.

He remembered he'd said something similar to her when she knew him as Thomas. The night he took everything away from her.

"Celina, can we—"

She moved into him, burying her face into his chest as he held her close, inhaling the scent of her hair. "I'm sorry. I should have told you sooner, but I was stalling. Part of me was terrified you'd be angry at me for attacking your realm. But more than anything, I didn't want to upset you and make what's left of our life together painful." Her voice broke into a sob, and Kai squeezed his eyes shut, composing himself before drawing her away.

"What do you mean by what is left?" he repeated.

"I can't stay here, and you can't go back and forth while trying to take care of Fenrir on your own." Large tears rolled down her cheeks. "You should find someone else. Someone who will—"

He slanted his mouth over hers, the heat of her lips grounding him as he took hold of his fury at her suggestion.

When their lips parted, she was panting, her face flushed.

"If you ever mention anything like that again, I will turn your ass so red, you will be unable to sit for weeks, dove."

Her eyes widened, and a small shiver ran through her. "Okay," she breathed.

He smiled, unsure if she was agreeing to never mention it again or agreeing to him spanking her.

Both.

She swallowed hard. "I could go back to the Venatores. Act as a spy to get—"

"Out of the question." He pushed her hair behind her ear, her skin cold against his own. "We have Jacob's brother. He may know what spell they used on you and how to break it."

"Spell?"

He nodded. "What your stepfather did when you were a child. It may be the reason you are poisoning this realm." He took her hand and sat on the stone bench, pulling her next to him.

She turned, determination lighting her eyes. "When he wakes up, I want to be there. I need to know why my stepfather did what he did."

"We will discuss it when the time comes."

She sighed. "You need to stop postponing things."

"Like you postponed telling me the truth?" he asked, smiling as she averted her gaze. He got to his feet and took her hand, pulling her to her feet. "But I agree. We will stop waiting."

They walked to the greenhouse. As soon as they were inside, every door slammed shut. He pressed his mouth over hers, kissing her hard and demanding her passion in return. She moaned against him, running her hands along his shoulders. He cupped her breasts through her clothes, and she shuddered. Taking his time, he slipped her dress over her head. Then he paused, taking in her body. He slid his pointed fingernail along her neck. Goosebumps crawled on her skin as he descended until he stopped near her navel.

She glanced down at herself and bit her lower lip. She wrapped her arms around her waist. Grabbing her hands, he pulled them away, and something like a growl vibrated through his chest.

"Do not hide from me. I have ways of keeping you immobilized, and I will use them."

"It's... I guess I'm feeling self-conscious since giving birth."

He traced along a few marks. "You are beautiful. With or without marks."

"That's easy for you to say."

He placed his hand against his shirt, and it vanished in a wisp of smoke, leaving him bare-chested. As she was about to speak, he turned to the side and folded his wings. Below his shoulder, an old scar ran near his left wing, and some surrounding skin had never healed.

She ran her fingers over it. "How did that happen?"

"I do not remember. It has always been there as far as I know." He faced her. "Your marks are perfect because they show you carried life inside you. You carried our son, and it makes you even more beautiful."

She rested her hands against his chest. "Thank you."

When he licked his lips, she slid her hand along his skin, resting her fingers on the hardness in his pants. He hissed through his teeth as she rubbed against his erections, his grip on her arms tightening.

"Careful how much you tempt me, or I will make sure the whole realm hears you scream."

He slid his hand to her back and unclasped her bra. Instead of tossing it away fast, he pulled it off slowly, her heavy breasts spilling out, her nipples hard. He cupped them, and she sucked in air. No matter how many languages Kai knew, none had a word to describe how breathtaking his wife was. The way she caused him to feel like he had a heart.

Leaning forward, he swirled his tongue around her nipple as she ran her fingers through his hair. He kissed along her breasts, licking and nipping as he descended a trail to her abdomen. Kneeling, he pulled down her panties and licked her sex. She was exquisite, and he'd spend every day showing her what she meant to him. The knowledge of their imminent separation took over his mind, and he clenched his jaw. Fury lit a renewed fire within, mixing itself to his desire for Celina. It was dangerous to bed her in anger, but he couldn't wait. Couldn't think of stopping this. Unless she told him to stop, there was no hope of taming his instincts.

Her knees buckled as she shuddered, and he grabbed her ass, then ran his tongue between her wet folds until he reached her clit. A moan ripped out of her as he lapped at her nub, and she tugged harder on his hair. She was delicious; her taste as perfect as she was. His wings wrapped around to her back, tickling along her skin as she threw her head back with a sigh.

"I could feast on you every day, and always want more," he said against her wetness.

She panted. "I need you inside me. Please."

When he stood, his pants had vanished, and Celina swallowed hard as she stared at his erect cocks. He followed her thoughts, wanting to be inside her in every way possible. It had taken time for her to get used to his anatomy, yet now it was all she could think of when they were intimate. The ways he took her, every time, claiming every inch of her. The things she wanted him to do with her—the things she'd let him do.

He growled. "Dove, I am trying to be gentle. But keep having those thoughts, and I will put you on your hands and knees and fuck you harder than you can imagine."

Taking her hand, he led her toward an armchair. He spun her back to him, and she gasped when he sat, pulling her on top of him. He pushed her hair to the side, kissing and licking along her neck. His hands slid to her breasts, and he cupped them, fondling her flesh between his fingers. She leaned her head on his shoulder, his hardness pressing against her ass. He felt a wave of anticipation flooding her core, her clit throbbing with so much need, he thought she'd explode. Lifting her hips, he pressed his cocks against her openings, and she cried out as he thrust inside.

"Don't stop," she moaned as she grabbed onto the armrest.

He rocked them slowly, the rhythm keeping them both on the edge. Sweat slid down their bodies as she gasped, crying out when he nipped at her neck. Sheathing himself deep, he stopped thrusting, his hand traveling from her hips to her breasts. He squeezed them hard, and she whimpered as his cocks throbbed inside her. She grabbed hold of his arms, rubbing his hands along her skin, begging for more of his touch.

He licked her earlobe. "Look at me."

She glanced over her shoulder and nibbled her lower lip. He grasped the back of her neck before trailing his fingers through her hair. Twirling it a few times in his hand, he grabbed a fistful and wrenched. She swallowed hard, exposed, goosebumps crawling on her flesh.

"Bite me."

He felt her lust and chuckled, grazing his teeth along her shoulder until she trembled. "You ask I mark you? My brand was not enough?" He licked at the crook of her neck. "Everyone will see and know who you belong to."

The scars left by the demon who had attacked her had faded, but he wanted his own mark over the spot.

His hands moved underneath her thighs, his pointed fingernails pressing against her soft flesh. He lifted her, then pumped faster and harder than before. She cried out, tears running from the corners of her eyes as waves of pleasure crashed against her.

When he bit into her neck, another orgasm flooded her before the last had even finished. A high-pitched moan left her as he groaned, spilling his seed to fill her.

Her body went limp.

Kai stood and carried her to the sofa. Selecting a soft blanket, he wrapped it around her. She closed her eyes, relaxing into sleep as he kissed the top of her head.

He didn't want to leave her, but she needed rest, and he had to tend to the newest massacre. After bolting the doors of the greenhouse, he left, knowing she was safe while he was gone.

I need to get her back to Demias.

Slaughter had occurred inside the house he had shared with Celina, a personal affront from the Venatores. Most of the house remained as he'd seen it last, their possessions untouched in rooms closed off behind police tape. Amongst the skinned corpses of Sanguis, a single human, face ruined beyond recognition, had been posed at the table where Kai and Celina used to dine. The redhead cradled a bundle of organs in her arms. Their message couldn't be clearer.

Kai would wipe them out.

Shiriki stopped near the human. "This one seems more personal than the others. They knew you had an interest in her, but perhaps they did not know your relationship. Either way, I suppose they would have to let her into their headquarters to finish the spell Dean Perry began."

Kai focused on the redhead, picturing his wife and nearly setting the place on fire. He moved to the patio door, staring out through the shattered glass. "Get out."

Without a word, Shiriki vanished.

Flames erupted as Kai stepped out onto the porch. The heat scorched his back.

It was just a house. Why am I feeling anything about it? A few scant years of memories, a life we built on a lie I created.

Smoke drifted to the ceiling and slid under the doors as fire licked the walls. A window burst nearby, and he glanced over at the paint bubbling inside the kitchen. His gaze landed on their wedding photo, the glass splintering within the picture frame.

Waving his hand with a flick of his wrist, a folded piece of paper appeared in his palm. He unfolded it, glancing from the sketch to the yard. The play structure Celina had drawn along with the swing-set he'd added. She'd spent so long out here alone, had wanted children and a place for them to laugh and play.

But he'd taken that from her.

I truly am a monster.

Dandelions poked through the grass, neglected in his wife's absence. A few birds landed on the edge of the birdbath but flew away when they found it empty.

A bitter smile curled his lips as the paper vanished. He walked straight ahead toward the woods where his tree stood. "We can still build it… together," he muttered.

26

BREAKING

Wyla's source turned out to be right, and Kai would reward the traitorous Venatore's wishes. Although, not quite in the way she expected. No deal with him ever ended as his victims expected.

He cornered three members who'd been hidden away since they were weaker than the rest. Too bad for the Venatores.

The source within was about to find out making any kind of exchange with his kind never ended well.

He waited outside the small house as she lowered the magic, then circled it with his own dark energy, keeping them trapped inside. And being the fair king he was, he allowed his subjects to join in the fun. His orders were clear: no one may harm any of them. But there were other ways they could subdue enemies.

The four Venatores sat on the floor, against the wall, unmoving. Shiriki lingered close, staring at them like he wanted nothing better than to shred them to pieces, but without permission, he didn't move.

The source, a woman named Grace, glared. "We had a deal."

"Ah, yes. The one you made with Wyla." He flicked his hand to the side, and the contract Grace had signed appeared. "Let us see what you agreed to. In exchange for the whereabouts of weaker members of your group, you want a guarantee that after everything, you will be left alone and not hunted."

"Exactly, so—"

"I am not hunting you, though am I? You are simply here." He chuckled as the contract vanished. "And while you remain in my dungeons, you will be by yourself."

Her eyes widened, filling with unshed tears. He could smell the fear radiating off of her and couldn't help widen his smile.

"That's not what I agreed to!"

"Perhaps, I can give you the chance to leave this place? To gain freedom instead of my dungeon." He crouched in front of her, and she pressed her back harder against the wall. "What are the Mackenzy brothers promising you? Both Jacob and Zachary seem so sure they can lead you to victory. Tell me why."

She swallowed visibly. "They've sworn they'll merge both worlds by taking over the dark realm. Get rid of your kind so we can rule."

Shiriki kept quiet, his expression unreadable. He looked ready to vanish, but instead, stepped closer to Grace, who stiffened. "Do you know about Dean Perry and his history with the Venatores?" When she nodded, he continued, "What was the plan for his daughter?"

"I—I'm not sure." When Shiriki's eyes narrowed, she jerked. "I was close to their group, but never a part of it. From what I'd heard, Zachary was supposed to fetch the girl if anything happened to Dean. But his daughter disappeared, and no one heard anything about her until recently."

Kai's energy rolled off him, barely able to contain his rage. "And what was the plan regarding her?"

"Dean wasn't known for his pleasant experiments… Zachary was worse." She trembled as Kai poured darkness into her mind. Shiriki's energy coiled around her, causing a few sparks on Grace's clothes.

"Now, here is the million-dollar question." Shiriki regained his composure so quickly, Kai wondered if he hadn't imagined the fury pooling out from him. "Who is your inside source within our kind?"

Grace pressed her lips tight, and Shiriki chuckled. Kai entered the Venatore's mind without mercy, searching through it for the source. But she didn't know. Both Jacob and Zachary seemed to have grown suspicious of her and slowly pushed her away from important information.

Kai got to his feet, and she jumped. "What was the spell Dean Perry used on Celina? The one Jacob finished when she was at your headquarters?"

"Finished?" Her eyebrows shot up. "I was inside the building when he and another member put a spell on her, but it wasn't to finish anything. It was just an untraceable spell. That's it. As for the one Dean put on her, I have no idea. He and Zachary were the experts on dark spells."

"We are done. For now. You are free to go." He called out to his subjects, instructing them to search the rest of the small building for anyone hiding within. "In the meantime, I will be… borrowing your friend here."

Her eyes widened, but before she could say anything, Kai vanished, materializing outside. He turned to Shiriki as soon as he appeared next to him. "Find Zachary. He is the one who would know what spell they cast on Celina, and I have the feeling he may know who the source is. I want him alive and unharmed. You get to do whatever pleases you with him after I am done."

The cruelest smile curled Shiriki's lips. With a final bow, he stalked away.

Kai wiped the rusty scalpel, the cloth stained with years of blood. Black ooze soaked most of his instruments, and he smiled at the continued whimpers of the Venatore. They'd found her hiding when Kai and his subjects attacked. People like her were easy and so pleasant to break.

The Viscus kneeling on the floor made rasping sounds, unable to do much else with his tongue ripped out and his face flayed. The Venatore had sobbed the entire time Kai tortured Ancus, her mind breaking with each cut. Dark spells made it difficult to read her thoughts, but as her sanity slipped, he'd caught glimpses of what they planned.

Once he'd carved into Ancus, prying his back open by detaching his ribs from his backbone, the woman edged close to insanity. He had assured her she would be next as soon as he finished tending to his own subject. The thought of what she'd suffer had been enough to break her.

He leaned against the bloodied table, focusing on the centipedes as they scurried across the saw and onto his hand.

Ancus had been locked inside his dungeon for some time, but Kai hadn't dared deal with his torture up to this point. His rage burned too hot after what he'd seen. Kai would have destroyed him on the spot, and there would have been no satisfaction in knowing Ancus hadn't suffered.

He glanced over his shoulder at Ancus, and his lips curled. A few tendons held together his subject's wrists and ankles. The woman shifted in the metallic chair, wincing as the pointed ends on the armrests punctured her skin. But her gaze never left the demon on the floor.

"Faustina." He chuckled when she yelped at his voice alone. "Why did your leaders declare war against me? Surely they know they cannot win."

Her lower lip trembled, her honey-brown hair sticking to her sweaty face. "I... can't..."

"Oh, you can." He took a large vial filled with a greenish liquid and walked over to her. "Jacob and Zachary are either insane and plan on dragging your entire group into extinction, or they think they can win. I want to know why."

She eyed the vial, pressing against the backrest despite the hooks tearing through her skin. "I won't… betray them."

"Flaying someone is agonizing," he cooed, taking a few steps closer to her. "But, unlike my kind, you would pass out from shock, which defies the purpose."

"Purpose?" she whispered, tears running down her cheeks.

He leaned forward, waving the vial. "To break you so you tell me what I need to know." His red irises reflected in her gaze. "You *will* answer my questions. Do you wish to scream them? Why not save yourself from the pain?"

She swallowed visibly, her focus on the vial. "What—"

"Acid." He tipped it, the liquid running to the rim. "A special kind. It peels skin faster so you have the fortune of staying conscious."

He allowed a few drops to fall on her thighs, and she screamed as it burned through her. Her skin blistered, blood oozing from the wounds.

She sobbed, tugging against the restraints. "He… Jacob said we're… getting help."

"Yes, from one of my subjects, but—"

She shook her head. "Not just a demon."

"Then from who?"

"An angel."

Kai frowned, allowing his essence to seep inside her mind without mercy as her screams filled the air. Having existed for so long, not much surprised him, but what he saw within her memories did.

Faustina told the truth.

He straightened and went to the instruments, placing the

vial on the rough surface. "Has your leader seen this supposed mythical being?"

"I don't know," she said, her voice cracking.

He took the curved blade. "And why had your group been looking for Celina?"

She turned her head to the side, straining to watch him. "Because the angel said we had to bring her to our headquarters and keep her there."

He went to Ancus and grasped his arm tight, digging his pointed fingernails into the demon's skin. Symbols glowed, then faded within seconds. "I have seen the messages written in Madka when your kind has left my subjects' corpses behind, but these markings," he motioned at the flesh, "are different."

When Kai had first seen them, thousands of explanations ran through him. His first thought was he'd found the traitor amongst his subjects, but after ripping through Ancus' mind, he found it wasn't the case. But the spell in question twisted already dark beings into killers who acted on instincts alone. They'd cursed Ancus, and the damage was already done to his mind. And Kai wasn't the type to forgive so easily after what his subject had tried doing to his wife.

"I don't know what those are. They aren't ours." She averted her gaze from Ancus, swallowing hard.

"Jacob did not tell me who your source is, but I know it is one of my subjects."

She held her breath and shook her head.

His lips curled into a thin smile. "I have not yet asked my question, but your actions speak louder."

He waved his hand to the side, and the restraints around her limbs vanished. She jumped to her feet and limped for the door, pulling on the metal handle. Her wounded leg trembled under her weight.

She screamed as Kai grabbed a fistful of hair and dragged her to the metal rack. Magic sparked between her fingers, and she aimed at him, but his darkness swallowed her measly light. He strapped her in, and she froze when he waved the curved blade.

"No! Please, no!"

He rested the metal against the side of her neck. "Flesh is less pliable than people think, but once it peels…" Cutting into her skin, he licked his lips as blood streamed down and she shrieked.

He exhaled long and hard, enjoying the smell of her fear. "Who is the source?"

Kai felt Shiriki approach, and he stepped away from his victim, enjoying the terror twisting her mind.

Shiriki materialized, staring at the piece of paper he held in his hand.

"Any information on Zachary?" Movement caught Kai's gaze, and he turned in time to see Faustina's eyes widen.

Shiriki lowered the paper, grinning ear to ear. "No, but she may know."

"I want her alive. She is my reply to Jacob's message."

The woman pressed her lips together, shaking her head.

"Has she given any useful information to be granted such a mercy?" he asked, ambling closer to the woman.

She flinched as he stood in front of her. "You're…" Her eyes glazed over for a second, and she passed out.

Shiriki continued staring at her, and Kai wondered why she'd fainted. After what she'd seen and suffered, Shiriki shouldn't have caused her that much fear. He pushed the slithering question from his mind.

Shiriki shrugged. "I suppose my reputation precedes me."

"She said Jacob is working with an angel," Kai said.

Shiriki raised an eyebrow, the ghost of a smile curling his lips. "Is that right?"

"Angels are myths invented by Lumen and Venatores to keep them in line. Obey their laws, or angels will wreak vengeance onto them." He grinned. "Or something like that."

"Once we find Zachary, it will be a matter of destroying them. It should solve quite a lot of problems, especially if he knows who the inside source is," Shiriki said with a shrug, staring at the paper. "Also, Rium perished after I extracted the substance keeping him from healing."

Kai frowned. "Rium?"

"The survivor we found in the alleyway after the Venatores' little art show of our brethren's corpses." Shiriki sighed. "Now then, you want me to break the members you are sending me and find Zachary. Will that be all?"

Kai clenched his jaw, appearing in front of Shiriki. "I am starting to believe you wish to be destroyed." He grasped his neck. "Is it why you continue to instigate me?"

Shiriki's eyes widened, his silver irises reflecting the red from Kai's. His usual calmness returned. "And roast over an open fire?" Shiriki said with a chuckle. "I prefer to save that for Christmas."

Kai released him, but neither of them moved. "Fire would be lenient. No, if you do not find Zachary soon, I will forbid any research on live victims."

"I see." Shiriki's expression hardened, but he bowed and vanished without another word.

He glanced to Faustina who was still unconscious. What had happened to her?

A mental connection formed with Adam, a request for permission to speak with him. Kai gritted his teeth but allowed it. He rarely let anyone into his private dungeon unless they were the victims.

Adam walked inside, his shoulders stiff. As soon as his gaze landed on the tortured demon, his face paled. "Ancus? Why have you—"

"Are you demanding an explanation from me?" Kai asked quietly.

Adam flinched. "No. I'm sorry. It's just… shock."

Kai smirked. Adam had a strange soft spot for their kind;

he supposed seeing one of his own in this state would shock any demon. Kai closed his eyes for a second, allowing what he'd seen inside Ancus's memories to slither inside Adam's mind.

Adam's hands turned to fists, his jaw clenched so tight his teeth grit together. "He… had always been a loyal subject, no?"

"He was already too far gone, but tasting my wife's blood was the final twist of his mind." Saying what happened out loud angered him further. Inside his own dungeon, he was less at risk for destroying his realm whenever he relinquished the control on his temper. But with Adam here, he risked destroying the Sanguis leader.

Adam averted his gaze. "I… Had your wife ever told you what had happened before we came to rescue you at Yonah Church?"

Kai scoffed. "Ah yes, the infamous rescue. If you had heeded Shiriki's advice, you would have saved her some pain."

"Celina made a contract for my help in rescuing you. In blood." He inched toward the door. "I have to admit, she had a different taste. It was the only thing I could think of for some time afterward, despite having only a drop."

"And are you telling me this so you may take your place alongside Ancus?" Kai asked in a dark tone.

He shook his head. "No, I'm just wondering why her blood does this. We've murdered Lumen before—had their blood. Why is Celina different?"

"None of your concern," he hissed through his teeth, letting go of his anger in a blast of energy.

Adam fell to his knees, bowing low. "I apologize for the contract, Mekaisto. It was completed, and nothing more would ever come of it. But I wanted you to be aware her blood is addictive to more than just the one who lost his mind."

"If you ever lay a finger on her, I will not end your existence." His irises flashed so brightly, the whole room glowed scarlet. "I will make it endless and filled with nothing but anguish. You will relieve your worst nightmares day after day without an end in sight. And as you recall, I know exactly what those are, *Hayden*."

Adam flinched, getting to his feet. "I… understand. Thank you."

"Now, then. I want to know more about one of your children. Eire." He took a scooping instrument from the tray and went to Ancus.

Adam rubbed his hands across his face, his expression pained. He cleared his throat. "Eire. I don't know her much. She appeared in the city years ago. I never asked too many questions since she isn't the sharing type. She keeps to herself, doesn't cause trouble." A small smile curled Adam's lips. "You want me to gather information on her?"

Kai twirled the scooper between his fingers, and Ancus's body shook, blood splattering to the floor. "My wife is fond of Eire. She is trustworthy, but that worries me. Find out more and return when you have something."

Adam left quickly as though Hell itself was chasing him.

Kai thought of what Adam had said about Celina's blood being addictive. The Sanguis leader was right, but he wasn't sure why it was. Delicious was an understatement, but why?

Lumen and demon blood mixed creates a fascinating cocktail.

Celina had once made a blood contract to save him. Even when she hadn't known who he was, she'd already been in love. She had done everything in her power to help him.

He leaned against the wall and closed his eyes.

She deserves so much more.

27

POISON

Celina rubbed her arms as they entered through the doors to Shiriki's dreaded high-rise. She'd left Fenrir with Nalie, and despite hating being away from her son, Kai had allowed her to come. She wasn't about to miss her chance to be included.

The security guard at the door bowed so low, she was sure he'd end up falling face first onto the ground.

Every time she was here, she sensed something unnatural about the place, but today tiny vibrations filtered through the ground.

A hand touched her back, and she yelped, staggering until Kai caught her.

"Are you all right?" he asked.

"Yes, sorry." She swallowed hard. "I get nervous in this place."

Shiriki walked past them. "I wonder why..."

She muttered a curse but focused on the floor. "Is there... I don't know, a connection to the dark realm under this building?"

"How would you know that?" Kai asked.

"I can... feel it. I always felt something when I came here

but never figured out what. It's got the same energy as your realm but different."

The grandfather clock ticked through the heavy silence. Whispers ran across the air, and Celina's neck prickled. From behind the archway, footsteps echoed, and Hilda strode inside.

"Celina?" Hilda's eyebrows shot up, but she smiled, going to her former ward and grasping her hands. "It's good to see you."

"You, too." Celina squeezed the woman's hands.

Shiriki cleared his throat, and they separated like a current shocked them. Hilda bowed, then waved toward the hallway she'd come from.

Celina tugged on Kai's sleeve as they followed Shiriki. "Who is Hilda anyway? I mean, I know she's Shiriki's caretaker, but that's it. What's her story?"

"She sold her soul to Shiriki decades ago in exchange for her family's safety from vampires. She gave up her life in servitude to him, and when she dies, her soul belongs to him."

"Vampires?" She froze in her step, her chest tightening. She remembered Adam's insistence Sanguis and vampires were different.

Kai nodded as though having followed her train of thought. "Sanguis are often mistaken for vampires, yes, but they don't need blood to survive. When they feast, they take a human's life essence. Vampires need to feed on blood alone and aren't connected to my realm."

"But she understands Demos, and I saw her vanish in smoke."

"Powers Shiriki granted her to keep her family safe. Though her life was also extended, her time grows near. I doubt Shiriki ever told her when she dies, so does the protection for her family."

Celina glared at Shiriki's back, hoping he could feel her disgust. "That's horrible."

"Humans never read the fine print," he said with a grin.

Remembering when she found out her body belonged to Kai in their contract, she gritted her teeth as heat filled her cheeks. "We should be more careful, but maybe demons should be honest."

He chuckled as they stopped in front of a metallic door. Shiriki pushed it open and stepped inside. Without a word, she joined the Viscus inside the bare room where a man sat in a corner, trembling. The man pressed his hands against his chest, gasping.

Celina shot Shiriki a nasty glare but stayed silent.

The man lifted his head, his dark-blue irises flashing in anger. "Come to torture me with an audience this time?"

"Tell me you tried talking to him before you jumped into your sadistic experiments," she muttered, staring at Shiriki.

He shook his head. "A waste of time with Venatores."

The man's gaze landed on Celina, and his eyes widened. "You… you're Celina."

Her eyebrows shot up. "How do you know my name?"

"My name is Oliver. I was an apprentice to Dean, your father. I was there when he…" He shifted and winced in pain, blood gushing between his fingers. "I tried to make him stop. I begged him, but he threatened to kill me. Zachary punished me every time I spoke up. I'm sorry for what they did to you."

"How… old were you?" Celina swallowed the lump in her throat.

"When he first brought you, I think you were maybe ten or eleven, so I must have been thirteen."

Celina shook her head. "You were a kid, too. You have nothing to apologize for."

"He certainly does," Kai rumbled from behind her.

Oliver's eyes turned to saucers. He inched to the side,

trying to escape Kai's wrathful gaze. Both Kai and Shiriki had changed to their demon forms. In the confined space with no way to escape, Celina understood the Venatore's terror.

"Kai, please stop. He's scared."

"And rightly so." He raised his hand, and the man's body flew up, pinning him against the wall. "I want to know what spell Dean put on Celina. And why?"

Oliver squirmed, his face paling.

"Kai! Let him go, please." Celina gripped his arm, shaking him. "No one can explain themselves when you're like this. It's terrifying."

His lips curled, and he turned his attention on her. "Speaking from experience, dove?"

"Yes." But she didn't waver. "Now, please put him down gently and let me talk to him. No more threats."

Oliver slid down the wall. As soon as his feet hit the floor, he pressed himself into the corner. "The… spell. Dark magic, something we're never supposed to use. Zachary learned it from a necromancer from the other world, Pyralis, but…"

Shiriki materialized next to him. "But what?"

He yelped and tried to run, but Shiriki grabbed a fistful of hair, wrenching him. "The necromancer…" He winced. "He said it was a spell from Oroth."

Kai snorted. "The Revenant Lord? He vanished over six thousand years ago. I doubt it came directly from that monster."

Celina's eyebrows rose. She'd never heard her husband call anyone a monster except himself. "Who's Oroth?"

"A powerful being. He always kept his power hidden, so no one knows how strong he was." Kai fixed his attention on Shiriki.

"Sound familiar, Your Majesty?" Shiriki asked with a grin.

Kai's eyes narrowed. "Please instigate me one more time. I am dying for an excuse to take away your little playthings."

Shiriki cringed, then bowed. "Noted." He turned to

Oliver, letting go of his hair. "As you said, I suppose it does not matter. Oroth is no more."

"What spell?" Kai demanded, taking a step closer to the Venatore. "Its name. Now."

"*Trado*. Zachary called it Trado."

Both Kai and Shiriki jerked, the reaction causing a shiver to crawl up Celina's spine.

Shiriki averted his gaze and murmured, "There is no reverting that spell."

Kai clenched his jaw, despair flashing behind his glower.

Shiriki turned to Celina, amusement vanishing from him. "It is a spell meant to destroy wherever you go. They use a host as a tool for destruction. It does not matter which world or realm you are in, you will inevitably drain it. Like a living poison."

Celina stared at her hands, and her shoulders slumped.

I'm a poison?

She was no good for anyone, anywhere. A cursed life of destroying whoever and whatever she loved. A monster. There was no reverting the spell by the man she'd believed was her real father. Someone she loved and trusted, only to find out he'd used her. Why did everyone end up betraying her? Was this her fault for being born?

Her mind flooded with images of Fenrir, and her throat tightened.

It's over.

Trying to not burst into tears, she asked, "Can... can you tell me why my stepfather did this?"

Oliver pressed his hand against his chest and winced. "Dean said you were half-demon. By the blood of one as powerful as him." He glanced at Shiriki. "Their opportunity to overthrow demons. He told Zachary he had your mother's permission to protect you, including using spells. Dean... he wanted to put *one of his own* into a place of power." He swallowed hard. "Apparently, your mother told Dean that

Mekaisto would try to claim you and bring you to his realm. He knew it would mean taking your soul, and he planned according to this assumption. Once you lost your soul, the spell would take over, and you would become a living time-bomb. Most members knew Mekaisto would have an interest in you, but only a few knew you ended up marrying him recently."

Tears blurred Celina's vision. Before anyone could stop her, she bolted from the room, running as fast as she could. There was no hope. It was over. Everything she'd fought for shattered beneath her as she tried to hold on to debris. The pain and joy. The fear and happiness. It was over.

I have been nothing but other people's tools. An experiment for Shiriki. A wife for Mekaisto. An assassin for my stepfather.

She slammed her hands against the doors leading outside and winced when they didn't budge. Instead, she turned toward the library. Once she reached her favorite reading nook, she slowed, her legs shaking. Leaning against the windowsill, she let her tears roll down her cheeks.

"Celina?" Kai said from behind her.

"I need to be alone."

"Oliver said more. You should know Dean never intended for you to die. He was supposed to reverse it once you destroyed my realm. Only the person who cast the spell can end it."

She turned to face him. "What happens to Oliver now?"

He cocked his head, amusement flashing across his gaze. "He dies."

"What? It's not his fault. He didn't have a choice."

"Then he should have died instead of working with them to kill my subjects."

She glared. "Is that what you'd want me to do? If they ever took me against my will, given the choice between spying for them or dying, I should choose death?"

He gritted his teeth. After a few seconds, he rolled his

eyes, raking his hand through his hair. "Humans and their moral logic."

"You don't need to kill him. Please, leave him be."

He stayed silent but then nodded. "I will interrogate the Venatores who were captured to find out if someone else besides Dean Perry put the spell on you. Perhaps Zachary was the one who did, and if it's the case..." He didn't sound hopeful.

She turned, looking out the window as the streetlamps in the distance blurred in orange starbursts.

It's not fair. I've never had a chance. I'm going to destroy a world or a realm, then die myself. And all because Dean wanted to use me. I'll never be a person to anyone, just a tool.

"That is not true, Celina."

"It is." She frowned. "What happens if I go to the Silence? Isn't it protected by strong magic?"

"You could not destroy that part of the realm, but eventually, it would drain *you* instead."

"Well, it's where I'll go then. I refuse to destroy somewhere that'll take the existence of anyone." She scoffed. "My failure would disappoint my stepfather. You know, dying for nothing and all."

He spun her. "I will not let you die."

"Face it, there's no way to reverse this spell without him and he's dead." She cupped his face. "I need to ask a favor."

"Celina—"

She pulled him close, burying her face in his chest. "Promise you'll take good care of Fenrir. I know a demon's love is a dangerous thing, but please, love him. For both of us. Give him the love he deserves and tell him his mother will always be so, so proud of him."

He withdrew, and her chest squeezed so tight, she was sure it would stop.

Tears rolled down Kai's face, and he cupped her cheek, leaning his forehead against her own. "I promise."

28

DANGEROUS WAY OUT

Kai drummed his fingernails against the wooden surface of the desk. He'd re-read the same paragraph too many times but still couldn't absorb any information. His wife preoccupied his mind—Celina, their son, their future together as a family. She was fated to die, and there was no solution in any of his tomes. He caused her so much pain, and for nothing.

Fenrir flashed through his mind, and he clenched his jaw. No, that wasn't true. She'd given him a child, and it was the greatest joy he'd ever felt. An emotion he didn't deserve to even glimpse.

He slammed the book shut, the room trembling under his building frustration. He'd given his subjects one task: find anyone who might have information about this Trado spell. Soon, Celina would need to go to the Silence to stop draining whichever world or realm she remained within. But it would destroy her.

A light bulb burst as his rage pulsed, and he gritted his teeth at the annoyance. Kai ran his hand across his face, sensing Shiriki approach before his second in command knocked on the door. "In," Kai snarled, his fingers curling, slicing through his skin as he gripped his hair.

The wounds healed as Shiriki entered, and although he arched an eyebrow, he didn't comment. "I have not seen this tome in quite some time," Shiriki said, pointing toward the dark-blue book. "Was this one not given to you by Zilar?"

"What does it matter?" Kai spat, bolting to his feet. A wave of energy blasted around him, sending everything on his desk smashing against nearby walls. "None of them have the answers I seek."

Shiriki crossed his arms. "Have you asked *him*?"

"I am not in any mood to deal with his egotistical ways."

"Coming from you, that is quite the insult," he said with an amused smile. "You may not care for him, but there is no denying he is well-versed in magic."

Kai wanted to shred Shiriki into tiny pieces as he stared into his smug expression but knew his second in command was right. The one person who'd have the answer to his question was *him*. And yet the very thought of the man grated on his nerves at the moment.

"Summon him to meet me in my dwelling. However, inform him this is a personal matter, and as such, I do not want him to divulge this meeting to anyone."

Shiriki bowed. "Consider it done."

Kai slumped into the chair once Shiriki vanished from the room. He avoided beings from the other world known as Pyralis; rarely did they have anything to do with his realm. But if what Oliver had told them was true, then a necromancer from Pyralis was the one who'd taught Dean Perry and Zachary Mackenzy the spell to begin with. Kai needed someone who was an expert on their magic, and although he wasn't looking forward to discussing his situation, Celina was worth every sacrifice.

Even if it meant speaking with Varek.

Kai threw his senses around as he stepped outside into his garden and strode to his meeting place. Varek sat at the table, chin resting against his knuckles as though already bored. As soon as his gaze locked with Kai, he smirked playfully.

Pulling out a chair, Kai took a seat across from Varek, allowing his power to seep from him freely. "I am surprised you agreed to meet so quickly."

"Not every day I get an invitation into your realm. Let alone your private dwelling." His blue irises gleamed. "I wouldn't miss the opportunity."

"You mean to request a favor?" Kai gave him a sardonic smile, and Varek half shrugged.

"I'm all for the old saying." He raised his hands, curving his fingers to look like claws. "You scratch my back, I scratch yours."

Kai scoffed. "What do you want, then?"

Varek reached into his jacket, and pulled out a rolled parchment, then placed it on the table. Without moving, Kai summoned the paper, and opened it. His gaze swept across a list, and he arched an eyebrow.

"Individuals to kill or protect?" Kai asked, rolling it.

"People to stay away from. You and your subjects." Varek picked a small piece of flint off his clothes, but iciness changed his irises to a pale blue. "Add these names to the little repertoire I know your second in command keeps. If I find out any demons go near them, we'll have problems."

Kai glowered. "Is that a threat?"

"I've started many wars, and well," he leaned his elbows against the surface, and grinned, "I've won them all."

Kai unleashed his power, and darkness slammed against Varek. Shadows coiled around his throat, tightening as Varek's magic pulsed in retaliation. Not wanting to damage his realm, Kai released him, and his guest sputtered as he tried catching his breath.

"No offense Mekaisto, but we don't have that kind of relationship. Besides, I do the choking. Not the other way around." He rubbed at his neck. "Kinky bastard," he muttered.

"I agree to your terms and will add the names to our list," Kai said darkly.

The vegetation surrounding the meeting place moved as he reeled in his powers once more and Varek did the same. The man was a mystery despite Kai having known him for years. Although, the only thing that mattered to Kai was the difference between ally and enemy. As it stood, Varek walked a fine line between both ever since they'd met.

Varek continued rubbing his skin as the lesions healed. "Now that we've shown our dicks, let's get to business."

Kai's lips twitched; the man was reckless and imbalanced. But he also didn't fear Kai, which was refreshing. In some ways, Varek reminded Kai of Shiriki.

"I have a source who informed me a Venatore was told by a necromancer—"

"Sounds like the start of a terrible joke, doesn't it?" Varek said with a laugh. "A Venatore, a necromancer, and you walk into the CrowBar—"

"Are you ever serious about anything?" Kai interjected as he ran his fingers through his hair, holding back the urge to dive into Varek's mind for answers instead.

"Serious? Me? Only when I have to be." Still, his smile vanished, and he leaned forward. "Does this perhaps have to do with your lovely wife?"

"Tread carefully," he hissed through his teeth.

"We both know you don't care for me. Though, one would never understand why since I am," he pressed his hand against his chest, "wonderful to be around." He chuckled at Kai's continued glare. "The only reason you'd summon me for a private meeting is if it was significant. I'm assuming your wife is important to you.

"Of course she is."

"If not her, then maybe this is about your son?" He lost his playfulness, and a true smile touched his lips. "Congratulations. Children are amazing gifts."

Kai searched his own memories, trying to recall Varek's family history, but he was so preoccupied with Celina, he couldn't focus on anything else.

"Thank you," he said quietly. Losing his wife tore at him, like the very core of him was rotting away.

Varek stared at him in silence for a few seconds. "What do you need my help with?"

"The necromancer taught a dark spell to a Venatore."

"I enjoy it so much when people spread dangerous teachings," Varek said with an exaggerated sigh that blew part of his black bangs away from his eyes. "Which?"

"One apparently learned from Oroth."

Varek's expression turned to stone and the white marble columns surrounding Kai's meeting area cracked. Kai had foreseen the reaction, considering the infamous history between Varek and Oroth, but the power pouring from the man sitting in front of him wasn't what Kai expected; it was stronger.

A slow smile curled Varek's lips, but it didn't reach his eyes. "Which spell?"

"Trado."

The pressure surrounding them outside vanished as Varek leaned back in the chair, staring up at the ceiling. Bright-red vines climbed the architecture, and he focused on a flower as its petals sparked with flames.

"Two ways to break it." Varek held up two fingers without looking away at the foliage. "One, I imagine you already know."

"The person who cast the spell died years ago," Kai said,

unable to contain his rage at the thought. Shiriki finally admitted to murdering Dean Perry and because of him, Celina was fated to die.

"Isn't that always the way?" Varek said, faint amusement crossing his features. He curled a finger, his index remaining up. "Well then, this leaves choice number two."

"Which is?" Kai snarled as his patience thinned.

"Dying."

The table flew to the side as Kai materialized in front of Varek. Kai grabbed the other man by his top, lifting him to his feet. His own red irises reflected in Varek's blue, turning them nearly purple.

"This is not a game," he spat, bringing him inches from his own face. "This is my wife's life. Her existence. I have caused her so much pain, lying to her for years so I could protect her. Everything I put her through to save my son. The thought of losing her…" Kai never had to breathe, and yet, it felt like something was choking him.

Rage poured from Kai in waves, but Varek didn't even flinch. Instead, he placed his hand over Kai's grip and smiled.

"The mind is quite a wonderful thing, isn't it?" When Kai remained silent, he continued, "It lets us know when a thing causes pain. Or when someone gives us joy." He pulled Kai's hands away from him, and once Kai let go, Varek straightened his shirt. "But it can also trick us. Convince us reality is a lie, and false memories to become the truth." Varek patted Kai on the arm and grinned. "You know what I mean. All you have to do now is act on it," he said with a shrug before walking away.

Kai stood in the middle of his meeting area, focused on the furniture lying amongst the ferns. He knew what Varek meant, but it wouldn't be easy.

This time, she won't forgive me.

29

DEATH

Celina watched as Fenrir slept, but when her neck prickled in warning, she spun. Shiriki stepped inside her temporary room of his seven-story building.

He smiled. "Mekaisto wishes to see you."

"I thought he'd gotten past the whole summoning thing." Celina glanced over her shoulder where her son slept. "Besides, I can't. Any reason he didn't come see me here in person instead of summoning me?"

He shrugged. "I will stay with the prince."

"Over my dead body."

His lips curled into a cruel smile. "Do not offer something you will not go through with, pet."

She glared at him. "I won't leave my son anywhere near you." She crossed her arms, taking a few steps back so she could be closer to her son in case Shiriki tried getting at him. "Why can't I bring Fenrir with me?"

Shiriki ran his fingers through his pale hair. "You are being rather difficult." In the blink of an eye, he materialized in front of her, grabbing her wrist. "You will come with me now, or I will drag you by force."

"Let go. I'm not leaving my child."

"Sometimes, leaving your child behind *is* the safest choice." He pulled her close, the shimmering in his irises blinding.

Before she could argue, he swung her over his shoulder and left the room.

"Stop! Put me down." She kicked and punched, but it didn't faze him.

He walked past Nalie who stood frozen in her steps, her eyes widening before she rushed toward Celina's room.

At least Fenrir won't be alone.

He dropped her to the floor, and she staggered to stand, backing away. She glared at him, wanting to throw all the curses at him, but he pointed over her shoulder, and she spun.

The barren wall was so at odds with the rest of what she'd seen of the dwelling. The interior was built of dark wood and had decorations. This was a white canvas.

Shiriki placed his hand against it and murmured a few words in Demos. He took a few steps back as veins spread across the wall. They coiled into strange spirals and familiar symbols, forming a black door. It opened on its own, and a terrible pressure surged from the other side.

She swallowed hard, glancing from Shiriki to the darkness. He stayed silent.

Her neck prickled as she stepped through the doorframe, jumping as the door slammed behind her. The ominous silence tugged at her core, yet she walked straight ahead into pitch darkness.

Light flashed ahead, as though an image came into focus. She approached it, squinting as her vision blurred. Pressing her hand against her mouth, she muffled a scream as she stared at Thomas's corpse, tied to a chair, blood streaming out of a bullet hole through his head.

Bringing her hands to her head, she squeezed her eyelids shut. "What… no! Stop!"

She fell to her knees, except, she hit nothing solid. Her scream caught inside her throat, and she fell, and fell…

She let out a shuddering breath. Heaviness settled in her limbs as she lay there, her chest aching with every beat. Tree branches wavered in the wind, darkness surrounding her with only the stars above.

Where am I?

The ground was cold against her back, branches and twigs digging into her. Her side throbbed, sending a shooting pain, and she pressed her hand against it. Warm liquid soaked her hands, and she brought it up closer to her face, the smell of copper bringing bile to the back of her throat. Blood.

Her brain scrambled to catch up.

I'm back where I started. Why?

She was dying all over again, the bullet lodged inside her. Staring up toward the black tree looming over her, she frowned. Red eyes had looked down at her last time.

But it was empty. No one was there to save her.

Her hand traced along her neck to the mark Kai had left during their lovemaking, but her skin was smooth. There was nothing there.

What was happening? Why was everything different this time? A branch cracked in the distance, and she tilted her head to the side. Her skull pounded, the pressure behind her eyes blinding her for a second. She slid her hand higher and hissed through her teeth as her fingers connected with a deep gash. Light flashed between the trees, and she squinted.

"Found anything?" a woman's voice called out.

Celina's heart hammered as she recognized it. Emily Pierce.

No. It can't be. I killed her. Got my revenge. Everything was… over.

Celina remembered pointing the gun at the back of Emily's head, not wanting to see Emily's eyes as life left her.

"No." Wayne's voice echoed inside the woods. "But I'm sure you shot her, so she'll die out here. Let's go."

Emily's husband. Shiriki killed him. He can't be here. This isn't real.

Celina remembered how Shiriki had rammed his hand through Wayne's stomach, murdering him where he'd stood.

The light between the tree trunks vanished, the footsteps moving farther until silence surrounded Celina once more. A throb sent a shock of pain to her side, and she pressed both hands against the gunshot wound as blood ran between her fingers.

She stared up at the tree, waiting for Kai. The branches wavered and cracked in the wind, but no one was there. She was alone.

Did I… imagine everything?

Tears streamed down her skin, and the pain in her chest worsened with every breath. The image of her husband tied to a chair, motionless, flashed into her mind. Her mouth went dry, and she pressed her lips together to stop from throwing up.

Had she imagined everything to cope with his death? Her body grew colder as images of Kai flew through her head. Had he been real? Was the love she felt from him a lie? And what about their son? Fenrir had to be real. She remembered holding him in her arms, the warmth of his tiny body against her.

"No… it's not… true."

How could it have all been lies?

She coughed, and blood splattered from her mouth, trickling down her chin. Her pulse slowed as pressure built in her chest.

"Kai?" She looked up at the tree, tears blurring her vision. "Please… come back."

But nobody came. With one last deep breath, her heart stopped. Darkness enveloped her.

ASHES TO ASHES, DUST TO DUST

Celina felt nothing, as though she was floating. No light, no air. She saw nothing. Even her thoughts were light, like they'd fly away on her.

What… is going on?

Warmth cocooned her, but she didn't seem to have a body. Not even a heartbeat. Images flew through her head, although she wasn't sure she had one anymore.

I'm thinking, so I must.

A baby's face floated in her line of sight, but he vanished as quickly, and she couldn't remember who it had been. The image returned, and she focused, her mind catching up. Fenrir. Her son. She hadn't imagined him. He was real. Her baby. Thomas' death—Mekaisto. Her husband. The information she'd learned from a Venatore about her stepfather, all lies. Infiltrating the members' headquarters and seeing Namika. How could that have happened? Celina died. Yet the memory of Kai renewing their vows… how could that have not been real? Kai was Thomas, no?

No. I died that night. Under my tree. None of these memories are real.

This was it. Her life had drained out of her as she'd waited for help, but no one ever came. Kai didn't exist. Never had. Her baby boy, a hopeful figment of her imagination. The child she'd wanted so much with her husband. But it had vanished when Thomas died. When Celina was killed too.

She waited, unaware of any time passing. How long would she hover like this? Was she in some purgatory for having even thought of making a deal for revenge with the devil? Had it been a test of faith?

None of it was real.

Would there be a tunnel of light? Her mother waiting for her? Would Thomas be there? Would he be angry at what she'd imagined? Disappointed?

A blinding light flashed, and Celina felt herself moving toward it, pulled by some invisible force. Her mother appeared, and she couldn't help but smile. It had been so long since she'd seen her.

Mom.

But blood streamed along her mother's face, her green eyes widening in fear as her face melted, and then she disappeared in a shriek. Celina wanted to scream but didn't have a voice.

Shiriki appeared instead, a cruel smile curling his lips, reaching forward to maim, and…

Celina bolted upright, panting. She was inside the bedroom at Shiriki's dwelling.

I'm back here? I don't even know what the hell is real anymore.

She pressed against where the bullet wound had pierced through her but found Kai's brand. Her memories washed over her in tidal waves, and she gripped her head.

Everything had been real. Losing her soul, the Venatores, her stepfather being one of them… She shuddered, then let out a bitter laugh. Both her biological father and stepfather were psychopaths, but only Dean had no problems hurting a child. Her mother sure knew how to pick them.

A shiver ran through Celina as the last of her memories

returned. Powerful magic lingered within, and anger filled her when she recognized it.

Kai.

He had done this to her. Making her believe she was shot and left for dead after they murdered Thomas… as though everything after that had been a figment of her imagination. That she had died alone under the black tree.

Yeah, I know how to pick them, too.

The basket-like crib caught her attention and tears blurred her vision. "You're still here Fenrir."

Swinging her legs over the bed, she went to where her son slept, her chest tightening when she found it empty.

"Fenrir?" She looked around, but when she couldn't find him, she rushed to the door.

A loud knock stopped her in her tracks, and she froze. Slowly, she approached and opened it. Fear trickled through her as she stared at Kai in his lowest demon form. Still, resentment won over.

"Where's my son?"

If he was fazed by her not saying *their* son, he didn't show it. "Nalie is with Fenrir. She will bring him in a few minutes."

"Then leave me alone." She slammed the door in his face but jumped back a few steps when he materialized inside the room.

"What was the point in knocking in the first place?"

"Still as feisty as ever."

"I want you to leave."

"I know you are angry—"

"You think?" she shouted. "And let me guess, you had to do it because you're a demon and it's in your nature. Yeah, heard that one before, and I'm sick and tired of it."

She expected him to react the same as he had every other time he'd hurt her for good reasons, but she assumed wrong.

So very wrong.

Her blood seemed to freeze in her veins as a dark expression shattered all gentleness she'd ever known from him. Even his playful cruelty vanished. Instead, she was left with something close to what Kai truly was.

The Devil.

He stalked toward her, and she dashed for the door, but the way out vanished. Turning, Celina pressed her back against the wall as he closed the gap between them. Although he didn't touch her, his burning glare pinned her to the spot.

"You. Were. Going to. Die." He bit out the words, one by one. The room turned pitch black, the only light coming from the hearth. "I found out the only way to break this spell was to kill the host. That meant having to break into your mind." He took a step closer. "Are you aware of what it takes to shatter a mind, Celina?"

She gritted her teeth. "You made me think everything that had happened had been another one of your lies. Do you know how that feels? Thinking you were never real? Thinking Fenrir never existed? I might not have died out there all alone, but it sure as hell felt like it."

"I needed to make you believe you died. Twist your mind into doubting itself so I could shatter the walls within." His pupils thinned. "You still have a beating heart as you did before, but your mind is a powerful tool. It believed you died, and this broke the spell. They cannot use you any longer. You will kill no one now."

"I wouldn't be too sure about that," she muttered through gritted teeth.

The ghost of a smile touched his lips. "Celina—"

"What about everything with the Venatores, killings, and that supposed angel?"

"The rest is business I will take care of," he said in a growl. "As for you… I did what I had to."

Anger continued boiling inside her, and she shot him a glare. "How nice of you to be so kind."

He leaned both hands on the wall at either side of her

head, nose to nose with her. "I told you. I did it to break the spell."

She crossed her arms, wanting to put some kind of barrier between them. Breaking the spell should've been good news; she didn't have to leave her family behind. But the way Kai had done it and the brutality of tearing her mind as he did… it was too much. Her fury with him pulsed inside her like a lingering poison.

"So now what?"

"I searched your mind and looked into the memories recovered." As though remembering them, a wave of energy crashed through the room. She pressed her hands against the wall, trying to keep upright. "You will no longer poison any realm or world. You are safe." He grasped her hands. "You can be with Fenrir in my realm. Is that not what you wanted?"

"Don't change the subject. I'm talking about the Venatores. But once again, I'll be left in the dark about what's going on because you won't let me help anymore. My plan got us in, and I'm sure—"

"Yes, your plan worked out so well," he muttered.

She could barely think straight with the anger coursing through her. "Fine. Deal with everything on your own."

He took a step back as the room reverted. His expression gentled, but she kept away from him. "Celina, please. I am sorry." He reached her before she moved again and cupped her face slowly as though terrified she'd slap him away. "Are… you all right? Are *we* all right?"

For the first time since meeting him, he sounded nervous.

Her mind flashed to when she died, alone in the woods behind their house. Thinking Kai never existed and that their son was a figment of her imagination. Kai had hurt her beyond what she could forgive. "There is no *we*. Not now. I…." She took a deep breath, tears stinging her eyes. "I need a break." She strode away from him and stopped near the window. If she stayed too close to him, her resolve would break, and she'd fall apart in his arms, seeking the comfort he always gave her. And yet, he was often the cause of that initial pain.

She glanced over her shoulder, trying to swallow the lump as she stared at his back. He didn't move for what seemed like a long time, and then the door reappeared. "If that is what you need."

Tears blurred her vision as he left. She slid down the wall, wrapping her arms around herself, thinking of their son as sobs wracked her body.

She clutched at her chest, unable to breathe. Why did he have to be so cruel? All the love in the world couldn't heal what he'd done. Yet, he loved her. She knew that without any doubt. But was it enough?

Memories flooded in as she pushed her face against her knees, crying until her eyes burned. The time he'd taken her out to a fundraiser, and they'd danced most of the evening, lost in each other's gaze. The thoughtful presents that weren't always material; for one Christmas, he'd read her favorite book as they cuddled on the sofa. Little acts meant to bring a smile to her lips. Even as Kai, he'd shown gentleness. Holding their son. Doing everything he could to protect them.

But when was love no longer enough to counter the hurt in a relationship? He'd lied to her for so long, and although she forgave him for it, the memories still stung. Leaving her with Shiriki, alone and pregnant, without a word? She was terrified and confused after waking up from the attack; why couldn't Kai have taken the time to leave a note? Explain things? No, because Kai had to do everything his way.

She clenched her jaw.

His way.

It had always been like that. Whether it was Kai or Thomas didn't matter. Secretive and only ever letting her in just enough that she wouldn't complain. Just enough she'd tolerate it because that's what a good wife did.

Her hands curled into fists, but when she glanced at the door, emptiness filled her. Kai had left to give her the space she asked for. Despite the sadness in his voice, he'd respected her wishes. He had done the worst time and time again all to save her, their son… their family.

Why does it hurt so much?

31

FATHERLY ADVICE

Celina walked through the gardens of Shiriki's private courtyard in silence. The place was walled up, but with all the cherry trees and flowers, she forgot she was trapped. She pressed Fenrir closer to her chest, smiling at him.

Eire visited with Brihan, and along with Nalie, all three followed close to her, speaking between themselves. Celina had grown fond of Eire since she had helped Celina and Namika after Ancus had attacked them, so the company of the group was welcome.

A few days had passed since she'd put a break on her relationship with her husband, and she needed distractions. She sighed for what felt like the hundredth time.

Nalie glanced at her, then rolled her eyes. "You made a mistake, no?"

"Want to tell me how you really feel?" Celina glared at the Viscus. They were his subjects, not hers, so they came to his defense.

Brihan cleared his throat. "Do you want my opinion?"

"Not so much."

Eire grinned and chimed in. "You had already set your

mind on ending things before you found out why he did what he did. In the heat of anger, you stuck to the decision out of stubbornness." When Celina opened her mouth to reply, Eire held up her hand. "It's understandable, but also rash."

Celina stopped, staring up at the cherry blossom tree overhead. "You don't understand. None of you do. And on top of it, he's your king. Of course, you'll side with him."

Brihan shook his head. "I don't side with him about everything. Sometimes, he's way too punitive."

Nalie flipped her platinum blonde hair to the side. "He may be my king, but there are many decisions I have never supported either. Take Shiriki, for example; he would have perished thousands of years ago if I had my way."

"We agree on that. Maybe we could form a 'Shiriki should die' group or something?" Celina suggested with a tiny, solemn grin.

Eire pressed her lips together, trying not to laugh, but Nalie and Brihan didn't hold back.

"I feel," an amused voice interjected from behind them, "the name should have more spunk."

They all spun at once, staring at Shiriki.

Nalie crossed her arms. "Why is it every time anyone speaks of you, you appear?"

"Talent?" he quipped with a grin.

Celina swallowed hard, staring at him as Brihan took a step back.

Nalie moved closer to Celina. "Why are you here?"

"To speak with Celina." Shiriki beckoned her.

"Not a chance," Celina said.

Nalie let some of her energy loose. "She will go nowhere with you."

"Do not try ordering me." His tone turned icy, and Nalie flinched. "I believe it is not uncommon for a father to speak with his daughter about leaving her husband."

Silence hung heavy, Nalie averting her gaze as Brihan and Eire turned to face Celina.

Brihan gaped. "Seriously? Is he serious?"

"He's your father?" Eire whispered.

"Biologically." Celina glared at him.

Why the hell did he bring it up?

Shiriki waved his hand dismissively. "We can go somewhere quiet to speak."

"Pretty sure I already refused." Her neck prickled, knowing he wouldn't take no for an answer. She glanced at Fenrir, worried he might hurt her baby to make her compliant.

When she raised her head, she flinched, surprised to find herself nose to nose with Shiriki. He stared at her son for a second. "I will not harm him."

"Glad to know you have a conscience when it comes to your grandson," she mumbled. Pressing her lips together, she cursed herself. Since when had she admitted any link to him? Especially when it came to her child?

He didn't comment, but his irises glowed whiter. "We will speak. Your choice how."

She turned to her friends. "I'll be back."

Brihan shot a sideways glance at Shiriki. "This is not a good idea."

Despite the cold chill going through her, Celina forced a smile. "It's fine." She waved her hand at Shiriki. "Lead the way. I want to get this over with."

He chuckled and made his way toward the path leading to more cherry trees. Celina glanced over her shoulder as Nalie, Brihan, and Eire walked away, then she followed Shiriki.

Cherry trees with different hues of pink swayed in the wind, the smell of flowers rich in the air. Moss climbed the bark, and Celina could smell the humid vegetation surrounding them. Ottawa was always damp during summer months, and she guessed he kept the cherry trees blooming with magic.

Once she caught up to him, she kept a good distance, watching his back.

"It will be difficult to speak with you back there."

"I don't care. I'm not coming any closer." She yelped when he materialized inches from her, and she nearly collided into him. She shifted Fenrir against her other shoulder, wanting him out of reach.

"You think distance would make any difference if I wanted to harm you?" He turned and continued walking.

She clenched her jaw before walking next to him. A cooling breeze pushed her hair aside, the ground beneath her feet uneven with spongy moss. She kept some space between them; he was right, but she liked the illusion of safety.

"What did you want to talk about?"

"The potential for ending your relationship with Mekaisto."

She stopped in her tracks as a bird chirped nearby. "Are you kidding me? I thought it was a joke. I'm not discussing it with you."

"Then how about we talk about your mother?" he asked.

Her heart hammered. "What about her?"

"You must be angry with her, after finding out the truth," he said with a shrug, not looking at her.

She frowned. "Why would I be?"

"She put you in harm's way." He turned toward her. "Now, now, there is no need to be so protective. What she did was terrible. She let a man she knew to be a Venatore with experience in black magic put spells on you."

Celina stiffened, resisting the urge to kick him. "That's not what Oliver said, and you know it. She agreed to let him help—"

"But she must have known what it would mean. Spells that can protect against demons are dark."

"She did it to protect me!"

"As did Mekaisto when he needed to break your mind to make you think you died."

She opened and closed her mouth, unsure what she even wanted to say. Instead, she fell silent, thinking of his words.

Her mother had let her new husband hurt Celina to keep her safe from the demons after her. The lesser of two evils. The only way Kai could break the spell was to make her believe she died. He faced a terrible choice, like when she'd gotten pregnant.

Shiriki seemed to follow her thoughts. "If your son was going to vanish and the one way to save him was to drain his blood in a painful manner, what would you do?" He took a step closer, and she didn't move. "Would you let him die, or would you hurt him, knowing he may resent you forever?"

She rubbed her son's back, staring into his bright yellow eyes. "I would… hurt him and live with the guilt. As long as he was alive and safe, even if he hated me, I'd love him." At her words, her chest squeezed.

He continued along the path. "You should have thought of that before you made a rash decision." Poison laced his tone.

Her hands curled into fists. "Why do you care whether I'm with Kai?"

In the blink of an eye, he was standing in front of her again. "Because being separated from the one you love hurts beyond all pain." He drew back, his expression guarded. "Or so I have been told."

Is he talking about my mom?

"I already told you it is complicated."

"You read minds like Kai?"

He smirked. "Your expressions are easy to read, pet."

"I told you not to call me that," she said through gritted teeth.

He plucked a blossom from the tree and watched it as it glowed white. "You have a chance to fix things. For the rest of

Mekaisto's existence, he will spend eternity trying to fix what he broke: your trust and love. How long will you make him punish himself for what he had to do?"

"What... what happened the day of my parents' car accident?" she asked quietly. He stared at her, the glowing blossom reflected within his cold stare. "Please tell me." She took a few tentative steps toward him but froze when he smirked.

"You do not need to know more than you already do."

A lump squeezed her throat at the memory of her mother hugging Celina before she'd left that day.

"I deserve the truth, don't I?" she whispered, tears blurring her vision.

The blossom caught fire and fell to ashes on the pathway. "The truth is sometimes much worse than the lies. Of all people, you should know that."

Without another word, he vanished.

32

WITHOUT WORDS

Celina tossed and turned, unable to get to sleep. Fenrir never woke during the night anymore so she couldn't use the distraction. After her conversation with Shiriki, she'd gone through the rest of the evening on autopilot, unable to focus on anything except what they spoke about. The doubts about her decision to take a break were all she could think of. And once in bed, they didn't ease up; guilt continued flooding her.

She sat up and groaned.

Grabbing the paper she'd set aside, she continued reading the page she had torn out of the tome from the Venatores' headquarters. The few artifacts listed didn't mean much until she stopped on the description of a talisman.

They described it as having a white quartz stone shaped in a half-moon encircling a ruby shaped like a drop of blood. It could drain magic from most beings.

Didn't I see this in the stuff Hilda was bringing to Shiriki's storage? In Kemptville, I think.

With a frustrated sigh, she put the page back. She got to her feet. Rubbing her arms, she walked across her bedroom, then opened the door. Nalie was leaning on the wall across, her icy-blue irises glowing.

"Late to be going out," she noted with a grin.

She wished she had a robe to cover herself better; the material of her nightgown was thin. "I need to speak with my husband. Do you know where he is?"

"He went to the private chambers Shiriki provided him." A knowing look flashed across her face, but she didn't comment. "Last doors at the end of the hallway."

"My son is—"

"No one will get in this room, and if he wakes, I will send Hilda to find you while I tend to him."

"Thank you."

Celina made her way to Kai's bedroom, all the while trying to think of why she was going. *What will I even say?*

The large silver doors came in sight, and she slowed, clutching her chest. Deciding she'd never feel brave enough to face him, she pushed opened the door, needing to get it over with.

The room was empty.

Stepping inside, she closed the door behind her, shivering. The balcony doors were open, the scent of cherry blossoms lingering in the air as the wind blew the curtains to the sides. Every movement and shadow caused her to jump. She assumed he wasn't in the room since she couldn't feel his energy but remembered how he could suppress it at will.

She made her way farther into the room, glancing out onto the balcony, but he wasn't there either.

Where is he at this hour?

The demon who had taunted Celina about Mekaisto's sleeping arrangements rang through her mind. Celina had told him their relationship was on hold; had he sought comfort with his favorite Viscus back in his realm? Was he with her now?

Her stomach clenched at the thought, and she swallowed the lump in her throat. Her chest hurt so much, she clutched at it, hoping she would just die.

"Mekaisto?" she called out, her voice cracking in a half-sob. Saying his real name felt wrong, but she'd lost the right to call him anything else after what she said to him.

His energy slammed against her so hard, she staggered. Her chest heaved as she stared, but frowned when she couldn't see him. She looked higher and froze when she spotted him, sitting in the crook of the high ceiling. The strange metallic beams on the ceiling slithered, but he sat, unmoving, his red glare burning into her.

In one quick movement, he flew and landed inches from her. Before she could take a few steps away, he grasped the back of her neck, holding her. His jaw clenched. She could feel him breathing hard as he stared at her. Cruelty flashed through his eyes, his pupils thinning.

She couldn't utter a single word. Raw emotions flew through her mind faster than she could make sense of them.

He placed his free hand against her hip, his thumb tracing along her nightgown. As the cloth moved higher, he slid his hand lower, his fingers gliding along her bare skin. She shivered at his touch, unable to look away from him. Her hand shook as she placed it on his bare chest, and it was all the permission he seemed to need. He slanted his mouth over hers, kissing her hard. Violent, possessive, and furious.

His hand climbed higher, and he cupped her breast, squeezing hard until she gasped into his mouth. She dug her fingers into his shoulders and arched against him.

The balcony doors behind him slammed shut, and she withdrew, taking a step back and panting as he let her go. His gaze turned animalistic as he advanced on her, and she continued backing away. She couldn't help but remember when she had attacked him, and he'd stared at her the same way. The way a predator tracked his prey.

When her knees hit the edge of the bed, she froze, and so did he. For what seemed like an eternity, they stared at each other.

I hate him. I need him. I love him.

Grabbing the hem of her nightgown, she pulled it over her head and dropped it on the floor next to her. His gaze raked over her naked body, and the dark energy coiling around him exploded.

Her knees buckled, and she sat on the edge of the mattress. He stalked toward her but stopped short as if fighting himself for control. He seemed to be losing.

His pants vanished in smoke, and he loomed over her, silent. He leaned forward, wrapping his arm around her before straightening, pulling her to her feet. Pressing his body against hers, he slid his fingers along her spine. Her breath hitched at his hungry stare like he wanted nothing better than to devour every inch of her.

He took off, still holding her, and she screamed, wrapping her arms and legs around him, burying her face in his neck. Her stomach seemed to plunge as they moved higher, and she gasped when he sat her on the edge of a nook within the wall. She withdrew just enough to glance down at the floor with wide eyes at how high they were. His wings hovered mid-air, the smoke swirling.

Grasping a fistful of her hair, he tilted her head back, exposing her neck. She trembled as she waited, but instead of biting like last time, he slid his tongue across her skin. He continued to trail down to her chest, kissing and nipping. She gripped the metal beams above her, terrified of falling as he lowered himself.

He grabbed her legs, placed them over his shoulder, and lapped at her wetness.

She moaned, her hands darting to his head and running through his hair, almost cutting herself against his horns. Pressing his face more firmly between her thighs, he sucked at her clit until she cried out, her toes curling. As he continued licking and sucking at her sensitive nub, his pointed fingernails dug into her hips. He sank his teeth into her inner thigh, and a hot piercing flash of pain ran through her before he thrust his tongue into her wet opening. Waves of pleasure flooded through her, and she tightened her grip on his hair.

As soon as she let go, he flew inches away from her face. The glower caused his irises to turn blood red, and behind it, wrath. A rage so strong she could feel it radiating off him. At the thought he hated her, tears blurred her vision, and he withdrew. He landed on the floor with Celina in his arms, let her go, and took a step back.

Without words, she knew he was giving her the choice to leave, the chance to stop if she didn't want this. If she didn't want him.

"Can… I stay?" she whispered, the lump in her throat painful.

A growl vibrated through his chest, and he pointed over her shoulder. "Lie on the bed and spread your legs."

She swallowed hard and stiffened to keep from trembling. He was so angry; she was terrified of what would happen next. Still, without hesitation, she went to his bed and lay on it. She did as he said but wrapped her arms over her breasts, vulnerable as he stood at the end of the bed, his gaze raking over her.

He crawled onto the mattress, his muscles rippling under his skin as he moved like a predator. As he lowered himself onto her, she pressed her knees against his hips, trying not to shake so much. Leaning against one arm, he took her chin between his finger and thumb, tracing her lower lip. The act was so gentle, she blinked back tears, but some rolled into her hair. His lips brushed hers, and he kissed her, cupping her face as though trying to maintain as much contact as possible.

His cocks pressed against her, and a throbbing desire pooled in her stomach. He slid his hand along the side of her body until he reached her thighs and spread her legs farther apart. Without ever breaking their kiss, he thrust his cocks into her, and she cried out against his mouth, grasping his biceps.

Time seemed suspended as he withdrew an inch, staring at her. She panted, the feeling of him filling her, warming her to her core. Then, he pulled out slowly and slammed in again. She moaned, lifting her hips to meet each thrust, running her hands along his arms. His wings came down on both sides, caressing her arms. When she arched her back, he wrapped his arm underneath her, holding tight as he continued the slow rhythm. He kissed her again, swallowing every moan and whimper.

They'd had intense sex, but this… this was different. It felt as though this was the final time.

At the thought of losing him, her throat closed, and tears streamed down the side of her face as her lips parted with a sob. He froze, his gaze searching her own.

"I'm… sorry. Please. I…" She could barely speak, choking on every sob. "I… love you, Kai."

He pressed his forehead against hers. This close, she could see flecks of black in his irises. "I'll always love you, Celina." His voice was husky, the anger in his tone gone now. "Stay with me. Please."

"Yes." She cupped his face with her hands and lifted her mouth to his, kissing him.

Their lips parted when he thrust into her, his rhythm increasing in speed and ferocity. She shut her eyelids tight as she cried out his name, lifting her hips higher so he could sheathe himself deeper.

"Look at me." His voice was rough, and she opened her eyes. With his forehead pressed against hers, he raised himself on his knees, pumping harder. He slid his fingers between her wet lips, and she gasped, so close to the edge. "I want to see your expression when you come for me, Celina." He rubbed her clit, and she screamed, rocking against an exploding orgasm. With a groan, he pressed his mouth against her neck and sank his fangs into her skin. Ripples of ecstasy flooded through her, and she climaxed as his cocks pulsated.

He pulled out, and she whimpered, pressing her face against the crook of his neck. Rolling to the side, he pulled her against his chest, holding her tight as she burst into tears. The cruel words she'd said to him repeated inside her mind without mercy. Every syllable she'd used to tear him apart for something he never wanted to do, when he had no other choice. The trembling in his voice when he had asked if they were okay and she'd shot him down.

She pictured herself in his position; if he had said those things to her, she would've gotten on her knees to beg him not to leave her. But she had done exactly that. She had accused him of being cruel, when she had been just as bad.

"I have you." He continued whispering sweet words, rubbing her back.

When she shivered, blankets materialized over them both. "I'm… I'm sorry. Can you forgive me?"

She held her breath, waiting. What if he said no? She hadn't forgiven him at first, refusing to look past her own hurt feelings. And yet, the intensity of their lovemaking had filled her with every memory of their time together, all the wonderful events that outweighed the bad. Kai held her like he never wanted to let go; she felt so loved, and the idea of losing that feeling—that safety—churned her stomach.

He pulled her closer and buried his face against the crook of her neck. His breath was shallow, and his muscles were stiff as he held her closer. "There is nothing to forgive, dove. You have every right not to trust me after all the lies." Something wet dropped against her skin and rolled down her back. "I am so sorry."

She pressed her face into his chest, holding him tight, and hoping he felt safer—as she felt with him.

We'll be okay.

33

THE SOURCE

Celina watched as Fenrir slept, safe in his father's arms. It was rare Kai went to sleep at all, but with all the massacres, it was draining him. She thought maybe it was because Fenrir himself absorbed his parents' energy as he grew, and even the great king wasn't so immune.

Or maybe it's by choice.

More bodies, both demon and human, were being found daily. In the last one, Venatores were amongst the victims. Apparently, some didn't want to continue, and they were killed for the betrayal.

The last message was clear: they would attack the dark realm soon. And knowing that, Celina was better involved. This was her family's home, and she would protect it.

She wasn't ready to go to sleep herself yet, so she went downstairs. She felt strange wandering around Shiriki's dwelling. Not so long ago, she would have avoided this place like the plague. But lately, it was a haven of sorts.

When she missed a step going downstairs, she slammed into the wall and winced as something hard pressed against her thigh. She slipped her hand into her pants pocket and frowned as she pulled out the obsidian shard.

"Forgot about you," she muttered.

She had grabbed the shard, wanting to ask Hilda about it. The woman seemed to know a lot about artifacts, and Celina needed to know more about the thing.

Once downstairs, she caught sight of Hilda standing in the lobby's doorway. The evening had come, but a warm breeze flitted through, and Celina smiled as she approached.

"It's a nice night," Celina said, stepping outside and standing next to the caretaker.

Hilda nodded. "It is. Sometimes, I like to stand here, and just… be outside. It's peaceful if you can learn to shut off all the city noises."

Celina wanted to ask Hilda about her life. Wanted to know if she'd ever regretted her decision to make a deal with Shiriki. Before she thought of how to ask, someone across the street waved in their direction.

"Oh, good," Hilda returned the wave. "Emanuel is back."

Celina squinted and recognized the security guard usually standing at the door. She frowned, wondering why the other guard wasn't here if one had left. Her neck prickled as Hilda smiled at her, red flags causing Celina's heart to hammer.

As she turned to Emanuel, Hilda pressed her hand over Celina's mouth, muffling her scream as the guard transformed.

Rupert. The Venatore she'd met back at the headquarters.

Celina shook her head, trying to free herself from Hilda.

No. It can't be Hilda. She wouldn't betray me like this.

She tried calling out to Kai mentally, but her arms glowed with the white symbols Jacob and Namika had put on her, and Celina's eyes widened.

Rupert laughed. "You don't think we planned this?"

They dragged her toward an alleyway near Shiriki's dwelling. Celina's breath caught when she spotted Hilda on the ground, tied and gagged.

What the…

Rupert pointed at Hilda. "If you make a sound, I hurt her. We know she can't die because she made a deal with a monster, but she can still suffer." He took out a dagger. "Do you want me to cut her up into little pieces?"

Celina shook her head, and the person holding her pushed her onto Rupert. He spun her around, putting his hand over her mouth. "Careful, Zoe. I almost didn't grab her in time."

The woman with black hair rolled her eyes, and Celina guessed she was another member.

Zoe grinned. "Clever spell, no? Cloaking. Doesn't last long, but does the trick."

Celina cursed, but Rupert's hand muffled it. She had the incredible urge to bite down but didn't want Hilda to suffer for it.

Zoe placed her hand on Celina's forehead, and pressure built until Celina squeezed her eyes tight from the discomfort. It vanished, and Celina blinked a few times as the hand covering her mouth slipped away. She wanted to open her mouth to say something, but it was as though she'd taken a back seat to her mind.

Her breathing came in steady, and she could still stand, and walk, but it wasn't by her own will.

Rupert laughed. "I love this spell. Makes people compliant for a while." He took out his cellphone. "We have to go."

Zoe nodded, and grabbed hold of Celina, pulling her toward the street. She glanced over her shoulder. "Make sure you don't leave until that one has been brought somewhere. We don't want anyone discovering her."

"Yeah, yeah. Just get to Kemptville on time."

Zoe hailed a cab, and she pushed Celina inside before getting in after her. "Bus terminal."

The drive didn't take long, and the whole time, Celina focused on one thing: Kemptville. Hilda had been bringing some of Shiriki's valuable objects to storage south of the city in that village. Had the Venatores found out?

She made a plan. If they brought her to the storage place, maybe she could grab the artifact that drained magic without being noticed. Then, once she had it, all she would need to do is get close to Jacob one more time.

Before long, Celina and Zoe strode inside the station, heading to an available counter.

The woman didn't even glance up from examining her nails. "How may I help you?"

Zoe squinted at the screen hanging behind the woman announcing the times and departures. "Two tickets for the bus heading to Kemptville."

The woman stared up at them. "The next one leaves in thirty minutes."

"We'll take it, please." Zoe glanced around the station as though expecting something to jump out and kill her. Celina couldn't help but hope Kai would show up and do just that.

Celina pressed her lips together. *No.* She had the opportunity to get that talisman, and then they'd probably bring her to Jacob. This could be her chance to stop them.

The woman glanced up, typing on her computer as the ticket printed. "Do you have any luggage to check?"

"No, we're good."

"You'll board at gate thirteen." She took Zoe's money, gave her the two tickets, and returned to her nail file.

With their tickets in hand, Zoe pulled Celina to the line, and they stood, waiting at the gate. Celina shot her a glare, and Zoe just grinned.

Soon enough, the station bustled, and they could board. Most seats were taken, but two were left at the front so they sat, Celina on the window side. The smell of perfume irritated Celina's nose, and she wanted to scream, but couldn't move of her own free will. She squinted to read the graffiti etched into the metal by the side of the window, trying to focus on something else.

Kai had planned to bring her and their son back to his realm in the morning since Fenrir was growing weaker. He'd already stayed too long in the human world and needed to get back. She pressed her lips together, hoping he'd take their son back before trying to look for her.

After about fifteen minutes, her eyelids drooped, and she leaned her head against the smudged window. The rocking motion lulled the stress away, even for a few seconds, as she plunged into a strange dream.

Celina stood inside her parents' cottage, her back against the wall, listening.

Her stepfather's tone sounded excited, and something in the pit of her stomach rolled. "Is it true then? Is Celina's biological father a demon?"

"Keep your voice down!" her mother hissed. "That letter was private, Dean. You had no right to read it."

He scoffed. "What does it matter? Is it true?"

"And what if it is?"

Celina was numb.

A demon. My father is a demon? Are the Lumen teachings true? Am I a monster?

"Is it why you married me? Because a Venatore would have a better chance of protecting you from demons?" he asked.

"I care for you, so I won't lie. And I won't pretend I love you either, but I think you knew it from the start. I'm still in love, Dean."

"I can protect her," he said. "Ward off the demons and make sure they never harm her."

There was a pause. "Really?" her mother whispered, a hint of hope Celina hadn't heard from her before.

"I'll need you to trust I'll do what's best for Celina. Can you promise me that?"

"Are you talking about spells? You know how I feel—"

"You don't understand." His voice rose. "This is an oppor —It's important to keep her safe."

"Okay. I'll trust you if it keeps her safe."

Before she had time to dash to her room, her stepfather loomed over her. "You were listening in?"

"I'm sorry."

"A ten-year-old should have better things to do than to stay indoors all the time. Don't worry. I'll make sure you can have a better life until the time comes."

She blinked a few times, trying to understand the meaning of his words. "I don't—"

He pressed his hands against her head, and a scream stuck in her throat as a white light invaded her mind.

The memory shifted, and Celina's vision blurred. Her pulse hammered as she relived more memories she didn't know had been sealed away.

They tied Celina to a chair, half-conscious after her stepfather had cast a spell on her, burning her from the inside. Dean leaned toward her with worry in his gaze. "Can you take care of the pain, Zachary?"

The blond-haired man came forward and stared at her. "Only if we want to disrupt the process. This should be the one to work, but I don't think we could try it a second time if I ease her pain."

"Why not?"

"It could kill her. Even with demon blood in her veins, she won't survive this twice." His strange eyes focused on her.

Celina's heart seemed to slow.

Kill me? Demon blood? What are they talking about? Please. Someone help. Mom.

Dean seemed to think on it a few minutes. "Fine. Leave her as she is now, and we'll hope she absorbs it."

"Dad. Please. It hurts," Celina whimpered, so weak she couldn't even cry from the agony.

He placed his hand on the side of her head and gave a sympathetic smile. "I know, honey, but you're doing great. Hang in there. You're so important, you know that? I just need you to get through this last bit. Try to breathe."

"I don't... understand."

You're hurting me. Please stop.

"I'm sorry I have to block your memories every time, but it's important for our plan to work."

Zachary let out a sigh. "The spell will take effect. We have to leave."

"Why? I can't leave her alone."

"You want to see her in that much pain? You'll break and let your emotions cloud your judgment and everything will be for nothing. This is our one chance." He grasped Dean's arm and pushed him to the side. "Go. I'll be right there."

Once Dean left, Zachary stared after him before turning a lewd smile on Celina. Her breath hitched as he leaned forward, his hand grasping her leg. His thumb traced along her inner thigh, and a shiver shot down her spine.

"Are you coming or what?" Dean called out.

Zachary clenched his jaw, but leaned closer, his lips brushing against her cheek. Celina thought for sure she'd throw up, and it wasn't just the pain anymore.

"We'll see each other again real soon... *honey.*"

He left, and she sat there, convulsing. The pain built as though acid melted her insides, fizzing her organs as she shrieked, sure her lungs would explode.

The bus hit a bump, and she straightened with a jolt, gasping as though out of breath.

Zoe frowned, giving her a warning look, and Celina turned away, in a daze.

Did I fall asleep? How long was I out? Was that a dream? No. Memories.

Her stepfather had betrayed her. She remembered now

what he'd done. The spells, the pain. And blocking her memory each time to keep it a secret.

And Zachary... always touching her when Dean wasn't around. Had undoing the spell unblocked those memories?

Celina focused straight ahead into the darkness, the city lights far behind them. A figure stood in the road. The bus driver yelled out, horns blasting and hit the brakes.

The man on the road waved his hand, and the vehicle flipped on its side. The glass fractured, the shock throwing everyone around. It threw passengers forward as gravity fell away. The crunch of metal and glass muffled gasps and screams shattering from the windows. Celina felt no pain as though a protective bubble kept her safe. Space vanished as the vehicle spun several times, her world blurring until she closed her eyes.

For a second, silence hung heavy in the air. Shattered glass fell to the floor as victims stirred. Celina grew aware of where she was, gagging at the smell of burned rubber.

The passengers moaned and cried. Most groaned, guttural and low, or begged for help. The bus lay on its side, a mess of twisted metal and glass shards. A few people remained still, either dead or unconscious, while others struggled to their feet. Her gaze focused on smears of blood on the seats, but she shook her head.

Zoe's eyelids fluttered open, and she gritted her teeth, trying to get her legs out from under the rubble.

Celina scrambled to a standing position but fell to the gritty floor, dizzy. The spell Zoe had put on her seemed to have been broken, probably by shock. But something told Celina the cause of the accident was also the reason she wasn't wounded like the others.

Did Kai send someone?

She frowned, staring outside the shattered window at the front. The untraceable spell was still on her, so how had one of Kai's subjects even found her in the first place?

She scanned the bus for an escape, getting to her feet more carefully this time while flexing her hands and trying to control their shaking as she moved to a window. Others joined in a flurry of panic and tried to open one of the emergency exits to the side while the driver yelled for people to stay calm.

As soon as a few people wrenched the door open, a man disappeared through it, as if sucked into a void, his terrible screams following. Celina backed away from the gaping opening. The passengers rushed for the emergency exit at the back, and she fought against the tide of people as she made her way to the driver.

"What's going on out there?" The driver's eyes were wild, blood staining the front of his shirt. He ran a hand across the top of his head, wincing as his fingers probed a laceration.

The windows shattered, and people climbed out into the dark.

"Wait, come back!" Celina staggered up the bus clutching at people's clothes as they prepared to jump.

More screams rang from outside, and the people within the wreckage backed away from the sound.

"We need help. Call 911," a man attempted to take charge, but she ignored him.

Zoe gritted her teeth, tears running down her cheeks and mixing with the blood. "Fuck."

Celina stared at her before going to the debris trapping her legs. She grunted, and with a final hard push, most of it toppled off.

"Why did you bother?" Zoe asked with a twisted smile.

Celina shrugged. "I've got enough blood on my hands."

The hiss of liquid spilling across the engine seemed to quiet the bus as a few passengers stared at the front. Steam rose from the engine, the smell of diesel getting worse. A crackling resonated around them as flames sparked. Celina's eyes widened, and she scrambled from the fire, despite people pushing her aside.

Zoe tried standing, but fell with a cry. Celina grabbed her hand, dragging her forward, and within seconds, flames engulfed the front of the bus, the heating metal painful at her back. People coughed as toxic smoke rushed into the bus, and she covered her mouth and nose, trying to give herself a better chance.

A nearby window broke open, and she frowned. It had opened from the outside.

The flames grew hotter, and she clenched her teeth, moving toward the opening. "You need to crawl out. I'll help you best I can, okay?"

Zoe nodded, crawling out through the window. A blast shook the vehicle, and Celina turned as it pushed someone into the fire. Flames engulfed him, and he shrieked, trying to roll as his skin blistered. People went to his aid, but he fell to the floor, unmoving.

Celina lay on her stomach and crawled out, the broken glass cutting through her clothes. The hot asphalt of the highway warmed her skin, and she winced at the heat on her legs.

She stood, trying to her bearings in the darkness, her gaze darting from side to side. The fire erupting from the bus cut through the darkness.

"Zoe?" She moved to the side, checking the ground, but she wasn't anywhere. "Zoe!"

The bus creaked, and her eyes widened as the metal bent and warped on itself. People inside screamed louder, trying to get out as the bus shrunk, crushing everything within. Bringing them closer to the flames.

Celina rounded the bus, and froze, coming face-to-face with the demon who'd caused the whole mess. She didn't recognize him but couldn't focus on that mystery. He was holding onto Zoe. Celina's mind urged her to flee, but she couldn't seem to move.

Zoe squirmed, barely able to keep upright. "Gabriel, what the fuck are you doing? Let go!"

Celina's pulse pounded in her ears, her breathing quickening.

Gabriel?

His hair was ashen blond, and his eyes a light brown, but there was something about this demon that raised all of Celina's red flags.

"Going on a trip without telling me? That's not nice," he cooed, and a shiver went through Zoe as her eyes widened.

"It was a last-minute plan, but—"

"With or without Jacob and Zachary's permission?" he asked in a cold tone.

Zoe dug her fingers into his arm, trying to get away. "No, we didn't tell them. I'm just as powerful as Jacob or Zachary. They don't get to decide everything." He threw her to the ground, and she screamed. "What the hell are you doing?"

Celina couldn't move, her heart hammering so hard she thought for sure she'd bruise.

Gabriel loomed over Zoe, a sadistic smile curling his lips. "Betraying Jacob and Zachary is signing your death warrant."

"What? No!" She crawled back, shaking her head. "We're all working together, and that includes you!"

He laughed and raised his hand. "Yes, but I don't play well with others."

The asphalt bubbled around Zoe, and she cried out as it melted over her. Her flesh reddened as the heated cement burned, melting onto her. She tried pulling away, but skin ripped off, leaving bloodied muscles gleaming in the bus's fire.

Celina turned her head, pressing her hand against her mouth as Zoe's shrieks of pain and begging echoed around the highway. A final gurgling sound from Zoe sent bile into the back of Celina's throat, and she couldn't help but look. She took several steps back at the sight. Zoe's maimed arm stuck out of the road, one blue eye wide and unmoving.

Gabriel materialized in front of Celina, blocking her view from the horrific sight. She swallowed hard, trembling.

"You… who are you?" she asked, her voice cracking.

White smoke swirled around him, and he vanished from view before it settled. Shiriki's smile curled over his pointed teeth as he took a step closer.

Celina's eyes widened, her mind catching up as her instincts continued screaming at her to run.

He chuckled. "No need to look so surprised. I have two different human forms, much like Mekaisto."

"You're… the source."

Her heart hammered as reality set in. The source within Kai's own subjects was his second in command. Shiriki was not just any demon. Having to go up against someone with his power wouldn't be easy. And if the Venatores were telling the truth, they also had an angel on their side. This would be one hell of a war.

"I am."

"How is that possible? I always recognize your energy, and I'm sure my husband can. How the hell have you not been found out?"

He shrugged. "One of my many skills is masking myself in this form. It takes more energy and drains me, so I cannot remain long in that state. But it has its benefits. I helped the Venatores to gain what I need." He glanced over his shoulder. "Though, only if it is to my benefit. Zoe bringing you out here was counterproductive to the plan, and so I am here to return you."

She took a step back. "Where?"

"To Jacob. He needs you for something."

"I'll tell him who you really are, *Gabriel*. He won't be going with your plan if he—"

"One tried telling him, but I made sure they brought her to your husband, and she lost her mind after he tortured her for information. She recognized me, but I terrorized her enough that she could never tell a soul." He grabbed her arm, digging his fingers into her arm until her skin punctured and she screamed.

"I'll tell him."

"At the cost of your son's life?" he asked.

"You wouldn't." She curled her hands into fists. "You said you'd never harm him."

He leaned forward, his teeth bared. "You have no idea what I would do to accomplish what I desire."

She clenched her jaw. "Fine."

"Good. Then we have a little trip to take."

White light flashed in her eyes and everything blurred.

34

PORTAL

S hiriki stopped in front of a small warehouse, pushing Celina forward. "Go inside and behave."

She narrowed her eyes on him. "And why am I here?"

"Shopping around for a commercial building to start a business?" he teased with a smirk.

"They… Rupert. He was taking Hilda somewhere," she said.

He looked out into the distance. "She is unharmed." He took a step forward. "Now go inside."

With a huff, she turned, ready to be rid of the traitorous bastard. She glanced over her shoulder. "Kai will kill you when he finds out."

His smile widened. "I am certain he will try."

She walked inside, and the heavy metal door slammed behind her with a clank.

One of the Venatores she had met, Terrin, stood from a table, eyebrows raised. "What… are you doing here?"

She opened her mouth, but closed it again, pressing her lips together. Telling on Shiriki was out of the question.

"Two members came to fetch me. Zoe and Rupert. But I don't know where they are right now."

"And you decided to come here and wait on your own?" he said with a snort.

"Gabriel *escorted* me."

"Oh." He glanced over her shoulder, face paling. "Well, that's good. Follow me, and if you don't want any problems, I suggest you try nothing stupid."

I wish I could've gotten that amulet so I could shove it down his throat.

They walked through the desolate industrial hallways, the commercial lights reflecting off Terrin's bleached hair.

"What happened to Namika?" he asked, not turning around.

She bit her lower lip, unsure what to say. "A demon attacked us. I got away, but I don't know what happened after."

Footsteps approached from behind, and she stiffened.

"She's probably dead," Jacob said in an icy tone.

Terrin gave a curt nod and left them.

Celina faced the Venatore, and her shoulders slumped. She didn't need to pretend she was sad. Leaving Namika behind scared out of her mind was a horrible decision she'd agreed to with her husband.

"I tried dragging her away, but he attacked me, and I ended up passing out." She pointed at the scar on her neck and had to suppress a smile knowing Kai had been the one to mark her. "He went insane. And it turns out, all demons are." She took a step forward, raising her head high. "I'm sick of demons destroying lives, and I want them all dead. They killed my parents, my family, took away my friends, and now, they think I'll just bend over and serve them. But they're holding my son hostage, and I don't know what to do anymore."

Jacob's lips curled into a smile. "You could be pretending to want to help us. Aren't you half-demon?"

"By blood, but it's not who I am. I am like my mother, a

Lumen, but I don't see eye-to-eye with their teachings. Restricting dark magic? Why? Demons are dark creatures, and we need to fight fire with fire."

"Hmm. The angel said you'd come back to us, wanting to make things right. Demons were never supposed to exist, and they should all be destroyed."

She fought the urge to flinch. "Will I meet this angel soon?"

"Still doubting his existence?" he asked with a grin. Motioning to the side, they walked through the large hallway, their footsteps echoing. "I can't say I blame you. The only reason I can believe is because he sends me messages. I've seen him several times, but he always wipes my memory of what he looks like."

She frowned. "Why?"

"Mekaisto is talented at searching people's minds. He'll destroy your mind with no difficulty if you try keeping him out. He'd see what the angel looks like and lock onto his energy. By wiping out my memory each time, it ensures he can continue to help us. The only one who has seen him and remembers is our source."

"You mean Gabriel?" When he arched an eyebrow, she explained, "He's the one who brought me here."

I hope they buy this bullshit.

He nodded. "Yes, Gabriel is our source for what demons are up to. But he has come into contact with the angel a few times."

Shiriki has met a real angel?

"What about the symbols on my arms? I've got the ones you put on me to be untraceable, but there are others I don't recognize." She lifted her arms, staring at her skin.

He shrugged. "I wouldn't know until something makes them appear."

Another Venatore strode forward and smiled. "Sorry to bother you."

"Ah, Lany. This is Celina Leviet."

Her eyebrows shot up. "Whoa. Dean Perry's daughter?"

Celina had to stop herself from cursing her stepfather, so she settled for a curt nod.

"And is it true Mekaisto murdered your husband and has been keeping you prisoner?" The woman bounced up and down in excitement.

"I escaped, but they took my son from me. I came here because I need help saving him," she said. She hated lying when it gave Kai a bad name. She turned away, pretending to wipe a tear but needing to suppress a grin. *Ha! Giving a bad name to the Devil.*

"We'll get him back once we destroy those monsters," he said. "With the angel's help, we'll win for sure."

Jacob stared off into the distance, his eyes turning white as he stiffened.

Celina took a step forward, but Lany held her back.

She frowned. "What's going on?"

"The angel is communicating with him. Puts him in a trance." She grimaced. "Kinda creepy, right?"

Jacob staggered, gasping for air as his mouth widened with a terrible smile. "He… wants us to set a trap for the demons. Now is the time."

Lany gaped. "Now?"

"He says he'll be using their powers once he lets us enter the dark realm, but we must set the trap."

Celina assumed Kai had taken Fenrir to his realm.

I have to warn him.

Celina cleared her throat. "My son is probably there right now. What if one of the members tries to kill—"

"I'll inform them not to harm any infant. They'll know to look for a child and bring him to us safely." He gave her a nod and assured her, "He'll be protected."

"I imagine once we set the trap, the angel will use his power to heighten your magic since Mekaisto is strong?"

"That would make sense. We'll gather power from the demons in our traps, too. It'll be our chance to wipe them all out." Jacob straightened and grinned. "More than one way to skin a cat—or demon, in our case." He turned his attention on Lany. "Send word to my brother to stand by. The angel will open a portal on his end with the members he's gathered. They'll join us in the dark realm to provide backup."

Terrin dashed around the corner, panting. "You'll want to see this."

Celina followed both into a large industrial room. The white dirt-covered cement floor was grimy even under the lights overhead. In the middle of the room, a large hole opened. It sparked, black shadows slithering out. A few members staggered back.

She gasped at the familiar energy pulsating from the void. It was the same as when she'd found the maimed demons inside Yonah Church's ruins, and when she'd been trapped within the void.

"Is it the angel?" one member asked, taking a step back.

Jacob closed his eyes, his body lit like a beacon against the darkness. "Yes, he's opened the way for us."

Celina twisted her fingers together.

"Now what?" Terrin asked, eyeing the darkness.

"Time to set the trap for the demons. Our powers will increase the longer we're in the realm, so we'll have an advantage."

Still, no one moved.

Despite the uncertainty in the air, Jacob took a step toward the darkness. "We've been working with the angel for years, and he's never steered us wrong. He heightened our powers, and gave us locations of Sanguis so we could eliminate them. No reason to doubt him now."

"Especially since he's giving us a way in." Terrin eyed the portal.

A few members walked into the large room, their eyes wide

as they stared at the portal. One or two strode toward it, despite the shadows wrapping around the few discarded machines in the room. Soon the shadows would grab onto the people.

Jacob clapped his hands together. "No time like the present."

White marks stretched out inside the portal, and Celina moved closer.

It's fading?

"Let's go," Jacob called out, his voice echoing around them. By then, more than a few hundred had gathered, ready to fight.

Celina didn't wait. She dashed through, the veil brushing against her skin as she pressed on. She opened her mind to let Kai see what was going on but hissed through her teeth as her arms burned. The markings on her arms glowed, searing her flesh, stopping her from warning her husband.

Shit. Why the hell is this happening now? I don't have a backup or...

Patting her side pocket, she remembered the obsidian shard. She had wanted to ask Hilda about it, but with everything that happened, never got the chance.

She barely got through before the Venatore poured through the portal, pushing her forward. Her senses heightened, and her instincts screamed to run. She dashed to the side.

A few followed her as a blinding light burst from beneath the void. Chains wrapped around the ones who hadn't moved fast enough, pulling them to their knees. The metal glowed white and their faces contorted in pain.

Jacob wrenched away, holding his bloodied arm against him as he rushed forward and out of harm's way. "What's going on?"

An explosion shook the ground where they stood, and Celina turned, a scream trapped in her throat. Someone had

35

THE KING OF THE DARK REALM

Celina strode forward, but Terrin grabbed her arm. "Where do you think you're going?"

"He said there are members already attacking in the centre and—"

"And you know where that is?" He pulled her closer, his jaw clenched. "Have you been here before?"

She was about to answer when the symbols on her arm glowed brighter, singeing his hand. As soon as he let go, she ran, ignoring the shouts at her back.

She needed to get to Fenrir.

Kai's dwelling was on fire. Her chest squeezed, hundreds of thoughts flashing through her mind. This was her home, the sanctuary that had taken over the last house she'd lost. Flames peeled at the exterior, black smoke billowing from the broken windows.

Fenrir.

She ran for the front doors. They opened, and a purple light flashed. Someone pushed her, and she rolled a few times before coming to a stop. Her sides ached, but she forced herself to her feet.

Kai stood in his true form, his hand stretched out in front

of him, blocking where the light had come from. She moved to the side and stared inside the dwelling. A woman stood near the doorway, her irises lit like she was on fire from the inside. She curled her fingers as purple light sparked between them.

Venatores were inside.

Her stomach clenched. Not willing to wait, Celina ran past the woman.

Celina needed to get her son and keep him safe. Taking the stairs two steps at a time, she froze when she came face-to-face with another stranger. She ducked to the side as he threw a spell at her. A crazed smile twisted his features as he raised his hand toward her.

A clawed hand erupted through his chest, and his eyes bulged for a second before he went limp and fell to the floor. Lokte stood behind him, panting. Deep gashes ran over his body, and most of his head was melted and charred. He gave her a wink, then his body disintegrated.

Shit. Shit.

She ran to the bedroom she shared with her husband. Barely through the door, she spotted a puddle of blood on the floor.

Where was Nalie? Or Eire? Why wasn't one of them here?

Clutching at her chest she dashed to the crib.

Empty. No time to cry.

Running through the room, she searched everywhere. She tore cabinet doors open and looked under furniture, hoping someone had hidden Fenrir.

"Fenrir?" Her voice sounded higher even to her own ears, and she cried out, still looking. "Fenrir!"

She ripped at anything and everything, desperation flooding her as her vision darkened. Someone grabbed her wrist, pulling her up, and she fought, needing to keep searching.

"Celina. Calm down." Kai's voice broke through her daze, and she blinked fast, trying to get him into focus.

"He's… Fenrir. He's not here." She grasped his arms and squeezed. "Please. Find him."

He closed his eyes, and his hair fluttered as his energy uncoiled and filled the space. Her knees buckled, and she landed hard on the floor. She barely felt any pain, needing him to find their son no matter what.

Maili, Kai's advisor, ran into the room, part of her arm hanging at a strange angle. "Mekaisto, the leader of the Venatores requests to see you and your wife."

"Not now." He opened his eyes, and rage burned behind them. Yet there was something more, something she couldn't place.

"They said they have your son."

Celina got to her feet. "Lead the way."

Maili nodded, then ran out of sight.

Celina turned to Kai, fury like she'd never felt burning through her. "I promise we'll talk about what happened when I disappeared. But after we get Fenrir back."

"You certainly will," he growled.

She took a step closer, despite her instincts urging her to flee. "Kill them. Make them suffer. Throw away any mercy you might have learned from me and destroy them all. Find our son. Please."

"That would put you in danger."

"It doesn't matter! Save Fenrir!" She wiped her tears. "I don't care if it kills me. Save him."

His gaze locked on her. "So be it."

Arcane symbols etched into his chest and along his arms, glowing red and pulsing as though having a life of their own. He rolled his shoulders as they paled, turning chalk-white all the way across his torso. As darkness coiled around his arms, those limbs turned ashen-black as though burned. His pointed fingernails curled into claws, and metal coiled along his wrists, cutting into his arms. Black hair flowed past his hips as though made of darkness, and as his wings stretched out, the feathers changed. Tiny hooks gleamed silver along the feathers, able to rip through flesh.

His head twitched, and he opened his eyes, pools of black filling them. Despite not having pupils, Celina felt his stare. Her pulse sped so fast, she was sure her heart would stop any second.

Bursts of energy crushed against everything, and she leaned on the doorframe to keep from hitting the floor, but she had to get to her son. She ran down the corridor as the wall next to her exploded. Maili grabbed her and pulled her out of the way as debris smashed where she'd stood seconds before.

Maili's face turned ashen as she stared over Celina's shoulder. "Oh. Oh no."

Celina spun and staggered.

Kai strode through the hole he'd blasted. In the blink of an eye, metallic shadows shot in their direction, and Celina screamed as they flew past her. The shadows coiled around a Venatore who'd been sneaking toward them from the back. He shrieked as they twisted until he fell into a sputtering pile of flesh and organs.

Maili grabbed Celina's arm and pulled her down the steps, running from Kai.

No. It's not Kai anymore. That's the King of the dark realm.

She didn't care. If it meant saving her son, it didn't matter what happened to her. They rushed through the doors and toward the path leading to the square.

"Where… are they?" Celina asked, her mouth dry.

Maili rammed herself against Celina, causing them to roll across the ground. Celina coughed as dust rose, her stomach tightening as she crawled away. Kai flew down, landing hard enough to flatten her to the ground. She glanced to the side, watching as Maili kneeled, her forehead pressed against the dirt.

As the dust settled, Celina swallowed hard. She stared at her husband. His black eyes now had a glowing red vertical pupil. The expression behind them held no mercy or kindness.

"Maili," he hissed, his voice laced with an evil Celina couldn't put a name to, "gather everyone to the center. They will be there or perish."

She straightened, and with one last pitiful glance at Celina, disappeared in a blur of motion.

Kai turned his stare on Celina, his energy pouring out in waves and tendrils.

A few demons dashed behind their king, but froze in their tracks, recognizing what he'd become. Even Tess's expression lost its usual smugness.

Kai didn't turn around. "Gather in the square."

Tess pointed toward Celina. "This is all your fault, you half-breed. You're the one who brought them here. That's what one of the members said when they destroyed—"

The Viscus's eyes widened, black veins pulsating beneath her skin. The others around her took a few steps back.

"I said the next time you instigated my wife the damage would be permanent," Kai said with a cruel smile, his gaze never leaving Celina.

Tess's scream was cut short when her head exploded, and her body turned to ashes before it ever hit the ground. He glanced over his shoulder at his remaining subjects.

"Now go."

They didn't wait, and vanished in a blur of motion, leaving Celina and Kai alone once more.

She staggered to her feet. "I… I'm going to run now."

"I think not."

Before she could think, he lunged at her. She yelped as he lifted them into the air. She wrapped her arms around his neck, pressing her face into his chest, trembling. This wasn't her husband. Only a fragment of him remained.

In less than a minute, they landed. When she tried to back away, he held her in place.

Fear flooded every pore in her body. "We… need to save Fenrir. If you need to kill me first, then do it fast."

His smile curled over his pointed teeth, longer and sharper than usual. "I already took your innocence and your soul. You ask me to claim more from you?"

"Are you still you?"

"I am." He leaned toward her ear, and she shivered. "But I am also the one who would sentence you to whipping. Would have used your body for my pleasure after we made our little contract. I am your nightmare, dove. The one you used to make that little rhyme about." He cupped her face and chuckled. "Shut your eyes and look away, the shadow monster will not stay?"

She raised her head higher as he straightened, holding his gaze. "As long as you save our son."

A voice called out, "There won't be anyone to save if you don't give us what we're here for."

Kai released Celina, and she turned to face an army of people standing in front of a large gray building. They were Venatores but not the ones Celina had come here with. They outnumbered the demons ten to one at least.

She glanced at Kai. The Venatores wouldn't survive this.

Celina dashed away from him, pushing through the crowd until she stood at the front. The one who'd spoken smiled at her.

"Zachary." She clenched her jaw, hatred filling her like boiling water.

His blond hair had grown, falling past his shoulders, but his eyes were the same gray with flecks of gold and green. And just as cold. "Oh? Do you recognize me? I'm pleased."

"Where is my son?"

He waggled his finger with a grin. "No, no, it doesn't work that way. First, you need to ask me what we're here for."

A few of the members behind him snickered.

The urge to butcher them overwhelmed her. "I don't care. I want my son."

When a blast of light shot past her, Nalie pulled her back. "What are you doing here without—"

Everyone fell silent when Kai landed next to Celina.

Zachary took a step back, but his grin widened. "Well, well. This is something we weren't informed of."

Wyla gritted her teeth. "Informed of?"

"You should know how the game works, demon. You have informants with each race, so why is it so surprising we would have one within yours?" Zachary crossed his arms. "Now then, we want this realm. It allows us to use our dark magic without draining our powers."

Lights flew at Zachary's group, but they blocked them with ease.

Jacob and his people strode forward. "Couldn't wait to start without us?" he asked, arching an eyebrow.

Zachary smirked. "The angel opened a portal, and after escaping a trap left behind for us, we thought we'd get on with it."

"Enough." Kai fixed his gaze on Zachary like he was prey. "Playtime starts now." He flew high into the air and lunged at Zachary. A red light, glowing like flames, burst from Kai's hands.

Blurred movement stopped in front of Zachary, and an emerald blast of energy exploded. Celina opened her eyes, and coldness spread from her core as she stared at Shiriki. The green light in his hand vanished as he lowered it.

"Killing him would be inconvenient." Shiriki glanced to the Venatore. "Though, if you wish to destroy some of them, feel free. I have no use for all of them since I trapped enough of their kind beyond the portal."

Kai stayed quiet, but the glare he aimed at his second in command was enough to singe a few people standing close.

"You're the source," Nalie said through gritted teeth.

"I am more than that."

Most of the members of Jacob's group gawked. "You? No, it can't be. Gabriel is the source. He—"

Shiriki's appearance changed to Gabriel for a few seconds before he turned back, then winked.

Kai will kill him.

"So, you have betrayed me." Kai raised his hand, the red light pulsing against the shadows that slithered from him. "Then you can perish."

The light blasted, and Celina shielded her face from the heat. A few of the demons staggered. Venatores' bodies caught fire, shattering as though made of glass. Kai's wings folded as white smoke billowed around them.

The dust settled, and Celina's eyes widened.

Shiriki's white hair fell past his chest, and his irises were bright yellow.

Like Fenrir.

Large white wings spread open behind him.

Shiriki sniggered. "You always guessed I was more than a Viscus, but you never thought I might be exactly as you are, Mekaisto." He unleashed his own energy.

The magic slithering from Shiriki caused her to wince; his was as strong as her husband's.

36

SACRIFICE

Celina couldn't think straight as she stared at Shiriki.

"It can't be." Jacob gritted his teeth. "How could you be the source *and* the angel? The being who's helped us for the past ten years? It doesn't make sense."

Shiriki shrugged and turned to his king. "It does not have to make sense to anyone but me."

"Interesting," Kai said with amusement in his voice. "Like me? I think not." He took a step closer. "You may be as strong as I am, but your energy is different."

"Let me tell you a story," Shiriki said, ambling to the side, making sure he stayed close to Zachary. "You do not remember this, but it begins after the guardians eradicated our kind."

Celina took a few steps closer, twisting her fingers together as she recalled the tome she'd read at the archives. "They imprisoned the two angel leaders." Her breath hitched as she stared at her husband. "One angel was cursed to darkness." She turned to Shiriki. "And the other was lost to time."

Kai frowned. "I remember nothing after we escaped those guardians."

"Nor did you even remember what you were by then," Shiriki commented with a shrug. "Surprise!"

Celina narrowed her gaze. "You can't be an angel."

"Why? Because angels are pure beings filled with love and mercy?" He chuckled and shook his head. "Lumen both feared and revered us. I created your group by sharing my blood and powers with a few humans who were not completely useless. From that time on, I granted both blessings and curses. If they disobeyed my rules, I destroyed them." In the blink of an eye, Shiriki vanished.

Celina yelped when he grabbed her from behind, holding her tight. She gripped his arm, clawing to get away. "Let go or I'll fry you."

"You cannot use your powers against another angel, Celina."

She froze and turned to stare into his gaze still fixed ahead. "Another angel?"

"Stay still or I will take more… permanent actions with you."

She jerked when Kai appeared a few feet away from where they stood. Most of the demons had taken several steps back, and even the Venatores stood transfixed.

Kai glowered at his second in command. Red light sparked in his palm.

Shiriki continued, "You were the first angel, Mekaisto, gifted with Zilar's blood. Given the ability to create. As a dark angel, all you could create were beings like you. It created an imbalance in the world." He grabbed a fistful of Celina's hair and yanked until she cried out. "So Zilar created me. And I created more of my kind."

Celina focused on her husband instead of the straining angle Shiriki twisted her head.

Kai's eyes seemed to swim. "We broke free of their prison after they used our blood to create new beings. We killed most of the guardians."

"Oh, ho, ho," Shiriki chuckled. "You are remembering. I was supposed to die, but you pushed me away. Because of your direct link to Zilar, they could not destroy you but instead cursed you to darkness. You may have lost your memory, but your powers grew. You became the dark realm itself."

Celina was sure he would crush her in his grip.

Kai's glare burned, and the shadows slithered out as though trying to reach forward. "Do not harm her."

"Oh, I would not dream of it. She has something I need. And I will take more of it for as long as I can."

Celina's vision blurred, and she blinked a few times, realizing they stood amongst the Venatores now.

"My research on souls brought me to the Venatores years ago. I discovered those brave enough to dabble in dark magic could perform the spell I need to fix it. All they needed was power. Your power." He glanced to the side, his lips curling into a cold smile.

Celina's grip on Shiriki's arm tightened. "A spell to fix what?"

"That burning question you always crave."

"What…"

Her husband's hands twitched as more energy sparked. "And what have you been taking from my wife?"

"I don't understand." Celina took a shuddering breath. "Taking something from me?"

Shiriki turned to Kai. "You are the first demon, Mekaisto. We are higher beings. Light or dark, angel or demon, it does not matter." He leaned closer to Celina's ear, making the hair raise along her neck and arms. "When you lost your soul, your Lumen blood mixed with mine. My angelic blood has been tainted by ages in the dark realm. But the Lumen? It is pure and untainted."

Her heart raced. "Lumen blood… but you're the one who gave your blood and powers to us."

"Indeed. And voila! A new angel was born to the light." Shiriki's tone grew excited, yet anger lurked behind his words. "When I found out your mother was pregnant, what you were did not make a difference. Not until she died."

Kai lunged at them.

Shiriki dodged to the side, putting a barrier in front of them.

Kai bared his fangs, ready to strike. "Why play my subject for so many years if you had the ability to overthrow me?"

Shiriki loosened his grip on Celina so she could turn her head toward him. "Because you are the reason I am standing here now. The guardians would have destroyed me. I served you out of loyalty."

Celina squirmed in his grip. "You call this loyal?"

Kai shot her a signal for silence, and she didn't argue with the murderous glare. "Why do you need the Venatores' powers?"

Shiriki motioned, and a member strode forward, holding Fenrir.

"No! Fenrir!"

Wrath surged through her whole being, and something inside her seemed to light up. As soon as the member handed her son to Zachary, she let the inner warmth flow from her, the energy tingling and sparking inside her core. Electricity flowed through her veins, and she focused on bringing the heat into her hands. Her fingers twitched, and she raised her arms up, unleashing a bright golden light.

She knew it wouldn't harm many, but she hoped Kai would use the distraction.

And he did.

The barrier exploded into tiny pieces.

With a yelp of surprise, Celina staggered as Shiriki vanished. Demons rushed forward, colliding with the Venatores, and Celina straightened. She searched through the chaos until she spotted Zachary retreating, still holding her son. Gritting her teeth, she dashed after him.

He ran all the way to the front of Kai's dwelling. The tree stood despite the fountain being shattered to pieces. Black oozed along the roads and plants, devouring everything in its path. Near the edge of the mansion, Zachary stared over the railing into the water below.

She ran toward them, her chest tightening with every second.

Zachary held Fenrir over the railing, dangling him. "One more step and I drop him."

When her son cried, his small hands curling tight, she thought for sure she'd die. "You don't need to do this." She moved slowly, hoping he was bluffing. She didn't want to believe he'd kill an infant. "I'll give you whatever you want. Please, just don't hurt my son."

He raised his hand, light shimmering from between his fingers. Her eyes widened, but before she could think of how to react, energy blasted from Kai's dwelling. The ground shook, and Zachary staggered back, the jerk of his body opening his hand. Fenrir disappeared from sight with one last echoing cry.

She screamed and ran, her mind refusing to accept what happened. The world tasted of bile and ashes. She reached the railing and tried to swing over.

Zachary held her back.

"No! Let go! Fenrir!"

Golden light scorched him, and he released her. He fell to the floor, squirming in pain.

Kai, back to his regular demon form, strode forward. She again went to jump, but this time, it was her husband who restrained her. "Celina, it is—"

She squirmed and fought. "No! Don't you dare! Let me go!"

Shiriki flew onto the railing, holding Fenrir in his arms.

"You will never guess what I found while I happened to fly by," he said with a smirk. Jumping down, he handed Fenrir to Celina.

She held him so tight in her arms she needed to remind herself not to hurt him. He'd stopped crying, but his eyes were wide. Kai wrapped his arm around her, cupping their son's head.

Zachary stirred, coughing as he got to his feet, trembling. "This… isn't over." He snapped his fingers and figures appeared from the black goo. The substance fell from them as it took a form of its own.

Celina brought her hand to her mouth at the sight of the people who had died because of her revenge for Thomas's death.

Father Christopher smiled, pointing a finger at her. His torso was exposed, revealing uneven stitching where Kai had ripped him in half. "My child, you should have listened to my warnings. Your unholy son can only be saved by baptizing him in boiling oil until his flesh melts, and he is reborn."

David Corval stood next to the priest, his body twisting as though his spine lay along his side. Lumen killed at Yonah Church stepped forward.

When Wayne and Emily Pierce limped into sight, Celina took a step back. Guilt replaced her vengeance. She had killed Emily in cold blood, and the hole in her forehead became Celina's entire world.

"You murdered us. For nothing. For a monster," Emily accused, her eyes wild and bulging.

One more person appeared. Her body was red, blistered so badly it bled. Her hair and eyes were burned away, but the cross around her neck told Celina it was her Aunt Marie.

Zachary pointed at her aunt. "Did you even try saving her, or did you let your demon burn her to death? He wanted to destroy the Lumen, and he did, including your aunt." Zachary glanced at Marie and grinned. "This is what we promised the angel." He turned to Shiriki, but his smile vanished, his face turning ashen.

"This," Shiriki took a step closer to the figures staggering around, "is what you promised me? Proof you could revive humans if you had the power of the dark realm?" His jaw clenched, his yellow irises glowing brighter. "They are not alive. They are mere shells. This is your dark magic?"

Celina took a step back, holding Fenrir against her, cradling his head. She'd never seen Shiriki lose his cool before.

An explosion sent her to the ground, and she curled her body to protect Fenrir. She bolted to her feet but froze. Shiriki shot a light, blasting it through her husband. Kai fell back, clutching at his chest as blood and black smoke oozed from the wound.

"Kai!"

Shiriki stopped advancing on Kai and turned, shooting his energy toward her. She screamed as Kai dove between them, blood spluttering from his mouth. His gaze gentled when it landed on her. Hands trembling, he took Fenrir in his arms. Then he collapsed, holding on to their son.

Celina dashed in front of him, shielding her family from Shiriki as he approached.

Shiriki narrowed his gaze. "You think you—"

She reached into her pocket, grasped the obsidian shard, and pointed it at him. "Stay the hell away from them."

His white wings fluttered, his energy pulsating. She narrowed her eyes. He had played everyone.

But why?

He glanced over her shoulder toward the walking corpses, his hands curling into fists. "It was… for nothing."

A few demons materialized, ready to strike, but Shiriki was fast. In a blur, he dashed for the tree that connected this realm to her world.

"Wait!" She ran after him, needing to stop him. As long as

he was out there, he was a threat to her family, and she couldn't let him escape.

When she grasped his arm, his eyes widened. Together they plunged into the void of the tree.

Celina staggered forward, clutching her chest. The room was small, painted in dark-gray and black.

Where am I?

Ahead, a figure lay inside a glass coffin. Wires hung out, and a glowing green light hovered at its base.

She approached, her eyes stinging. "Mom?"

Her mother looked the same as the last time Celina had seen her. Her eyelids were closed. With no visible wounds, she could have been sleeping.

"Mom." Celina pressed her hands against the glass, blinking back tears.

A door behind her slammed, and she spun, trembling.

Shiriki leaned against it, his head down so she couldn't see his face. "It did not work. I could not bring her back," he whispered.

She swallowed hard. "What's going on? What is this?"

He lifted his head. Fear trickled through her whole being. She'd never seen him furious, and she wished she hadn't now.

He appeared next to her, his fingernails digging into her arms. "I tore everyone and everything apart to bring her back. Your blood was supposed to revive her. All those samples Nalie took and Elizabeth did not stir once."

Celina glanced at her mother. "I don't understand. There was a body at the scene of the accident. We buried her." She had said something like that to Kai. But he'd put Thomas's features onto Martin Kent's body when faking his death.

He squeezed harder until the pain made her squirm. "Why did she sacrifice herself to save you? Why?"

He threw her and she collided hard against the wall, gritting her teeth. "Because my mother loved me." The lump in her throat grew so tight, she swallowed several times.

"And what about those you leave behind?" His glare burned into her as he lunged, slamming her again. "What about the consequences of leaving a being who has nothing left to lose?" He wrapped his hand around her throat. "I have wanted to rip you apart since that promise, Celina."

She grasped his wrist. "What promise? Why?"

His body seemed to glow with a white fire, his pupils thinning to slits. "Because it is your fault Elizabeth is gone. She tried to keep you safe and died for it. You did the same for Fenrir, so willing to throw yourself over a balcony, knowing you would never survive."

"It's what we do for the people we love." Her voice was calm to her ears even though she screamed inside. "It doesn't mean we don't love those we leave behind. If I'd died saving Fenrir, Kai would've understood, and he would've known I loved him, too."

He clenched his jaw. "It—"

"You loved my mother." She didn't ask. "Let her go. You did what you could, and I'm sure, wherever she is, she knows it." She placed a trembling hand on his arm, holding her breath.

The energy diminished, and he leaned his forehead against her shoulder. "You look so much like her. I hate you for that."

"I'm not." She swallowed as the lump in her throat grew more painful than Shiriki's grip around her neck. "Whenever I look in the mirror, I remember her easier. I remember her laugh, her smile, tears, everything." When he lifted his head to look at her, she held his gaze. "You must have fond memories of her. Remember those. Keep her alive that way instead."

He released her and backed away. "The Venatores promised to revive her if she had enough angelic blood inside her. With Lumen blood and mine flowing in your veins, you have the purest I could obtain." His yellow irises dimmed. "But all they can revive are puppets. They lied."

"Please, I—"

"I tried." He raised his hand.

She pressed her back against the wall. White light hit her, and she passed out, her scream dying inside her.

37

STERN WARNING

Kai sat on the sofa, Celina curled into his arms as Fenrir slept cuddled between them. She had refused to let go of their son, and he didn't have the heart to argue.

He had found her in their bedroom, asleep and alone. The fact she was unharmed was surprising, but he didn't want to push her to explain what had happened. When he'd watched her disappear through the void with Shiriki, he'd nearly imploded his realm to stop them.

Kai wanted answers but had given her time to recuperate from the shock. Whatever had happened seemed to have shaken her.

"Did he harm you?" he asked.

She glanced at him for a second but averted her gaze. "No. Not physically."

"Then what did he do mentally?" He ran his fingers through her hair. "I will see it for myself. Close your eyes."

She scooted away from him. "I don't want you inside my mind. You already do it more than I like, and I'm asking you to respect—"

"It has nothing to do with respect." He wrapped a strong

arm around her waist, pulling her hard against him. "It has everything to do with understanding."

Leaning her head against his chest, she sighed. "Please don't make it hurt."

He entered as flashes of light and colors flew in his line of vision. Images, memories; all Kai needed to know filled his mind and within seconds, it was over. The room was quiet, save for the crackling fire.

Everything he had seen sent his emotions in different directions. On the one hand, Shiriki had betrayed him, yet he'd also saved Fenrir from dying. The love his second in command felt for Elizabeth could only rival what Kai felt for Celina. "Are you all right?"

"I think so. I guess it'll just take time for me to come to terms with everything I learned. Everything he did… it was all for my mother." She pulled away from him. "I'm sorry I left the dwelling. It was stupid of me, and that's why the Venatores could take me away. As soon as I was going through the portal, I tried opening my mind to you so you could know what was happening."

He pushed against his fury. "I thought you ran away."

"Why? We had fixed most of our issues."

His lips curled into a smile. "You did not choose this life, and I did not give you a fair chance to get out at any point. I thought maybe you wanted to get away from me."

"I didn't choose my life, and I hadn't planned on it being one big lie or having it crumble." She took his hand. "I could've chosen not to go anywhere with you when we met at the bar. Left when our marriage became difficult, or when I'd become secluded or as I became nervous around you at the end. Though now I know why, and…"

"And what?" he whispered, cupping her cheek.

Her pulse sped. "I could've left you every day since I got here. In fact, I told you I wanted a break, and you gave me space, respected my wish. If I had wanted out of this relation-ship, I would've left."

"Are you saying you do not want to leave me?"

"I don't want to leave. I love you."

"I love you, too. I promise to always be here for you, and I will not go back on my word."

She sighed against him.

"I need to go out." He ran his fingers through her hair.

She pressed her face against his chest. "What for?"

"I have to destroy the Venatores. It would be rude to leave them rotting in my dungeon for all eternity."

She straightened. "What? But not all of them had anything to do with this. Some are innocent. They trusted Jacob and Zachary; it was a bad choice and not something they should die for. Namika doesn't deserve to die. Please."

"They have always been power-hungry. Generation after generation, they seek powers they should never have. This has been a long time coming; I must wipe them out."

Clenching her jaw, she got to her feet and strode to the large window, her arms crossed. "So, you'll kill them? Just in case? Why not do that with humans, too, since there are murderous ones out there?"

"Humans could never cause the same damage." He kept his voice steady, unwilling to argue in her state. With a sigh, he placed Fenrir in a comfortable position on the sofa, protected from rolling off by a few cushions, and went to his wife, wrapping his arms around her. "Very well. I will not kill the ones who are innocent, including your friend Namika. But they will get a stern warning."

She glanced over her shoulder. "Promise?"

"I have been making many of those lately," he said in exasperation but nodded. "I promise. Just a stern warning."

He wondered when he'd become so powerless to his wife. Perhaps when, after dating for a few years, she was no longer just his future wife, but someone he'd fallen in love with.

"Thank you." Her soft smile warmed him as she placed her hands against his arms and leaned into him. "Please wake me as soon as you get back, okay?"

"Of course." With another kiss, he turned to leave, glancing at his son before heading out.

Kai stopped in front of his tree. The liquid poured out at his feet, creating the portal he needed to get to his dungeon. His wings opened, and he flew through the darkness.

He refused to feel guilty about what he had to do. There was no choice. He would wipe out the Venatores, but not in the way she imagined. This way, he'd keep his promise to her while getting rid of dangerous people.

The descent didn't take any time, and when he emerged, he changed to his true form.

Kai reached the prison cell where he'd put Jacob Mackenzy. He grabbed the iron-barred door, ripping it off its hinges. The metal clanged against the stone floor once he dropped it.

Jacob stood, pressing his back against the cold wall.

Kai raised his hand, and blood splattered out of Jacob's mouth as he clutched his chest.

Jacob's dark-blue irises flashed in anger. "If you're going to kill me, then do it. Don't drag it out."

Kai chuckled until Celina's face flashed through his mind. Guilt filled him as he watched Jacob desperate to stay alive. Still, giving Fenrir a safe place to live and grow until he reached the age of immortality drove Kai onward.

Lunging forward, he grabbed Jacob and threw him across the small room. The wall cracked on impact. Unable to move, the man hissed through his teeth.

Kai moved fast, crouching in front of the Venatore. "This is the end." He placed his hand against Jacob's chest, ripping the energy from him. "You and your brother are the leaders, connected through a bloodline of black magic. Once both of you are dead, this will sentence your people to live as mere mortals."

Jacob's eyes closed, and he fell to the floor, an empty shell. Kai opened a portal, and shadows slithered from it, wrapping around Jacob and disintegrating him.

The rest of the captured members Kai deemed innocent would lose their magic but would be taken back to Demias to live out their lives as mortal humans. One brother was dead, now all he had to do was murder Zachary.

With a smile, he left his dungeon.

Celina needed him, and he needed to be close to her. His plan had been to kill them all, but he would keep his promise. The monster inside him protested, fury flaring, but he pushed it away.

As soon as he arrived into his realm, familiar energy coiled in the air, and he bristled.

Shiriki lurked nearby.

Kai strode through the old temple used for court thousands of years before. When the first demons he'd created had tried overthrowing him, the damage he'd caused was irreparable. It served as a reminder of what happened when taking on his spiritual form.

Red vines grew in the ruins. Most of the marbled black floor remained covered in the ashes of the subjects who'd dared to betray him. Part of the roof hung overhead, decorated with skeletal remains secured with chains. The torture and destruction that had occurred here so long ago was forgotten.

Except by him and the demon sitting on the decrepit stone steps ahead.

Shiriki raised his head and smirked. "I apologize. It took

time to answer your summons. Did you want to try destroying me now?"

"We have the same level of power. Destroying you would be no easy feat." Kai faced a bank of shattered windows. "No one has wounded me since the guardians. It was refreshing after all this time."

"Our energies are not equal. You became more than powerful. You are a deity of sorts because of Zilar's direct link to you." Shiriki shrugged. "That is why I passed myself off as one of the first demons you created. A Viscus."

Kai materialized a few feet away, glowering. "Why?"

"I was… tired of fighting. We had banded together to defeat a common enemy, but after? We would have been at each other's throats all over again, fighting for power to surpass one another." He stared at his hand, a green light pulsating over his palm.

Kai chuckled. "I never knew you to be sentimental."

"What I am is loyal."

"Yet you betray me?" He cocked his head.

Shiriki's gaze focused on a vine. "I never said I was loyal to just you."

"To Celina's mother as well," he said. "You had Ancus try to kill my wife."

He shook his head as he stood from the steps. "No, that spell was to bring her back to the Venatores. But my powers overwhelmed his mind. After tasting blood so pure, he broke."

"Speaking of her blood… why did you not go after Fenrir? He is powerf—"

"His blood is tainted with the curse the guardians placed on you." His gaze held Kai's. "You know Celina cannot stay in this realm forever. She is as close to a light angel as I once was. For a time, she will stay with no ill side effects, but one day, she will perish."

Kai curled his hands into fists. "And do you have any

solutions to keep that from happening?" He didn't bother hiding the desperation in his voice.

"Have you killed the Venatores yet? The ones who tried killing your son?"

"Jacob Mackenzy is dead, and I will sentence the ones who did not cause much damage to have their powers stripped from them. But the others? I have not killed them… *yet*." Kai ignored his unanswered question. Shiriki didn't have a solution, then. "Care to join me?"

Shiriki arched an eyebrow. "Oh, am I still your second in command then?"

"I have not decided what to do with you yet." Kai sighed. "I could try destroying you, and we would fight until the end of days. But for now, I need to focus on killing my enemies and finding a solution for my wife in the long run."

They walked in silence.

How can I save her?

When they strode into the court, the few demons talking amongst themselves bowed. Then they straightened, most of them glowering at Shiriki.

He chortled. "If anyone would like to attack me, now would be a good time."

A few lunged, but Kai uncoiled his energy and blasted it against everyone in the room. "Attacking my second in command is a direct attack on me. Make your next choice wisely."

Wyla frowned. "Shiriki betrayed you. Why—"

"And since when have I ever needed to explain myself to any of you?" he demanded, allowing the darkness to slither around their feet.

They bowed, mumbling apologies, but Kai didn't listen as he continued toward one of the far doors.

Once they reached the bottom of the public execution dungeon, Shiriki's smile widened at the scene. The Venatores Kai had deemed guilty were chained at their necks, anchored to the parts of the floor not covered by grills. Most of them crouched, covering themselves as they'd been stripped naked. A few glowing stones embedded in the walls gave the room a sinister blue hue.

"I have always liked your creativity, and this does not disappoint."

Kai chuckled, staring at his own masterpiece. "Years of practice." He pointed at the far back of the room where a small platform stood. Zachary hung against a cross, bound and gagged. "After he has the pleasure of watching his people die, you may have fun with him. I gave you my word you would get a prize, and that my laws would not apply for this Venatore. However, Zachary did more than torture my wife when she was just a child, and I will deal with his final sentence myself."

Kai brought his finger to his thumb. The first grill lit underneath a man. He screamed, jumping up and pulling at the chain, but with every yank, it tugged him closer to the flames. His feet cooked over the metal, flesh and muscle searing. He fell to his hands and knees, then his face pressed against the burning grill. With a final shriek and tug at the chain, his head crushed against the grate, and what was left of his body stilled.

The rest of the members whimpered, most begging for mercy.

Kai smirked. "Enjoying this?"

Shiriki chuckled in amusement. "Oh yes, very much."

Finger to thumb, the second grill lit.

Three hundred and forty-one to go.

38

THE PAST

C elina woke shivering and turned her head to the side, staring at Kai as he slept. He looked so peaceful. At the thought, a tiny smile curled her lips.

The Devil looks peaceful?

Part of her wanted to wake him, just to talk, but she couldn't bring herself to do it.

She got out of bed and caressed his cheek. "I love you."

Moving to her son's crib, she stared at Fenrir. They were home, yet she still felt the heaviness from the dark realm pushing against her.

I'll adapt.

She rubbed his back and smiled. When he stirred, she held her breath, taking a step back. After a second ticked by, she strode to the door, glancing over her shoulder at her family, then walked out.

I'm lucky.

She wandered, unable to sleep. Finally, she went to her favorite place: the greenhouse. There, she grabbed a book, lay on the sofa, and pulled a blanket over her.

She lost herself in a story, a book she'd read hundreds of times back in the home she'd shared with Thomas. As the hours ticked by, she leaned her head back, closing her eyes. The cushion near her hip moved, and she froze.

"Kai?"

Silence.

She opened her eyes, and her stomach clenched. Shiriki's irises shone bright silver in the twilight-illuminated room. He'd reverted to the demon form she'd learned to fear.

She pulled the blanket higher, the urge to pull it over her head and hide from the monster stronger than she wanted to admit.

"Did you come back to kill me?" she asked quietly.

"Time will do that for me." He locked gazes with her. "You know what you are now. A light angel. One that cannot survive in this realm for all eternity as you would like."

"But how can you survive, then?"

"I was tainted long before Mekaisto created the dark realm. It only added to my thirst for revenge against what the guardians had done to us."

He pulled something from his pocket, silent as he looked at the obsidian shard. Even in the dimness, it absorbed every bit of light.

Why does he have that?

She tried remembering the last time she had it. Shiriki had attacked Kai, and she'd placed herself in front of her family, pulling out the shard to attack Shiriki.

"This is the piece I pulled out of Mekaisto when the guardians cursed him. I only broke off the part sticking out of him." He twirled it between his fingers. "Do you know how a curse works?"

"No. And I don't care."

He moved so fast, she didn't scream as he impaled the shard through her chest. Her bones cracked, and blood splattered out of her mouth as her nerves caught fire. She curled and uncurled her hands, gasping for air.

"You are what I once was." He gave one last push against

her chest, and the shard vanished in a wisp of smoke. "You were the last light angel left, but now, with your heart giving one final beat…" He stared at the spot where he'd rammed the shard. "You will be like us. Die to reawaken as a tainted angel. A true demon."

"But why… now?" she panted.

"It would need to be done one day. Why not now?" He averted his gaze. "To curse someone is also to expose yourself. Memories of important events. Regrets I did not want to reveal to anyone. But I made a promise, and for her, I will not break it." He leaned closer. "I never wanted to relive these moments."

Her heart gave out. She hovered over her body and closed her eyes tight. Feathers caressed along her skin, but there was darkness… sadness. She opened her eyes and looked around as though watching a movie. She didn't have a body. She was just—there.

The city bustled even late at night, and Shiriki walked past her. In the human form Celina had seen many times, he never looked far from the cruel demon she knew. Blond hair tied in a loose ponytail and his silver irises the same shade she saw every day in the mirror.

He walked past a familiar night club and slowed. The CrowBar was demon central, and she was sure he'd go inside. He stopped. For a second, he seemed frozen in place, but a smile curled his lips. Instead, he continued forward. He walked through crowds of people, some staring at him with unease while others didn't even give him a second glance.

Downtown had safe places to enjoy at night: bars, nightclubs, food trucks. He continued to the less-traveled roads with fewer lights, and soon he was alone. He turned into an alley, the one lamppost at its edge giving the place an eerie aura. The brick walls were spray painted, and debris lay on the ground.

Shiriki drew closer to a break in the walls. A low roof

came in sight, crates stacked against the building to create a makeshift ladder. A girl crouched there, her red hair tied in a high ponytail. She jumped, the glint of steel flashing as she lifted it high and struck.

Shiriki turned to the side and grabbed her wrist in the blink of an eye, the movement bored. The girl glowered, and she kicked out, trying to wrench away.

He chuckled. "Hello, little girl." With no effort, he threw her aside.

She slid along the ground until she hit the chain link fence at the edge of the alley.

Celina stared at herself at the same young age, yet… the green irises. It was her mother. Celina wanted to call out to her, but… it was just a memory.

"Crap," her mother muttered, wincing in pain. Taking out another blade, she bolted to her feet but cried out and fell to her knees.

Shiriki crouched in front of her. "Ah, a Lumen." He pressed his finger against her forehead, and she toppled backwards. "You're young. Are your people getting so desperate they'd send a little girl to attack demons and lose?"

"No one sent me. I felt a demon, so I followed," she said through her teeth. "And I won't lose."

"Is that right?" He grinned. "You can't even stand." Shaking his head, he grabbed her throat and squeezed. "No. It's over. You shouldn't be out here alone. Besides the obvious monsters you hunt, humans are not always so nice either. Do you have any idea what some would do to a sweet-looking little girl?"

She squirmed against his grip. "I don't care."

"You shouldn't have come after us. Especially not me."

Her green irises shone with anger. "I *will* kill you."

His grip loosened, and a smirk spread over his face. "You're not even afraid of me. How interesting." He straightened, and for a second, it seemed like he might strike, but instead, turned away.

"Hey, wait!" She gripped her weapon tighter and crawled forward. "Don't you dare run away."

He glanced over his shoulder, and she froze as his irises flashed white. "How old are you?"

"Fourteen."

He seemed to ponder. "Train harder for another ten years."

"I will! I swear it," she shouted, getting to her feet, clinging to the fence for support. "What's your name?"

"Why does it matter? You can find me by tracing the same energy you sensed tonight." He took a few steps toward the end of the alley.

"I want to know the name of the demon I'll kill." Her voice didn't waver, and despite her young age, she was fearless.

He materialized inches from her. "Shiriki."

She didn't flinch. "I'm Elizabeth Tayen."

"Well then, Elizabeth, when you'd like to try your luck again, find me."

The scene in Celina's vision vanished, replaced by a decrepit house. Crusty paint peeled from the walls. Wooden boards creaked under Shiriki's feet as he spoke to Adam. In his usual business suit, Adam looked out of place in the dusty area, but his red irises betrayed his nature.

"I request you stop taking my children for those… experiments of yours." Adam kept his voice steady.

Shiriki arched an eyebrow. "Where else will I find viable immortal creatures such as Sanguis?" Shaking his head, he stared up as dust fell from the ceiling. "We're done here."

"But—"

"If you have any issues, take them up with the one who ordered me to conduct those experiments."

Adam swallowed hard, and his shoulders slumped. "I... never mind. I'll leave you, then."

Without another word, Adam left, but Shiriki stayed inside the room. He eyed the door hanging from broken hinges and crossed his arms, waiting.

In a flash of movement, a figure rounded the corner near where he stood, a blade swinging at him. He raised his hand to stop that one, but a second rammed into his arm, anchoring it against the wall.

"You're greeting me with a dagger again?" he asked with a smirk.

Elizabeth grinned. "Old habits."

Shiriki had said he'd hated how much she looked like her mother. He was right. Her hair was longer, and her eyes were green, but she could be Celina's twin.

"You've gotten quicker." In less than a second, he pulled the blade free and threw her across the room.

This time, she spun mid-air. Crouching, she slid across the floor. Dust rose as she straightened, glaring at him. "Took less than ten years, too."

"Oh? How long has it been then?" He twirled the weapon between his fingers, staring at it.

She took out another blade. "Seven."

"I feel like I've interrupted something," he said with a grin as he pointed at her. Her short green dress had ripped, and a strap hung off her shoulder.

She dusted off her clothes and shrugged. "I was out clubbing with my friends, but I felt your energy, and couldn't miss the opportunity."

"I'm afraid your evening won't end well." The blade twisted in his grip like cheap plastic, and he dropped it to the floor with a clang. "You survived once because your lack of fear interested me, but you won't get lucky twice."

She tilted her head to the side, a smile curling her lips. "That's my line."

He laughed—genuine mirth, not cruel or sadistic—and shook his head. "I'll keep you alive a little longer then."

"Try me."

"Oh, I will." In a blur, he appeared next to her, grasping her neck as she turned.

She swiped at him, but he caught her wrist and slammed her into the nearest wall. He opened his mouth as though to say something, but she kicked off. They rolled into a heap, then both straightened, locking gazes, hunting.

Her breathing was heavy, but he didn't seem the least bit affected. She rubbed at a bleeding spot on her leg and winced. "You had to be somewhere I'd get this many splinters, didn't you?"

"If I had known you were visiting, I would've picked an appropriate place." He lunged, and she gasped as he threw her against the discarded furniture.

The sofa toppled, dust rising in the air.

He strode forward but frowned when he looked behind the sofa. It was empty.

A dagger impaled him, blood pulsing from his abdomen.

"I told you I'd kill you," she hissed from behind him.

His shoulders shook as he burst out laughing. This time, the sinister sound caused Elizabeth to take a few steps back.

He pulled out the dagger, the hilt tearing the hole from his back to his abdomen bigger. Then he tossed it on the floor. It landed with a thud, his blood dripping.

"You're right." He turned to face her. "If I'd been a Sanguis, I would've fallen face down, and you could've decapitated me. A Lumen spell could then have put me out of my misery." He materialized in front of her and slammed her on the ground. Before she could get up, he pressed his foot against her chest, holding her in place despite her clawing at his leg. "But I'm not a Sanguis."

Smoke rose around him, and Celina shivered at Shiriki's demonic appearance. His white hair flowed past his shoulders, a silver glow in his irises contrasting against the vertical pupils.

"Doesn't matter." She twisted her body, trying to stand, but he straddled her, keeping her pinned under him. "Get off me, fucking demon!"

"Such language from a Lumen. Do not let them hear you speak like that."

She tried to punch him, but he grabbed her wrists, holding them on either side of her head. Tears filled her eyes, but she blinked them away quickly.

"They teach us how to kill Sanguis, but I figured with you, it wouldn't be so different."

He cocked his head. "You thought it would be the same for a Viscus despite—"

"No." She shook her head, trying to yank from his grasp. "You're not a Viscus either. Maybe a Tenebris, but we learned they were extinct."

His eyebrows rose. "If you knew how powerful I am, why attack me a second time?"

She grinned. "I like a challenge."

"I can see that." He stood.

She staggered to her feet, taking several steps back. "Do I get to grab my weapon?" She glanced from one of her daggers to Shiriki, sweat beading her forehead.

"There is no need." His energy uncoiled from around him, pressing against her so hard, she couldn't move. He stalked forward and stopped inches from her. "All I want is to hear you scream once before I kill you."

When she grinned, he stopped unleashing his essence.

"I won't ever scream for you, Shiriki. I've trained myself never to cry out in pain, no matter how much it hurts."

"There is more than one reason to scream and cry out, pet."

Her cheeks turned pink. "I know."

"I have met no one who has blushed around me. Most

pale and die in fear." He slid his hand into her hair and stared at it like it was the most interesting thing in the world. Leaning forward, he pushed her hair to the side, whispering in her ear, "Why do you smell like lust?"

When he straightened, she grinned. "Sucker for punishment?" She shrugged, but the anger in her gaze faded away. "I liked the nickname… pet."

"Careful with the tempting words you use. Dressed like this, alone at night, you might attract the wrong attention." He slid his hand along her arm.

Pain flashed through her gaze, but it was distant, as though remembering something in the past. "I know that, too. Father Robert's apprentice, Theodore… he likes to train the girls at my church. He… touches us, and when we reach the legal age, he…" She bit her lip, letting a tear roll down her cheeks. "He said it was important we weren't virgins, so if men ever did that to us while we were hunting, we'd already be used to it. Not distracted by our… weakness, he calls it."

The energy around Shiriki changed, and his irises flashed as his gaze turned to a burning glare. For a second, he stared at her, then backed away. "You are not ready to fight me yet. Try later."

"You're running away again?" She wiped tears though she grinned at him.

Shiriki stopped in the middle of the room. "Train, then find me again, Elizabeth."

Celina didn't have a body in her state, yet she'd felt her stomach churn. The lump in her throat squeezed tight. Her mother had suffered at Yonah Church, but she still brought Celina to protect her against the demons hunting her.

Yet Shiriki's actions seemed… out of place. Even her mother showed no revulsion.

What happened?

39

GUARDIAN ANGEL

As though knowing Celina had been waiting, a new scene appeared. Elizabeth looked the same as before, leaning against a parked car in a sparse lot. The man with her cursed, his hands curling into fists.

"What the fuck? I take you out on a date, and now you're saying we can't go to your place?" He took a step closer, glaring. "You owe me."

She crossed her arms. "Is that what you think? Go fuck yourself."

He raised his hand, but before he struck, Shiriki appeared, grabbed his wrist, and snapped it to the side. The man screamed, falling to his knees, his face paling.

In his demon form, Shiriki's glower held no amusement. Without a word, he backhanded the man, and he fell to the ground with a loud thud.

Elizabeth had pulled out her dagger. She pointed it at Shiriki. "What the hell? You didn't have to interfere. I was about to slap this asshole all the way back to his ancestors."

He raised his eyebrows but grinned. "I thought humans considered it a good trait to help others."

"Ha! Yeah, my own guardian angel," she laughed as she sheathed the dagger at her back.

"You have no idea how accurate that is." He took a step closer. "Are you all right, then? Did he touch you?"

She placed her hands on her hips. "He didn't. Because I can take care of myself, you know." Her body stiffened as though thinking of something. "Father Robert's apprentice, Theodore, disappeared a few months ago."

"Tragic," Shiriki commented, his smirk terrifying. "I hope he has not found himself in a few jars on the shelf in the laboratory of a twisted individual."

She sighed. "I knew it was you, but I have to say, I'm not sorry he's gone." Taking a few steps closer, she crossed her arms over her chest. "Why did you do it?"

"Do I need a reason?"

"No. I'm asking if you had one."

His gaze locked on hers. "Because he hurt you."

She closed the gap between them and wrapped her arms around him. "Thank you."

They stared at each other before their lips brushed together in a kiss.

Celina couldn't process what she was seeing. The way Shiriki acted with her mother and the way she was with him… none of it made sense.

In a flash of light, the scene changed. Part of Celina wanted out. She couldn't take the emotions flowing through her, the confusion and hurt. Yet she had craved the truth for so long, she couldn't bear to look away.

Elizabeth paced through a tiny bachelor apartment. The small room had a low water-stained ceiling, and most of the furniture had clothes thrown over it. She stopped, then resumed her pacing, clutching something in her hand. Celina didn't have a beating heart, but it almost jolted to life seeing the pregnancy test clutched in her mother's fist.

Shiriki appeared nearby, holding a bouquet of red flowers. "You seem angry."

"What. The. Fuck?" She marched to him and shoved the test in his face. "Care to explain this? What did you do?"

Surprise flashed across his face, but by the time he looked at her, it was gone. "You are assuming this is my doing? Why?"

"Because you're the only one I'm fucking!" She threw the test against the wall and went back to her pacing.

"Is that what you call this?"

She stopped in her tracks and clenched her jaw. "What else do you want to call it?"

"Love."

Her breath hitched, and she stared around, as though trying to find an escape or a solution. She gave him a bitter smile. "I guess I should be happy, but I'm just scared."

"As you should be. You have studied enough about my kind to know what it means." He closed the gap between them but didn't touch her. Instead, he held out the flowers. "It means I am possessive and will destroy anything I consider even a slight threat to you."

She rolled her eyes but took the bouquet. "I know how you are. And I don't want to imagine how much worse you'll get with me carrying our child."

"Oh, so you consider me the worst when I am protecting you?" he teased.

She placed her free hand on her abdomen. "How did this happen? There've been no records of your kind and mine being able to reproduce."

"I injected myself with an experimental concoction in hopes for this. I originally created it so we would use it on the female but changed the base signature because I did not want to cause you any pain."

Taking several steps back, she gritted her teeth. "Why the hell would you do that? And without even telling me?"

"The Lumen do not allow abortion, so I knew you would keep it either way." When she opened her mouth as though to scream at him, he cupped her face. "I wanted to give you something to make you happy, something we could share."

Her shoulders slumped as she placed her hand against his. "We need to go over basic, normal, human gift-giving."

Shiriki leaned forward and kissed Elizabeth, wrapping his arms around her waist to bring her closer. When their lips parted, his gaze searched hers. "Are you happy?"

"I am, but for future reference, a baby isn't a gift. The flowers are, though, thank you." She flushed. "Oh… and I love you, too."

A new scene appeared in a flash of light. Celina's stomach churned less with this transition, growing accustomed to the sensation.

Her mother was covered in sweat, crying out as her abdomen contracted. Blood soaked the sheets of the bed where she lay. She clutched at the blanket as another wave hit her.

The door crashed open, and Shiriki rushed inside. Without a word, he put his hand against her swollen belly. A white light glowed around her, and she fell onto the pillow.

"What… took you so long?"

"The usual. A few Sanguis out of control." He frowned. "You have lost a lot of blood." Closing his eyes, the white light flowed out of him faster and brighter.

She let out a breath. "Thank you."

He reached between her legs. "You are doing fine. A few more pushes."

"Easy for you to say." She squeezed her eyelids tight. She tried pushing until, with a shudder, she slumped.

Shiriki held a newborn Celina in his hands, her head fitting in his palm. She cried but not as loud as most infants. Elizabeth propped on her elbows, looking toward her.

"Is it okay? A boy? Girl?"

Shiriki stared at Celina, and as soon as their gazes locked, she stopped crying. "She is perfect."

Elizabeth smiled, closing her eyes. "She? A girl. What should we call her?"

"Celina." He pressed his forehead against hers and whispered something in Demos.

"I like it." She sat against the headboard. "Let me hold her… please."

He cleaned Celina and wrapped a clean blanket around her before handing the baby to Elizabeth. She beamed at her daughter, tears rolling down her cheeks. "I was so worried. I mean, it's not like I could go to the hospital. How would I explain a half-demon, half-human to a bunch of doctors?"

Shiriki's brow furrowed. "She will not have an easy life, being who she is."

"I know, but we'll share our love with her and do the best we can."

He stayed silent, sitting on the edge of the bloodied bed. "Let me take her with me to my realm."

"What? What are you talking about?" she asked, one eyebrow arched.

He got to his feet. "If I take her there, she will adapt to her future life better."

"Her future life? What are—"

"Living in the dark realm with Mekaisto."

She gaped at him, then shot him an icy glare. "What does any of this have to do with your king?"

"He… ordered me to make a human who was half-demon so he could have a bride who could live in our realm." He took a step closer. "I want Celina to be happy, and by letting her grow up in my realm, it would—"

"You monster," Elizabeth whispered, tears streaming down her cheeks. "You used me. This whole time, I thought you loved me." She shook her head. "I should've known demons can't love. You used me to make…" Elizabeth stared at her daughter and took a shuddering breath. "Get out, Shiriki."

He frowned. "I promise I will find a way for you to visit—"

"I said get out!" she yelled, and Celina cried, her tiny hands turning into fists.

Shiriki's pupils thinned. "Give her to me, Elizabeth."

"No." She held Celina closer to her chest and shifted her body. "Leave us alone and never come back. Ever."

He took a step back. "I... still love you."

She let out a bitter laugh, mixed with a sob. "It doesn't matter. I hate what you did, and I'll protect our daughter... even if it means keeping her away from you."

A look of despair crossed Shiriki's face, but without another word, he vanished. The sound of Elizabeth's sobbing echoed in the darkness.

Celina swallowed hard, trying to get rid of the lump in her throat. Shiriki had told her mother the truth, and it had broken them apart.

Her spirit form stumbled inside a familiar bedroom with white walls and a light, wooden floor. It creaked underneath her feet. Decorations hung on the walls: paintings of butterflies, a child's drawings, and hammocks holding some stuffed animals.

A blinding flash of light forced her eyes shut for a second, and she gasped when Shiriki appeared in the room. He was in his human form, yet his cold stare betrayed his disguise. Sitting on the rocking chair, he waited.

Movement caught her gaze, and Celina watched herself stretch on the small bed, waking from a nap. At around three years old, she had the same red hair as she did now, but it was cut much shorter.

Glancing from herself to Shiriki, a part of her wanted to hide. But it was a memory, and nothing she could do would change the past.

Young Celina smiled when she saw Shiriki and slid off the bed. She made her way to a small colorful table, found a drawing among the pages, and brought it to the demon.

"You, Daddy," she said, beaming.

Celina stared at the page, a drawing of what looked like her as a child holding hands with Shiriki and her mother. She clutched at her chest as it tightened.

I… remember this now.

"That's nice of you, Celina. Is it for me?" he asked, leaning forward so he was at eye-level with her.

She nodded. Without waiting, she went to her toy chest and took out a stuffed animal.

Shiriki glanced from the drawing to her a few times before folding it and putting it away in his pocket. Clouds passed overhead, and the room darkened as if night had fallen. Young Celina dashed to the window, holding onto her stuffed polar bear.

Less than a second after, Kai materialized inside the room.

His jaw clenched as he stared at Shiriki. "What are you doing here again?"

"Curiosity," he said with a shrug. Getting to his feet, he bowed his head.

Young Celina gawked at Kai as he crouched in front of her, then touched the top of her head. She passed out, and he caught her before she fell. Glaring at his king, Shiriki approached as Kai lifted her. He placed her back on the bed, and young Celina's eyelids fluttered as Kai turned to his second in command.

"I ordered you to stop coming here," he said in a dark tone. "This is your third and final warning."

Shiriki's gaze lingered on her form, but Celina hadn't

fallen asleep. She'd been listening. She just hadn't understood at the time.

"Why not take her to the dark realm now?" Shiriki asked, his tone dull as if he'd asked many times before. "She could live with me, and I could—"

The white walls turned a dark gray as Kai's jaw clenched. "No. She will already have to go through a difficult life. One day, she will discover everything she has ever known is a lie. The least I can do is let her have a childhood. Something she will hold on to when the time comes." He took a step toward Shiriki, his vertical pupils thinning. "If you return to visit her again, I will take away the one thing you cherish." And without waiting for a response, he vanished.

The door burst open, and a woman lunged at Shiriki with a dagger held tight in her hand. He grabbed Elizabeth's wrist and slammed her against the wall.

Celina's breath hitched as she stared at her mother.

"You need to stop greeting me with pointy weapons."

The ghost of a smile turned her expression to something dangerous. "Why break old habits?"

He chuckled as he let go but he didn't move away, and she didn't push him back. "I won't be coming back again, pet," he whispered.

"Good." Something behind her gaze turned to sorrow. "I won't let either of you take her away, ruin her life. She may be half-demon, but it won't change the fact she'll be a good person." Tucking the dagger inside the sheath on her belt, she sighed. "She has your blood, but it doesn't make her evil."

Shiriki cupped her cheek. "I never said she would be. You're a good mother, and you'll raise her to be kind and strong, like you; I have no doubt about that. But when the day comes, and you know it will, nothing will save her."

"We'll see about that," she said with a grin.

"Keep her away from Lumen. They'll kill her if they find out what she is."

"They won't find out, and if it keeps her safer from you both, then I'll take my chances."

Everything blurred again, and darkness surrounded Celina once more. She dreaded the next memory she'd see, knowing his final regret.

The sun beamed on a country road, a car traveling along the tall trees. Celina's mind numbed, recognizing the vehicle she'd wanted to borrow from Dean so many times.

Shiriki appeared in the middle of the road, far from the car, but it stopped. He let his senses unfold, and Celina appeared next to the vehicle.

"What? Why is he here?" Elizabeth whispered.

Dean reached into his pocket and took out a familiar talisman.

The one that drains magic.

Holding it between his fingers, he raised his hands in front of him and muttered an incantation. Blue chains rose from the road and wrapped around Shiriki, entrapping him as flames coiled around his body.

Dean grinned. "It's working."

"Tell me what's going on. We were supposed to go talk to him. You said you had a way for him to stop trying to take Celina away."

He shot her an exasperated look. "Yes, but I didn't want to tell you all the details in case it didn't work. I've got him immobilized, but it won't hold long." His gaze turned crazed. "The next spell will turn him mortal for a short time. Once he's dead, I'll take his blood and mix it into Celina's potion."

"What are you talking about?" Her chest heaved. "What have you been doing to my daughter?"

"Our daughter!" He ran his free hand through his hair. "Look, what did you think I meant when I had said I could keep Celina safe from demons that powerful? I needed to do a bit of experimenting, and this is the last step. You should be happy."

Her hands curled into fists, and she clenched her jaw. "Happy you've been experimenting on her? How long has this been going on? What have you done? Why didn't she ever tell—"

"I blocked her memories; I didn't want her to remember the pain. I care about her, you know. Soon, Mekaisto will come for her. Once she's in the dark realm, she will be the perfect tool to defeat those monsters." He closed his eyes and mumbled a few sentences.

Spikes shot from the road and impaled Shiriki where he stood, trapped. His eyebrows rose, and he tilted his head, staring at the sky.

Dean pressed on the gas, and the tires peeled against the asphalt as the car surged forward.

Celina seemed to hover, watching as her mother glanced from Shiriki to her husband. Tears filled Elizabeth's eyes, and she yanked off the pendant she'd borrowed from Celina. As Dean glanced at her with a frown, she grabbed the wheel, jerking it hard.

The car flipped and rolled, smashing, crunching as it tumbled across the road. Metal grated against the asphalt, sending sparks as it came to a stop. The spell on Shiriki broke, his wounds healing fast.

Dean crawled out of the car, coughing up blood. Deep gashes ran across his body. He fell forward, his head hitting the cement. He was alive.

Not for long.

Shiriki loomed over Dean. White smoke swirled around him for a second, so bright it looked like snow. When it vanished, he stood in his true form, his white wings spread out, irises glowing yellow. His hands curled and uncurled as though fighting himself.

With a growl, he rushed to the other side of the car, reaching into the twisted metal.

As soon as he pulled Elizabeth out, she smiled and

pointed at his wings. "I was right. You were my… guardian angel."

He ran his hand across her body. "Hold on." Desperation filled his voice.

She placed her hand over his, and he froze. "I'm sorry… for what I said. You are a monster, but… you were *my* monster."

"You are not healing. Why are you not healing?" He looked around as though he might spot the answer. "I can get Mekaisto. He—"

"Don't leave me. Please." Tears rolled down her cheeks, turning pink as it mixed with her blood. She cupped his cheek and smiled. "Just stay with me, please. I don't want to… die alone. I want to remember you… remember us."

"You are not allowed to leave me, Elizabeth. I forbid it." He clenched his teeth. "Why did you do it? You could have let him kill me. Why?"

She traced along his jaw. "Celina… she's been in danger this whole time. Between him and you… at least, I can hold you to a promise."

"Trusting a demon's word?" He shook his head. "You should never have come back to try killing me."

Blood trickled out of her mouth. "Which time? We never finished our fight. But I don't… regret having loved you. And Shiriki…" She looked at the sky, and a sob left her. "Promise you'll make sure Celina… lives. Promise me."

"I promise, but I will not let you—"

"I…" She mumbled a few words, a gurgling sound muffling them as blood dripped down her lips. "So… very much."

Her eyes closed, and her hand dropped to her side. He squeezed her arms and shook her. "Elizabeth? Elizabeth! Wake up! Please…" Tears rolled down his cheeks, and he pressed his face into her neck. "No. Come back, Elizabeth. Please. Come back to me."

Celina watched, and despite not having a body, she cried, unable to breathe even though she didn't need to. Emotions not her own flowed through her, and she realized they were Shiriki's. The years after Elizabeth's death had twisted him further, her loss having torn him apart.

Celina's spirit fell.

When she opened her eyes, she was lying on the sofa once again. The wound in her chest had healed, and her limbs tingled as though coming back to life. Shiriki stared at her, no expression on his face.

She burst into tears and grabbed his hand, squeezing hard. "I'm… so sorry."

He looked away. "It is in the past. It has long been over." And without another word, he vanished.

Moments later, Kai cradled her in his arms as she sobbed. He didn't speak, didn't ask questions; he just let her cry.

40

NEWER BEGINNINGS

Celina waited inside a large living room within the CrowBar's basement with Brihan by her side. Brihan had business with Adam, so he offered to accompany her since she needed to see Namika. While Kai had been less than pleased, he'd agreed that with the Venatore threat gone, and her becoming a true demon, there wasn't a legitimate reason not to let her go. So, while he stayed in the dark realm with their son, Celina crossed into the human world.

And she made her friend promise he wouldn't tell Kai about her throwing up when she'd seen the Inferno. Hell indeed.

Adam walked inside the living area, followed by Namika. Without waiting, the two friends ran to each other, holding tight. Celina hated what she had to do next, knowing this could tear them apart. But she had to tell her friend the truth.

"Are you okay?" Celina asked, pulling Namika away to look at her.

Adam scoffed. "Are you insinuating I'd break my word and harm your friend?"

"I'm saying no one reads the fine print." She ignored Adam and Brihan's laughing as she pulled Namika away. She wanted privacy, despite knowing both demons could hear for miles if they wanted to.

They went through an archway leading into a smaller area, and Celina regretted her choice of location, staring at the rusted chains hanging on the wall. Still, Namika didn't seem to mind as she sat at the small wooden table.

Namika pointed at Celina's belly. "You had your baby?"

"A boy. His name is Fenrir." She took a deep breath. "There's something… well, lots of things I need to tell you."

"Oh?"

So, Celina told her everything. The deal for revenge, and how Thomas had been Mekaisto the whole time. How she only found out about it at the end, and how Shiriki was her biological father. The story of her mother poured out, including what she'd learned about her stepfather. Everything.

Silence hung heavy between them until Namika leaned back in her chair. "Wow."

"Yeah."

"So, you're half-demon, and your son is a little more than half. You're married to the Devil, and your biological father is the infamous second in command who turned out to be our source, and also an angel." She shook her head, a slow smile curling her lips. "Sounds insane."

"You're telling me," Celina muttered. She bit her lower lip. "Did Adam explain what happened? Like, what you felt a few days ago?"

"Mekaisto took away our magic source. I felt it leave me. It was horrible… like I'd lost a part of myself. But Adam talked me through it. I don't mind it so much anymore. I want no association with Venatores after finding out not all demons are bad." She winked. "You're proof of that alone."

Celina smiled, not commenting on the small blush creeping up in her friend's cheeks. Apparently, Namika had changed her mind before she found out Celina was a demon herself, which meant Celina bet another demon changed her mind. Adam, perhaps?

"What are you going to do now?"

"I found out Yasuo died during all the attacks. A lot of my friends are gone, and the group I called family are either dead or they've dispersed out of fear. I was doing my Master's degree in business, but that was being paid for by the group... they figured I could help with the business side of things."

She gave a half-shrug, but sorrow was etched all over her face. "Adam said I can stay here until I find a place to live, and he even gave me a job working in the club during the day. For some reason, he doesn't seem to want me up there at night, though," she said with a frown.

Celina pressed her lips together. She could guess why Adam wouldn't want her there: to keep Namika safe.

"I have to stay in the dark realm for Fenrir, but I'll try to come visit you with him as soon as I can."

Namika swallowed visibly. "With your husband?"

Celina couldn't help grin. The first and last time her friend had seen him in his true form, he'd been terrorizing them all at the Venatores' headquarters. "Well, he's as bad as he seems, but in a way... not."

"That made me feel so much better," Namika said, giving a small tap on Celina's arm. "Well, by the time you all visit, I might be more used to demons if I work here."

They both stood, and Celina pulled her friend into a hug. "Take care of yourself, and if you ever need anything, tell Adam. He can pass the message along."

"I will. Thanks." She smiled. "And same to you. If you need me, I'm just an Adam away."

"I don't think the Sanguis leader will appreciate being used as a messenger," Celina quipped, walking back toward the main living area.

Namika paled, inching closer to Celina as she tried

pointing to where Adam and Brihan were speaking. "Wait. He's the… first Sanguis? The leader?"

"I am, buttercup," Adam said with a wink.

Celina gawked, wondering what possessed Adam to use a pet name like that until she remembered. Namika had a buttercup tattoo on her shoulder blade. He must have seen it. Celina arched an eyebrow at him, but Adam only grinned as Namika turned a deeper shade of red.

Pressure tingled along Celina's skin distracted her, and she frowned. Kai was in the human world, somewhere nearby. He'd told Celina he needed to find Shiriki, and she guessed where he might be.

"I have to go. Remember what I told you. Anytime you need me, okay?" Namika nodded, and they embraced one final time.

Using her newfound powers, Celina focused on where she wanted to go, the room around her blurring. She squinted in the sudden sunlight and hid behind a tree, keeping her energy suppressed so no one would feel her nearby. In the human world, it was harder without being able to use the dark realm's essence. Tainted by the same shard the guardians had used on her husband ages ago, she had become a demon and a powerful one at that. But she still needed practice.

Shiriki stood in front of her mother's grave, the freshly dug earth contrasting against the old plots. With his back to her, she couldn't see his face, but his shoulders were tense.

Kai appeared and stood shoulder to shoulder with his second in command.

"You tried murdering me. And Celina. You betrayed me. Tried to merge my realm with both worlds. Sided with Venatores against me…" Kai sighed, giving him a sideways glance. Despite his human form, Kai's irises flashed red.

Shiriki nodded. "I did."

"Celina begged me not to punish you."

He stiffened. "What did she tell you?"

"Nothing." Moments passed in silence and then he turned, facing Shiriki. "She didn't need to. In her broken state of mind, I could read it."

Shiriki chuckled. "And now you're here to kill me in secret? I doubt you'll do nothing after finding out all I've wanted to do for years was—"

"I didn't know what I was asking of you," he whispered, "ordering you to keep away from Celina and her mother. I believed I was protecting them. From you. Maybe I was, maybe not. But if anyone would've told me I couldn't be with my son and the woman I love…" His irises grew bright. "I know it doesn't matter anymore, but I *am* sorry, Shiriki."

Celina swallowed hard, her fingers digging into the tree bark. It wasn't what she'd expected of Kai. He rarely admitted he was wrong, and never once had he shown vulnerability to his second in command as far as she was aware.

"I wish…" Shiriki scoffed. "Seems odd for a monster to wish anything, doesn't it? And it won't change what happened." Glancing to the side, he grinned. "I had given the shard to Celina's mother, so she could defend herself against our kind. I suppose that has to warrant execution, no?"

"If you remain in your position as second in command, I will sentence you. If you prefer to vanish from my sight, never to return, I won't hunt you."

"Since when are you so forgiving?" he asked with a grin.

"I owe you debts. Consider one repaid." He shook his head and glanced over his shoulder. "And even if you suppress your energy, I can still sense you, dove."

Shiriki turned, glaring as Celina came out from behind the tree. She avoided their stares, wrapping her arms around her waist. It was like she was a child caught trying to eavesdrop.

"Old habits die hard?" Shiriki asked with amusement in his voice.

She looked at him, her mother's words echoing through her mind. "Can… I talk to you in private?"

Kai smiled. "It can't wait until we're—"

"No, I mean… talk to Shiriki alone."

Both looked taken aback, but Kai rolled his eyes. "If I say no, she'll do it anyway."

Celina raised her head high. "*She* will."

He chuckled, turning his attention on Shiriki. "I'll break my promise to Celina if you cause any harm to her ever again." And without waiting for an answer, he vanished.

She stepped forward and stopped a few feet away from Shiriki. "You once told me you couldn't read minds, but I'm sure it was a lie."

"It was. I can read most, save for a few powerful exceptions here and there." He cocked his head. "Is this what you wanted to ask me in private?"

"If I focus on a memory, can you see it?"

"What is it you want me to see?" he asked with a smirk. In a flash, he appeared a foot away from her; she had to fight the urge to recoil. "If it's anything too risqué, I'm afraid Mekaisto may gouge my eyeballs."

"That's vile, and you know it." Letting out a sigh, she shook her head. "There's… there's something you need to see."

Without waiting, she closed her eyes. She focused on one memory of her stepfather. The scene went through her mind, and Celina froze on a particular bit.

"*Is it why you married me? Because a Venatore would have a better chance of protecting you from demons?*" Dean asked quietly.

"*I care for you, so I won't lie. And I won't pretend I love you either, but I think you knew it from the start. I'm still in love, Dean.*"

Celina had assumed at the time her mother meant she was still in love with her stepfather to an extent, but it wasn't true. Until her dying breath, Elizabeth had loved Shiriki.

Celina opened her eyes, and Shiriki turned his back on her. He went to the grave and crouched in front of it, his hand gripping the top of the tombstone. "She tried telling me something as she... died. I didn't think it was what I hoped..." He straightened. "I suppose it's... good to know." Then he vanished.

Celina walked closer to her mother's grave, staring at the bouquet of red flowers Shiriki left behind. The same ones he'd brought her when Elizabeth found out she was pregnant. Celina frowned at the folded piece of paper next to the bouquet and picked it up. Her chest tightened, and she took a shuddering breath. It was the drawing she'd given him as a child: a young Celina holding hands with Shiriki and her mother.

He kept it all those years? The life that could have been his with my mother. And me.

A tear slid along her nose, but she smiled.

The court was silent as Kai drummed his fingers against his throne's armrest.

Celina had asked Nalie to bring Fenrir to court later and had snuck in ahead of time. Kai had ordered her to wait until he came to fetch her, but she wanted to see the monster punished.

"Bring Zachary Mackenzy." His smile turned her blood to ice as Lokte dragged a large rectangular box forward.

Celina was glad Lokte hadn't been destroyed after one of the Venatores had wounded him. He was a dutiful guard and also a friend.

A few of the demons murmured amongst each other, but everyone fell silent again when Kai raised his hand. Lokte moved closer to the rectangle and pulled the sheet off, letting the cloth drop to the floor.

Celina gagged on bile as she stared at Zachary. They'd impaled a spike through his backside and out his mouth. A gag had been shoved inside, muffling his shrieks. The spike, placed on two poles, rotated with the same rhythm as Kai's fingers, cooking the Venatore over a roaring fire. His skin blistered, some of it melting, yet it reformed so the agony repeated. His hair had singed away. The only way she recognized him was the eyes that had kept her awake at night ever since she had gotten her memories back.

Kai's gaze fixed on his prey. "I searched your mind. Not only had you been using Celina for her blood, but you also forced yourself on her whenever her stepfather brought her."

She wrapped her arms around her waist and shuddered at those memories.

Kai released some of his energy, and the whole room seemed to flinch at once. "I sentence you to death. You will join the damned in the Inferno Realm and spend eternity roasting."

Something deep down inside Celina lit up with satisfaction. He deserved the pain and death.

Kai stood. "Bring him to me."

Chains slithered from the ceiling, wrapping themselves around the Venatore. They lifted him off the fire, letting him float in front of Kai.

Zachary's eyes bulged, his shrieks piercing through his gag.

Kai took a step closer. His smile twisted his features into that of a sadistic monster. He rammed his hand inside Zachary's chest, keeping it there as the air around the room sparked. Kai's limb acted like a black hole of sorts, and the Venatore's body compressed inward. His face contorted in anguish, and his eyeballs burst, his head and limbs twisting at horrible angles as his body twitched. Soon, he disappeared into Kai's palm. When he opened his hand, black ashes flew upward.

He sat again and swept his gaze along his subjects.

Nalie moved through the crowd, accompanied by Eire and Brihan, and she handed Fenrir to Celina. After what she had witnessed, Celina needed to hold her son close. She'd gotten revenge, and the monster had paid the price but seeing someone die like that had been horrifying. Did everyone who made deals with demons share this terrible fate? Her mind flashed to Hilda, and she bit her bottom lip.

Kai locked gazes with her, a knowing look crossing his face, but he didn't seem angry. The court fell silent again, watching Shiriki as he ambled forward until he was a few feet away from the throne.

Nalie stood by Celina. She'd become more than a protector, and now she gave Celina an encouraging touch. Brihan gave her a thumbs-up, and Eire smiled. With Fenrir in her arms, Celina strode next to her husband.

Shiriki stared. "Are you the one to sentence me? Seems fair."

Kai leaned his elbows against his knees. "I warned you if you remained in my realm, I would sentence you, so we will hear your crimes." Straightening, his gaze burned red. "You have caused unnecessary fear and pain on my wife. On more than one occasion, threatened her. You even tried murdering her, planning to use her blood and let her die." He ignored a few of the mutters going through the room. He had ordered every single one of his subjects to attend this court, and so it was at full capacity. "You attacked a charter bus and wounded her during the incident you caused."

"I admit to it, yes."

"You also worked with the Venatores and helped them invade the dark realm. Because of you, many of our own perished. You betrayed me when you stopped me from destroying Zachary. He attempted to kill my son because you let him live. You tried murdering me." Kai waved his hand. "The list goes on… it is quite extensive."

The ghost of a smile touched Shiriki's lips. "Guilty."

Celina took a step forward. "But your other actions tell a different story."

The crowd murmured louder, but Kai cleared his throat and they fell silent.

"Is that so?" Shiriki's gaze turned cold as though daring her to mention anything she'd seen in his memories.

"You saved Fenrir when Zachary threw him off the railing."

His eyebrows rose, but he grinned. "As I said, I happened to be flying by."

One of Kai's subjects stepped out of the crowd, gawking. "You saved the prince?"

"I did."

Kai let out something between a growl and a sigh. "For your betrayal, I had sentenced you to death."

Shiriki cocked his head. "A fair sentence considering my crimes."

Celina placed her son against her shoulder and rubbed his back. "When Kai told me your sentence, I asked he reconsider. Between saving my son and me and giving me the information I needed from my past, I asked for a new sentence."

"Oh?"

Kai rolled his eyes. "She did. Despite being a demon now, she still has the sentiment of a human." He shot her an amused look.

Celina beamed at her husband; the trust and understanding he'd given after she explained why she wanted Kai to reconsider was more than she could put into words. He listened and although he'd countered her arguments, in the end, he agreed. For the first time in their relationship, she felt like his equal.

She strode to Shiriki. "I forgive you."

He stiffened. "I suppose there is still a consequence, despite your good graces. So, what is my punishment?"

She let out a small laugh. "You'll be banished from this realm for a hundred years. No more experiments on any beings for that time. I also have requests. Release Hilda; I want her free and alive to enjoy the rest of her years as she sees fit. And you'll continue to protect her and her family until the vampires no longer threaten any of them."

"Who will clean my messes, though?" He chuckled. "Consider it done."

She grinned. "Oh, and if you ever torture me again... I'll kill you myself."

"Noted." For a second, the smile on his lips became the one she'd seen him give her mother. Then it turned cruel again. "I look forward to that day."

She shook her head and grinned.

Kai stood and wrapped his arms around Celina's shoulders, staring at their son. "This has been long overdue." His gaze swept the room. "I present Celina, Queen of the dark realm, and our son, Fenrir, Prince of Darkness."

The room burst with applause.

Celina caught Shiriki staring toward a window in the cathedral ceiling. The twilight seemed to fade, light bathing the room, and her chest tightened. Red flower petals scattered through the open windows. Deep down, she felt her mother now lay at rest, wherever she was.

With a small bow, Shiriki vanished.

Fenrir squirmed in Celina's arms. She turned to Kai, who stared at the petals with a sad smile.

"They're beautiful," she whispered.

He looked at her, leaning forward so their foreheads touched. "So are you, dove." He kissed the top of her head. "I have a gift for you."

"Now?" She glanced at the room and grinned.

With a mischievous smile, he picked her up, and she tightened her hold on Fenrir. In a blur, the scenery changed, and she shivered as he put her on her feet. They were inside his dwelling, standing in the main entrance.

"This way," he said, then strode to the right of the staircase.

She frowned. There had been nothing there before. Now, a door stood, painted in a familiar dark green. He pushed it open, and she gawked, entering the living room she'd shared with Thomas. Without a word, she went through the house, everything similar but not quite the same.

"Why?"

"I did not want it bringing up unpleasant memories. I also promise I will never face you as Thomas to avoid causing you further pain." He cupped her face, and she leaned into it. "You were calling this place my dwelling, but I want to share a home with you, a place that belongs to us so we may start anew."

He'd placed a few of their old belongings throughout the house, and she laughed through her tears. "There's a house inside your house."

"Anything for you, dove." He kissed her forehead, then did the same to their son. "And I have a surprise for you, too, Fenrir." Taking his son in his arms, Kai walked into the kitchen. He grabbed the heavy curtains over the patio door and opened them.

Sunlight.

Celina rushed forward, looking out into the backyard. Grass and trees from her world grew under a bright blue sky as the sun beamed. Kai slid the door open, and they stepped outside.

"How is this possible?"

"An illusion, but it is eternal so long as you like it." He wrapped his arm around her shoulder and turned her to the side. "And this is Fenrir's gift."

A lump formed in her throat as she stared at the play

structure she'd sketched. Everything was there, from the climbing wall to the upper clubhouse with a small lookout and a slide. Even the swing-set Kai had added as Thomas was there, and a baby swing hung, waiting.

"I am sorry I got impatient and built it without you."

She looked at him. "It's perfect. Thank you."

"I love you." He cupped her cheek and smiled.

"I love you, too." She smiled, then stared at Fenrir. "And we both love you."

Kai took his son's small hand, his gaze softening. "Very much."

Despite no longer beating, her heart swelled. A demon's love was a dangerous thing, but to her, it was also perfect.

AUTHOR NOTES

If you liked the story, please leave a review!

I am so excited too share this story with you. This was originally supposed to be the last in the series, but I am happy to announce a third and final book for A Demon's Love: MY LOVE TO KEEP. There is no release date for this upcoming book, but since the story will take place several years after many other books within the same universe, it may be a while.

As always, I have to thank Wendy Vogel and Nikolas Everhart who both read and critiqued this manuscript. It is thanks to them that it was turned into the story it is today. I will never be able to express enough gratitude for the help and support they've provided through the years, but I hope this small acknowledgement goes toward it.

To my readers: thank you so, so much! I honestly believe writers are nothing without their readers. I appreciate you all so much.

ABOUT THE AUTHOR

M. A. Fréchette writes the darker side of romance.

Being an extremist, she loves both the dark aspects of life and everything sweet. All her stories are either set in Canada where she lives or in alternate worlds she made up while living within her imagination. When not writing, she thinks of the next scene or plot while enjoying her work as a cover designer. Although she has a fascination for monsters, with a bachelor degree in criminology, she understands there's no need to create the paranormal; humans are capable of inflicting nightmares of their own.

Please feel free to reach out through any social media. I truly love hearing from readers!

facebook.com / AuthorMAF

twitter.com / authormaf

instagram.com / authormaf

amazon.com / author / authormaf

bookbub.com / authors / m-a-frechette

goodreads.com / authormaf

A Demon's Love series

MY SOUL TO GIVE (book #1)

Unbroken series

A THOUSAND WORDS (book #1)

www.ingramcontent.com/pod-product-compliance
Lightning Source LLC
Chambersburg PA
CBHW050903130726
47900CB00015B/1938